RIGHT MAN RIGHT TIME

USA TODAY BESTSELLING AUTHOR

MEGHAN QUINN

Published by Hot-Lanta Publishing, LLC

Copyright 2023

Cover Design By: RBA Designs

Cover Illustrations By: Gerard Soratorio

Prologue

SILAS

"I don't know, dude. Maybe I should have gone with the princess cut," I say into the phone as I head up the elevator to my penthouse apartment that offers expansive views of the Burrard Inlet.

When Sarah and I found this place, she told me we had to get it. Not only were the views everything we could have asked for, but the privacy was also a huge bonus, especially since privacy doesn't come so easily anymore. Not when you're the star right wing from the Vancouver Agitators.

"Do we really have to go through this again?" Pacey Lawes says through the phone, clearly irritated with my inability to settle on the right ring.

"I want to get this right." The elevator shoots me up to the penthouse. "I know Sarah has been waiting for this, and I'm finally in a place in my life where I can get her the ring she deserves. I want to make sure it's perfect."

"How many times do we have to go through this? She sent you pictures of that halo ring. That's what she wants, and what you got matches that. Don't change anything."

"Yeah, you're right." I sigh. "Shit, I'm nervous."

"Are you doing it tonight?"

"No." I shake my head even though he can't see me. "I have to figure out her ring size first."

"That would have been job number one," he says just as the elevator dings and the doors begin to part.

"Probably." I scrub my hand over my face as I step off the elevator. "This is my first and last proposal, so I'm not quite sure of the timetable here."

"Don't think that's part of a timetable. Just common sense, man," Pacey says as I set my keys on the side table next to the elevator, kick off my shoes, and then head toward the kitchen where I find one of Sarah's bras discarded on the counter.

That's weird.

She's a bit of a neat freak, so finding something like a bra on the counter and no other laundry feels out of place.

"You there?" Pacey asks.

"Uh, yeah." I clear my throat and pick up the black lace, a bra I don't think I've ever seen her wear before. And I know because I've been with her since high school. I've seen the ins and outs of this woman's wardrobe, and I would have easily remembered a bra like this. "Hey, I have to go."

"Everything okay?" Pacey asks with concern, obviously hearing the change in my tone.

"Yup, just, uh, realized I forgot to take the meat out of the freezer." A simple lie that I know will do the trick.

"Oh shit, dude, you're in trouble."

"Don't I know it," I say right before hanging up and setting my phone on the counter.

I examine the bra, tracing my fingers over the lace. *Have I seen this before?*

No, definitely not.

This is different.

This is not the Sarah I know who *only* wears nude-colored undergarments. That's all she's ever worn, and I've been fine with it. I couldn't care less. I just wanted to see what was under the undergarments, and lately, there's been a drought in that department.

She blames it on hockey, saying I'm never around. But I don't see how my schedule is any different from last year. Sure, I might have acquired more deals that have brought in an exponentially higher income, and those commitments have stolen some of my time, but I still make an effort to make time to be available for her.

She's the one who tells me she's tired.

She's the one who offers me her cheek when I try to kiss her good night.

I spoke to the guys about it. How she never initiates intimacy, how she rolls away from me at night, and we concluded that maybe she was tired of waiting for a true commitment from me.

Hence the ring.

But this bra . . . maybe she's trying to spice things up for the both of us.

Maybe she left this here, knowing I was coming home and would believe it's a clue.

A smile stretches across my face as I stick the bra in the back pocket of my jeans and move toward the bedroom.

"Sarah, babe, you here?" I ask, heading closer to the shut bedroom door. "Found your bra."

"Mmmmm." I hear her moan, which makes me pause in my path to open the bedroom door.

Was that moan for me, or was that moan . . . something else?

Confused, I reach for our bedroom doorknob and twist it just as I hear her again. "Yes, right there."

What the . . .

I part the door open, just enough to see Sarah spread naked on our bed with a woman's head between her legs. *What. The. Fuck?*

My mouth drops to the floor, my heart sputters to a stop, and I can feel all the color draining from my face.

"That's it, baby, keep up that pace," a male voice speaks from the side of the room, nearly knocking me back on my ass.

I glance toward the window and find a naked man sitting in the chair I use to put my fucking shoes on, stroking his mediocre erection.

"What the actual fuck?" I say, unable to stop myself.

Sarah's head pops up, and her eyes connect with mine. Fear crosses her pupils right before pure ecstasy. The woman doesn't stop eating Sarah's pussy, the man doesn't stop stroking his dick, and it's as if everything is playing out in slow motion like some sort of fucked-up porn video.

Sarah's eyes remain on mine as she bites her bottom lip and her cheeks flush, a look I haven't seen from her in I don't know how long. And for the life of me, I can't look away as her chest lifts, nipples puckered, skin slick, and her mouth falls open as a low, feral moan slips past her lips. A sound so erotic that I honestly wasn't sure she could make it.

Her head falls back to the bed, her fingers grip the sheets tightly, and then, to my absolute horror, I watch her come, getting off from another woman while a man in the corner does the same, he groans even louder.

At a complete standstill, unsure of what to fucking do, I stay rooted in place, waiting for this nightmare to end.

"Oh God," Sarah says as she fondles her breasts, plucking her nipples. "So good," she mumbles before she finally catches her breath.

So good? Is she fucking kidding me right now?

The naked woman between her legs pulls away and turns toward me. Her fake breasts are *way too* large for her body.

That's what you notice, Silas? She stands up and then starts fingering herself. With a coy look, she asks, "Do you want to be next?"

"The fuck?" I ask. "No!" I look past the busty redhead and over at Sarah. "What the fuck is going on?"

Hand draped over her face, she closes her legs and then rolls up to a seated position. She's flush, satisfied, and it makes me so fucking mad. My vision starts to tunnel. She's my girl, and someone else made her look fucking satisfied. That doesn't settle well with me. Nor does her hair looking a mess. Or the wild expression in her eyes. Gratification rings clear in her voice as she says, "I needed a good fuck, Silas."

She needed a good fuck?

That's her excuse?

"Then why the hell did you not ask me? Your boyfriend?"

I stare Sarah down, looking for an answer, but she doesn't give me one. The redhead walks up to me seductively and rests her hand on my chest. "You seem tense. Let me fix that for you."

Keeping still, I speak through my clenched jaw. "I suggest you get the fuck away from me right now."

"Do not talk to my woman like that," the man says while standing and stuffing his now flaccid dick in his pants.

"Test me, dude. Seriously, see how far it gets you. I've bashed more skulls in my lifetime to even count. You do not want to fuck with me."

"Maybe I do," the man says, acting like a stupid fuck. He steps toward me, and without even thinking twice, I cock my arm back. Sarah inserts herself between the man and me before I can hit him.

"Don't," she says, her voice stern.

She can't be serious.

"You're protecting *him*?" I ask. In my fucking house? My fucking bedroom? What the hell is happening?

5

Without answering me, she turns toward the man and woman. "I think you two should leave."

"Are you sure?" the woman asks. "If you're in trouble, we can stay."

"She's not in fucking trouble," I yell. "I'm her goddamn boyfriend, and if you don't leave in the next five minutes, I will physically remove you myself."

"Go," Sarah says.

While they pick up and leave, Sarah grabs a robe from the bed and tosses it over her body, covering up the bite marks along her rib cage and breasts. Breasts I've spent years worshipping.

Pain, anger, and confusion all lace through my body, putting me through a mental fuckery of a roller coaster as I try to pick one emotion to focus on.

When I hear the elevator doors close, I know which one to run with. Anger. I turn toward her and say, "What the fuck was that?"

Arms crossed defensively, she answers, "I've . . . I've been feeling neglected. Todd and Nancy have—"

"Todd and Nancy?" I shout.

"Yes, Todd and Nancy." She secures the tie around her waist. "They've made me feel supported, fulfilled, and not so alone."

White-hot rage shoots up my spine. "Don't fucking come at me with that. I've tried to make you feel . . . fulfilled, but you won't let me. You push me away, turn me down, you won't even fucking look at me. I mean, what the hell, Sarah? How long has this been going on?"

"Four months," she says without even an ounce of apology in her voice.

"Four months?" I ask. "Jesus Christ." I step away, running my hand through my hair. When I look at her, I don't see the same person I fell in love with years ago. I see someone jaded,

6

someone manipulative, someone who had no intention of protecting my heart.

After everything we've been through, all the ups and downs of trying to make it in hockey, the hardships, the joy, she's going to act like cheating on me for four months is nothing?

That it's my fault when I've put in the effort?

That I'm the one to blame even though we both agreed that my goal to be a professional hockey player is what we both wanted?

She knew what this life would be like. I didn't see her complaining when she got her expensive purses and brand-name shoes.

I stare at her, the woman I gave my heart to, and as anger fills me, I say, "Fuck you, Sarah."

"Excuse me?" she asks, shock registering across her face.

"I said . . . fuck . . . you."

"You're mad at me." She points at her chest. "You're mad at me when I'm the one who has to stay here all alone?"

"You knew what you were getting into," I yell. "You fucking knew this is what life would be like, and you agreed to it. We had an in-depth conversation about what to expect. We agreed this was what would be best for our life together. And to help the situation, to make you feel more comfortable, I got the fancy apartment you wanted. I got you the car and the clothes. I got you everything you ever asked for. So yeah, Sarah, fuck you. We were supposed to be monogamous."

"As if you've never cheated on me," she says offhandedly.

"Never," I answer with a low growl in my voice. It feels like the hair on the back of my neck is standing to attention. "I've never once touched another woman, looked their way, or even thought about it because I love you, Sarah. You're my girl. You're the one I want to be with."

Hand propped on her hip, disbelief in her voice, she repeats,

"You never cheated on me? That's hard to believe. I've heard what the other girls have said about all those women running around the hotel rooms looking to hook up with your team."

"Yeah, that's true, but I have fucking loyalty," I snap at her. "I promised myself to you, and I've kept that promise. Wait, have you been cheating on me with other people besides Todd and Nancy?" When she glances away, I have my answer. I throw my arms up and turn my back on her. "Un-fucking-believable." This whole time, I thought she was loyal. I thought we were in this together. I thought that maybe she was pulling away because of the change in popularity I've received. *But she's been fucking unfaithful all this time. What the actual fuck?*

Everything I've known about love comes crashing to a fucking standstill. I feel so . . . betrayed. *Broken.*

I take a few deep breaths. "I want you out."

"What?" she asks.

I turn around to face her. Feeling absolutely gutted inside, I repeat myself. "I said I want you out. You have an hour. Get what you need and get the fuck out. We're done, Sarah."

"This is my apartment too."

"You know what? You're right, it is." I smile demonically. "I'll call the landlord right now and tell her to switch the name on the lease to yours. Enjoy paying rent."

Her face falls flat. "You can't do that. I don't have a job. I put my life on hold to support you."

"I didn't know supporting me meant you got to fuck around with other people. I think we have a different view of what supporting really means."

Not sure if it's me asking her to leave or the realization that she has nothing without me, but panic lights up her eyes. "Listen, Silas, we can work this out."

"The fuck we can. Now you either pack up and get out of here in an hour, or the apartment is yours. Rent is due in a week."

And with that, I storm out of the apartment and as far away from her as I can get.

We are so fucking over.

And I'll be damned if I ever let anyone treat me like that again.

Chapter One

OLLIE

"To the worst internship of our lives," Ross says, holding up a shot glass.

I hold mine up as well. "And may Alan Roberts's teeth fall out for creating the toxic workspace we've suffered through all summer."

"Cheers to that." Ross clinks his glass against mine, and together, we take down a tequila shot, quickly counteracting the bitter taste with some lime.

When we finish, I let out a large breath. "I can't believe the fucker is making us work extra to earn our internship credit."

Ross licks the lime before setting his down. "That's what happens when you're fucking the head of the journalism department. You get what you want."

I grip Ross's arm. "Do you really think Roberts is fucking Professor Wheeler?"

Ross purses his lips and gives me his telltale look for "girl-llll." "Please, Yamish saw them in her office last spring. That's how Roberts nabs all of those summer interns to do his dirty work because he siphons them straight from the department."

"We were siphoned," I say.

"Exactly, and look where that got us. Sure, we worked a paid internship for college credit. That was great and appreciated, but at what cost? We lost one of the greatest summers of our life to Alan Roberts and his coffee order of steamed milk with a teaspoon of espresso. And now, when we finally have a chance to take part in writing something for his elusive website, we have to do it when school starts to earn our credit. What the fuck is that about?"

"Poor time management," I say as I pick up my margarita and twirl my straw. Our drink of the summer has been a margarita on the rocks with a shot of tequila on the side. It gets the job done with no hangover in the morning.

Ross and I met our freshman year. We were put into a study group together and immediately hit it off. We bonded over face creams, fashion trends, and workout routines that gave us the best results with the least possible injury.

"Have you even looked at your assignment?" he asks.

I slip the envelope handed to us when we left work today out of my purse and hold it to my chest. "I have not. Have you?"

"No."

"Want to do it together?" I ask.

He nods and reaches into the back pocket of his perfectly pressed dress slacks and pulls out his envelope. "I'll read yours, and you read mine."

"That seems fair. It lessens the blow."

We exchange envelopes, and he nods at me. "You read mine first. And if it says anything about sports, just end me now."

"Same," I say as I pull out the letter. "Ahem. You, my

12

friend, have . . ." I pause, scanning the letter . . . "Oh shit, you have fall fashion trends."

"Shut up," he shouts before ripping the letter from my hands and reading it himself. "Holy fuck, a five-hundred-word spread on fall fashion must-haves." His eyes widen when he looks up at me. "Ollie, do you understand how big a deal this is?"

I chuckle. "I do. I worked with you this entire summer. Everyone is going to see that article, and I have no doubt it will be syndicated."

"Holy . . . fuck," he breathes out. "And here I thought Roberts hated me. He just made me get his coffee every morning so he could make sure I had the style to back up the article. This could only mean if I got fashion, you probably got lifestyle. That list of books you've been putting together will pay off." He rips open my envelope, and I wait in antici-pation because I truly hope he's right. Lifestyle would be my ideal topic, the one I know the most about. I've kept up with all the reading, beauty, and exercise trends. I'm my very own Andie Anderson over here.

He clears his throat, tosses the letter open with a shake of his hand, and smiles at me.

"Ollie, my dearest friend who has the glowing complexion of an angel—"

"Thank you, plant-derived squalane."

Smiling, he says, "You will be working tirelessly, writing about . . ." He pauses, and I know it's for dramatic effect. Ross doesn't know any other way to operate. At least that's what I think until his brow creases in concern, and his smile flattens into a frown.

Uh-oh, that can't be good.

Unless he's trying to fake me out.

Would Ross do that, though? He's not much of a prankster.

Oh God, what if I got something bad?

"What, uh . . . what is it?" I ask nervously.

His eyes slowly lift to mine. "I think they messed up."

"What do you mean you think they messed up?" I snag the letter from Ross and scan it until my eyes land directly on the assignment. "No, this can't be right."

"Looking at assignments?" we hear a cheery yet shrill voice say as she walks up behind us.

Candace Roundhouse.

The bane of our existence.

The suck-up of the summer.

The brown-nose that belongs to Alan Roberts.

Abhorrently annoying and a compulsive inhibiter of all fun, Candace has been the second main reason Ross and I came up with a drink of the summer. Roberts is the margarita. Candace is the shot of tequila on the side.

Plastering on a smile because even though we can't stand her, we have to pretend to get along, I turn toward Candace and say, "Oh hey, didn't think you were going out tonight."

She flips her fake fiery-red hair over one shoulder and gives me a slow once-over. "Yes, thought I would introduce my boyfriend to all my work peeps."

Ew, who says peeps?

"How fun," Ross says with his genuinely fake smile. I know it's fake because his teeth clench tightly together while the corners of his mouth twitch ever so slightly.

"Can you believe Roberts allowed me to put together the assignments? He just tossed it on my desk and said have at it."

The bitch.

Of course she put these together. I should have freaking known.

"You put these together?" I ask, still trying to hold my composure. I want to flick that red lipstick right off her pursed lips.

"I did." She smiles brightly. "I knew you would be

amazing with the fashion piece, Ross. The minute I saw it, I thought you needed to have it."

"Yeah, thank you," he says quietly because sure, she did him a favor. But what about me?

She did this on purpose, I know she did, and it's all because of the stupid freaking Post-it Notes.

Want to talk about petty?

Candace Roundhouse is the definition of it.

You see, Candace was very particular about her office supplies. So particular that she took in her own, which is fine. If you want to use the stupid gel pens like a girl who grew up in the two thousands, have at it. I'm not going to stop you. But one day, I was running around the office at everyone's beck and call, and I was on the phone with an advertiser who needed me to pick up a product from a warehouse downtown. I needed something to write the address down on. I was right next to Candace's desk, and since she wasn't there, I picked up a pen and a Post-it Note and wrote down the address. When I hung up and turned around, Candace was right behind me, staring me down as if she was one of the twins from *The Shining*.

I smiled awkwardly, begging for forgiveness.

She folded her arms.

Nothing was said between us, just a stare down still ingrained in my memory as one of the top five scariest moments of my life. There is nothing like utter silence to gain the upper hand when facing a competitor, especially me because I can't stand the silence.

Ross told me he heard Candace offhandedly mention to one of the girls in the office how I used her Post-it Notes and didn't bother to replace them. She sounded irritated.

It was ONE Post-it.

See what I'm talking about?

Petty.

Clearing my throat, I say, "So . . . with all due respect, what were you thinking when you gave me my assignment?"

Her amused eyes turn toward me as she says, "Well, all I heard all summer was how much you enjoyed the male form, objectifying men in every which way." What the hell is she talking about? "I thought your assignment would be perfect for you."

"I wasn't objectifying men," I say because if anything, I was professional all summer, and that was exhausting. There were many times I didn't want to be professional.

Like when Candace bossed people around for half an hour while her fly was undone. I could have asked her if she was attempting to win the boss's affection, maybe offer a panty parade, or even looking for singles ready to mingle. But did I open my mouth? Nooooo, and that's because I was a professional.

I didn't tell her it was down either because just that morning, she'd yelled at me for taking the last Green Mountain blueberry coffee pod. Someone had to take it, and that someone just happened to be me.

"I distinctly remember you going into great detail about the contours and crevices of Chris Hemsworth's body."

I shake my head, trying to comprehend her idiocy. "That was on a lunch break, and it's because he just came out with a series of pictures in *Men's Health*. How does that have anything to do with my assignment of . . . hockey?"

Yup, she gave me hockey. A sport I know absolutely nothing about other than . . . skates, uh . . . puck . . . stick . . . and lots of ice. That about sums it up.

She smiles. "Figured you could study the contours and crevices of hockey players. After all, hockey is a national treasure in Canada. You could really do something special with the assignment."

Petty. She is so freaking petty.

I can be petty, you know. I could . . . uh . . . I could kick her right in the crotch. Not sure if that's petty, but it sure as hell would make me feel better. A toe to her camel toe. Blamo, instant joy for me.

"I know nothing about hockey, and you know damn well if I turn in a fluff piece about muscles and perfectly proportioned man nipples, Roberts isn't going to give me credit for this summer internship. Everything rides on these last assignments." I can feel myself losing my cool.

If I don't do a good job on this assignment, I might have to repeat the internship, and I can't do that. Repeating would put me behind, and I need to graduate at the end of this year. *I have a strict schedule.*

She taps her chin. "Hmm, you might be right about that. Looks like you need to learn some hockey."

Stepping forward, I point my finger at her. "You did this on purpose, all because of a Post-it. Honestly, how could you—"

"Darling, there you are," a male voice says. A familiar male voice. A voice so bone-chillingly familiar that I feel my stomach bottom out as I slowly look up to see Yonny Biliak standing in front of me.

Actually, not just standing in front of me but wrapping his arm around Candace and kissing the side of her cheek.

No fucking way.

Who is Yonny Biliak, you ask?

A self-proclaimed rising star in the legal field, horrid offender of crisscrossing suit patterns, expert dribble pee-er, and my ex-boyfriend of two years. He broke up with me this summer, stating we were going our own ways. *He* thought it'd be best that we focus on our careers and not each other.

Funny how it's the end of summer, and he seems NOT to be focusing on his career but rather the backside of Candace Roundhouse.

Like I can actually see him rubbing her ass. Right here, in the middle of a bar, as if we're in the privacy of his stuffy bedroom where he chose to show affection because PDA was forbidden. He had to uphold an image, after all.

"The beefy sweetheart of my life," Candace coos back as she lifts her hand to his ill-shaven face and kisses his dry, crusty lips. At least that's how I want them to be, but they actually look quite moisturized, which just irritates me even more. Looks like the man found chapstick. Also, can we please pause for a moment and lament over the pet name "beefy sweetheart"? Blech. "I'm so glad you found me. I'm lost without you," Candace continues.

Oh, come on.

Are they trying to make the bar collectively dry-heave?

I feel Ross lean into me, his hand slowly falling to my back protectively. I appreciate him. He knows how I was after my breakup with Yonny. Yonny never treated me right, yet I still gave him all of me, so when we broke up, I didn't take it that well.

I spent more time holding a bottle of wine to my lips than I care to admit . . . and yelling at innocent birds just trying to put in a day's work of finding twigs and worms.

When the two sugarplum sweethearts of our generation are finally done cooing at each other, Yonny looks up, only to be partially stunned when I come into view.

"Ollie," he says, straightening up. "Didn't see you there. How, uh, how are you?"

Lovely.

Bubbling with euphoria.

On the precipice of so much joy that my soulless heart—as you once called it—might combust into micro pieces of merriment.

"Great," I answer louder than I want. "So great. The greatest, actually. The greatest of all time. GOAT. I'm the GOAT of all GOATs."

"Stop saying goat," Ross whispers.

I smile with just my lips, regaining my composure, and say, "Just wonderful."

Yonny drapes his arm around Candace and pulls her in close to his chest, clearly trying to make me jealous.

Well, try harder, sir, because you're not much of a prize to fight over.

Yet . . . even though I know he's not a prize and more of a jerk than anything, I feel myself gearing up to do something stupid, say something stupid, anything to save face in front of the man who once told me it was normal to have pee drips all over his underwear.

"I'm really great, actually," I continue because they can't hear that enough. I push my hair behind my ear. "Yup, everything is wildly awesome for me right now. Just got the assignment of a lifetime thanks to Candace, living my best life in the heart of Vancouver, rolling in lavish food from sponsor after sponsor, and easily having the best sex of my life." His brow turns down, and that spurs me on because nothing feels better than seeing an ex displeased with your success. "Yup, so much sex, crazy sex too. Sex that actually makes me convulse like an electric shock but straight to my pu—"

"A semblance of class," Ross says, cutting me off.

Yup, okay, I can admit when I've gotten a touch out of hand.

"Well, that's nice," Yonny says, looking uncomfortable. Yeah, that's right, feel uncomfortable. Regret life. Reconsider all of your choices.

"That's funny," Candace says, a smarmy look on her face. "Last I heard, you've been in a drought since you and Yonny broke up."

Freaking office gossip.

I get drunk one night and tell a few girls that it's been the Sahara Desert between my legs all summer, and it just happens to get back to Candace Roundhouse. What is she freaking doing? Paying people for information? Does she pay them in Post-it Notes? I wouldn't put it past her. She's vengeful, folks, and not one to mess with.

Yet here I am, going all in.

"This was recent," I say. "He's actually here, right now, the man I've been losing many nights of sleep to. The man who has stretched me in more ways than one. The man who I've purposely called daddy in the middle of fu—" Ross elbows my ribs. Right, stay on track. I clear my throat. "So . . . yeah, anyway, I bet you two have a lot of public rubbing you want to get on with, so I'm just going to go—"

"Where is he?" Candace asks, the challenging look in her eyes telling me she doesn't believe me one bit. What a freaking frump. "I would love to meet him."

Of course she would.

"Oh yeah, I would love for you to meet him. Unfortunately, my little cuddle bunny is shy," I say, offering an apologetic smile.

"What are you doing?" Ross whispers under his breath, clearly concerned for me. He has all the right to be because I have become unhinged.

"Oh, I'm sure he's shy," Candace says with a roll of her eyes. "So shy that he doesn't exist." She pats Yonny's chest. "Let's go before she embarrasses herself even more."

"He does exist," I say, anger pulsing up my spine. My voice sounds so convincing that I almost believe he has magically appeared from my imagination and parked it right here in this bar.

Candace glances over her shoulder. "Okay, Ollie. Enjoy your assignment. I'm sure you'll do a wonderful job with it." Her condescending tone tips me over the edge, and I feel my body go absolutely feral.

Teeth snarling.

Hair raised.

Bloodshot eyes.

Ohhhhh no, she doesn't walk away from me with the last

word, not when I have to conjure up a fake boyfriend who has given me the best sex of my life.

"He is. Actually, there he is," I say, aiming my gaze at the first man I see. And before I can stop myself, I charge toward the far end of the bar.

Better watch out, man, feral beast incoming.

Chapter Two

SILAS

Silas: *Did you see the press announcement from the Agitators?*

I pick up my glass of Scotch as I stare down at my text thread with my boys, willing them to respond. I'm all sorts of fucked up.

The moment I saw the press announcement come in, I dropped everything I was doing, slipped on my shoes, and walked to the closest bar where I've been ever since, wallowing in how the universe is so fucking unfair.

No, not unfair, just fucked up.

My phone dings with a message.

Pacey: *Dude . . . what the actual fuck?*

Pacey is the star goalie for the Agitators. Last summer, when we were spending our time off the ice at my cabin in Banff, he met the love of his life, Winnie. He recently proposed, and she said yes. Not sure when the wedding will be, but I do know their disgustingly cute love makes me want to throw up.

Pacey: *Are you okay?*

Shaking my head, I text him back.

Silas: *No. All kinds of fucked up right now.*

Hornsby: *Wait . . . SARAH is working for the Agitators now? HOW?*

Eli Hornsby—defenseman, pretty boy, and the guy who got Pacey's sister pregnant. Yeah . . . sore subject, but everything seems to have worked out now. Penny is due soon, and throughout all the years I've known Hornsby, I've never seen him this protective over anything . . . even his gleaming, Prince Charming-like smile.

Oh, and if you didn't catch his text, yeah, my ex, the girl who destroyed me, is working for the Agitators in the marketing department. Hence the heavy glass of Scotch in my hand.

Posey: *Whoa, whoa . . . whoa. *pinches brow* How? How the fuck?*

Levi Posey—teddy bear on the inside, absolute bruiser on the outside—acts like the innocent one of the group with his love for bologna sandwiches and his penchant for helping old ladies walk across the streets of Vancouver when, in reality, he's the biggest ladies' man of them all.

Pacey: *Do you think she used your name to get the job?*

Hornsby: *She better not have. Who can we talk to about this? How can we get her fired?*

Posey: *You can't get someone fired because of a personal relationship.*

Hornsby: *You sure as hell can if this new hire is going to fuck with Taters's head. You know it is. No offense, bro.*

Silas: *None taken because you're fucking right.*

Holmes: *Just catching up. Sarah is working for the Agitators? Dude, are you okay?*

Halsey Holmes, besides me, is the quickest skates out on the ice. A former twin, he lost his brother in a horrible car accident. Halsey turtled in on himself and focused on hockey and only hockey. That was until this past summer when we discovered that Halsey has a huge fucking crush on Penny's best friend, Blakely. The only problem is Blakely is massively in love with her boyfriend. Yeah, he's in deep.

Silas: *Yeah, not doing great. I mean, what the actual fuck? Why would she do this?*

Hornsby: *Isn't it obvious? To fuck with you, man.*

Pacey: *I hate to admit it, but I'm with Hornsby.*

Hornsby: *So how can we take her down?*

Posey: *Once again, you can't take her down. Her personal life isn't the Agitators concern.*

Holmes: *I'm with Posey. There isn't much we can do.*

Hornsby: *What the fuck? What happened to band of brothers?*

Silas: *I appreciate your willingness to charge after her with a bayonet at the end of your hockey stick, but bro, they're right. Nothing can be done.*

I set my phone down and bring my glass to my lips. Absolutely nothing can be done other than hope and pray I don't have to interact with her. And how the fuck did she get the job? As far as I know, she has little to no job experience. Are the Agitators just hiring anyone now? I want to see her credentials.

After taking a sip, I set it down on the bar in front of me as a hand presses to my back. I turn just in time for a woman to speak closely to my face as if we've known each other for years and we're in cahoots.

"My name is Ollie. I'm in a really tough spot, and I'm so sorry, but I'm about to kiss you because I need to save face in front of my ex-boyfriend, who is now dating my nemesis. If you don't stop me in three seconds, I'm going in." She says this at such a rapid rate that I almost don't understand what she's saying.

As I turn to face her, I catch a glimpse of thick wavy brown hair and a flash of red lipstick, and then her lips are on mine, her hand shifting to the back of my head.

Whoa, what the hell is happening?

I'm caught off guard, but it's only a moment because once her soft, plush lips move along mine, I turn toward her and smooth my hand around her narrow waist as my lips move along hers.

And for a brief second, I'm stunned, brought to another world where Sarah doesn't exist and my worries are nowhere to be found. Instead, I'm lost in the most perfect pair of lips I've ever tasted.

My hand grows tighter on her waist as her fingers toy with my blond locks. She steps in closer, her mouth parting just slightly. I part mine as well while her other hand falls to my chest. Hell, this woman tastes good, like tequila and promises.

Just as I reach to pull her in even closer, she breaks away but keeps her face close as she whispers, "Please pretend to be my boyfriend for a second. Also, you're the best sex I've ever had."

That makes me smirk. "Damn, and I didn't even have to do anything to earn the title." I catch her glance over her shoulder, so I quickly say, "I'm Silas."

"Nice to meet you," she says before turning around and sinking into me, my open stance on the barstool welcoming her as I slip my arm around her waist and pull her in even closer. Not sure why I'm going with her demands. Maybe I'm a bit drunk from the kiss . . . and the Scotch, but I hold still, ready for what's to come.

Three people approach us.

One is a woman sporting a shocked, disapproving glare—must be one of the offenders.

Behind her is a lanky man whose brow is pinched together so tightly that I bet it could hold a quarter if I slipped it in.

And the other man just keeps blinking . . . rapidly, as if he can't quite comprehend what he's witnessing.

From a guess, I think Cranky and Lanky are the people

Ollie—that's her name, right?—is trying to save face with, and the blinker has to be a friend.

"See, told you he was over here," Ollie says as she places her hand on mine. "He's just shy, is all."

Ehh, shy? Not really, but I'll go with it.

I nod at them, not saying anything while still acknowledging their presence.

"Well, I, uh . . . I don't know what to say," the girl says.

"You're . . . you're dating Silas Taters?" Lanky asks. Honestly, I'm shocked it took this long for the guy to say something.

"Oh, you know each other?" Ollie asks, clearly having no idea who the hell I am.

"Everyone knows who Silas Taters is," Lanky says.

Clearly, not everyone.

"It's . . . it's a pleasure to meet you," Lanky says, holding his hand out.

Out of respect for my image, I take it and offer him a solid shake. "Thanks, pleasure is mine, man."

I feel Ollie stiffen against me, probably wondering what the hell is going on and how her ex-boyfriend knows who I am, so I decide to help her out a bit.

"Ollie and I don't talk about hockey much . . ." I leave it at that, letting them fill in the blank.

Cranky's eyes narrow. "Wait, if you're dating a hockey player, then why are you so up in arms about your assignment?"

Hmm, wonder what the assignment is. Also, really curious why Ollie and Cranky are nemeses. Who threw the first punch? Who wronged who? Was it because the ex-boyfriend was stolen? Not to be a dick, but he doesn't seem like much of a prize to me.

"Uh, because he just said we don't talk about hockey much," Ollie says, and I'm somewhat impressed with her ability to think on her feet. "I clearly don't want to bother him about it."

I bring her in tighter and lightly stroke her stomach with my thumb, catching Lanky's eyes falling to the movement. Huh, the guy has some jealousy showing, so hopefully, this helps her out.

And keeping with the shy guy mentality, I quietly say, "You can bother me, babe."

She turns a few inches and cups my cheek while saying, "Thank you." And then, once again, her soft, delicious lips touch mine, and she lightly kisses me. It's short, but goddamn, is it sweet. I could easily kiss this girl more. She wouldn't even have to ask me to pretend.

"Well," the girl huffs. "We should get going. We have plans."

"Yeah, okay," Lanky says, his eyes never averting from Ollie's and my connection.

"Good luck with your assignment. I think you'll need it," Cranky says right before she turns Lanky around and pushes him toward the bar's exit.

Once they're out of sight, Ollie turns toward me, grateful-ness all over her face. And hell . . . she's beautiful, but I only get a quick glance before she's pulling me into a tight hug, her tits pressing into my chest. "Oh my God, thank you so much. You completely saved me."

Not sure what to do, I return the three-second embrace.

When she pulls away, I get a good look at her.

Petite, toned body. Large chest for her size, beautiful long brown hair that seems to be naturally wavy, green, almond-shaped eyes, and plump lips. She's an absolute smoke show.

"Uh, yeah, glad I could be of service."

"What the hell is going on?" the friend says as he steps forward. "What was that, Ollie?"

Biting the corner of her lip, looking coy as shit, she says, "I took a chance, and by the grace of good luck, it worked out for me."

"So you don't know each other?" the guy asks.

Ollie shakes her head. "No."

"Never seen her before," I add.

"Well, hell, you convinced me. I thought you were hiding something from me, Ollie."

She chuckles and shakes her head. "Nope, just a random guy."

"Hell," the guy says while pulling on his hair.

Yeah, hell is right.

I could have convinced myself we were together just from that kiss and the way she cuddled into me. I hate to admit it, but it felt good for a second to have someone need me again. To have someone touch me, cuddle into me, treat me as theirs.

Turning back toward me, Ollie says, "Well, I'll let you get back to your drink. Thank you so much again. I can't tell you the kind of favor you just did for me. I truly appreciate it." And with that, she takes her friend by the arm and starts to pull away.

I'm not sure what comes over me.

Maybe it's the kiss.

Maybe it's the thought of having to see Sarah around my sacred space.

Or maybe it's the Scotch.

Before I can stop myself, I say, "You owe me."

She pauses and looks over her shoulder. "What?"

I grip my glass and lift it to my mouth. From over the rim, I say, "You owe me." I take a sip. "I did you a favor, so I think you should do me one." I kick out the barstool next to me and nod toward it. "Take a seat."

Her eyes flit from the seat and then back up to me. "If you think I'm going to sleep with you, you better think again."

"I don't want to sleep with you," I say, even though the

prospect of it is appealing. Wouldn't mind tasting those lips again.

Her friend leans down, and even though it seems like he tries to keep his comment quiet, I can still hear him. "I think you should at least listen to him. He did just let you sexually assault him with your mouth."

"Hey, I gave him three seconds to say no. There was no sexual assault. That kiss was consensual . . . right?" she asks me on a wince.

I nod. "It was consensual."

"See. Consensual. Everything is on the up and up." She gestures toward me. "Now, if you'll excuse us, we have some drinking to do tonight, and I'm sure you have the goal at hand. Have a good night."

"Sit. Down," I say in a firmer tone, which stops her.

She slowly turns on her heel. "Uh, excuse me?" she asks, a spark of fire lighting up her burning irises. "Did you just try to use some alpha-hero voice on me?"

"Alpha-hero voice? What the hell is that?" I ask.

"I don't think he reads romances like you," the friend says. "And I think he has a point. You owe him."

"Ross, whose side are you on?" Ollie asks, flapping her hands.

Ah, his name is Ross.

Man, does he look like a Ross. The name fits him perfectly.

"Yours, Ollie. But he's right. You do owe him. At least listen to what he has to say."

"And what if he's a predator, huh? You're just going to let me sit next to a predator?"

"If anyone is a predator, it's you," I say. "You're the one who kissed *me*."

"Oh please," she says, exasperated. "You kissed me back, and don't even pretend you didn't like it."

Ross, being of sound mind, says, "He's a hockey player.

Pretty sure he isn't going to risk his reputation on being a predator."

"That's what he wants you to think," Ollie says, putting up a pitiful fight. When Ross just gives her a look, she grunts out in frustration. "Fine." Ollie throws her arms up in the air. "But I'm agreeing to nothing." She gets a few inches from my face as she says, "You hear that? I agree to nothing!"

Reluctantly, she takes a seat on the barstool and slaps her clutch on the bar top. She turns toward me with her arms crossed under her breasts, which perks them up even more.

"Well, I'll leave you two to it," Ross says, slowly backing away.

"Wait, you're leaving?" Ollie asks. "You can't leave me with this guy. For all we know, he could be a murderer ready to drug me and take me back to his lair, where he'll sell my body parts on the black market."

First predator, now a murderer. She sure does have a high regard for men who help her out.

"Yet . . . you kissed me," I say.

"Out of sheer desperation. You saw the disbelief in Candace's eyes. She needed to be put in her place."

"I'll be right over there," Ross says, pointing to the end of the bar.

Ollie turns her attention toward the end of the bar. "Oh, near Fernando from accounting? The guy you've had a crush on all summer?"

Looking guilty as shit, Ross says, "He has his top three buttons undone. It's clear he's open for business tonight."

"Dear God," Ollie says while pinching the bridge of her nose. "Fine, go flirt. But you are not to leave this bar until I'm safe from this overlord."

"Overlord?" I ask. "Jesus Christ."

"Well, come on. Can't you just be a good Samaritan and do something for a damsel in distress without needing something in return? What happened to white knights?"

"Equal opportunity for all. That's what happened," I answer.

"Ugh, men."

"So . . ." Ross says, rocking on his heels. "Am I good to go?"

"Yes, go. But don't leave me."

"I won't." He kisses Ollie on the head and then takes off, leaving me alone with the now disgruntled woman with the perfect lips.

"Okay, you have me. Now, what do you want?" she asks with a snap to her tone.

Yeah, what do you want, Silas?

I'm not even sure. I just know that I couldn't let her walk away, not when I feel like I could use her the same way she used me.

Needing to collect my thoughts, I say, "Want a drink?"

"Actually, yes. Margarita on the rocks, no salt."

That I can do. Facing the bar, I grab the bartender's attention with a nod. I give him the order and request a refill for myself. While that's being filled, I say, "Want to properly introduce yourself?"

"If I must." She brushes the hem of her tight dress that has ridden up to her midthigh from crossing her toned legs. Just from a quick glance at her shapely shoulders, small waist, and muscled legs, I can tell she works out. "I'm Ollie Owens. I absolutely despise the woman who was just here because she's a know-it-all anus who is mad at me for using one of her Post-it Notes. And I think out of spite, she decided to date my ex, who I'm over, just so you know. Nothing like freeing the guy who acted like a dead fish in the bedroom."

I nod. "And what is this assignment she speaks of?"

Ollie rolls her eyes just as the bartender places our drinks in front of us. I offer a thank you and bring my glass to my lips as she says, "Just the stupid end-of-the-year assignment for our internship that's worth all of my credit."

I nearly spit out my drink as I attempt to swallow, choking on the burning liquid. After a few coughs, I say, "Internship? As in you're . . . in college?" When she nods, I mutter, "Jesus Christ, please tell me you're of age."

Her brows narrow. "Of course I'm of age. All college students are, you nitwit."

Huh . . . she's right. They are.

"How old are you?"

She tilts her head. "Twenty-one. How old are *you?*"

"Thirty-one," I answer.

"Ew, you're in your thirties?"

The fuck?

"It's not like I said I was sixty," I snap.

"Still . . . thirties, so old."

"It's not *that* fucking old," I shoot back. Although, I'm starting to really feel those long nights on the ice lately.

"Still, ten years difference? That means when I was born, you were hitting the double digits. You could have been my babysitter. You're a decade older than me, a near generation. Ew, I kissed an old man."

"You kissed an *experienced* man," I point out, growing irritated. "More than I can say for your ex who looked like he still watches *Rugrats* on Saturday mornings."

"What's *Rugrats?*"

"For fuck's sake," I say, dragging my hand over my face. "So what are you doing in college still? Getting your master's?"

"No, bachelor's in journalism, heading into my senior year of college."

Jesus fuck.

She's so young.

So fucking young that I *know* my boys would ask me what the fuck I was even doing talking to her. They'd give me so much shit if they knew.

"Bachelor's." I nod, trying to convince myself she's way

too young and I should just send her on her way. But as my phone dings next to me with incoming text messages, I'm reminded of my dilemma.

Sarah.

Sarah is back in my life even though I don't want her to be.

"So you have an assignment?" I ask before taking a sip of my drink to help wash away my worries.

"Yeah. It's the end-of-the-year article we need to write to earn our credit. Candace decided who got what topic, and as you can imagine, she deliberately gave me hockey as my assignment, knowing I know nothing about the stupid sport." Not reading the crowd around her, that's fine. "I hope her teeth fall out."

I chuckle. "I could help you with that, you know. Since I play hockey and all."

"But really, how experienced are you?" she asks.

"Pretty experienced. It's my job."

"Like . . . you're a professional hockey player? I thought you were just, I don't know, some club player or something people knew."

I slowly nod. I've never met anyone who has at least not seen my face or heard my name. Vancouver plasters it all over the place.

"I play for the Vancouver Agitators."

Her eyes widen slightly, and then they give me a slow once-over. "Like . . . the actual Agitators?"

"Yes, the actual Agitators."

Her lips purse to the side. "Prove it."

With a heavy sigh, I pick up my phone, ignore the texts from my boys, and type my name into the search engine. When it comes up with results—my face and Wikipedia info the very first thing—I turn it toward her.

She takes my phone and studies it. Her eyes flit up to me,

then back to the phone. Then up to me, then back to my phone.

"Your hair is longer in person," she says.

"That's because hair grows."

"You don't have scruff in this picture."

"Razors have to be used for something."

Her eyes narrow. "I don't see any tattoos in this picture."

"Because they're covered up. Jesus Christ." I take the phone from her. "Are you really going to be that difficult?"

"Excuse me for wanting to make sure you're not some impersonator trying to score women with a false identity of some poor schmuck who plays hockey for a living."

"Poor schmuck?" I ask. The fucking audacity of this girl. "I have millions in the bank to prove I'm anything but poor or a schmuck. Also, you're the one who came up to me. You're the one who kissed me, so why the fuck am I the one defending myself?"

"Because in this day and age, you can't trust anyone," she says before taking a drink of her margarita.

"So what makes me think I can trust you?"

"Oh, you can't." She shakes her head and sets her glass down. "I'm a total wild card. Truly, the most ornery in the morning, especially after drinking. I tend to focus more on my needs than others, and even though I say I don't want something, secretly, I always do. Completely untrustworthy, so if we're done here, I shall retreat to my friend to see how he's doing with his conquest to sit on Fernando's penis."

She starts to move, but I place my hand on her thigh. "Not so fast. You can't scare me away with your nonsense."

"Nonsense?" She dramatically clutches her hand to her chest. "How dare you speak of my life like that—"

"Cut the shit," I say. "I did you a favor. Now you need to do one for me."

She rolls her eyes. "Okay, I can see we haven't given good thought to the whole white knight thing." She rolls her wrist for me to continue. "Please, regale me with your demands."

Yeah, regale her with your demands, Silas.

I take a long, slow sip of my drink.

How the fuck can she help me?

My phone lights up beside me, and my eyes catch a glimpse of a text from Hornsby.

Hornsby: *What the fuck are you going to do about the welcome dinner?*

And just like that, a light bulb switches on in my head.

The welcome dinner, where everyone in the organization comes together before the season starts, and we toast to a healthy, successful year with ice skating, hot cocoa, and all that bullshit.

Which means Sarah will be there.

And the last thing I want is for Sarah to think I'm alone and unattached, possibly still pining for her.

No fucking way.

There's only one solution I can think of, and I'm rolling with it.

"I need you to pretend to be my girlfriend."

"What?" she asks with a laugh. "You can't be serious."

I swallow down the rest of my drink and say, "I'm dead serious."

"Pretend to be your girlfriend?" She blinks a few times. "Dude, I kissed you for like five seconds, and you want me to pretend to be your girlfriend? You're supposedly famous," she says, using air quotes. "Hire someone."

"I'm not going to hire someone. Do you know how lame that is?"

"Lamer than asking a girl in a bar ten years younger than you to be your pretend girlfriend?"

I pinch the bridge of my nose because, dammit, she has a point. This is all lame.

"You know what? Never mind. Forget I even asked." I turn

back toward the bar and try to flag down the bartender to order another drink. Anything to help forget this awkward conversation and the fact I'll have to deal with Sarah at the arena. We don't always interact with the front house staff, but from the description of Sarah's job, it seems like she'll be out on the ice for certain games with sponsors, so I'm bound to run into her.

"Why do you need me to pretend to be your girlfriend?" Ollie asks.

"Don't worry about it," I say. "Go see how your friend is progressing with the penis sitting."

I feel her hesitate like she doesn't quite know what to do, so I encourage her.

"Seriously, go."

"Okay," she says softly while stepping down from the barstool. But she doesn't walk away right away. Instead, I feel her eyes on mine. It's like she has more questions that she wants to ask but is trying to pluck up the courage to ask them.

"Ollie, I'm serious. Leave."

"I can see that you're serious," she says. "But I feel like I should stay."

"Why?"

I finally get the bartender's attention and ask for another Scotch. He gives me a concerned look but fills me up without a word.

"It seems like you're maybe in a bad mood."

I lift my glass to my lips. "What gave you that impression?"

"Hmm, I wonder," she says sarcastically, staring at my drink. "So what is it? What's causing you to drink this much and ask strange women to be your pretend girlfriend?"

"Nothing you need to worry about."

"Is it a girl?"

I grumble under my breath. "Ollie, please, for the love of God, just go."

Because she's a defiant ass, she takes a seat on her barstool again and pokes me in the side. "Tell me. It's a girl. What did she do to you?"

"Do you really think I'm going to tell a complete stranger that?"

"Well, you did ask me to be your pretend girlfriend, so I assume, yeah, you would."

For how annoyingly young she is, she's quite clever and quick on her feet. Absolutely terrifying.

"Just an ex who has re-entered my life," I say, keeping it simple. She doesn't need to know the details.

"Were you in love with this ex?"

"Yes," I answer. "She was my high school sweetheart."

"Oh," Ollie says softly, empathy evident in her voice. "I'm assuming she's the one who broke your heart?" I nod. "Yeah, that's pretty obvious. Okay, how did she re-enter your life?"

"Got a job with the Agitators."

"As in your hockey team?"

I nod again. "Yup." *I wonder if the bartender will pour me another drink after this one.*

"Knowing full well that you are on the team?"

"Yup."

"Wow," she says, and I catch her shaking her head. "What a wench. That's all kinds of messed up."

"It is. And the reason my phone keeps blowing up is because my teammates know, and now it's going to be this big fucking thing."

"What do you mean?" she asks.

I turn toward her again and rest my arm on the bar while keeping a solid grip on my glass. "They're protective of me. They saw what she did to me, they saw how she came back this summer and messed with my head for a goddamn second, and there's no doubt in my mind that she searched out this job to continue to fuck with me. And they'll be up my ass, making sure I'm okay."

"Aah, I see." She glances to the side. "So . . . would I be

your pretend girlfriend to fend off their concerns? Make her jealous? What's the proposal here?"

"You don't have to. It was a stupid idea," I say.

Her hand lands on my thigh, drawing my attention back to her gleaming eyes. "Maybe it wasn't."

"What do you mean?"

"Well, I feel like we could help each other out. I have this assignment to take care of, and I know nothing about hockey. You have friends to fend off and an ex. I think we could, you know, work things out. But . . . the offer has to be good." She lifts up and smiles.

"Why do I feel like I'm going to be indebted to you?"

"Because isn't that how it always is? You truly need more from me than I need from you."

"What about that doofus of an ex of yours and that Candace girl? Pretty sure you needed me first."

"Semantics." She waves her hand at me. "So what do you have to offer?"

"You're not kidding?"

She shakes her head. "No. I need to see your offer, and if I think it's worth my time, I'll take it."

"Are you sure you're studying journalism? Not law?"

"Positive," she says with a wide smile.

"Well, the fuck if I know." I lift my drink. "Frankly, I'm kind of drunk at this point, so I don't think I'm in the right mindset."

"Great, so why don't we talk this over tomorrow when you're fresh?"

"Not quite sure you understand how hard it is for a thirty-one-year-old to bounce back from a night out."

"You'll be fine." She grabs her clutch and pulls out her phone. "Here, enter your phone number and your name. What is it again? Simon?"

"Silas," I say. "Jesus Christ, every hockey fan in the city is crying right now that you got it wrong." I type my phone number into her phone.

"Ooo, sorry, Mr. Big Shot. Wasn't aware you were so popular."

"You need to pay attention more. My face is on quite a few billboards around the city."

"That's cute," she says, patting my cheek. "I'll text you tomorrow, and we can figure this all out. Bring your best proposal."

"How can I bring a proposal when I know nothing about you?"

"That's fair. Umm, let's see." She hops off her stool and straightens out her dress. "I like working out. I like sandwiches. Like all kinds, especially ones with lots of meat. I enjoy interior design and reading books. I also really like anything concerning lifestyle trends. Oh, I love a good face cream. Anything to keep those thirty-one-year-old wrinkles away, you know?" She presses her finger to my brow, and I swat her hand away.

"When you have to skate on the ice with two-hundred-pound men, you're bound to get wrinkles."

"Don't quite see the connection, but hang out with me, and I'll get that face looking fresh."

"What the fuck? It does look fresh."

"Okay." She smiles at me. "See you tomorrow . . . Simon."

"Silas," I call out.

"Yeah . . . Silas." She twiddles her fingers at me and takes off toward her friend.

I'm pretty sure I'll regret all this when I wake up, especially the three glasses of Scotch.

Chapter Three

OLLIE

"Alexa, play today's hits," I say as I throw my hair into a messy bun.

It's Sunday, which means it's reset day.

I woke up this morning, fresh as a daisy, so I went on a run followed up by a simple ab workout, then walked to the dining hall and picked up a protein smoothie.

What I love about the dorms is that they are for upperclassmen only, and the dining hall is open year-round because most of us stay through the summer for our internships. Not to mention, I have my own room. Which means I don't have to be bothered by anyone other than my neighbors.

I remember when I first toured my dorm. It was an immediate yes for me. Not only do I have my own suite, but I have my own bathroom as well. The rooms are equipped with a mini kitchen, bathroom, desk, and a double bed, not even a twin—see what I'm talking about. It's total luxury for college. And when we don't cook, we can grab something from the dining hall or the convenience store right here on campus. I have everything I need at my fingertips. The only thing missing is a gym.

If I were a student athlete, I'd have access to the best gym this area can offer, but unfortunately, that's not the case. Instead, I pay fifteen dollars a month at a gym ten minutes away and deal with a bunch of meatheads who believe they know more than me about lifting weights.

First things first for my reset day—strip my bed and replace the sheets with clean ones.

Music on in the background—thank you, Alexa—I get to work. Nothing is better than preparing yourself for the week ahead. I love starting a Monday on a fresh start—room clean, fridge stocked with my quick grab items, and laundry done.

Sheets in hand, I stuff them in my laundry basket, and I pick it up along with my other laundry. Grabbing my detergent and keys, I head to the laundry room.

Luckily, I wake up at a decent hour on Sundays, which bypasses everyone else in the laundry room who might be curing a hangover. My trick is tons of electrolytes and a run to sweat it all out. I know not many people can run after a night of drinking, but even if I feel like I'm going to puke, I still go for my run. It's the best cure.

I take the elevator to the basement, and when I step off, I spot a familiar face in the laundry room.

"I'm surprised to see you here," I say to Ross as I set my basket on one of the folding counters.

Shoulders slumped, he replies, "Yeah, last night didn't end as I'd hoped."

"So I'm guessing you didn't hook up with Fernando?" I ask as I open one of the washers and stick my sheets inside. Another great thing about our dorms is that laundry is free.

"Not so much." Ross starts his washer, walks over to the folding counter, and takes a seat. His eyes scan my outfit, and a small smile passes over his lips. "Your hard nipples in your crop top are telling me very clearly that it's laundry day."

I glance down at my favorite crop top and then back up at him. "What's the point of wearing a bra on Sundays?"

"A motto I live by," Ross says.

"A great one at that. So tell me about last night. What happened?"

"Fernando is shyer than I expected him to be. He flirted a lot and even touched my arm a few times, but when it came to making a move, he backed down and said he had to get home. I don't know, it was weird."

I fill up the washer with detergent and turn it on, then move on to the next washer. "I'm sorry. I know you've been crushing on him all summer."

"It's fine. I'd rather have a guy who takes charge, you know?"

"Yes, I get it." Poor Ross, I think he's struck out all summer. Not sure he's had one hookup. The boy needs some love too.

"What happened with the hockey player last night?"

"Oh, I almost forgot," I say as I reach for my phone at the bottom of my laundry basket. "I was supposed to text him this morning."

"Why?"

"Oh, he wants to talk about me being his fake girlfriend or something. But you keep that between us."

"Who the hell would I tell? I barely like anyone these days. Hell, I hardly tolerate you."

"You can't get rid of me even if you tried," I say as I pull up his name and shoot off a quick text.

Ollie: *My place, noon, bring sandwiches.*

I send another text with my address and suite number and go back to the washer, filling it up with my clothes. I know my mother taught me to sort my laundry, but let's be honest. It can all go into one giant pile, and you just set it on cold water without any ramifications for laziness. I don't have time to separate.

"Uh . . . are we going to discuss what happened last night?" Ross asks. "Or are we just going to ignore the fact that you went up to a complete stranger and made out with him?"

Made out is a bit extreme. Kissed a bit? Now, that's more accurate. And between you and me, the man was a good kisser. I was going in expecting the worst and was very pleasantly surprised. Talk about lucking out.

"I mean, we can talk about last night if you want, but there's not much to say. I wanted Candace to eat her words, so I made sure that happened. Simon . . . errr, I mean Silas, was a great kisser, thank God."

"How can you be so nonchalant about this?"

"Because it was a kiss. It's not like I stuck my hand down his pants and twirled his dick around like my own personal pepperoni stick. It was a simple kiss, and he thankfully went with it. Candace ate her words, and Yonny got to watch me make out with a hot guy. It was a win-win."

"And him asking you to be his pretend girlfriend, that's what you owe him?"

"We're going to discuss details later today." I grab my laundry basket and nod toward the exit. "You coming?"

Ross hops off the counter, grabs his things as well, and together, we take the elevator up to our floor. Lucky for me, Ross lives a few suites down from mine, so when we get to our floor, he follows me to my room.

When we arrive in my room, my phone dings with a message. I set my basket down and read it.

Silas: What kind of sandwiches?
Ollie: Meat ones. See you at noon.

"Was that him?" Ross asks.

"Yeah, he asked what kind of sandwich I wanted. Oh shoot, I forgot something."

I pick up my phone and type out another text.

Ollie: *Don't forget the deli pickle. I'll scream if you show up without it. Thanks.*

"Pickle?" Ross asks.

I smile at him and grab the clean sheets from my closet. "I have you so well trained."

I lift the sheet in the air and let it float down to the bed.

"You realize I can see the underside of your breasts, right?" Ross asks.

"Can you? Huh." I shrug. "Do anything for you?"

"Not really."

"Shame. I have great tits," I say with a smirk.

"Hence what you're wearing. You like to show them off."

"No, I don't like to show them off. I just like to be comfortable, and this shirt is comfortable."

"Are you going to change before your hockey friend gets here?"

"And give me more laundry to do? I'm good, thanks." I fit the sheet over my bed, then pick up the flat sheet. "So what are you up to today?"

"Are you really going to change the subject like that? Ollie, you realize you kissed a very popular hockey player last night, and he's coming to your dorm today. Do you honestly have nothing to say about that?"

"Not really. I don't know the guy or know of him. I'm grateful he kissed me back last night, and I feel bad for him. It seems like he's going through a tough spot, so I thought I'd listen to what he has to say. Plus, he can possibly help me with my assignment. It's all business."

"That's until you find yourself crushing on him."

"Oh please," I scoff while neatly making hospital corners on my bed. Nothing is more soothing than sleeping in a properly made bed. "I have better things to do than fall for some guy ten years older than me."

"Ten years?" Ross asks. "Huh, I wouldn't have guessed that. But you know what that means? Ten years older . . ."

"What?" I ask while placing my white comforter back on the bed.

"Experience."

"So?"

"I mean . . . bedroom experience."

I roll my eyes. "I knew what you meant."

"You should be excited about that. After being with Yonny, who was subpar at best, this should give you some joy."

"First of all, I have zero intention of sleeping with this man. If we do any kind of agreement, there will be nothing sexual about the interaction. All business. And second, who's to say he's even good at sex?"

"Did you see his forearms?" Ross asks. "They were all ripply and muscular. Trust me, he's good in bed. I bet he has a piercing."

"Oh my God, you've lost it." I move around him.

"He has the tattoos and the scruffy hair. Broad shoulders. Wicked lips. Roguish eyes. There is no doubt he also has a pierced cock. And with the way you love giving head, could you imagine if there was a piercing on it?"

I do love giving head. I don't know why. Something about the control of it all, but I've never given a guy a blow job who had a piercing. It might be fun. *Wait, what am I thinking?* No. That's not something I'm going to imagine.

"Listen, Ross. I have too much going on to even consider a relationship at the moment. This whole fake dating thing might actually be good. We could use each other when needed without the pressure of having to . . . you know . . . be all couple-y. He needs help. I need help. With the holidays coming up and the stupid parties we'll have to go to, it might be beneficial."

"You're serious," Ross deadpans. "You're actually thinking about doing this?"

"The more I do, the more I believe it might be a good

idea. Although, I want to hear his proposal first of course. Milk this thing for all I can."

Ross shakes his head at me before sitting on my desk chair. "You're unbelievable, you know that? I don't think I could be like you. Act like I'm dating someone and not get feelings for that person."

"What's there to get feelings about? This is business. It's like purchasing the perfect winter slippers. But instead of slippers, I'm purchasing a fake boyfriend. Simple. And it's not like he'll want to start a relationship, hence the need for something fake. I know nothing about hockey other than the fact that it's a long-ass, never-ending season, and I'm sure he'll be quite busy. It's beneficial for both parties."

"And what happens if there's an event he can't show up at because he's so busy?"

"Uh, duh, I just say my boyfriend is playing a game, simple as that. It's not like they'll assume I'm lying. They can look it up on the Internet. Seriously, this might be the best plan I've ever had. I can keep Candace pissed, learn about hockey, use him for parties and gatherings when I need to, and then wash our hands of the agreement when we're all done. Simple."

Ross shakes his head in disbelief. "I think you're making it out to be that simple, but you're forgetting one thing."

"What's that?" I ask as I finish fitting my pillows in their fresh cases.

"You're a romantic at heart, a daydreamer, someone who gets lost in her feelings. If you truly think you can make an arrangement with a man like Silas Taters and not catch feelings, you've lost your damn mind."

I plop my pillow on my bed and smile at him. "Watch me."

Chapter Four

SILAS

She lives in a dorm?

A fucking dorm?

Jesus Christ, what the hell am I doing?

I rub my hand over my forehead, absolutely humiliated as I sit in my Tesla. Staring at the dorm entrance, I wonder if I'll be able to muster enough courage to walk up to those doors and go in.

I spent the morning figuring out where to get a meaty sandwich and pickle combo. When I found a place, I ordered five different sandwiches because I was unsure what she would want.

The boys asked me how I was this morning. I told them I was great, that I didn't think Sarah would be a problem, and not to worry about me. I think they bought it. At least, I hope they did because if the number of text messages I got from them is any indication of how they're going to play this Sarah thing out, I truly hope they bought it.

No way in hell was I going to tell them about Ollie and what happened last night. Or the fact I'm sitting in a dorm parking lot with a bagful of sandwiches and pickles, looking to make a college girl my pretend girlfriend. They'd believe I've lost my mind. They'd probably try to have me committed if I'm honest. Some sort of intervention would occur.

Maybe I need it, though.

Because is this really how low I've stooped?

Is this rock bottom?

For my own sake, I truly hope so. I don't think I could go any lower than this.

I glance at the clock and swear under my breath. If I don't leave now, I'll be late, and I don't want to be a dick since she's expecting me—and her stupid sandwich and pickle. So on a groan, I slip my hat on, glasses, and hood over my hat—can't be too careful—then take my bag of food in one hand and head toward the entrance of her dorm, where security personnel man the door.

"Post Mates delivery?" he asks as I approach.

Sure . . . why not.

"Yup," I say. "Suite 305. She asked me to bring it up."

The door buzzes, and I'm let in. Okay, that seemed too easy.

I spot the elevators and press the button for the third floor. When the doors close, a nervous energy bounces in me as I ride to Ollie's floor. When the doors part, I'm surprised by the wide, bright hallways and the common space full of couches, chairs, and tables. Not that bad.

I follow signs for her apartment and spot it at the end.

Fuck, what if she has roommates?

Would she invite me over if she has roommates? No, right?

Jesus, I hope not. If she does, I'm dropping this food off and bolting. No thirty-one-year-old man should be in a dorm room full of women . . . ever.

Palms sweating, I knock on her door and stand there, waiting for her to open up. It takes a few seconds, but when she does, I bite the inside of my cheek to keep in the inappropriate sound that wants to escape. Standing in the doorway, wearing a crop top with her nipples erect, is Ollie. Her sweatpants hang low on her hips, her toned stomach is on full display, and she looks so comfortably hot that it's almost painful.

Jesus.

Is this something she wears on the daily?

And where's her bra? I can see nearly her whole nipple against the sheer fabric of her shirt.

"Between the way you're inconspicuously dressed and the full-on once-over you just gave me, your vibe is screaming pervert looking for his next prey."

And then there's that snappy wit of hers. How could I possibly forget?

"Just let me in," I say, irritated that she's right.

She pushes the door open even more and lets me into a quaint studio suite. With a kitchen on the right of the wall, bathroom on the left, the room parts open into a space just big enough for a desk, double bed, and dresser.

So . . . no roommates. Thank fuck.

The bag of sandwiches is taken from my hand and set on the counter. "Make yourself comfortable, and when I say that, I mean get rid of the hood, glasses, and hat. You look ridiculous."

"I didn't want anyone to recognize me."

"You are giving your stardom too much credit. I don't even think that many people like hockey."

I nearly choke on my own saliva. Is she kidding? We're the most successful team in the league, and we live in Canada. Hockey is in the blood of every Canadian.

"You realize you live in Vancouver, right? Everywhere you

look, someone is wearing something branded by the Agitators logo."

She just shrugs her shoulders. "Never noticed, I guess. Oh, is this pastrami? Yes, please."

The pastrami was for me, but that's just fucking fine.

"What do you want? Plain ham? You seem like a ham guy." She slips the sandwich on a plate and turns toward me to hand it over when she notices I haven't disrobed. "Oh, for fuck's sake."

She sets the sandwiches down on her bed, then steps up to me and tears my hood and hat off in one fell swoop. Then she removes my glasses.

"There, now take a seat and eat."

"Where?" I ask as I pat down my hair. "There's no dining table."

"Dining table. God, could you be any more of a snob? It's a dorm room, jackass. There's my bed and my desk chair. Take your pick. Unless you want to have a picnic on the floor, those are your choices."

I think I'm still too hungover for this conversation.

"I'll take the desk chair." There is no way I'm getting on that bed. It looks far too comfortable, and I can see myself falling asleep.

"Then I'll take my bed." She hops up and then brings her plate close to her. She lifts the sandwich and takes a large bite before leaning back and moaning.

Jesus, that sound. It has the blood in my body pumping harder.

"Did you go to Tony's around the corner?"

"No, the Brooklyn Pickle." I walk over to her fridge to look for a drink. When I see nothing but hot sauce, I glance over at her. "Anything to drink?"

"Glasses are above the sink. Water is great. Thanks."

Okay. I grab two glasses and fill them up with sink water. I give one to her and then set one on the desk for me before grabbing my plate from the bed and taking a seat.

"Aren't you hot in that sweatshirt?"

"Yeah," I say.

"Then take it off. God, I can't watch you eat in that."

I set my plate down again, grab my hoodie from over my head, and pull it until it's completely off. I adjust my shirt that rose, and then I fold the sweatshirt and put it on the desk.

"You know, if you don't want to get recognized, maybe don't wear an Agitators sweatshirt."

"It's all I had," I say before taking a large bite of my ham sandwich, wishing it was pastrami.

"So . . . how was the hangover? Brutal?"

"More than I care to admit," I say.

"I was perfectly fine, in case you were wondering. I went for a run this morning, did some light ab work, took a shower, and had a protein shake. I've also done my laundry, cleaned my room, and ordered my online groceries to be delivered later today. What have you done?"

"Searched sandwich shops with pickles on my phone."

She smirks and holds up her pickle. "Well, then you accomplished more than I would have expected. Don't you have practice or something?"

"Sundays we have off. Once the season starts in a few weeks, things get more intense."

"Do you drink during the season?"

"Yes," I answer. "I try to be as healthy as I can, but there are nights when nothing will cure a tough loss like a pint of beer."

"Soaking your sorrows, I get it. Do you do this sorrow drinking at a bar or at home?"

"If we're away, it's at a bar. If we're home, it's in my apartment."

"Makes sense, and do you ever pick up women at the bar?" Her brows wiggle.

"If you're wondering if I often ask women to be my pretend girlfriend, the answer is no."

"I'm not asking that. From how you reacted last night, I knew it was the first time you'd asked someone to be your fake girlfriend. I'm just curious about your sex life."

"Why are you curious about that? Interested?"

"God, no," she says, as if that's the most preposterous idea she's ever heard. "You're far too old for me. I'm just curious to know what it's like to be a hockey player. Do you get a lot of action?"

"Some players do," I answer, not wanting to use names, ahem, Levi Posey. "Some are in relationships. And then there's me. I only hook up if I really need it. But I don't like fucking random women because it's too risky. The last thing I need is a random kid."

"So your pleasure is mainly from your hand."

"Is this really how we're going to start the conversation? Masturbation?"

"I truly believe the best way to get to know someone is through their orgasms, so yes. How many times a week do you come?"

"Jesus Christ," I mutter. Is this really what the dating world has come to—not that we're dating—but have I really been that out of the game that we're now comparing orgasms?

"Are you shy? Fine, I'll go first. I have a healthy appetite for pleasure. I would say at least every night. Now it's your turn."

Every night? I nearly choke on my sandwich just thinking about her getting herself off so often. I'm pretty sure Sarah didn't even know how to touch herself, let alone want to touch herself that often, or even once a week for that matter.

"How does this pertain to fake dating?"

"It has everything to do with fake dating. Before I sign on for anything, I need to make sure you're pleasuring yourself so you don't come sniffing over here, looking for someone to place their hand on your dick. Because if we do this thing—guidelines still to be determined—then I need to know that there is no chance in hell you'll be a horndog, sniffing up this tree."

"Wow," I say under my breath. Not sure I've ever had a woman talk to me like this before.

"So if you don't mind, please tell me how many times you masturbate."

I pull on the back of my neck. "Probably same as you."

"Ooo, healthy. Good to know. Now that we have that out of the way, I'd like you to convince me why I should agree to this farce."

"Honestly, I have no idea," I say as I lean back in her desk chair and kick my feet up on the foot of her bed. "The more I think about it, the more I know it's ridiculous, but fuck . . ." I shake my head lightly. "There are some events I'm going to, and it would feel so fucking great to show up with a girlfriend."

"I understand that feeling. I experienced it last night when I shoved my lips onto yours. It felt great to kiss another man in front of my ex. It's like silently laughing in their face."

"That's how I imagined it would be." I take a bite of my sandwich, chew, and swallow. "I know it would be asking a lot, but I could help you out as well. I'm not sure if your ex and that Candace girl will be at anything you're attending with the holidays coming up, but if I don't have a game and I'm in town, I can go with you. I can also offer you help on your assignment."

"Which I'll probably need," she says. "Sucks that you're out of town a lot coming up because there are some events I could use you at."

"And I have some too. Plus, if I told my friends I'm dating you, then they won't harass me over my personal life, which they've tended to do a lot since Sarah and I broke up." I stare down at my sandwich. "I feel like I need to sweeten the deal for you."

"I could enjoy a little sweetening."

I twist my lips to the side, thinking about what I can offer her. I have lots of fucking money, but that would be borderline prostitution, and I'm not into that. I have a nice car, a home gym . . .

Hmm, maybe that would be of interest.

"Do you need to borrow a car? You can always borrow mine when I'm out of town."

"I have a car, but thanks."

"Yeah, figured. I have a home gym, not sure if—"

"Tell me more about that," she says, setting her sandwich down and wiping her fingers with a napkin.

"Uh, I have a gym in my apartment with practically brand-new equipment. I don't use it as often as I want, but just enough to warrant the money I spent on it. I mainly work out at the arena."

"What kind of equipment?"

"Everything," I say.

"Even cardio?"

"I need to keep my legs in shape to ensure I keep up late in the third period. Yeah, there's cardio."

"And you would give me access to your apartment so I could use the gym? You don't think that's weird or anything?"

"I have nothing to hide," I say. "My cabin up in Banff feels more like home than my apartment here in Vancouver."

"You have a cabin in Banff?" she asks. "Like in the mountains?"

"Yup." I smirk at the awe in her eyes. "Not so bad knowing a thirty-one-year-old now, is it? Bet your little pipsqueak friends don't have a cabin in Banff, do they?"

"I don't even think they pay their own phone bill."

That makes me chuckle. "Anyway, the gym is yours if you want to use it. Tack that on with helping out on that assignment and going to any event I'm present for, and that's what I can offer."

"And what would you require from me?"

"Being available when I need you."

"For . . ."

I roll my eyes. "Nothing sexual. Remember, my hand owns that job."

"As does mine." She winks. "Well, that and my seven-inch, neon-purple vibrator that I've promised myself to use only once a week to keep my expectations low."

"Probably smart." I take a bite of my sandwich because I'm tempted to ask her if I can see it. Seven inches? The girl likes a touch of length. "But nothing sexual. I think you established that early on in this conversation. But we'd have to be intimate around people."

"Describe intimate."

"Holding hands, maybe a kiss here and there. You'll have to look at me as if you find me attractive and not some old man you're trying to help across the street."

She smiles. "It might behoove you to know that I do find you attractive. I'm just able to control myself, unlike you, whose eyes wandered immediately to my breasts the moment you saw me this afternoon."

"You're not wearing a bra."

"So?"

"So that's hot. I looked."

"Well, at least you're honest." She takes a sip of water. "Okay, so are we doing this?"

"You tell me." And for some reason, I hold my breath, waiting for her answer.

It's not like it matters if she says no. It's not like my career or my life depends on her answer.

But I also find the idea of having someone by my side when I'm around Sarah very appealing. I'm still not over what Sarah did to me, and it would feel like such sweet redemption if I showed up to an event with Ollie on my arm.

So yeah, maybe I do hope that Ollie says yes even though this is an asinine idea. Probably a terrible plan in the long run.

"Seems like a ridiculous thing to agree to," she says. "But I'll be honest, I think the gym won me over. You have no idea the type of misogynistic behavior I deal with all the time at the gym."

"What kind of behavior?" I ask.

"Oh, you know, random men coming up to me, mansplaining proper form even though they're over in the corner, attempting bicep curls by swinging their entire body to get the weight up. Or men who think they can move my stuff to the side to use the bench I'm occupying. Or stealing equipment or blatantly trying to hit on me. It's frustrating. I just want to work out."

I run my tongue over my top teeth. "Well, you don't need to worry about that with me."

"So I can count on you not attempting to show me how to squat?"

"I probably won't be there very often at all, so no, you won't have to worry."

"How close are you to my dorm?"

"Ten minutes," I say. "Not very far at all."

She sighs and leans against her headboard. "This feels too good to be true. My very own gym, help on this stupid hockey thing, and a guy to take to random events. I should have signed up for this a long time ago."

"Guess you kissed the right man at the right time."

She smirks at me. "I guess I did."

Chapter Five

OLLIE

From my purse, I pull out the picture frame I bought last night and filled with a picture of Silas. It was a random thought after he left, and I couldn't think of anything more perfect for Candace to see while she walked by my cubicle this sunny Monday morning. Sure, we have a few weeks left before the school year starts, and I won't be in the office that much longer, but it felt . . . apropos to solidify this boyfriend thing with a picture. Really shove it in her face.

And I must admit, I picked an amazing picture.

Shirt pulled up halfway, showing off the deep V in his waist and his endless stack of abs. His wet hair hanging around his shoulders, the scruff on his face defining his sharp jawline, and those freaking eyes of his, crystal blue and sparkling, as they dangerously look at the camera. He's fucking hot.

Yup, I said it.

So hot.

Like *take me to the hardware store to purchase an A/C unit for my nether region* hot.

And broad. Huge actually. I didn't notice it until he was in my dorm yesterday, soaking up what little space I had.

Tall.

Muscular.

Just overall, a very large presence of body mass and attractiveness.

And he just so happened to leave his sweatshirt at my place yesterday, so I might have tried it on, you know, just to see how things fit. It was the most luxurious piece of clothing I've ever put on my body. Oversized, it came down to my thighs and smelled like high-end cologne that makes women weak in the knees.

Good thing I'm immune to it.

There are no weak knees where I'm concerned.

I can admit when someone is sexy, and he is. And I can admit that wearing his sweatshirt felt nice because it did. But I also know where to draw the line, and no way in hell will I be mixing any business with pleasure.

For one, the man seems complicated. Let's face it, he's looking for a pretend girlfriend to make an old girlfriend jealous. He probably still has feelings for said old girlfriend, and that's a tangled web I want nothing to do with. It's messy, and I don't do messy.

Also, he's on a different path than I am. It seems that playing professional hockey sucks all the time from your life. Even though I have school and an internship, I still very much like having fun. I like to go out and party and have a good time. I'm pretty sure his good time is staying at home and fiddling around with knitting needles—this has not been confirmed, just an assumption.

And finally, I'm not sure we have a lot in common besides an appreciation for gym equipment. You can only talk about your favorite kind of racking system so many times. Therefore, to sum the last few paragraphs up, there is no way, on my two perfect nipples, that I will ever find myself in the arms of Silas Taters—unless it's for business.

Glad we're on the same page.

I glance at the picture, focusing longer on his abs. His regimen must be insane to have such little body fat. It's hard to hold back my smile because in all honesty, I feel like I'm getting the better end of the deal.

"My, oh my, what do we have here?" Ross asks, coming into my cubicle space. He picks up the picture and stares at it for a few seconds. "I don't think this is suitable for work. At least, that's the angle Candace will take to get you to remove this brain-melting picture."

"Ew, do you really think she will?"

Ross raises his brow. "Please, she's probably already figuring out a way to tell you what she saw last night was an illusion and not reality."

"You're probably right." I reach into my purse and pull out a stack of photos. "Good thing I printed multiple copies yesterday."

Ross chuckles and shakes his head at the same time. "God, I love you so much."

I wave the pictures in front of my face. "Always come prepared. You never know what the tyrant Candace might throw at you during any given day."

"Did I hear my name?" Candace says, appearing out of nowhere.

Good God!

Evil!

Who does that? Who can hear their name and quickly appear out of thin air?

Witches, that's who.

Tacking on a pleasant facade, I say, "Why, yes, Candace, you did."

"Hopefully all good things." She offers me a smile that seems more condescending than anything.

Good things . . . I'm not sure I can utter one nice thing about the woman. Even her precious Post-it Notes are an irritating color. Seafoam green? Always go with neon. Post-it Notes are meant to be SEEN, not used as an aesthetic.

"Of course, we only ever say great things about you." I smile back.

"Oh, is that a picture of your boyfriend?" She points at the picture of Silas.

"Yes, it is. Since we're now out in public, I figured it would be okay to bring in a picture to remind me of what a fine piece of ass I get to grab every night."

Ross coughs and hides his grin. Candace is not amused.

"Were you hiding your relationship before?" she asks.

I nod. "Yup. Since he plays professional hockey, we figured we'd keep it quiet until we were ready to announce."

"I see." She folds her arms and stares at the picture. "Seems a little crude for the workplace, don't you think?" Ross called it. Candace, the pearl clutcher, ruining everyone's life.

I glance at the picture and then back at her. "I don't think so. It just reminds me how I get to lick those abs every chance I get."

Ross chokes out a laugh while Candace's eyes narrow. "That's inappropriate, Ollie."

"Oh, did I offend you?" I ask. "Is it because Yonny doesn't have abs to lick?"

"He's actually put on some muscle." Oh please, the man has ramen noodle arms, and we all know it. "Now that he's shed an old relationship, he can focus on himself and not play second fiddle to the ego he used to date."

Oh.

My.

Fuck.

No, she did not.

Where the hell does she get the nerve?

I lean back in my chair, nostrils flared. "I know you're talking about me, Candace."

"Good, because I was." She folds her arms tighter and juts out her hip. What does she plan on doing with that stance? I could take her down with one swipe to the leg. One knife-hand to the throat. One sharpened pencil straight to the tit.

My hand itches for an attack, something she's not expecting. Teach her a freaking lesson on who to mess with.

"Ehh, you know, maybe we should all get to work," Ross says, clearly aware of the building tension. But guess who doesn't want any part in calming down? The Post-it Note Prostitute.

She leans forward, coffee ripe on her breath, and says, "I don't buy it for one second that you're dating Silas Taters. You either know him or struck up some sort of deal."

What sort of wizardry does this woman possess? Has she bugged my dorm room? Tapped into my text messages? Become a mind reader and can hear and see my every freaking thought? In all seriousness, I fear for Yonny because this woman has the potential to take down empires.

But of course, being the prideful woman that I am, I can't possibly show her that she's right. I will take this secret to my grave.

To the freaking grave! *pounds finger into table* There is no way in hell Candace Roundhouse will ever know that I struck a deal with Silas Taters. She will only think that he is the love of my freaking life.

"Wow, what a fantasy you're living in," I say. "Does it make you feel better, trying to come up with some sort of storyline like that?"

"I'm not coming up with a storyline. You know how I know you're lying?" she says, taking a step closer, her burgundy wool skirt scraping across my knee. Hideous, Candace, just hideous. "Because you were panicking the moment you saw that I assigned you hockey. If you were really dating Silas Taters, there wouldn't have been an ounce of panic in your eyes."

If only she weren't so clever—cunning—it would make fighting with her so much easier.

"There was no panic. There was shock because I assumed I would be assigned something in lifestyle, not sports. Also, the last thing I want to do is bother my boyfriend with hockey questions. He has better things to do like . . . win championships."

"Your boyfriend is a hockey player?" a deep, recognizable voice says.

Oh no . . .

All our heads turn toward where Mr. Roberts is standing, cup of coffee in hand, a permanent crease in his brow. Known for wearing only dark gray suits, he combs his slightly thinning salt-and-pepper hair neatly to the side while his well-trimmed mustache twitches with his question. Some interns in the office have believed that his mustache is its own organism that just lives on Roberts's face. I'm not a believer . . . at least that's what I tell myself.

"Mr. Roberts," I say, my body wavering between sitting, standing, and possibly curtseying. We never see him down here among the company peons. He's a high and mighty kind of dude, not one with the people. "Uh, good morning."

He sips his coffee, scanning all of us. "Good morning." He glances at the name tag on my cubicle and says, "Ollie, is it?"

"Yes, that would be me."

He nods. "You wrote that piece about romance books and how they apply to everyday life, didn't you?"

Good God, he knows of my work. The curtsey is feeling more and more necessary.

"Guilty," I reply while raising my hand.

"My wife liked it." Oh, the wife you cheat on with the head of the journalism department? How lovely.

"Oh . . . well . . . thank you to your wife." I dip my head in a slight bow, hating myself.

"What's this about a hockey player?"

Smiling a devilish gleam, Candace says, "Our very own Ollie Owens is dating Silas Taters from the Agitators."

Roberts's eyes widen as he takes another sip of his coffee. "Are you, now?"

I swallow hard and nod, suddenly feeling the pressure of this lie. It was all fun and games when it was just to make Candace jealous, but I don't particularly enjoy the look on Roberts's face. He's . . . beaming with excitement.

"Yes, Silas and I are dating," I answer because what else can I say? Candace is watching my every move.

He nods again, and it's the kind of nod that says he's thinking, not just taking a general interest in my life. And that's terrifying. You should never have your boss think about you . . . not in the conspiratorial way Roberts is.

Finally, he taps the top of my cubicle wall. "Make an appointment with my assistant. I'd like to speak to you today."

And my nipples just shriveled up.

"Oh sure, I'll, uh, get right on that," I say, stumbling over my words.

He doesn't offer me a reassuring response. Instead, he takes off down the hall, leaving me in a wake of "oh fuck."

"Well, that should be a fun conversation," Candace says while adjusting the waistband of her skirt.

"Why do you say that?" I try to hide the panic in my voice, but I do a poor job of it.

"Roberts has a vendetta against the owner of the Agitators. Despises the man. Did you not know that?" Candace smiles again. "Roberts is also a huge Agitators fan despite hating the owner. Looks like you should do some more research, then you wouldn't be put in these situations. Have a great day."

She's vile.

When the know-it-all is out of earshot, I turn to Ross. "Oh my God, do you think I'm fucked?"

Ross folds his hands together, and I can sense some uneasiness in his shoulders. "What could Roberts possibly do? Not give you internship credit because you're dating an Agitator? That's not a thing."

"Are you sure? It's Alan Roberts we're talking about. He once fired someone for wearing cologne that smelled too much like his late father."

"For the record, it was not an appealing cologne. I think everyone was happy with that decision."

"Ross, I'm being serious. Do you think this is going to mess with me? Should I call it off with Silas?"

"Can you?"

"We didn't sign a contract or anything. Just kind of shook on it."

"Do you think you could cut things off with him? Would he be okay with that?"

I think back to the way Silas looked at the bar, then at my dorm, like this was the lifeline he'd been looking for. Even though I barely know him, I feel like I also owe him for what he did for me at the bar.

Goddammit, look at me having a conscience. This is why I'll never be a killer businesswoman. I don't have the instinct to only take what I want and not let emotions get in the way.

"I don't think he'd put up a fight if I called it off, but I'd feel guilty." Really guilty.

"Then why don't you figure out what Roberts wants first and go from there. Because thinking up ideas of what he might possibly say to you is not going to get you anything other than a stomachache and anxiety."

"You're right," I say. "I need to make that appointment as soon as I can, then I can worry after the meeting."

THREE HOURS, five cups of coffee, and four nervous pees later, I'm sitting outside Roberts's office, waiting for him to call me in.

I considered texting Silas at least a dozen times while I waited. I drummed up every possible way I could break the news to him that I couldn't go through with the deal, but every time I came close to considering sending him a message, I chickened out and told myself to wait it out. No reason to ruffle feathers if I don't need to.

"Mr. Roberts will see you now," his assistant says while buzzing his door open.

I quickly stand, pen and paper in hand, and open the door to his expansive office.

I've never been in here . . . ever . . . but I heard he has the best view, and whoever I heard that from was right. It's a corner office with floor-to-ceiling windows, rich mahogany furniture, and a wet bar to the right decorated with cut-glass tumblers and beautiful decanters. Fancy . . . just like his combed mustache.

"Miss Owens," he says while lifting his head. "Please, take a seat." He gestures toward the black leather chair in front of his desk. His office reminds me of an old-timey cigar salon. Not that I've been in one, but this is what I would envision. Deep, rich woods and leather, the smell of success in the air, masculinity oozing from the floor, seeping into your feet. Lowly interns like myself don't belong here.

Once seated, I rest my pad of paper on my leg and poise my pen, ready to take down any notes.

"I see that you have chosen hockey as your final assignment."

Chosen, ha!

More like rudely forced.

"Not to brazenly correct you, but it was assigned to me. As I'm sure you're aware, I've focused more on lifestyle while working here. Sports hasn't necessarily been my thing."

"Some might challenge you that hockey is a lifestyle." He picks up a pen and clicks it as he leans back in his chair.

Uh, I beg to differ, but then again, who am I to argue with the boss?

"I suppose you're right, Mr. Roberts."

He stares at me for a few moments. "How long have you been dating Taters?"

I always find it odd when people use last names when talking about individuals. Probably a boys club kind of thing.

"Just a few weeks," I answer, my palms starting to sweat.

"A few weeks. Why haven't I seen anything in the news about it? You know who the Agitators are dating is always circulating."

"Yes, well, we wanted to keep it really quiet at first."

"I see. What made you want to come out with your relationship?" Is this really appropriate work talk? Feels more like a gossip sesh.

Like, where's the HR representative? I have no idea what my *fake* personal life has to do with my job. If I wasn't so terrified about fucking up this internship opportunity, I would ask him what his intentions are with this conversation. You know, really stick up for me and "my man."

"What made us come out with our relationship . . . well, we were spotted out in the world and figured we couldn't hide forever." That is somewhat true since we were spotted kissing in the bar by Candace, Yonny, and Ross. There was no hiding after that.

"Well." He leans forward and rests his forearms on the desk. "Were you aware that I was going to purchase the Agitators?"

Huh, that's news to me.

"I was not aware of that. Are you a hockey fan, sir?"

"I am. I played my entire childhood and a little in college on a club team until I hurt my knee."

"Oh, I'm sorry to hear that." Empathy is a beautiful thing in moments like this.

"It was always my goal to stay within the world of sports, but somehow, I deviated from that and ended up in print and now online journalism."

"You've done a wonderful job in providing a safe place for people to visit for information and fun articles," I say, feeling my head start to slip right up his ass.

He must notice it as well because his brows turn down as if he disapproves of my compliments. Maybe tone it down a bit, Ollie.

"Either way, I'm not a huge fan of the owner of the Agitators. We've had our quarrels in the past, and I've always wondered how he's operated and managed the team. How he's been able to keep the media at bay when it comes to his players. There is never a scandal. He also has a winning record, more championships than any team in history. The refs seem to always call penalties in their favor, and I believe he's doing something to maintain relationships so his team is always in favor of the winning side of the ice."

But aren't you a freaking Agitators fan? Who cares? Praise the man if he's paying off the refs.

"Oh, really?" I ask. "Yeah, I truly know nothing about hockey. I didn't even know the Agitators were that good. I don't think I've ever watched a game, so I don't have much input on what you're talking about."

"Well, you will," he says while moving his mouse around. "I want you to focus your assignment on the inner workings of the Agitators. I want you to immerse yourself into the team and dig up any information you can."

"Oh," I say. "Well, I don't really feel comfortable doing that, given I'm dating one of the players. It might be a conflict of interest. Best you give this assignment to someone else."

His eyes flash to mine. "You're dating Silas Taters. You're

not dating the organization or the owner. There's a difference."

Is there? Because it seems to all fall under the same umbrella if you ask me.

"I don't know," I say. "It makes me uncomfortable."

"Are you saying you're not going to complete the assignment?"

"What? No," I say quickly. "I just . . ." I chew on the corner of my lip, feeling all my hard work slip from my fingers. "Maybe I could take a different angle. You know, one that doesn't impose on my relationship with Silas."

"Then don't involve him. Simple as that. The less he knows, the better. We can even change the byline so it's not reflecting you as the writer."

"That doesn't sound ideal," I say, feeling my stomach churn at the thought. "What if there's nothing to find?" I barely know Silas, yet for some reason, I feel this sense of loyalty toward him.

"Well, it's up to you, Miss Owens," Roberts says as he directs his attention back to his computer. "But I would tread carefully because your journalism career and graduation depend on this internship. So I would make the decision that's best for you." Threaten much? Jesus. He clicks his mouse a few times and then says, "You're excused."

Oh . . . well, okay. I guess that's that.

Awkwardly, I thank him, not sure why, and head out of his office. I offer a wave to his assistant, then take the elevator back to my floor, feeling the weight of the world on my shoulders.

When I signed up for this internship, it was for the fluff. I wanted to write about the best aftercare for a hangover. Or what books can get your motor running when experiencing a drought. Or even how to balance the pH on your scalp for better hair growth.

I didn't come in here thinking I would break the code on

the underbelly of a national hockey team. I wouldn't even know where to begin. I'm not an investigative journalist when it comes to real-world problems—if you consider refs falsifying games real-world problems. I came here to talk about the things that interest me, and I don't know, spread a little joy. Not overturn the sports mafia—if that's a thing. Who knows, I sure as hell don't because I know nothing about this!

"How did it go?" Ross asks, coming up to me in the break room, where I took a quick detour. I grab a bag of Skittles from the snack drawer and hold it close to my chest.

"He wants me to write a 'gotcha' article about the Agitators and how they're cheating the system."

"Stop. What did he really want?" Ross asks, clearly assuming I'm joking. If only.

"That's what he wanted. He said I could get the inside scoop."

"Isn't that a conflict of interest?"

"Uh, yeah. And it also breaks all trust I have with Silas. Which sure," I lean in and whisper, "I've known him for a weekend, but still, I'm not that person. I don't step on people to get ahead."

"So what did you say?"

"That I wasn't comfortable doing that, and then he of course reiterated that this was for my school credit."

"That's some shady shit."

"Tell me about it." I open my Skittles and pop a lime and grape one in my mouth.

"So what are you going to do?"

"I'm not about to overturn the Agitators organization. I just need to think of a different angle that will appeal to Roberts and one that doesn't lose me all credibility with my fake boyfriend."

"Sounds like a task. I don't envy you."

"I don't envy me either."

AFTER A LONG RUN TO clear my head and a cold shower to appease my muscles, I lie flat on my bed and stare up at the ceiling, my mind still whirling about my conversation with Roberts today. I wrote down some ideas of what I could write about, one having promise. I kind of liked how he spoke about the media not covering any player scandals. There could be a story that doesn't include some dark alleyway money shuffling.

There is probably a good reason for it, and I plan on figuring that out.

In the meantime, I pick up my phone and text Silas.

Ollie: *Hey, not sure what your schedule is like, but I just realized I know nothing about you. People were asking about you at work today, and I was talking out of my ass. Maybe we should, I don't know, go on a fake date to at least get our stories straight.*

Once I press send, I reach for my water bottle and down half of it just as my phone dings with a text.

Silas: *People were talking about me at your work? Why?*

Ollie: *Um, maybe because I put a picture of you on my desk, you know, as a way to solidify the relationship.*

Silas: *What picture?*

Ollie: *Some picture I found on the Internet of you lifting your shirt up. It really put a bee in Candace's bonnet.*

Silas: *Are you pleased with yourself?*

Ollie: *Massively. Anything to make her mad is a win in my book. I might have mentioned licking your abs whenever I want, but that's neither here nor there. Anyway, can we go on a date? Or you just come over here?*

Silas: *How about you come over to my place? I can give you a key, and you can check out the gym. Get you situated, and then we can talk.*

Ollie: *That sounds perfect. When?*

Silas: *You available tomorrow?*

Ollie: *I can be. Send me the time and place, and I'll be there.*

Chapter Six

SILAS

Should I light a candle?

That seems like I'm trying too hard.

But what if it smells weird in here?

I don't want her first impression of my place to be associated with an odd smell.

I stare at the beeswax mahogany teakwood candle on my living room coffee table. It smells really good. It could make a great first impression, even if it screams trying too hard.

"Fuck it," I mutter as I pick up the candle as well as the lighter in the wood box I keep it in and light the stupid candle.

Once I put the lighter away, I lift my arm and check that I put deodorant on after my shower.

Yup, smells good.

Hands on my hips, I look around my place, seeing if I can do anything else to get it ready.

As usual, everything is in its proper place.

So why the fuck do I feel so nervous?

This is stupid.

I don't even like the girl. I don't know her, so I shouldn't be nervous.

But something about inviting someone into your personal space exposes you in a different way. I feel vulnerable when I shouldn't. Compared to her dorm room, I truly believe her mind will be blown when she sees my penthouse apartment.

For the seventh time in the past hour, I fluff my throw pillows just as there is a knock on my door.

I glance at the clock.

Fuck, she's early.

I walk over to the entryway and catch a glimpse of my T-shirt and jeans in the mirror and wonder if I should have opted for sweats. Doesn't matter now.

I grip the handle to the door, take a deep breath, and open it.

"There he is, our man," Pacey says, charging through the door, followed by Hornsby, Holmes, and Posey.

Shit.

What the hell are they doing here?

That's when I notice the pizza and beer in their hands.

"Uh, what are you doing?" I ask while shutting the door.

"What does it look like?" Hornsby says while kicking his shoes off and taking a seat on my couch. "Keeping you company." He glances around. "Man, it looks good in here."

"I don't need you to keep me company," I say as panic sets in. Ollie will be here any moment, and the last thing I want, before Ollie and I can even figure out our story, is my boys meeting her and questioning everything about our relationship.

"That's exactly why we're here," Pacey says while flipping open the pizza box, the sausage and onions ruining any improvement the candle had made in my space. "You act like everything is okay, but when you left practice today, you bolted. And you haven't really talked to us at all in the last few days. You're retreating because of Sarah, and we're here to make sure you're okay."

I'm not retreating.

I don't give a fuck about Sarah—sort of.

And the last thing I want is company.

"And we brought pizza, so that's fun," Posey says as he grabs a slice and takes a huge bite. Through a full mouth, he moans, "Fuck, that's good."

"Doesn't his place look nice?" Holmes asks. "These pillows are perfectly fluffed as if you're trying to impress someone."

"Are you?" Posey asks.

"No," I say quickly.

"Don't you think the pillows look nice?" Hornsby asks, harping on the goddamn pillows a touch too much.

"I think they look great," Pacey says, clearly trying to be the super positive one. "Best pillows I've ever seen."

"Where did you get them?" Posey asks. "Target?"

"Target?" Hornsby scoffs. "These are West Elm quality."

"Target has great quality pillows, you jackass," Posey replies.

"I don't think we're here to talk about the pillows, remember?" Pacey says, giving them both looks.

"Oh . . . right," Hornsby says. "Uh . . . how's life?"

Jesus Christ. I pinch my brow, irritated that I must deal with this.

"You okay?" Holmes asks, the more levelheaded and quieter one of the group.

"I'm fine. I actually—"

Knock. Knock.

The guys all pause, and with confused looks in their eyes, they glance over at the door.

Shit.

Using his finger, Posey counts us, making sure we're all here. Hornsby sits taller, staring at the door as if he has X-ray vision, and Pacey fluffs the pillow next to him while whispering, "Who's that?"

"Uh . . ." I say, unsure of how to respond. They all turn to me, looking for an answer, and I don't know what to say. Their stares and confused expressions shift to anger, which causes my back to break out in sweat.

"If you tell me that's Sarah, I'm going to have a fucking conniption," Hornsby says.

"Oh shit, I didn't even think about that," Posey says. "Tates, that can't be Sarah."

"Dude, is it Sarah?" Pacey asks, his fist clenching at his side.

"No," I answer, exasperated.

"Then answer it," Hornsby challenges.

"No need. I can," Pacey says, moving right past me and toward the door.

"Wait," I call out, but it's too late. He opens the door, revealing Ollie standing on the other side. Long brown hair tied up into a tight pony on the top of her head, she has minimal makeup on her face and is sporting a pair of leggings and a plain black V-neck T-shirt.

"Oh, is this the wrong apartment?" she asks, looking confused.

"Who are you looking for?" Pacey asks.

"Me," I call out, knowing there's no use telling her to run for her life. "Let her in, Pacey."

A collective quiet hangs over the room as Pacey moves to the side and Ollie steps into my apartment, her hands clutching the thin straps of her mini backpack.

"Uh . . . hi," she says with a cute wave. "I didn't think you would, uh, have company."

"I wasn't expecting them as well."

Looking more confused than ever, Pacey says, "Who's this?"

Well, this is what I wanted, right? To tell my boys that I'm seeing someone so they don't assume I'm lonely and barge into my apartment with pizza and beer. Or fret over me getting back together with Sarah. This is the moment . . .

So I guess here goes nothing.

"This is Ollie," I answer. "My, uh . . . my girlfriend."

"Girlfriend?" Posey croaks, choking on his pizza.

"You have a girlfriend?" Pacey asks, brows pulled together. "How come you've never told us about her?"

"Yeah, what the fuck, man?" Hornsby adds. "You've just been hiding her from us?"

I pull on the back of my neck, trying to gather my patience. "We, uh . . . we wanted to make sure we were committed before going public."

Ollie awkwardly smiles and then waves. "Hey, I'm Ollie, nice to weirdly meet you all."

Finding his manners, Pacey lends his hand out to her and says, "Hi. I'm Pacey. The guy with the pizza is Levi Posey. The one on the couch is Eli Hornsby. And the shy one over there in the corner, that's Halsey Holmes."

"Nice to meet you all." She rocks on her heels as silence falls between us all. This is so fucking uncomfortable. "Do you want me to wait out in the hallway until you're done?"

"No," I say quickly. "They were all just leaving."

"Wait, I didn't even get to crack my beer open yet," Posey says.

"You're leaving."

"Now that Ollie's here, I really want to stay," Hornsby says.

Yeah, over my dead body.

"Leave. Now. Before I physically remove you myself."

"I think he's being serious," Posey says while looking among the boys and me. "I think he wants us to leave."

"I think he does," Hornsby says. "That's fucking rude."

"Come on," Holmes says while picking up the pizza and the beer.

"Are we really just going to let him slide by with this new information?" Hornsby asks, the ever-present questioner in the group.

"We can talk about it later," Pacey says, eyeing me.

"What about the pizza?" Posey asks while standing.

Glad to see where his priorities are at.

"We'll finish it at my place," Holmes says. "Come on."

Thank God for him. Collectively, they shuffle out the door, all saying bye to Ollie. Pacey is the last one out, and when he turns to me, he has a very serious look on his face as he says, "You will be explaining this tomorrow."

"Can't wait," I say right before shutting the door on him.

Jesus, they treat me like an absolute child. There will be explaining, though I owe them nothing. Although I know they're going to harass me until I do explain, so . . . something to look forward to.

Slightly embarrassed, I turn toward Ollie and push my hand through my hair. "Sorry about that."

"Why are you apologizing? That was a lot of fun."

"For you," I say. "Not really the way I wanted to greet you into my home."

"I don't know. It had some pizzazz that I wasn't expecting." She kicks her shoes off at the door and takes her backpack off, which she sets down next to her shoes. "Wow, your view is incredible."

"Thanks," I say, grateful she's so easygoing. And *clearly* not a hockey fan. When was the last time a college student had been among my teammates and not swooned with a thousand *oh my Gods* spilling from their lips? Ah, that would be never. Until Ollie. So weird.

"Is your place always this clean? Or is this all for me?"

"Usually this clean, especially during the season when I'm not here that much."

"Hmm, fake dating an older man does have its pluses. Nice, fancy apartment with a gym, clean, smells good." She turns toward me. "It's a real step up from what I'm used to when it comes to men."

"Men . . . or boys?"

"Good point." She moves over to my couch and sits cross-legged. "So what's for dinner? That pizza smelled good. Should have asked them to leave it."

"I can order some. I wasn't really sure what you would want."

"Pizza now."

Pulling my phone from my pocket, I sit on the couch as well and pull up my delivery app. "Do you want just pizza, or do you want a salad too?"

"Salad would be amazing. Italian dressing, please."

"Got it." I finish putting the order in, then set my phone on the coffee table before turning to face her.

She turns toward me as well and smiles brightly. "So . . . those are your teammates?"

"Yeah. They're evasive as fuck."

"I don't know about that. They seemed like a good time," she says with a cute smile.

"Not when they're up my ass."

"Why were they here? Seemed like they were planning a guys' night."

"They were here because they thought I was depressed and needed some cheering up."

"Are you depressed?" she asks.

"No." I shake my head. "I've been occupied with our agreement and bolted from practice today so I could shower and make sure everything was ready before you came over. They took that as I was avoiding them because of the whole Sarah thing."

"I could see the correlation. But that wasn't the case?"

"Not even a little."

"So Sarah working at your arena doesn't make you want to run for shelter?"

I shake my head. "Not really. I'm dreading seeing her, that's for damn sure, but I'm a man, so I can face her."

"At least you can admit that." She folds her hands in her lap. "So how did we meet?"

"What do you mean?" I ask, confused.

She rolls her eyes. "Dude, we need a story to tell everyone. People will ask how we met, and if we're not on the same page, we'll look like fools. People will be able to see right through us."

"Ah, I see. Why don't we just say we met at a bar? That's true, so it won't be hard to remember."

"Kind of boring, though, don't you think? We have an opportunity to reinvent ourselves. We could say something like . . . we were both at a deli, you got the roast beef, I got the meatball sub. You took too large of a bite, started choking, and I was there to save you. To pay me back for giving you a proper Heimlich, you asked me out to dinner, and the rest is history."

I feel my brow crease as I stare at her. "That doesn't sound appealing to me."

"You know, it doesn't make you less of a man to admit being saved by a woman."

"I understand that, but I also don't want to put choking out there in the universe."

"Aw," she coos. "You're one of those guys. Superstitious, are we?"

"Sure," I answer.

"Okay, then you come up with the way we met."

"Easy. At a bar. You thought I was hot, couldn't live life another second without saying hi, so you came over to me and made the first move."

"Ew, I would never."

"Uh . . . you did. You're the one who kissed me."

"That's different." She dismisses me with a wave.

"How so?"

"That was an act of desperation. It wasn't a move. It was survival instincts. Much, much different."

"So you're saying, if you just randomly saw me in a bar, without having to fend for your life, you wouldn't have come up to me?"

"Never." She shakes her head. "I don't do that, and you would have seemed far too old for me."

"Bullshit," I say. "I don't look that old. Stop using that as a thing."

"Only old men get bent out of shape about being called old."

I roll my eyes. "If you don't like the bar story, then come up with something that doesn't involve me choking on a fucking sandwich."

"Fine." She leans her shoulder against the back of the couch. "Let's see. Hmm . . . oh, how about this. You were driving and blew a tire. I helped you change it. You were so grateful for my presence and blown away by my sheer beauty that you asked me out."

"First of all, I know how to change a tire. Second, I own a Tesla. They don't have spare tires, so we would have had to call a tow truck."

"Really? That's stupid." She taps her chin. "Okay, what about this. You were shopping for a gift for your mom, and you couldn't decide between a candle and a gift card, so you asked me. I told you to stop being a thoughtless asshole and directed you toward those sentimental Willow sculptures."

"My mom prefers gift cards."

She tosses her hands up in the air. "Fine, you come up with something."

"We met on a ferry. You were seasick, and I held your hair back. After you threw up on my shoe."

"Or . . ." she says, holding up her finger. "You threw up on my lap, and I guided you to the toilet, where I rubbed your back and told you all was going to be okay in the world."

"How come you're the hero in this story?"

"Uh, isn't it obvious?" she asks. "Women are the true heroes in this world."

"Really? Because I'm pretty sure I was your hero the other night."

"Wow, you're just going to keep bringing that up, aren't you? What about this? I'm your hero now."

"How so? You're getting the better end of the deal."

"Excuse me?" she asks, her brows rising. "You're the one who came up with the fake dating cockamamie idea in the first place. If anyone is getting a good deal, it's you because I'm going along with this deranged plan. Therefore"—she points at herself—"hero."

"Why can't we both be heroes?"

That makes her straight-up guffaw. "Have you ever heard of a storyline with two heroes?"

"*Miracle.*"

"Huh?" she asks.

"The movie *Miracle*. It's about the 1980 Olympic hockey team. All those guys are heroes in my book."

"Never seen it."

"What?" I ask. "You can't be serious."

"Look at my face." She points at her serious expression. "I am."

Groaning, I drag my hand over my face. "Fuck, that's annoying."

"I'm pretty sure you haven't seen movies I like."

"Name one," I challenge her.

"Okay . . . *Pride and Prejudice.*"

"With Keira Knightley? Seen it."

"Okay, what about *Two Weeks Notice?*"

"I've seen every Hugh Grant movie ever made."

"*Pretty Woman.*"

"Big mistake . . . huge," I say, quoting the movie.

"Oh yeah, how about . . . *Sixteen Candles?*"

"There's something about Jake Ryan that makes you weak in the knees, isn't there?"

"Ugh, of course you've seen that. You're old. I need something recent." She taps her chin. "What about *Bridgerton*?"

"I got a boner during one of the sex scenes. Chills when their fingers touched in front of the art."

She grumbles, "God, you're annoying."

"What you're failing to remember is that I was in a committed, long-term relationship ever since I was in high school. I've seen everything she wanted to watch and then some."

"Fine, so you're well-polished in romance. Still doesn't mean we can both be heroes."

"How about no one is a hero, and I saw you in a bar and hit on you, simple as that."

She taps her chin in thought. "It has merit. I think we could make it work."

"Well, thank God for that."

—

"SO WHAT BROUGHT US TOGETHER?" Ollie asks as she blots her pizza with a napkin.

I gave her a quick tour of the apartment, saving the gym for last because I knew she would love it, and she did. She was in total awe and could not wait to work out in the space without being bothered.

She was testing out some of the weights when the food arrived, so we retreated to the dining room to eat.

"What do you mean? We saw each other in the bar. That's what we agreed upon. We're not coming up with something else," I say.

"No, I mean, initial attraction clearly is what got us talking, but how did we hang on to the conversation? Obviously, I know nothing about hockey, so it's not like we can bond over that. And I doubt you're a lifestyle guru."

"Are you?" I ask.

"Maybe not the guru status yet, but I do know a thing or two about the proper way to use a bobby pin."

I scratch the side of my jaw. "Yeah, I don't know much about that."

"But you do know how to create a kick-ass home gym, and that's hot."

"So I have one thing going for me." I take a bite of my salad. "Where are you from?"

"Portland, Oregon. What about you?"

"Minnesota."

She chuckles. "Not the same thing."

"Not so much."

"Do you have any siblings?" she asks.

"I have a sister," I say. "But we're not super close."

"Yeah, I don't have any siblings."

"What about childhood? What did you like to do?" I ask, fishing for any commonality now.

"Take pictures of moss. Collect stickers. Pretend that the sticks I found were a wand, and I was Hermione Granger."

I pause and glance at her. "You're a Potter head?"

She grips the edge of the table. "Please, for the love of all that is holy, please tell me that you're a Potter head as well."

"Eh, not so much."

She groans. "Ughhh, really?"

"No, I actually am."

"Stop, are you?" she asks.

"Yes, and I read some of the books when they were first released. That's how old I am compared to you. I have some first editions."

"You're a liar," she yells, excitement bustling in her eyes. "Seriously?"

"Yes, they're my prized possessions. Have you been to Harry Potter World?"

"No," she bemoans. "But when I graduate, I plan on going. I'm assuming since you're rich and can do whatever you want when you're not playing, you've been?"

"I have."

"Is the butter beer everything I think it would be?"

"And then some," I answer. "Harry Potter World is probably one of the best things that has ever happened to fandom. It feels so real."

"Urrghh, I'm so jealous. Did you get sorted into a house?"

"Yeah, Gryffindor."

"Of course. You seem like an overachiever. I know I'm Hufflepuff through and through, and I'm damn proud of it."

"Do you ever feel bad for people who get Ravenclaw?" I ask. "No one ever talks about it. Gryffindor is clearly superior, Slytherin has its own merit because it's evil, and then Hufflepuff is for all the fun-loving people. What about Ravenclaw?"

"You know, now that you mentioned it, I don't think I ever hear anyone claim they're from Ravenclaw. That's sad."

"It is."

She tilts her head to the side. "I think we figured out what we bonded over."

I scratch the back of my head. "Yeah, the guys will love that. Harry Potter. They always make fun of me for being such a Potter head."

"Aw, poor baby. The boys are picking on you."

"It's rare," I say. "I'm usually the one being a dick."

"Is that so?" she asks. "From what I've seen, you seem quite sensitive."

"I'm not sensitive," I defend. "That would be Posey or Holmes. I'm anything but sensitive."

"Okay, keep telling yourself that."

"Why the hell do you think I'm sensitive?"

She holds up her finger. "First of all, it's not a bad thing to be sensitive. No need to shed some toxic masculinity between us, thanks. Second of all, you *are* sensitive. If you weren't, we wouldn't be in this predicament. If you were truly the dick you claim to be, you wouldn't care about Sarah being around the arena or what the guys think. Maybe your problem is you don't like to be vulnerable. Therefore, you attempt to hide it by being a dick."

Jesus.

Is she sure she's in lifestyle journalism and not psychology?

I shake my head. "I don't think that's what's going on."

She chuckles. "Okay, keep thinking that."

"DO YOU REALLY, in all honesty, like that picture?" she asks as she stares at a piece of art hanging in the dining area. The dark blue paint has been smooshed into the canvas. There's no rhyme or reason to it, just a bunch of texture.

I shrug. "It does the job."

"And what job is that?" she asks while picking up another piece of pizza and dabbing the grease off with a napkin.

"Aesthetic. Brings color into the space."

"Is that what you think, or is that what your interior decorator thinks?"

I take a sip of my water. "Who says I used an interior decorator?"

Her lips fall to the side in disbelief. "Please. Sure, this might be the nicest place I've ever been, but I'm not stupid. Your decor screams professionally done. Nothing in this space is personal. Your apartment could really be anyone's home."

"I know," I say. "There's a reason for that."

"What's the reason?" she asks.

"Everything I had that was remotely personal involved

Sarah, and I didn't want that in my new space. I wanted a fresh start."

"Ah, that makes sense. You wanted to eliminate her from your life."

"Exactly."

She studies the space again. "Well, you could use a picture of yourself here or there."

"Why would I want to look at a picture of myself?"

She shrugs. "You're hot. Don't you want to look at the beauty of your body?"

That makes me laugh. "Do you have pictures of yourself in your dorm?"

She nods. "With Ross. I also have some items from my childhood home that I brought with me. Little treasures I couldn't part with."

"Like what?"

"Like . . . a box full of Polaroid pictures from high school. My scrapbook. A few significant decorative items I had growing up that remind me of my childhood. Just simple things."

"Anything really sentimental?" I ask.

She wipes her fingers on a napkin. "I have a blanket my grandma made for me. I keep it in my closet because it's fragile, barely holding together. It provides zero warmth, but it's always been with me, so I keep it close. On occasion, I bring it out and just look at the faded quilt blocks, running my fingers over the hand stitching."

"Were you close to your grandma?" I ask.

"Yes, I was. My dad was always tough on me, and my mom didn't have much to say. She was loving, but she let Dad take the lead on discipline and life in general. My grandma was the one I could go to and just hug. To escape the pressures from my dad."

"When did she pass?"

"Right before I graduated from high school," she answers.

"I still don't think I've fully recovered from losing her. A piece of me died with her. She was honestly the only person I've felt was 100 percent on my side. She was tough but so, so kind and helped me believe in myself. I've missed that over the past three years." She lets out a soft sigh. "Anyway, she would have thought this whole arrangement was hilarious and would have encouraged it." Ollie looks up at me. "And she would have loved you."

"Really?" I ask.

"Oh yeah. She had a thing for guys with toned muscles. She would have hit on you for sure."

That makes me laugh. "Your grandma's type. Maybe that's why you zeroed in on me at the bar. Runs in the family."

"You were the only guy in the bar who was alone, that's why I zeroed in on you, but it's cute that you're trying to make more sense of it."

"Have you always been a ballbuster?" I ask her.

"Yes. It's the reason I've only ever had one boyfriend, was never asked to prom, and why boys never tried to take me out. I was too much for them."

"Seems like they missed out, then," I say.

"Aw, look at you buttering me up." She flips her ponytail over her shoulder. "No need to. I know they were all losers. Anyone I date needs to be manly enough to deal with my strong personality and all the intricacies that go with it. Yonny wasn't that guy. It doesn't make our breakup any less hurtful, but I know he wasn't the one for me."

"Strong personalities are sexy," I say.

"This coming from a real man."

"I'm going to take that as a compliment."

"You should," she says, her eyes meeting mine. "See, look at us. We have all the potential to crush this fake dating thing. We have a mutual appreciation for one another. That's the first step to a successful business relationship."

"You think so?" I ask. Fuck, she's entertaining.

"I know so." She winks. "They'll use us as the model couple. Just wait, you'll see. Books will be written about us."

Got to love her enthusiasm.

⸺

"WHAT GOT YOU INTO WORKING OUT?" I ask as I finish cleaning off the dining room table.

"Jamie Terrance."

"Who's that?" I ask. "An influencer or something?"

She laughs and shakes her head. Sitting across from me at the bar, she watches me work around the kitchen, putting away the leftovers and washing the dishes. "No, Jamie Terrance is my nemesis from high school. She was a rotten bitch with a shit family, so instead of trying to make the best of the people around her and be positive, she did the opposite. She would make fun of me all the time for having . . . as she put it . . . rolls."

"Fuck off. Are you serious?" I ask.

"Yup, she would walk by me in the cafeteria and say rude things about what I was eating. Unfortunately, I let it get to me. I started going on one-mile runs around my neighborhood early in the morning before school started. I walked half of it, but I felt good doing something to combat the negative thoughts in my head. And the more I started to enjoy the feeling of working out, the more I pushed myself." She sighs. "I hate that it started from a place of negativity, but I'm grateful I found the love of working out. It truly helps me when I'm stressed."

"How often is that?" I place our plates in the dishwasher.

"With this internship, more often than not."

"Is there a reason this internship is so important? I know it's for a grade, but why do an internship in a place that stresses you out?"

"It's the company name," she says. "If you have Alan

Roberts on your résumé, anyone will pick you up. The jobs flow right in, and the last thing I want to do after I graduate is go back to my hometown to live with my parents."

"Didn't like it there?" I ask.

"I did, but I made a big deal about leaving and never coming back. You know, dramatic teen stuff. Now that I'm a touch older, I see how stupid it was, but this girl has pride, and I'll be damned if I have to go back there and eat my words."

I chuckle. "I can feel you on that. I was the same way with hockey. Bound and determined to make something of myself, I wouldn't stop until I did, even if that meant practically killing myself in the process."

"Well, you made it," she says while drawing a circle on the counter with her finger. "But the real question is, are you happy that you made it? Because even though this internship has opened many doors for me, I'm anything but happy. I just keep telling myself there are days we'll be unhappy to obtain the happiness we want. So . . . have you obtained that happiness?"

Am I happy?

I think maybe from the outside looking in, it could seem that I am. I have the car, the house in the woods, the penthouse apartment, the glory, the fame, the championships. Yet . . . I find myself acting like a dick more and more.

Happiness eludes me.

Never feeling settled.

Not feeling adequate enough for anyone . . .

Fuck.

"Yeah, maybe we shouldn't talk about this," I say, not wanting to dive deep into my feelings, especially with Ollie.

"Ah, right, that would make you vulnerable, and you don't do vulnerable."

"Right," I say as I close the dishwasher. I grip the counter and stare at her. "Do you feel like we have our story straight?"

She doesn't answer right away but tries to study me. I can

see her wanting to ask more, to bring up the vulnerability thing and dive deep into why I'm so guarded, but I refuse. There's no need to get into that with her. Our relationship is surface level. Business. We don't need to delve into deep-rooted emotions.

"I think so," she finally says. "Met at a bar, you hit on me because you're a horny bastard and couldn't control yourself—"

"Didn't think we added the horny thing in there."

"And when I finally gave you the time of day because I felt bad that you were drooling while looking at me—"

"Also, not something that happened."

"That's when you made a move and told me you admired my beauty and strength and wit and that it reminded you of Hermione."

"That's not something I would say."

She presses her hand to her chest. "And I thought . . . wow, this guy. He's clearly trying far too hard to make an impression. Maybe I should give him a chance. So I let you buy me a drink. You ordered Shirley Temples—"

"Oh fuck off," I say while laughing.

But she continues. "It was a bit of a turn-off, watching a man slowly sip a Shirley Temple with utter delight in his eyes, but I decided to give you a chance since you seemed like you needed friends . . . or rather attention."

"It's amazing how much this story has grown."

"Just spitting out facts."

"Yeah, if you want to spit out facts, why don't we just stick to the actual truth that you attacked me with your lips out of desperation?"

She stares up at the ceiling, giving it some thought. "I think my story is better." She hops off the stool and heads toward the entryway. "Well, thanks for the pizza and the key." She holds up the key I gave her so she could work out here. "It's appreciated."

"Just wipe down when you're done. I don't need your sweat all over my equipment."

"I don't sweat," she says while she slips her shoes on.

"Everyone sweats."

"Not me." She slides her backpack on and heads toward the door. "Keep me updated on what you need from me, and if I could have your schedule, that would be ideal. I'd prefer to come here when you're not around."

"You're such a good girlfriend."

"I know." She throws up a peace sign. "See you later." And then she takes off, just like that, without another word.

My life had order and structure a few days ago. Same place to live, same friends, same job. Now? It's been somewhat upended.

Where the hell did Ollie Owens, the pint-sized ballbuster, even come from?

PRE-WORKOUT DRINK in one hand and a protein bar in the other, I head down the hallway toward the locker room, knowing I'll have to face the boys today.

They were dead silent last night.

Not even a text to warn me they'll have questions today, which is even more nerve-wracking because now I have no idea what to expect.

I would have preferred the guys not find out about Ollie like that last night. I wasn't prepared, and now I feel like I'm walking into the lion's den as a giant piece of raw meat ready to be torn apart.

Bracing myself, I open the door to the locker room and then pause at the entrance as I spot Hornsby, Pacey, Holmes, and Posey all sitting in chairs around my locker.

Super.

Head hanging, I walk toward my locker, knowing what's coming.

"There he is," Pacey says. "The guy we've been waiting for."

"He looks fresh. Doesn't he look fresh, boys?" Hornsby asks.

"Very fresh," Posey says before biting into an egg and sausage sandwich. "Fresher than ever. Don't you think, Holmes?"

"I don't want to be a part of this," Holmes replies as he folds his arms across his chest.

"That's because you don't want us to treat you the same way when it comes to your crush," Pacey says, pointing out the obvious. And because Holmes doesn't ever want to engage in whatever shenanigans we have going on. He prefers to stay silent.

"Back to Taters," Hornsby says. "I would say he is the most fresh we've seen in a while."

"Can we cut it with the fresh shit?" I say as I sit at my locker. The guys waste no time closing in on me.

"So . . ." Pacey says, "care to tell us what the fuck happened last night?"

Yup, getting straight to the point.

"Not much to talk about," I say. "My girlfriend came over, we ate some pizza, and we talked."

"Why haven't you ever talked about her before?" Posey asks. "That's shitty, man. We're your boys."

"Because I didn't need you butting in on my life like you do all the time. Like right now, the four of you, breathing in my space."

"Oh, so it's okay for you to do it?" Hornsby asks, knowing full well I gave him plenty of shit when he got Pacey's sister pregnant. "But the moment we give you any sort of shit, you try to shut it down?"

"Glad you can see it that way." I pat him on the shoulder. "Now, get the fuck out of here so I can get ready."

"Uh, do you really think that's going to work on us? You didn't even tell us where you met, how long you've been dating, or what she's like," Hornsby says.

"Well, seems like you have something to look forward to, then," I answer as I stand and tear my shirt over my head so I can get ready for weight training this morning.

Pacey stands, puts his hand on my shoulder, and pushes me back onto my seat.

"Nice try. You're not leaving this room until you answer questions."

Hell.

"How long have you been dating?" Hornsby asks.

"A few weeks," I answer.

"Where is she from?" Posey asks.

"Portland," I say, glad I know that answer.

"She's young," Pacey says. "Just how young are we talking?"

I swallow. "Uh, twenty-one."

"What the fuck?" Hornsby says as all the guys shift back.

"Dude," Holmes says with a shake of his head.

"I know, okay? I don't need shit from you four about her age. I didn't know she was that young at first. It doesn't seem like it matters, though. You can't even tell." Lies. Going to her dorm makes me feel like some sort of creepy pervert. I don't belong there.

"Is it serious?" Hornsby asks.

"Very," I answer and then stand. "I've answered enough of your questions. Now leave me the fuck alone so I can get my training done." Clothes in hand, I storm off toward the bathroom, where I'll get changed to avoid them.

That could have been way worse, although I don't think it's over.

Chapter Seven

OLLIE

To: Ollie Owens
From: Alan Roberts
Subject: Internship
Miss Owens,
I'm writing to advise that I've chosen to extend your internship through the end of the college year. I assume you'll be able to handle the workload. I've already been in touch with your adviser. I suggest you accept.
Roberts

I stare blankly at my computer, confused, elated, worried .
. .

It's rare for an internship to get extended. I know it happens, but only to a few choice candidates. And when they're extended, you'll most likely be offered a job at the end of the year.

A job straight out of college would be everything I ever wanted.

It's what I've been working toward. To prove to everyone, especially my dad, that I don't need their help and can make it on my own.

Yeah, I might not have been entirely truthful with Silas last night. I don't want to go back home because I don't want to hear it from my dad, who has told me time and again that a job in journalism will get me nowhere. That I was wasting his money and my time by going to school up here. He couldn't understand why I wouldn't want to follow in his footsteps and take over the family business when I graduated from high school.

The family business is a small print shop in Oregon where he prints menus, brochures, and any other miscellaneous things he can get his hands on. The business was passed down from his dad, and he was hoping to do the same, but I have zero interest in it. Last Christmas, we got into a huge fight about it. He told me I was wasting his money by going to school for something that would never pay the bills. I told him his business was a dying trade, and then we parted ways.

So this is a huge opportunity . . .

"I see you got my email," Roberts says behind me, startling me right out of my thoughts.

"Oh Jesus," I mutter and catch my breath. "I didn't see you there."

"You are one of two who got the email. Don't take it for granted."

One of two . . . I can only imagine who the other person is. *Mentally grinds teeth together* Seems like I'll be spending more time with Candace since there's no way she didn't get it.

"I won't," I say. "I'm very grateful. Thank you."

He nods. "We have a fundraiser tonight at the Walton. I suggest you bring your boyfriend to it. I'll be expecting him."

"Oh, uh . . . sure." I swallow hard.

"Connect with Candace, and she'll give you the details."

Great.

"Wonderful. Thanks." I wave awkwardly, and he turns on his heel and walks away as I slump into my chair.

A fundraiser? Roberts attends many events during the year, and I've never been invited to one. But now that Silas is in the picture, I'm invited. I don't like how this feels, not even a little.

Yet . . . I'll also do anything to move forward in my career, so it looks like I need to get in touch with my fake, doting boyfriend.

Phone in hand, I head down the hall toward Candace's cubicle, where she's typing away on her computer. Tacking on a smile, I knock on the side of her cubicle and brace myself.

When she turns, she says, "Oh, Ollie, didn't expect to see you."

"Roberts came by my desk. Told me he wanted me at the fundraiser tonight and said to get the info from you."

"Ah, I see," she says as she turns back toward her desk and grabs a Post-it Note. She scribbles something on the paper and hands it over to me. "Here you go. It's black tie. Do you have something to wear?"

No.

"Of course," I say as I glance down at the information. "Uh, do I have to come with an invite or anything?"

She shakes her head. "Just say you're with Roberts, and you'll be let in."

"Are you sure?"

She rolls her eyes. "Yes, would I tell you the wrong information?"

Yes, yes, you would.

"I suppose not."

"Will you be bringing your boyfriend?"

"Roberts requested me to, so yes," I say, hoping Silas isn't doing anything tonight. They're still in preseason training—that's what he told me last night—so unless he has another engagement, he should be free.

"Great," Candace says with a smile. "Then I'll see you two there."

"Yup, see you there," I say. "Thanks for this," I add because she seems to be acting nice, so I'll return the favor.

Moving away from her desk, I bypass the kitchen and head into one of the private conference rooms. I lock the door, then pull out my phone and click on Silas's name. I have no idea what he's doing, but at least I can leave a message.

The phone rings a few times, and then he picks up.

"Hey," he says quietly. "Everything okay?"

"Umm, sort of," I reply. "Are you busy?"

"I have a second."

"Okay, well, long story short, my boss invited me to a fundraiser tonight and kind of made it a requirement that I attend . . . with you. And I'm sure you're busy or whatever, but—"

"I'll be there. When and where?"

"Seriously?" I ask, my breath escaping me all at once.

"Yes, we agreed to help each other out, so I'll be there. I can't promise I'll be as flexible when the season starts, but I can do this."

"Wow, okay. Thank you. This means a lot to me."

"Of course," he says softly. And for the rough and tough exterior he exudes, he really is a softy at heart.

"I'll text you the details. It's black tie, though. Is that going to be a problem?"

"You fail to realize the number of events I've gone to just like this. I have everything I need."

"Okay, awesome."

"Want me to pick you up?"

"Hmm, we should probably show up together, huh?"

"Might look best."

"Okay, sure. That would be great."

"Just send me the details. Gotta go."

"Okay, thank you, Silas."

"Any time," he says before hanging up.

Instead of returning to my cubicle, I sit in the silence of the conference room for a moment, gathering myself. In the matter of a week, my life has drastically changed. Before all of this, I was gearing up to finish up my final assignment, happy I was able to intern with Alan Roberts. Now I feel like I'm living in this tangled web that's becoming increasingly complicated with no escape.

The only lifeline I have is the man who I felt helped me get tangled in the first place.

No, let's be honest. I brought this on myself.

I was the one who wanted to show up Yonny.

I'm the one who kissed Silas.

I'm the one who agreed to Silas's fake relationship terms.

If anyone is to blame, it's 100 percent me.

If only I didn't *need* to keep Silas on the hook to impress Alan Roberts.

And I just wish I didn't care so much about proving my father wrong. If I didn't care, then keeping my hockey-legend fake boyfriend wouldn't be a necessity.

With a heavy sigh, I head straight to Ross's desk from the conference room. If anyone can get me black tie ready, it's him.

———

OLLIE: *I'm going to have a nip slip. I know it.*

Ross: *You're not.*

Ollie: *How do you know that? This dress wasn't made for a girl like me. My boobs are big. This was made for someone with a flat chest.*

Ross: *You'll be fine.*

Ollie: *But what if I go to shake someone's hand, and then out of nowhere, my boob decides to have a mind of its own, slip out of my dress, and then wink at the person in front of me?*

Ross: *Boobs can't wink.*

Ollie: You don't know that. You are not the one with the boobs. You prefer a penis.

Ross: I've been around enough models, even busty models, and I know for a fact the double-sided tape we used will hold up.

Ollie: This dress isn't classy. Candace said black tie, and this is more like . . . hooker behind the dumpster in the back alleyway where watches are traded for dime bags.

Ross: Are you really questioning my taste in fashion?

Ollie: I'm questioning my life decisions.

Ross: I think you're just nervous.

Ollie: Of course I'm nervous! I've never been to a fundraiser before or any sort of black tie anything. Nor do I take dates to functions this fancy. And the only reason Roberts invited me was because he found out I'm (fake) dating Silas. How am I supposed to handle this?

Ross: With a shred of dignity. Pull yourself together. You're wearing a beautiful plum dress that will grab the attention of every person in the room but also doesn't pull too much attention. You've worked hard on your networking this summer, and you have a very popular man at your side. You'll be fine.

Ollie: What if I say something stupid?

Ross: Sneeze.

Ollie: What?

Ross: Pretend to sneeze and blame it on that.

Ollie: That has got to be the worst advice I've ever read.

Ross: Be happy I found you a dress on such short notice. Now stop bothering me. I'm trying to watch The Crown.

I'm about to text him back when another text comes through.

Silas: Out front.

I told him not to bother coming up to get me. Since this isn't a real date, I don't need the fanfare of him knocking on my door and all that crap. Plus, from what I could tell from the last time he came here, he didn't want to be recognized. No need to put the pressure on him when he's doing me a favor.

After texting him back so he knows I'm on my way, I grab my clutch and glance at myself one more time in the mirror. The plum dress Ross chose for me has a strapless, structured top that splits at the cleavage. It has boning sewn into it, so it holds to my torso nicely, but the split of the dress to offer cleavage makes me nervous. It's why I used the tape, just in case. When the dress hits my hips, it flows in a gauzy-like material and appears to almost be Grecian. It's beautiful, but not something I've ever worn before.

Knowing I can't go back now, I leave my dorm and take the elevator down to the first floor. I pass a few people who eye me in my dress, but I move past them and right out the front door where a black Tesla Model X waits for me. I peek into the window and spot Silas, so I wave awkwardly, and when I go to open the door, it pops open for me.

"Oh . . ." I chuckle. "Uh, hi."

"Hey," he replies, his voice gruff.

I slip into the warm vehicle and smile over at him. "Thank you for doing this. You have no idea how grateful I am."

"Not a problem." I catch his Adam's apple bob as he turns away from me.

"Is, uh . . . is everything okay?"

"Yeah," he says, pulling on the back of his neck before he glances at me again. "That's a really nice dress, Ollie."

I glance down at it as if I haven't been staring at myself in the damn thing for the past half hour. "Thank you. Ross helped me find it. I didn't have anything that was black tie appropriate."

"You should have told me. I could have helped."

"Why would you help? I'm the one who asked you for a favor."

"I still could have helped."

"Well, it's fine. Everything worked out."

He nods and grips the steering wheel a touch tighter. Confused about his stiff attitude, I ask, "Are you sure everything's okay? If you don't want to do this, I totally get it. I just—"

"No, I don't mind," he says and then sighs. "Christ, I just wasn't expecting you to look so hot. That's all."

"Oh." My cheeks blush. "Well . . . I guess I'll take that as a compliment."

"Sorry, that was a shit way to say it." He turns toward me, and with a genuine look in his eyes, he says, "Ollie, you look beautiful."

"Thank you," I reply, feeling shy and awkward and good God, why is this so hard? "You look very nice yourself, so if we can move on from this because I feel really weird, that would be great."

"Sorry." He chuckles. "Still trying to figure all of this out. How to approach things. I feel like you should know you look good, but that's also something a real boyfriend would say, so . . . fuck . . . I don't know how to handle this."

"Ah, yes, I get it," I say. "How about we just treat this like a business transaction? Like would you tell your colleague that he looked good in a suit?"

"Hornsby demands I pay attention to his outfits . . . but I get what you're trying to say."

"I wish I knew which one of your teammates you were talking about. I know I met them, but it was brief. I retained nothing."

Silas pulls away from the curb and says, "Eli Hornsby. Look up a picture of him on your phone. He's the pretty boy of the group. Somehow, in all the years he's played hockey, he's never managed to get his face bashed in, giving him that perfect movie star look. Earlier this year, he got Pacey's sister pregnant."

"Really?" I ask. "Who's Pacey again?"

"Our goalie."

I type away on my phone to pull up a picture of him. "How did he handle the news?"

"Not well. Things were rocky within the group for a bit, but luckily, we helped them work it out."

"Does Pacey have a girlfriend? He's pretty cute."

Silas side-eyes me. "He's just as old as I am, so stop knocking on the doors of grandads." I laugh out loud. "And he's attached. He and Winnie are engaged. She actually got lost in the woods right outside of my house in Banff and wound up needing help in the middle of the rainstorm. We thought she was a murderer, and she accused us of being murderers. But in the end, Hornsby was the one who suggested she was good, and Pacey just so happened to hit it off with her. And smitten . . . the boy was all over her on day one."

"Really?" I ask. "Has he ever had that reaction to a girl before?"

Silas shakes his head. "No. It was an interesting thing to experience. He was never the doting boyfriend, but Winnie came along, and he was like a goddamn grizzly bear. He didn't want anyone going near her."

"That's hot," I say. "Too bad he's taken."

Silas shakes his head. "And then there's Levi Posey. He will eat anything you put in front of him, truly loves food, but not refined food. He likes things like bologna and Swedish Fish."

"There is nothing wrong with Swedish Fish."

"He eats the Swedish Fish on his bologna sandwich."

"Oh." I wince. "Ew, that's gross."

"Exactly. And he seems like this loveable guy who is nice to everyone, which is true, but the boy gets around."

"Like sleeps with a lot of women?"

"Yes, but he's never mean about it. He never hurts women's feelings. They know what they're getting into. And people always assume it's Hornsby who is the biggest player, but really . . . it's Posey."

"Where do you fall in line on that scale?" I ask as he makes a right.

"I met Sarah back in high school. I was never with anyone else. It was me and her up until we broke up. I've fucked around a bit since, but nothing like Posey or Hornsby before he met Penny."

"Interesting. So you've had sex with other women besides Sarah?"

"Yes."

"Who was the lucky girl after your breakup? And how did it feel?"

"Some girl I picked up at a hotel bar. It was really fucking weird at first. I was drunk. She was drunk. I fumbled a lot, so it probably wasn't her best experience."

"Aw, poor Silas. Did you find your stride after that?"

"Yeah." His hand falls to his thigh. "Sex for me is way different now. I don't feel like I have to stay in a box. If I want to talk dirty, I won't get chastised for it. If I want to spank a woman's ass, I don't feel bad about it. If I want my cock sucked, I'm going to ask and won't have any regrets."

I fan myself. "Ooo, tell me more."

He chuckles. "When you're with someone for so long, you get in a groove and forget that you can explore other options. I've explored. I know what I want now."

"I know what I want, just haven't had the chance to ask for it," I say.

"Why not?"

"Haven't found a guy worthy of my time," I answer.

"At least you have standards."

"I do." I clear my throat. "So there is one more guy in your group. What was his name again? Uh, it began with an H."

"Halsey Holmes," Silas says. "He's a tough one. He lost his twin brother a few years back. Holden. We were all devastated, but Halsey really didn't handle it well for obvious reasons. He's never been the same. He's focused on hockey and hockey alone. Some of the championships we have are because of him. When he comes up to the cabin during the off-season, he keeps to himself a lot of the time, always reading, and we just let him because we know if he needs something, he will come to us. Surprisingly, out of the guys in our group, he's the most levelheaded. Well, he and Pacey. If you need advice, they're the ones to go to."

"Huh," I say as I stare down at a picture of Halsey. "He's also really handsome. Is he dating anyone?"

"No, but he has a huge crush on a girl who is actually dating someone else."

"Aw, that makes me sad for him. Does she know?"

"Probably not. We barely know about it. It slipped out of him earlier this year, and it's something none of us have been able to let go because we're pretty sure he hasn't had sex since his brother died."

"Interesting," I say. "I mean, that's not the end of the world. I've barely had sex."

He stops at a red light and looks over at me. "What do you mean you've barely had sex?"

I shrug. "Yonny wasn't that into it. I love the act of sex and living through a heart-beating orgasm. It's the best feeling ever, so I never understood him. It really irritated me that he didn't want to have sex that much. I started to think I was repulsive or something."

"Not the case," Silas says as we start moving again. "The dude probably had some sort of complex."

"Maybe. Hard not to blame yourself, though, you know?"

"Don't," he says. "That's all on him, trust me."

"Thanks," I say quietly, then stare out the window. I appreciate his reassurance, but I still can't help to think it had something to do with me. Maybe my expectations were too high? "Do you remember the first time you looked at porn?" He coughs and pats his chest, causing me to laugh. "Sorry, that was kind of out of the blue. It was a bit of a rabbit trail in my head."

"You think?"

"I was just thinking that maybe my expectations were too high with Yonny because of porn," I say. "My friend showed me my first video our freshman year in high school. Her older brother had it all over his computer. I was fascinated. I remember going home and looking at it myself. I thought it was so hot. These people just getting off with each other. But when it came to the actual act of sex, I always felt intimidated. It took me a second to lose my virginity, and when I did, it was not the kind of experience I wanted to give myself."

"No guy is good at sex when they're younger. None."

"I guess so. And with Yonny, he was . . . well, less than interested to say the least. I love playing with my nipples so much, and he never paid them any attention. He was in and out. Honestly, the only orgasms I've ever felt have been hand-delivered by me."

From the corner of my eye, I catch his grip on the steering wheel tighten even further.

"Am I making you mad?" I ask, sensing the tension in his shoulders as well.

"Yeah, only because I can't stand guys who don't put in the effort."

"Are you saying you put in the effort, Silas?" I ask teasingly.

He makes another right, then slowly pulls in front of a lavish hotel. When he puts the car in park, he turns toward me and says, "I don't come until she comes." And with that, he's out of the car and moving around the front to open my door.

⊏⊐

"ARE YOU SURE THIS IS OKAY?" I ask, my palm feeling sweaty as I hold Silas's hand.

"Can you stop asking?" he says. "Couples hold hands."

"I know, I know, but this was supposed to be your ruse, not

mine. I feel like I'm abusing the situation now. I owe you something, like . . . a new pair of skates."

"For the love of God, don't purchase me new skates. And you owe me nothing. This is the deal we made."

"I know," I whisper. "I just feel like we need to make more of a deal." I spot an empty high-top table and tug on his hand. "Over here."

I guide him through a crowd of people I know are staring at us. They started staring the moment we walked into the ballroom. I wasn't aware of Silas's popularity until we showed up here. There's whispering, pointing, and talking behind hands. Apparently, I'm an absolute dumbass.

"Does this work?" I ask.

"Whatever you want," he says just as a server approaches with glasses of champagne. Silas picks up a flute for each of us and hands me one.

I hold the glass up to him and say, "Thank you for coming here tonight."

"No need to thank me. It's part of the deal," he says before clinking his glass against mine and taking a long sip of champagne.

"About that," I say as I pick up a napkin from the table and pull a pen out of my clutch. Always come prepared. That's what I say. "I think we need to make some ground rules."

His brow rises. "Is that really necessary?"

"It would make me feel better because right now, I feel like I'm using you."

"Jesus Christ, Ollie, I told you—"

"I know," I say. "But please just humor me."

"Fine." He nods at the napkin. "You're going to take notes?"

"No, I'm drawing up a contract."

"On a napkin? Wow, really official."

"Hey." I tap the napkin and say, "We will live and die by this napkin. Got it?"

"Sure," he answers while taking another sip of his champagne.

As I write, I talk out loud. "This hereby napkin will formally and legally bind Ollie Owens and Silas Taters to the following agenda below."

"Agenda . . . fancy."

I lean in and whisper, "I took one class in law as a prerequisite."

"It's like you've practically passed the Bar." Silas grins.

"Right?" I smile and go back to the napkin. "Silas Taters, hereby known from here on out as Puck, will deliver the following to Ollie Owens, hereby known from here on out as Lipstick."

"Are the nicknames necessary?"

"It's called having a sense of humor." I poke him with my pen. "Try having one."

"Be funny, and I will."

My eyes widen, and he smirks while sipping his champagne.

"Oh sir, you better watch yourself." He laughs some more while I focus back on the napkin. I clear my throat and continue, "Puck allows Lipstick full access to his home gym. Puck agrees to answer any question about hockey, even if it seems like a dumb question."

"Can't wait for that," he says.

"Puck agrees to attend any event/outing/date requested by Lipstick as long as his hockey season schedule allows."

"It's going to become quite sparse when the season starts."

"I understand that." I hand him the pen. "Please initial next to each line." He initials, then I take the pen from him and do the same. "Okay. Lipstick will deliver the following to Puck. Attend any and all events requested by Puck. Lipstick will dress as slutty—within reason—as Puck wants to make

Sarah last name unknown, from here on out known as Witch-bag"—Silas snorts—"jealous." I glance up at him. "What else do you want?"

"Nothing," he replies. "That's fine."

"It's not fine," I say. "There has to be something else I can do for you."

"Everything is already done for me."

"What about something like social media? Do you need help with that? Or a website? I know how to make one. Or I can help you with any lifestyle things like . . . how to, uh . . . fold a fitted sheet."

"I'm good."

"Ugh, come on, can't you think of something? I mean, I'd offer sexual favors at this point." He raises one brow in question. "But as we established, this is a business transaction, not a whorehouse."

"Maybe you should write that on the napkin."

I tap my nose with the pen and point at him. "You're right." I leave a space for him to put in another request, then underneath that, I write about not being a whorehouse. I hand him the pen. "Initial, please." He initials and hands me back the pen. "Okay, so now that we have no sex written in stone, we need one more thing for you."

"I want nothing."

"Urgh, you're infuriating," I say as the room around us erupts in laughter. We both glance to the right where Roberts has walked into the room. "Shit, my boss. Make it quick."

"I told you, I don't need—"

"Lipstick owes Puck one favor not related to events. Lipstick must comply. There," I say, dotting the sentence with a period. "Now sign here."

I give him the pen, and as he signs, he says, "You realize I will never cash in on that favor."

"Your problem, not mine." I sign the napkin as well and then seal it with a kiss.

"Is that your version of notarizing the document?"

"Yup." I place the napkin in my purse just as I feel the crowd part behind me, and Roberts steps in.

Tacking on a smile, champagne flute in hand, I turn toward the right, where Roberts waits. "Mr. Roberts, so nice to see you," I say, feeling awkward since I saw him just this morning. "I'd like to introduce you to my boyfriend, Silas Taters. Silas, this is my boss, Mr. Alan Roberts."

Silas sets his champagne down, snags his arm around my waist, and then holds his hand out for Roberts. "It's a pleasure," he says. "Ollie has said nothing but great things about her internship with you."

"The pleasure is all mine," Roberts says with a huge smile. A smile so large, it almost seems like he's fangirling. "Please, come over to my sitting space. I'd love to get to know you better."

Ooo, sitting space. He makes it sound so luxurious.

"Of course," Silas says as he slips his hand into mine and guides me through the crowd, sometimes pausing to shake a hand or two. It's probably one of the most surreal experiences I've ever had. I went into this thing with Silas completely blind, not knowing a damn thing about him and hockey or his presence in this city. Yet here I am, pretending to be his girlfriend as grown-ass men and women fawn over him as he walks through a crowded room. No wonder he tries to hide his face when he comes to my dorm. He doesn't want to be mauled.

When we arrive at Roberts's sitting area—a small section of the ballroom blocked off by fern trees and bushes and decorated in rich black velvet couches—Silas helps me down to one of the couches. Roberts takes a seat across from us, and a beautiful woman in what I can only assume is her fifties takes a seat next to him.

"This is my wife, Gloria. Gloria, this is Silas Taters, as you know, and his girlfriend, Ollie Owens. Ollie works for me as an intern."

"Lovely," Gloria says while folding her hands on her lap. I wonder if she knows about Roberts's affair. If she's compliant about it because she doesn't want to start over or lose the luxury of being with someone like Roberts. "How long have you two been dating?"

"Just a few weeks," I answer, my nerves spiking immediately because we didn't really talk about that. As I opened my mouth to answer, I just prayed that Silas didn't answer at the same time. That could have been disastrous. "Still newish. We just actually told our friends we were dating."

"Ah, I see," Gloria says in a disbelieving tone and pursed cheeks.

I'm going to tell you right now, I don't like her vibe.

I don't like the way she's studying us.

I don't like her clipped tone.

And I don't like how she's sitting there with a gleam in her eyes like she's ready to catch us in a lie.

How can she be so jaded, so disbelieving within seconds of meeting us?

I know when someone is challenging me, and I believe that's what she's doing.

How can she see right through me, through us? Does she not believe the validity of our fake relationship? Did she speak to Candace?

Will she go home tonight, and while she's brushing her teeth and Roberts is combing his mustache with mustache oil, is she going to tell him that we're frauds and that he should fire me?

Will I have a job tomorrow?

Will Roberts meet me at my cubicle with a box and a sardonic laugh as he watches me pack my pathetic desk up, noticing the one pack of light blue Post-it Notes I stole from Candace a month ago because Ross dared me?

I slip my hand into Silas's, scared for my freaking life.

It's bad enough Roberts is going to fire me, but there's no way I can allow him to see those Post-it Notes. He'll know the sort of deviant I actually am.

"How did you two meet?" Gloria asks, snapping me out of my thoughts and forcing me to face-plant back into this conversation. But now, instead of surging with waving confidence, I'm teetering on the brink of nerves.

How did we meet?

Great question.

Sweat forms on my upper lip as I attempt to remember the story Silas and I agreed upon, but for the life of me, my mind goes blank.

Black.

It's all faded.

"The doctor's office," I nearly shout. The moment the words leave my mouth, Silas stiffens next to me. I don't blame him because I'm pretty sure we're about to go on a wild ride. "Yup, the doctor's office. Weird, I know, but I was there for a routine checkup, and Silas was there because he got a rock stuck up his nose." Silas shifts next to me, and I can only imagine what's going through his head. "Now, some might think that's a sure-fire way to get a first-class ticket to the emergency room, but not Silas. He's a real saint and believed his GP could assist him with his needs. I remember seeing him in the waiting room, wondering how a grown man got a rock stuck up his nose. Come to find out, it wasn't from morbid curiosity or a nose fetish on his end. He just happened to sniff at the wrong time while a car drove by, lodging a rock right up the nostril. What are the chances, right?"

"Very . . . odd," Gloria says while Roberts studies me carefully. God, he can probably see right through me as well. He's mentally dialing HR, telling them to pull my file because a firing will occur.

"Anyway, I told him good luck with his nose, then went on

my way. Hard to make a love connection with a guy who was mouth breathing the whole time, am I right?" Silas slips his arm around my waist and squeezes me tight. *Yeah, he's not happy.*

Don't worry, dude. I'm not happy either because now I need to run with this story.

"So how did you two connect then?" Roberts asks, seeming more into the story than I initially thought.

I nod slowly and say, "The zoo."

"The zoo?" Gloria asks.

"Yup. We were both marveling at the domestic donkeys when we turned to leave and bumped into each other. The earth nearly shook as we fumbled to gain our footing. I knocked a chicken tender out of his hand, he accidentally sneezed on my face, and when all was said and done, I cleared my eyes, he pushed his hair out of his face, and it was like angels sang around us. It was rock nose guy . . ."

"Aw," Gloria says.

"And he had his fly down."

"Oh," Roberts replies with a chuckle. I know, I think a fly down is hilarious as well. Real classic comedy.

"Yup, there he was, not one single rock stuck up his nose, munching on a kid-size chicken tender, staring romantically at the domestic donkeys with his fly down." I wave my hand in front of my face, chuckling. "What an ass . . . am I right?" I laugh a little harder because that was funny. Thankfully, Roberts and Gloria join in.

When the laughter dies down, Gloria says, "What happened next?" And right there, I see that I've hooked her. She's no longer sneering in judgment or trying to see through me but rather leaning forward in interest. She's invested. Roberts crosses his ankle over the opposite knee and looks positively entertained.

Huzzah.

Now it's time to really kick it up a notch.

"Naturally, after the angels stopped singing, I told him his fly was down. Befuddled with embarrassment, he gripped his zipper and yanked it up . . ." Gloria and Roberts lean in. "I know what you're wondering . . . he zipped up too much, right?" I shake my head. "Luckily, that was not the case, but while he zipped up, I bent down and picked up his chicken tender for him. Poor thing was barely nibbled on. When I offered it back to him, he told me we'd surpassed the five-second rule, and he couldn't finish it. A decision I respected, given the amount of animal feces probably scattered throughout the walkways. He then proceeded to tell me how he was at an expert level of zipping his fly and wasn't sure why it was down in front of the donkeys. I gave him a reassuring pat on the shoulder, told him not to be embarrassed, and then . . . took off."

"You left?" Gloria asks. "After the angels sang?"

"Crazy, right? But there was something in his desperation to clear the air about his fly being down in front of the domestic donkeys that had a mini red flag waving over his head. I didn't want to subject myself to someone who might have . . . an animal fetish, if you know what I mean." Silas sharply coughs, and I take that as a solid "shut the fuck up right now, Ollie."

But I can't stop.

It's like a dam that's collapsed.

"You didn't know who he was?" Gloria asks.

I shake my head. "No idea. And as I started to leave, he called out . . . you owe me." See, there's some truth to this story. "When I asked him what for, he told me I owed him a chicken tender." I talk behind my hand and say, "Clearly a desperate attempt to spend more time with me. Despite the possible red flag, I saw right through it but was marginally interested. I've always been into a little freakiness. After all, he did have a rock stuck up his nose and flirted with me in the doctor's office. The confidence this man has is astounding. So

I told him of course I'd buy him a new tender. Together, we walked over to the concessions, and I purchased more tenders. He asked me to join him, and I did. I watched him mix mayonnaise and mustard together for a dipping sauce concoction I can still smell to this day. Positively putrid. But as he ate, he told me how much he loves donkeys. Their petite stature, unruly hair, and mind-of-their-own ears. As I listened to him go on and on about donkeys, I thought to myself, you know . . . he's kind of cute, so when he asked me for my number, I handed it over."

"That's sweet," Gloria says.

"But that's not really how it ended."

"Jesus Christ," Silas mutters under his breath.

"His attention to grammar in his text messages truly got my motor revving. Nothing is more erotic to me than the proper usage of punctuation in a text message. A lost art if you ask me."

"Makes sense, given your profession," Gloria says. "Well, that was quite a story."

"Yes," Roberts says with a smile on his face. "Seems like Silas will need something stronger if that story keeps getting repeated."

"Something like Scotch," Silas says.

"I'll have the finest brought to you." And with a wave of his fingers, Roberts orders Silas a Scotch while I feel a drop of sweat scoot down my back.

Well, that didn't go as expected.

"WHAT THE ACTUAL FUCK WAS THAT?" Silas asks while Roberts and Gloria are pulled to the side to meet with another couple. I heard mumblings of a big sponsor from one of Roberts's assistants, which means Roberts needs to shake hands.

"I'm sorry," I murmur. "I was nervous."

Silas leans close to my ear, his hand still curved around my waist so he can pull me in even closer. "How the fuck was that nervous? That was a disaster."

"Disaster seems a bit drastic," I say. "More like a great story."

"Says the girl who didn't have a rock shoved up her nose."

I wince. "Yeah, that is slightly problematic for your image, but hey, it garnered some sympathy. Instead of a run by fruiting like in *Mrs. Doubtfire*, this was a glide by rocking."

"Are you trying to be funny?"

"Is it not working?" I ask, his nose now mere inches from my cheek.

"Not even a little."

"Can I offer you an apology?"

"Not sure an apology can cure the damage done."

"What damage?" I ask. "You came off endearing."

"That was not endearing," he says, his voice dripping in anger. "It's not the fucking rock that I'm overly concerned about. It's that you practically said I had my penis out while marveling at donkeys. They're going to assume I'm some sort of public voyeur with a sick animal fetish. And domestic donkeys? Really?"

I turn toward him so it looks like we're having an intimate conversation rather than him scolding me in my ear. "First of all, I did not claim you were jerkin' your gherkin while staring at the donkeys. All I said was your fly was down. If you took that as something else, that's on you, sir."

"While eating a goddamn chicken tender. That's weird behavior, Ollie."

"I couldn't think of the word of that stick dough thing with the cinnamon."

"A churro?" he hisses.

"Ohhh . . . yeah, that's it. Churro would have made much more sense."

"So you wanted to say churro but opted for chicken tender instead?"

"What the mind wants, the mind gets," I respond. The way he snorts steam in my direction makes me believe he doesn't like that response. "Also, why are you breathing all heavily at me when you could have stopped me and taken over the conversation at any point. Almost seems like you wanted to hear the rest of the story. I can't be completely at blame here."

"The fuck you can. This is all on you. Jesus fuck, Ollie, you said I dip tenders in mustard and mayonnaise. Do you know how vile that is?"

"Made me gag just saying it out loud."

He stares at me, those ice-blue eyes screaming murder. "We had a fucking story, a simple one, so what happened?"

I pat his arm and kindly say, "It's called panic. Welcome to the show that is my life. Strap in, it's going to be bumpy."

"Jesus," he mutters under his breath just as Roberts and Gloria come back to sit down.

"Sorry about that," Roberts says while placing his arm behind Gloria.

It's odd to see your boss outside the workplace because if I didn't know Roberts professionally, at this moment, I'd believe he seemed like an easygoing guy. He's relaxed, in his element, and enjoying himself. There's no crease between his brow, no pep in his step to yell at someone for doing their job inadequately. He's . . . dare I say it? Chill.

I honestly don't think I like it. It's throwing off everything I ever believed in.

"Have you two thought about what the season will be like and the toll it will have on your relationship?" Roberts asks, the question quite specific. Makes me wonder if he's fishing for anything.

Is that why he seems so relaxed because he's trying to

loosen us up, make us feel comfortable so we say something we might not want to say?

Well, too bad for him. The boning of this dress has released from its confines and is digging into my side, putting me on high alert.

"We've spoken about it," Silas says, clearly wanting to take the lead now on answering questions.

Go ahead, man. I'm exhausted.

"She understands the schedule and that I'll sometimes be gone on longer trips, but the days I'm in town will be spent with her when I'm not required to be at the arena."

"Balance is important," Roberts says and smiles. "But so are championships."

"They are."

"Think you'll win another one this year?"

"That's the goal," Silas says while taking a very tiny sip of his Scotch, something I appreciate since he's the one who has to drive me back to my dorm. After the chicken tender–donkey debacle, he could be guzzling it.

"Mr. Roberts," another assistant says, "the chair would like to speak with you about your speech."

Roberts sighs and places his hands on his legs. "Duty calls. I'll let you two have some time with the rest of the crowd. Thank you for coming, and we'll catch up some more later."

"Sounds great," Silas says, and together, we all rise. Silas and Roberts shake hands one more time. I smile at Gloria, she nods at me, and then we part.

Silas takes my hand in his and keeps me close as he walks us through the crowd and over to the far wall, where we can scrounge up a touch of privacy.

"Was it worth it?" he asks when we're finally out of range of other ears.

"Was what worth it?"

"Embarrassing me. Was it worth the minuscule leap you must have taken in his eyes?"

"Hey," I say, pushing at his chest. "Don't be mean. It's a stupid story about your fly being undone. It's not the end of the world."

"It is when I have people all over this goddamn city trying to find information to print about me." He shakes his head. "You don't get it, Ollie. I'm not like you. I can't float around this world without a worry or care. I have to watch my image at all times."

"I don't float around without a worry or care. I care very much, hence why I brought you to this stupid thing. And I panicked. I didn't say those things to purposely embarrass you. It just happened."

"Well, control yourself. Jesus. If you're going to make moves in this world, in this career, then you'll have to grow up, Ollie."

I take a step back, his words hitting me harder than I expected because they sound like something my dad would say.

Journalism? Grow up, Ollie. Pick a real job.

And just like with my dad, it's not something I take lightly, nor will I let slide.

"Don't talk to me like that," I say. "Just because you think you're wiser than me doesn't give you the authority to treat me like a child. I fucked up tonight because I thought Gloria could see right through us. That panic made me try to think of a more elaborate story that seemed more believable. I'm sorry that I didn't paint you as the golden boy of Vancouver. My apologies. I didn't know you needed your ego stroked that badly."

I pick up my skirt and turn on my heel, heading in a different direction. Any direction to get away from him.

"Ollie, wait," I hear him call out, but I ignore him.

I then spot the buffet.

Bingo.

This girl needs a freaking crab cake.

With one thing on my mind, I bolt to the buffet where I pick up a plate and examine all the fine foods expertly crafted.

Fruits, cheeses, crackers, fancy vegetables cut to look like flowers. Mini beef things that look tempting, shrimp in a dollop of cocktail sauce, and . . . crab cakes.

Come to mama.

Don't mind distracting the hurt Silas just caused by a delicious, perfectly fried crab cake.

"I heard the beef Wellington is delicious," a familiar voice says. I glance up to find Yonny standing beside me, plate in hand.

"Ah, beef Wellington, I couldn't think of the name. Doesn't that take a while to cook?"

"Apparently, that's why it's such a delicacy to have as an appetizer at a buffet. Although, I've never seen it like this, in bite-size nuggets." He smirks at me, and it feels . . . odd. The last time he smirked at me was when he found out he could eat prepackaged cookie dough and not get sick.

So what's with the smirk?

Is he flirting? No, he can't be flirting. That's not what he does. He's just being nice.

"Have you had a lot of experience with beef Wellington?" I ask. Might as well partake in the conversation. It's not like the last person I talked to was being polite.

"Not as much as I'm making it seem." He leans closer with a smile playing on his lips. "Am I fitting in okay?"

"Uh . . . yes," I say, smiling back because, good God, he's actually being playful. What's going on with him? He must be high.

"Fantastic. I wasn't sure about attending tonight, but Candace told me I didn't have an option." He looks over his shoulder and says, "I borrowed this tux from my dad. Does it smell musty?"

I chuckle. He's definitely high. I lean in closer, giving his tux a sniff. "No, it smells like your cologne."

"I can't tell if that's a good or bad thing."

"A good thing," I say just as a strong arm wraps around my waist, pulling me in tight to an even stronger chest.

"Hey, baby," I hear right before a pair of lips presses against my neck.

I might be irritated with the man, but oh my God, that little kiss sends a tsunami of chills up and down my legs. Damn him.

When he pulls away—and when I say away, I mean like an inch—he asks, "Can I get you another drink?" His thumb makes small circles over my waist.

So we're just going to ignore our little conversation from a minute ago? *Not going to act like you just told me to grow up? Going to assume all is right in the world?*

Super.

"Sure," I say, feeling my breath catch in my throat from his proximity. It's easy to forget just how large he is, how his presence can eat up all the air around you. I realized that the moment I first kissed him, and I'm realizing that now as he holds me protectively in front of Yonny.

Not just protectively but . . . he's claiming me.

He's showing everyone in the room exactly who I belong to.

"Be right back." He lays another kiss on my neck before taking off.

"So," Yonny says, clearing his throat. "You seem to be happy."

I pick up some cheese and crackers, mindlessly putting them on my plate as I try to shiver off the feel of Silas's warm, delicious lips on my neck.

"Yes, I am," I answer.

"I'm glad you found someone," Yonny says. "I know I didn't treat you the way you deserved." He glances down at me, our eyes connecting. "You deserved so much more than what I could offer you at that time."

"At that time?" I ask, confused. "What do you mean by that?"

He just shakes his head. "Nothing to worry about. But I'm glad you found Silas." He glances over my shoulder at something behind me. I look as well and catch Silas leaning against the bar, his eyes glued on me. He doesn't waver or hide the fact he's staring. Instead, it's almost as if his gaze grows more intense with each passing second. "He seems infatuated with you."

I turn away as I feel this tingling sensation pour through my body. "He's, uh . . . very protective."

"I can see that. I'm pretty sure every person in this room knows you're off limits."

"That's only because he commands the attention."

Yonny shakes his head as he picks up a beef Wellington nugget. "No, he commands nothing from the room other than *your* attention." He picks up a napkin. "I guess I'll see you around, Ollie. Oh, and since I didn't say it enough when we were dating, you look stunning tonight."

My cheeks heat, and as he walks away, I find myself watching him. Silently, even though he can't hear me, I mumble, "T-Thanks." *What was with that? You look stunning tonight?* Obviously high. It's a good thing I no longer crave his attention.

I finish filling up my plate, and just as I turn around, Silas is at my side with a drink. "Follow me," he says, and because I feel all out of sorts, I do. I follow him to a private seating area to the left near an expansive window that grants us a view of the city. He takes a seat on an open couch and sets the drinks down on a coffee table in front of it, then helps me down as well. He sets my plate on the table and slips his hand into mine, tugging me close so he can speak quietly in my ear.

"I'm sorry," he whispers gently. "I wasn't prepared for your story, and it embarrassed me."

The cold, rough exterior I erected the minute we started

fighting melts away, and I reply, "I'm sorry too. It wasn't my intention to embarrass you."

He pulls away just enough to cup my cheek and stare into my eyes. From an outsider looking in, it looks like we're head over heels in love. But I like this. I like that this gentle man, who I'm coming to see could have an ego the size of Mike Tyson's, has chosen to make our moment of apology look like something romantic. I certainly chose a good one for my fake boyfriend.

"I know you wouldn't intentionally try to make me look like a donkey-loving pervert."

That causes me to snort. I lean my head against his shoulder, and he cradles me as we both chuckle.

"If the headlines tomorrow say Silas Taters is a donkey-loving pervert, I'll take full responsibility." I lift away from his shoulder and catch a slight smirk on his lips.

"If the headlines read that, the worst of my problems isn't what the public has to say. Facing the boys would be an absolute nightmare."

"Just direct them toward me, and I'll be able to explain."

"Pretty sure you lost all credibility when it comes to explaining or telling any kind of story. You're a loose cannon, and I won't allow it to happen again."

"Probably the best move you can make at the moment." I grab the plate and lift it between us. "Cheese and cracker?"

"Sure."

———

"DO you go to those kinds of things often?" I ask as we sit in Silas's car, sharing a large fry and sucking down milkshakes we got from a local joint that happened to be open.

"I go to more than I want to, that's for sure."

"So was that painful for you?" I pick up a fry and shove the crispy potato in my mouth.

"Parts of it." He lolls his head to the side to smirk at me. "Other parts, not so bad."

"I think we all know the painful part, and I'm pretty sure we're over it, so there's no need to bring it up again."

"You're the one who brought it up." He nudges my leg with his index finger knuckle.

"No need to be right all the time, Silas. It isn't an attractive quality."

"Good thing I have no need to be attractive around you since we have a strict no whorehouse policy."

"A policy I feel very strongly about."

"Is that why you were flirting with Yonny tonight?" He sips from his straw as I stare at him in shock.

"Excuse me, sir, I was not flirting."

"Could have fooled everyone in the room, even Candace. She stormed off to the bathroom when she saw you two at the buffet."

"Stop. No, she didn't."

Silas nods his head. "She did."

"Well, I wasn't flirting. If anyone was flirting, it was Yonny. I was just being polite."

"Flirting when he knows you're attached? That's fucked up."

"Is that why you came over to me?" I ask, still curious about the neck kiss.

"I didn't like that my girl was talking to another man," Silas says immediately as if he didn't need any time to think about his answer.

"Uh, I'm not your girl."

He picks up a fry and says, "You are when we work a job together. I would never let that happen in reality, so it's not going to happen when we're fake dating either. I had to stake my claim."

"Is that what was happening?" I ask, the back of my neck growing hot at the thought of him possessing *and acting* on that sort of attitude in real life. I've read about these possessive men who want to control you but also give you space at the same time, but I've never experienced one. Now, as I live and breathe, Silas Taters is stepping up.

And that feeling that flew through me with the feel of his lips on my skin was very . . . arousing.

"Fuck yes, it was," he says. "I'm not about to have anyone thinking you belong to anyone but me when we're in public. Now here, in the car, I can sit for twenty minutes, not giving two shits that you have dried milkshake crusted on the tip of your nose."

"Oh my God!" I shout as I grab the visor and flip down the mirror to look at myself. And sure as the day I was born, I have chocolate milkshake on my nose. I pick up a napkin, lick it, and then rub. "Why the hell are you just letting me sit here with milkshake on my nose?"

He leans back in his chair with a grin. "Donkey pervert, Ollie . . . donkey pervert."

Chapter Eight

SILAS

"Are you bringing Ollie to the family skate welcome party?" Posey asks as he sits next to me on the bench, water bottle in hand.

"We're in the middle of drills, and that's what you're asking me?" I pick up a water bottle and squirt some water in my mouth.

"What am I going to say? That I can feel the bologna sandwich I ate before stepping on the ice lodged in my stomach, acting like a two-ton brick and slowing me the fuck down?"

"Dude, you have a problem. Stop eating those."

"I do have a problem. I got a new pack yesterday, and it was calling me to open it this morning. I have no control."

"You're vile."

Our coach blows the whistle, letting the third-string line take a turn. First string is up next, so I stand from the bench, sweat dripping down my face with my helmet perched on the top of my head.

"So, are you?"

"I haven't thought about it," I answer.

"You should. She could meet everyone. I know Penny and Winnie will be there. Penny won't be skating, but it might be nice for Ollie to meet them."

"Yeah, maybe," I say.

"Don't be that way."

"Don't be what way?" I ask, confused.

"Not go because Sarah will be there."

I turn toward Posey. "She's going to be there?"

"Yeah, everyone is."

I run my tongue over my teeth just as the whistle sounds. I pull down my helmet, slip my mouth guard in, then hop over the boards and onto the ice.

If Sarah will be there, this might be the perfect time to introduce Ollie to everyone. After all, this is why we're doing this whole thing, right?

SILAS: *Hey, what are you doing this Saturday?*

Ollie: *I was planning to go on a long run. Why? Do you need something?*

Silas: *The team hosts a family skate welcome party before every season starts, and its Saturday. They make a big thing of it. Hot chocolate, s'mores, catered dinner. Wasn't sure if you could make it?*

Ollie: *Of course I can. But there is one big problem.*

Silas: *Don't tell me you don't know how to skate.*

Ollie: *Guilty.*

Silas: *Jesus Christ.*

Ollie: *Uh, pardon me for not growing up on the ice like you. I spent my youth being teased . . . remember? The last thing I wanted to do was flop around on the ice.*

Silas: *Well . . . good thing you have me.*

Ollie: *Are you telling me you're going to teach me how to skate in front of your entire organization and their family members? You understand how humiliated I'll be if you make me use one of those kid walkers.*

Silas: *Consider it payback for donkey pervert.*

Ollie: *Listen here, mister. *points finger* You can't use that anymore. Donkey pervert is off the table for negotiations.*

Silas: *I've barely used it.*

Ollie: *Well, this is your last time. No more.*

Silas: *Fine, but I think I'm getting the short end of the stick.*

Ollie: *The sooner you realize the world revolves around me, the better.*

Silas: *This is a partnership, not a dictatorship.*

Ollie: *Cute that you think that. Send me the deets and what I should wear. Slutty or non slutty. I have both covered.*

Silas: *It will be cold. Non slutty.*

Ollie: *Oh Silas, you truly have no idea about women, do you? Doesn't have to be warm to be slutty. Let me ask you this. Will Sarah be there?*

Silas: *Yes.*

Ollie: *Slutty it is!*

———

SILAS: *I'm here.*

Ollie: *Tucking my tits in. Give me a second.*

Tucking her tits in? What the hell does that even mean? Do I want to know?

Probably not.

I lean my head against the headrest and let out a large sigh.

I'm fucking exhausted. Practice was brutal this week. Not sure if Coach was trying to prove something or if he's not pleased about our performance, but I'm wiped out.

My legs are sore. My back is on fire. And after a heavy round of lifting, I feel like my upper body can barely move.

The last thing I want to do is skate around some more, but I know everyone will expect me to show up and bring Ollie. Pacey told me how excited Winnie is to meet her, which just adds to the pressure of it all.

And then there's Ollie and what might come out of her mouth. I decided to have a friendly chat on our way to the arena about what we say and don't say.

From the corner of my eye, I catch Ollie walking toward me, so I open the door for her from inside the car. It pops open, and she fully comes into view . . .

Jesus fuck, is she hot.

"What do you think?" she asks as she twirls in place, showing off her perfect ass and toned legs.

"Uh . . . good," I say as my eyes float down to the low-cut crop top sweater she's wearing. It shows off an abundance of cleavage while also offering a view of her toned stomach. Her leggings sparkle in the sunlight, and she paired them with fluffy white leg warmers that match her sweater or what little sweater she has. And then there's her long, bouncy, and volu-minous chestnut hair with the ends curled and curtain bangs framing her gorgeous face. Her green eyes stand out against the dark of her mascara, and her glossed, shiny lips pull my attention for a second longer than I care to admit.

"Just good?" she asks, then lifts her breasts. "I have cleavage in a crop top sweater. Do you know the kind of bra I had to wear to make this happen?"

"Something made of magic?" I ask as I stare at her round tits.

"Exactly, so I would appreciate a little more appreciation."

Mouth dry, my eyes move from her stomach, back up to her tits—tits I wouldn't mind fucking exploring—and up to her face, where I catch a smirk. "You look fucking hot," I say.

"That's much better," she replies as she slips into my car

and sets her mini backpack on her lap before buckling up. "So you approve of the outfit, then?"

"Yes," I say, putting the car in drive and taking off.

"Then why do you seem all frowny?"

"Tired as fuck," I say. "Sore. Hungry. Just irritable."

"Oh, fun for me, especially since you're supposed to teach me how to skate today."

"Don't worry, I won't be grumpy when we get there."

"Ah, so the grumpiness is just for me to experience."

"Yeah," I say. "Not like I need to impress you or anything. I already have a signed napkin stating you're mine."

"Something you should be grateful for."

"Trust me, in that sweater, I'm very fucking grateful."

I catch her smile and then turn to look out the window, clearly satisfied with that answer.

"So do we need to have a conversation about what's appropriate to say in front of people?"

"No," she groans. "I have it under control."

"Are you sure? Because that's what you thought when we went into the fundraiser."

"Listen, I might be a loose cannon, but now that I'm seasoned, I totally got this."

"That's what you're calling it?" I ask. "Being seasoned?"

"Yes, the perfect description. Now, if you don't mind, I'd like to turn on some Taylor Swift to pump me up."

"Taylor Swift for pumping up?"

"Uh . . . yeah. And if you piss me off, I can go into the party with *Reputation* on my mind, or we can be friendly and fly in on a *Lover* high. Take your pick."

I tug on my hair and sigh. "Do *Lover*."

"Good choice, Silas. You're so good at pleasing your fake girlfriend."

"SO I KNOW I EXUDE CONFIDENCE," Ollie says as I hold her hand and walk her down the hallway toward the rink. "But I'm going to tell you right now, I feel like I could throw up."

That causes me to pause and turn toward her.

"But we played the *Lover* remix featuring Shawn Mendes on repeat." She squeezes my hand and looks up at me in a panic. "Wait. Are you serious? Do you need a bathroom?"

"I think I just need a second," she says as she backs up to the wall and leans against it.

I continue to hold her hand and rub my thumb over her knuckles.

"Sorry," she says while taking a deep breath. "I just got really nervous all of a sudden. You would think I would be more nervous at my event, but this just feels so . . . intimate."

"We can leave if you want."

She shakes her head. "No, this is what I signed up for." Her eyes connect with mine. "Can you do me a favor, though?"

"Anything," I say, feeling her nerves course through me as well. She's so good at being vulnerable. It comes so easily to her that whenever she is vulnerable, it's almost like those feelings transfer over to me as well.

"Please don't leave my side. Yonny would do this thing where he took me to events and expected me to hit it off with other people without him. It's intimidating. I'm much better around people when I'm comfortable." She blinks, and those green eyes nearly bring me to my knees when she says, "This might sound weird, but I'm comfortable with you around."

"I'll be at your side the whole time. I promise."

"Thank you. I just know that Sarah will be here, and I'm not sure I'm ready for the whole you go flirt with her thing while I watch. I know it seemed like I did that with Yonny, but I didn't and—"

I reach up and cup her cheek as I say, "When I say I want

nothing to do with Sarah, I fucking mean it. I'm not leaving you. You'll be by my side the whole time, okay? Remember, you're doing me a favor, so I'm here for you."

She nods. "Okay, yeah." She lets out another deep breath. "God, I'm sorry. I'm stronger than this." I watch as she steadies her shoulders, lifts her chin, and poises herself for what's to come. It's interesting to see someone just drop their fear and anxieties like that, as if to say, I'm done worrying and now I'm moving on.

Not sure I even can do that.

"Okay, I'm ready."

"Are you sure?"

She nods. "Very sure. I'm taking a page out of your book and not showing any vulnerability."

For some reason, that doesn't settle well with me. Maybe because I have seen her vulnerable before or maybe because I know what it feels like to hold those feelings in. Either way, I don't want her to feel like she needs to deter from being herself.

"Don't take a page out of my book," I say. "It's not a healthy way to live."

"You say that," she says, tilting her head as she looks at me, "yet you don't listen to your own advice."

"Never said I was an expert at handling emotions. I just know if you have feelings, you'll feel better when you get them off your chest." I run my thumb over her cheek.

"Well, I'm nervous. What if people don't like me? I'll be letting you down."

"Trust me, the last thing you can do when dressed in that sweater is let me down."

That puts a smile on her face. "Really a fan of the sweater, huh?"

"Everyone is a fan of the sweater."

"Told you I could dress warm and slutty."

"You continue to prove me wrong." Now that she's feeling a touch lighter, I ask, "Ready to do this?"

"I am." She nods. "And thanks, Silas, for understanding."

"Listen. We're both doing each other a favor here. Working out all the kinks will take a second, but once we're comfortable, it will be easy moving forward."

"I hope so." She pushes off the wall and snuggles into my arm as we hold hands and head down the hallway again. "Remember, no ditching me."

"Babe, trust me, I'm not going anywhere."

"Babe?" she asks, with a raise of her brow.

I just shrug my shoulder, choosing not to address it because honestly, the term of endearment just slipped out. I didn't mean for it to come out like that, but unfortunately, there doesn't seem to be much I can control these days.

Like the way I keep glancing over at her stunning eyes.

Or how my gaze drifts down to her shirt and her mouth-watering tits.

Or how I can't wait to get out on the ice despite being sore, so I can show her how to skate.

Ollie is fun to be around, and I appreciate her keeping my mind off my demons.

"So this is where we enter on game days," I say. "And that"—I point at our logo on the wall—"that is what we tap before we enter the arena."

"Is it a good luck thing?"

I nod. "Yeah, good luck, tradition, all of the combined."

"And these heavy mats on the floor, is this because you wear skates?"

"Yup," I say as we pass a few employees. I nod and smile at them.

"Do you ever stop to talk to fans?"

"Before the game, not really. I'll toss pucks over the boards to fans after warm-ups, but conversations and autographs?

No. I'll save that for after games . . . games that we win. Coach doesn't like us hanging out on the ice after a loss."

"I can understand that. Good thing you win a lot, or at least that's what I've heard. I haven't really paid attention to your stats."

"Shame, I could really impress you."

"Stats mean nothing to me. How you treat the people around you, now that's something to talk about."

I lead her out onto the ice. The staff has truly made something special out of the event, they always do. Half of the ice is a rink for family and friends to skate on. Covered by rugs, the other half has a mix of couches, chairs, tables, and of course, hot cocoa and s'mores stations, which are really more for the kids. Food is up in the club section. I've been to this event a few times with Sarah, so being here with Ollie feels slightly awkward.

"Oh wow, this is . . . this is bigger than I expected," she says as she glances around the arena. "You play hockey here? Look at all those empty seats. Are they usually full?"

"Every home game," I say.

"It must get loud in here."

"Very loud, but the cheering fans only spur me on to work harder."

"Sexy," she coos as I take her over to the skates section. Of course, the players all have their skates on display and below them are their respective family and friends. We had to provide the team with sizes prior to arriving to make it easier.

"Mr. Taters, are you ready to skate?" the attendant asks.

"I am," I say. "And please, call me Silas."

"Sure thing," she says as she retrieves the skates and hands them off to us.

"Thank you." I guide Ollie to a couch, then kneel in front of her.

"What are you doing?" she asks.

"Helping you put your skates on," I answer and then carefully slip her shoe off. When I glance up at her, I notice her cheeks are blushing. I don't know how much of that has to do with me kneeling in front of her or the chill of the ice beneath us.

"Oh, that's not necessary."

"Have you done it before?"

"No," she answers.

"Then let me help you . . . *babe*."

She chuckles. "Really going with that, aren't you?"

I'm about to answer when I hear, "Oh my God, Pacey, look, he's helping her with her skates."

Winnie.

Here we go.

"Hi," Winnie says, walking right up to us and holding her hand out. "You must be Ollie. I'm Winnie, Pacey's fiancée."

"Hi, Winnie," Ollie says with a bright smile. "It's so nice to meet you."

"Good God, she's gorgeous." Winnie knees me in the side. "Potato, she's so freaking pretty."

Ughhhhh, Winnie.

"Potato?" Ollie asks. There it is.

"Oh yes, that's what I call Taters. Just reminded me of a potato." I glance up at Ollie to see her smiling from ear to ear.

"I rather like that nickname."

"Don't even think about it," I mutter under my breath as I pick up her foot and help her insert it in the skate. When it's fully in, I lace her up.

"When Pacey told me Potato was bringing you, I could not stop thinking about all the things I want to talk to you about."

"Winnie," Pacey says. "Give her a second to breathe."

But Winnie takes a seat right next to Ollie and says, "How on earth did you two meet? The first time I met Silas, he was a total ass. Sure, I was crashing his guy vacation, but God, he was a tough one to break."

"And you think you've broken me?" I ask with a raise of

my brow.

"It's adorable that you think I haven't." Winnie pats me on the head and turns back to Ollie. "So how did you two meet?"

Here we fucking go . . .

"Well, it was at a doctor's office," Ollie starts, and I take her other foot and slip it into the skate as I hear her tell the story of how we "met." Pacey and Winnie are laughing the entire time.

"Dude . . . what were you doing with your penis out near the donkeys?" Pacey asks.

"My dick wasn't out," I groan as I stand, my muscles firing. "My fly was just down, that's all. Right, Ollie?"

She nods. "There was no perverting over the donkeys."

"I'm wondering why you were holding a chicken tender," Winnie says. "That doesn't seem like something you would eat. You're fancy."

"I like to switch it up when I'm at the zoo," I say, just going with the flow at this point.

"I didn't even know you like to go to the zoo by yourself," Pacey says.

"Who goes to the zoo by themselves?" Posey says, walking up alone.

"Taters," Pacey says.

"Really?" Posey asks. "That doesn't seem like something you would do."

"And he had a chicken tender with his fly undone while jerking off to the donkeys," Winnie adds, causing me to pinch the bridge of my nose.

"Jesus, dude . . . come on. There are children at the zoo."

I stand from where I was helping Ollie and hold out my hand to her. "Ready, babe?"

"Oooo." Winnie claps her hands. "He calls her babe. Pacey, did you hear that?"

"I did."

"I still can't believe it. Potato has a girlfriend."

"Glad you're not making a big deal about it," I say to Winnie.

"I'm happy for you. For both of you," she says. "Let's chat some more. I want to hear about all of the romantic things Potato does for you."

Ollie smiles. "There's a lot. He's easily the best boyfriend I've ever had."

Winnie clutches her chest and then, out of nowhere, comes up to me and gives me a hug. Unsure of what to do, I awkwardly pat her back as she squeezes tight.

"I'm so happy for you," she quietly says. "I hated seeing you so upset over the summer." She looks up at me with tears in her eyes. "I can't wait to learn more about your girl."

Okay . . . someone is super emotional today.

Winnie and I had a rocky start, but a lot of it had to do with the fact that I was still trying to get over my breakup with Sarah and what happened that summer. It was supposed to be spent with my guys. But it was interrupted on day one by Winnie. It took me a while to accept her into the group, but after I got to know her better and saw how much she cared about Pacey, I knew she was a keeper.

And now, as she hugs me tightly, I can honestly call her a friend, even though a lot of the times she drives me nuts.

"Thanks, Winnie."

She pulls away and goes to Pacey, who hugs her into his side. "Let's get your skates," he says. "Ollie, I expect to see you more later."

"Of course."

And with that, I take her hand in mine and guide her toward the edge of the carpet.

"So . . . potato, huh?"

I chuckle. "Winnie is something special. She's the only one who gets to call me that."

"And what nickname should I use for you?"

"You might have to get to know me better to find out."

"Why do I feel like that's an innuendo to call you daddy?"

I nearly choke as I glance down at her. "How the hell did you get that?"

She shrugs. "I don't know. You just seem like one."

"Can't tell if that's a good thing or a bad thing."

"In my world"—she pauses and smirks—"it's a good thing."

That smirk makes me believe there's so much more to this girl that I will never find out about. I already know she likes to fuck, she likes to come, she likes to be sexual, but even though I know these things, it doesn't mean I'm going to experience it.

"Are you ready to go out on the ice?"

"No," she answers as her hand trembles in mine.

I glance over at the open ice where kids and families are already skating.

"Do you trust me, Ollie?"

"I think so," she answers.

"Then know when I say I won't let you fall, I'm not going to let you fall."

Her eyes connect with mine, worry etched in them. "You promise?"

"Promise."

"Okay," she says. Guiding her out on the ice, I skate backward while her wobbly legs skate toward me. "I have no idea what I'm doing."

"Just glide with me," I say. "Bend your knees a bit, yes, just like that. And let me bring you around the ice. Rely on the strength in your glutes, thighs, and ankles from all your workouts."

Her hands tremble in mine, but I keep her steady on the ice as I swivel around.

"How are you feeling?"

"Okay," she says and glances up at me, her lips barely forming a smile.

"Relax. It'll be a lot easier if you're not so stiff."

"I want to make a joke about stiffness and donkey pervert, but my brain can't seem to connect the two at the moment."

"Well, thank God for small miracles. Maybe I should always have you on the ice." I bring her closer to the boards so if she wants to grab on to them, she can.

"See those kids over there?" she says, nodding to the right.

"Yes," I answer.

"Please, for the love of God, keep them away from me."

I chuckle. "Understood."

"I can't believe you do this for a living."

"I started young. It just feels like second nature now," I say as she grips my hands tightly.

"I wish I had done something like this when I was young. I don't think my parents cared enough to get me involved in any sort of sport."

"Were they mean to you?" I ask, just as a kid flies by us. "I got you," I whisper, letting her dig her fingers into my forearms.

"No, they weren't mean per se." She pauses and takes a breath. "But you know how there are super involved parents, and then the parents who have kids but don't get very involved in their lives? Those were my parents. They weren't mean, just not interested."

"I'm sorry," I say, wondering what it would be like if my parents didn't take an interest in me. I'm not sure I'd handle that. "Well, you have me if you ever want to move further in your ice-skating journey."

She glances up at me, those beautiful eyes of hers penetrating right into my soul. "I can say with full confidence that this will be the beginning and the end of my ice-skating journey."

I let out a low chuckle and continue to skate backward as I say, "At least you know your limitations."

We spend the next fifteen or so minutes skating around the

ice. She tries moving her legs, but when she almost falls on her ass, she thinks better of it and asks me to just move her around, which I have no problem doing. We joke around. Talk about hockey and what a game day looks like. We go into detail about the gear, which I think is funny. Once I notice her shivering from being out on the ice for so long, I ask her if she wants some cocoa and receive an emphatic yes.

"Sit right here, and I'll help you with your skates."

"You know I can manage it, right?" she asks.

"Yes, but if you were my real girlfriend, I'd take these off for you. Therefore, I'll do the same in this situation."

Once I finish, I slip our shoes back on, drop off our skates, and then head to the cocoa bar.

"Wow," she says, taking in all the fixings. "I'm overwhelmed. I don't think I've ever seen so many hot cocoa options."

"It's more popular than the s'mores," I say. "Let me give you the tour. You have milk chocolate and dark chocolate cocoa as well as white chocolate to choose from. From there, you have caramels, peppermint sticks, espresso shots, raspberry syrup, cherry syrup, chocolate chips, five kinds of marshmallows ranging from Martha Stewart's homemade recipe to Lucky Charms. And then there's Cool Whip, whipped cream, sprinkles, caramel drizzle, fudge, twizzle cookies, Oreo cookies, and coconut."

"Dear God," she says, causing me to laugh. "I don't know where to start. What do you usually do?"

"Are you asking for the Silas special?"

"Is that a thing?"

"It is in my head."

She smirks at me. "Then please, delight me with the Silas special."

"Okay. First up is milk chocolate cocoa." We fill up a glass mug that we get to keep. "Then it's cherry syrup for me."

"Oh interesting," Ollie says as she follows me.

"Two cordial cherries."

"You didn't mention those."

"Because it's a surprise." I plop two in her mug.

"Then Martha Stewart marshmallow followed by whipped cream, chocolate drizzle, and chocolate sprinkles." I load her up and then sink a paper straw into her drink. With her hand in mine, I bring her over to one of the couches and help her down.

Music plays in the background, offering a festive atmosphere in the very large arena.

"This is nice," Ollie says. "I know nothing about professional sports, but it's really cool that your team does this for family and friends. It must make them feel special."

"It does," I say. "They always bring it back because of the positive response, and it seems like the hot cocoa bar gets bigger and bigger every year."

"Was the first year just a canteen of it that everyone had to share?"

"Almost," I say with a smile. A smile that seems to catch her attention because I sense her staring at me as I take my first sip. "Can I help you?" I ask when our eyes meet.

She lifts her hand and presses her finger along my cheek. "I never noticed your dimples before and how deep they are."

"I got them from my mom," I say.

"Your eyes too?"

"Yes," I say. "How did you know?"

"Because despite the stark color that gains someone's attention from across the room, they're soft, warm, inviting, the type of eyes I'd expect to see on a mom."

"Not sure anyone has called my eyes soft or warm."

"Then they haven't been looking hard enough," she says right before taking her first sip of her cocoa. I watch as her lips wrap around the straw and her cheeks hollow out as she sucks. It gives me a brief glimpse into what she might look like sucking my cock. Those bright-green eyes satisfied, her cheeks flush but contoured, those lips passing up and down my shaft. It would be so hot.

"Are we interrupting?" I hear Hornsby ask. I look up to find him gripping a very pregnant Penny.

"Not at all." I stand. "Penny, would you like to sit down?"

"Would love to," she says while sitting next to Ollie. She presses her hand to her stomach and says, "I'm Penny. That hunk of meat over there got me pregnant, and I'm ready to not have this baby in my belly anymore."

Ollie chuckles. "I'm Ollie, and I can't imagine how you feel at the moment. For what it's worth, your boobs look amazing."

Penny claps her hand over her chest and, in a choked-up voice, says, "Thank you, that means so much to me."

"Could you imagine if I met you for the first time and told you your dick looked nice in your jeans?" Hornsby asks.

Hands in my pockets, I say, "Wouldn't hurt to hear it every once in a while."

"Ahhh," Ollie coos. "Silas, your dick looks fantastic in your jeans."

Well fuck me, that makes me smile.

Smile and blush, because she didn't just tell me my dick looked good. She also let her eyes fall to my crotch and paused for a moment and stared.

I rock on my heels and say, "Thanks, babe."

"Oh my God, I love them already," Penny says, clapping her hands, and I kind of feel bad at this moment, my friends meeting Ollie and thinking we're a real couple. I can see the girls becoming attached. And when this is over, whenever that is, what the hell am I going to say to them? "So how did you two meet?"

Ah, fucking hell . . .

"Well, we were both in the doctor's office," Ollie starts, a conspiratorial look in her eyes.

Here we go.

Chapter Nine

OLLIE

"You okay?" I ask as we travel through the arena and up to the clubhouse.

"Yeah," Silas answers, a slight hobble in his step.

"Are you sure? It feels like you're limping."

"Just really fucking sore and exhausted."

"Your eyes do look tired. They're slightly bloodshot."

"They are?" Silas asks. "Fuck, they feel heavy."

"Do you want to leave?" I ask, even though I want to spend a touch more time with Silas and his teammates.

Coming into today, I was nervous, scared, and so frightened to make a bad impression that I knew I was trembling as we walked into the arena. I don't know what came over me. I'm usually not the kind of person who settles into their feelings and exposes them on the outside. Maybe it was the way Silas handled himself at my event that I felt like I had to match his energy. I don't know, but now that I'm here and have met everyone, I feel a lot more comfortable. So comfortable that I want to get to know them more.

"I would love to leave," Silas says, "but that's not an option. I have to show my face upstairs."

"Well, after that," I say. "You just let me know when."

"I will," he says as he presses the up button for the elevator. "Are you having a good time?"

"I am. I think your friends are awesome. Penny and Winnie are pretty cool too."

"They are. Penny is all over the place right now with her pregnancy hormones. Hornsby has been dealing with a lot."

"She's carrying the baby. He can suffer through it."

"Very fair point," Silas says. The elevator dings, he slips his hand into mine, and we walk into an open hallway together. Off to the right is a glassed-off suite, and from the outside looking in, I can see purple, black, and silver decorations, resembling the team's colors—something I just learned today. It's embarrassing how clueless I've been.

"Smells good," I say as we approach the door.

"The food is always amazing here." He opens the door for me, and he ushers me in, a crowd of people by the tables and the buffet. Holding my hand tightly, he guides me in that direction.

"Is that a catering dish full of meatballs?" I ask, my eyes zeroing in, my stomach growling.

But Silas doesn't answer me.

He doesn't even acknowledge me.

When I glance up at him, I immediately notice the clench to his jaw and the stiffness in his shoulders. I follow his line of sight and spot a woman over by the plates and napkins. Long blonde hair, gorgeous pouty lips, and a curvy body shown off by high-waisted pants and a skintight long-sleeve bodysuit.

I know, without even having to ask, that's Sarah.

And she's so freaking gorgeous.

Filled out in all the right places. Poised. Confident. Styled. I feel like a child compared to her.

And experiencing the way Silas reacts when he sees her, it makes me feel . . . inferior in so many ways. This is ridiculous because I shouldn't care how he looks at her or his reaction to her, but here I am, growing an army of insecurities in my head when I shouldn't. I mean, they were high school sweethearts, which means Sarah is ten years my senior as well. *What does that matter, Ollie?* We aren't romantically involved. Although, how will I make Sarah feel inferior when the woman standing in front of me is superior in looks?

I'm about to ask him if he wants to leave, but then she turns and spots Silas. I watch as her lips turn up, and she sets down the plates she's handing out to walk up to Silas, completely ignoring me standing right next to him.

"Silas, oh my God," she says as she steps right up and throws her arms around him.

He lets go of my hand and returns the embrace, leaving me standing there watching them, feeling foolish.

His hand falls to the small of her back, and his head drops down as she squeezes him tighter.

"It's so great to see you," Sarah says. Even her voice is sexy. When she pulls away, I notice just how breathtakingly beautiful she is with her ocean-blue eyes, full lashes, and carved cheekbones. She has an air of sophistication about her that I know I don't have. She's grown-up, mature, her own person, and I'm over here, still trying to figure out my life.

This was not what I was expecting when I considered meeting Silas's ex-girlfriend. I thought I'd float in, show off, and make her jealous. Somehow, it feels like the exact opposite.

"Hey," Silas says, his voice gruff.

"I'm glad you came. I was afraid you might not, given how I work here now." She completely ignores me, and to my horror, so does Silas. "And that's a stupid assumption since this is your home, but I want you to know I didn't intentionally seek out this job. A recruiter approached me. I wouldn't have taken it if it wasn't a dream opportunity. The last thing I want to do is invade your space."

"It's fine," Silas says as he pulls on the back of his neck while his eyes travel the length of her.

It almost seems like a hungry look.

She toes the ground, and it's so fucking cute it makes me feel like an ogre, standing off to the side, wondering if he's going to introduce me.

"You look good, by the way," she says as she reaches out and touches his sweater. "I always thought dark blue looked the best on you."

He nods. "You look good too, Sarah."

Well . . . fuck.

It's one thing to say hi.

It's another thing to completely forget that your fake girl-friend is standing next to you, watching you interact with your ex-girlfriend that you've said you have no feelings for. Uh, it looks like someone needs to check themselves again because from where I'm standing, no way in hell is Silas over this girl.

Finally, after what feels like hours, Sarah spots me and smiles sweetly. "Oh gosh, I'm so sorry." She holds out her hand. "I'm Sarah."

As if that snapped Silas out of his Sarah-induced coma, he places his hand on the small of my back and says, "This is Ollie . . . my girlfriend."

"Girlfriend?" Sarah says in surprise. "Oh wow, I just assumed she was your assistant or an intern." She shakes my hand, then gives me a once-over. "You're so young."

God, do I want to grow claws and scratch her across the face. It might not be obvious to others, but it's obvious to me. She's trying to make me seem less than I am, and to hell if I'm going to let that happen. If there is one type of person I know how to deal with, it's a bitchy one.

"Thank you, I can give you the name of my night cream if you want. It works wonders."

Her face falls flat.

"I know the eye area is so hard to combat when you get older," I add for the hell of it.

"That would be sweet," she says, plastering on a fake smile. She then turns her attention back to Silas. "Well, I'll let you get back to your meal." She touches his arm. "It was so nice to see you, Silas. Good luck this season. I can't wait to cheer you on."

"Thanks, Sarah," Silas says, sticking his hands in his pockets.

And as she walks away, I watch Silas watch her.

Wow, just . . . wow.

After a few seconds, I say, "So . . . that's Sarah."

He nods, then presses his hand to my back and leads me toward the buffet where we quietly fill our plates. He assists me, scooping the food out that I want. He grabs us silverware and napkins, and when he finds us a seat, he grabs us drinks as well. It's like he's on autopilot, frozen in his thoughts with nothing to say.

Thankfully, after a few minutes of silence while we eat, Winnie comes over to our table and takes a seat. "Aren't the meatballs divine? They have them at every gathering."

"They're really good," I reply, feeling awkward and uncomfortable. Even though Silas sits next to me with his hand on my thigh, I catch him looking back at Sarah every so often. If this was a real relationship, my ass would be walking out that door so fast. I'm actually tempted to call it a day. Silas and I aren't attached, but I do feel embarrassed. Anyone observing us would see that Silas is clearly distracted, like I'm not good enough to hold his attention.

"Hey dude, you okay?" Pacey says as he sits down and sets a plate in front of Winnie.

"Yeah, I'm good," Silas says as he pushes a piece of broccoli around on his plate. "Pretty tired, though. I think I'm about ready to go."

"I actually was hoping to talk to you for a second," Pacey says and clears his throat. "In private."

Silas glances at him, and they exchange some sort of secret conversation that forces Silas to nod and stand. And without a second thought to me, he and Pacey walk off.

What happened to not leaving me behind? Good God, this man.

When they're out of earshot, Winnie leans in. "Are you okay?"

"Of course." I smile at her because I'm not going to make a big deal out of being around Sarah—that would just mean I'm intimidated by her. And even though I am, I'm not going to show it.

When I imagined Silas's ex-girlfriend, I assumed she'd be this average girl who maybe broke his young high school heart. I had no idea she'd be as stunning as she is or sophisti-cated with one of the most sultry voices I've ever heard. I truly felt like a tenth grader trying to gain her crush's attention while standing next to him.

"You're so much stronger than I am," Winnie says. "I'd have a coronary if Pacey's ex-girlfriend was near us."

I just shrug. "He's not with her. He's with me. That's all I need to know."

"You know, I might have a girl crush on you."

That makes me chuckle as I take the last bite of my meatball.

"So now that they're out of the way, I want to get to know you more. What do you do?"

"Well, I'm actually still in college."

"What?" Winnie asks, her eyes widening. "You're in college?"

"Going into my last year. I'm majoring in journalism. I have an internship with Alan Roberts."

"Impressive. I know exactly who that is. Wow. I thought you were young, but I didn't know you were that young. Does Silas visit you on campus?"

"Only at my dorm," I say.

"Why do I find that so hot?" Winnie asks. "Just the thought of dating an older man and having him visit you on campus is like something you'd read about but never see in real life."

"You should see him when he comes over. He's all covered up so he's not recognized."

She chuckles. "Now that I can see. Are you from around here?"

"Oregon, actually. I knew I wanted to be in journalism, and Roberts was the best in the Pacific Northwest, so I applied to college up here. Luckily, I got in and worked my ass off to earn that internship. It was actually just extended."

"That's fantastic," Winnie says. "Congratulations."

"Thank you."

"Are you ready for the season to start?"

"I am," I say. "I honestly don't know much about hockey. I didn't even know who Silas was when I first met him. So I don't know what to expect."

"I have one year under my belt. The key to making it through the season is lots of communication. And trust of course. Pacey and I like to keep things interesting. We have dates every night when he's away, and we tend to get . . . frisky over the phone."

I smile. "I love that. Do you get each other off?"

Winnie perks up as if this is the first time she's been able to talk about this. "Yes, every time. I like to surprise him with different lingerie."

"Do you strip for him?"

"Yes. But he honestly just likes it when I play with myself. I just prop up the camera and listen to him tell me what to do."

"That's so hot," I say, feeling jealous. "The guy I was with

147

before Silas never wanted to try anything beyond missionary. And even at that, we didn't have much sex."

"Travesty." Winnie leans in. "Believe me when I say these hockey men are insatiable. Especially after a win, all they want to do is fuck, and fuck hard." My mouth waters at the thought.

Too bad we have the no whorehouse pact.

Dammit, I didn't think this through.

Just then, the guys come back, and instead of taking a seat, Silas says, "Are you good to go?"

"Sure," I say, sensing how off he is.

He holds his hand out to me, and I take it. "We'll catch you guys later."

I offer Winnie a smile and a wave and allow Silas to guide me out of the room and to the elevator, where we wait. When it dings, a few players come off, including Posey. They do a quick fist-bump, and then we're on the elevator, headed down.

The entire time, Silas stays silent. I wish for the life of me I knew what he's thinking because I know a lot is swirling through his head. I also want to know what Pacey said to him, but that's none of my business and not something I'm going to pry into.

After we get off the elevator, we head down the hallway and out the door to the parking lot full of some of the most expensive cars I've ever seen. Row after row.

When we reach Silas's car, he moves to the passenger side and opens the door for me. I take a seat, and he shuts the door before moving around to his side. His silence is deafening right now. I have no idea how to handle this or what to ask him to see if he's okay. I'm not sure he even wants to talk at this point, so when he gets in the car, I don't say anything.

I just let him drive.

And that's what he does.

We drive in silence to my dorm, and the entire time, I replay the night. I think about how he so carefully helped me skate, how he was attentive and sweet when I was nervous and scared, but all of that vanished the moment he saw Sarah. And after that, it was almost as if I didn't exist or I was just an accessory to his night.

And maybe I was.

I shouldn't be offended by that. It's a job after all. This is what I signed up for.

When we reach my dorm parking lot, he parks instead of pulling to the front and then gets out of the car. I wait for him to open my door, assuming he wants to talk, but when he just helps me out and walks me up to my dorm, I'm more confused than ever.

He follows me up the elevator, and when we reach my room, I expect him to say goodbye. Instead, when I open the door, he follows me right in and kicks off his shoes at the front.

Done with the silence, I turn toward him and say, "What's going on?"

"I'm exhausted," he says as he walks over to my bed, hops up on it, and lies down.

Uhhh . . .

I enter the main space, and with a hand on my hip, I say, "You realize you have a home, right?"

"I can't fucking drive there right now," he says as he closes his eyes and drapes his thick arm over his face. "Just give me an hour. Okay?"

"Just give you an hour? You want to sleep in my bed for an hour?"

"Please, Ollie," he says, sounding more exhausted than I realized.

What can I really say? It's not like I can force him out of my dorm, the man has major muscle, so I just step away and move toward my closet. I pull my sweater up and over my head, leaving me in my bra, and then I dig around for one of my comfortable shirts, but all I have are crop tops. That will have to do.

I glance over my shoulder and notice he's already knocked out, so I keep my back toward him, remove my bra, and then slip my crop top over my head. I glance back at him again just to make sure he's not looking and change out of my leggings and into a pair of sweats.

Comfortable, I slip on my slippers and turn to look at him again. His thick chest rises and falls as he curls into one of my pillows. The scruff on his face looks thicker as he lies there, his arm draped over his eyes. It's no wonder Sarah was blatantly flirting with him tonight. He's incredibly attractive, not to mention very fit. With his arm lifted, a small patch of skin on his flat, muscular stomach is exposed. And as I stare at him, I wonder if I would have flirted if I had randomly seen him at the bar that night rather than using him to prove a point.

Probably not.

I would have thought him out of my league for many reasons. One of the biggest ones being that he seems too complicated. Too complex. Just from the pinch in his brow and the tightness of his jaw, you can tell he's dealing with things. Today was a good example of that.

One moment he was showing me off, being the attentive boyfriend every girl dreams of, and then the next, he was aloof, staring at another woman, and completely shut down. If that doesn't scream red flag, I don't know what does.

Good thing I'm not attached.

Good thing I can let the day roll off me even though it was embarrassing.

Phone in one hand and e-reader in the other, I head out of my dorm and to the community space, where I text Ross.

Ollie: *I'm assuming you're not home?*

I open my e-reader and settle into my chair just as my phone buzzes next to me.

Ross: *Out with Zachary getting dinner. Everything okay?*
Ollie: *Yup, just checking in.*

Ross: *You sure, because you went to that hockey thing today, right? How did it go?*

Ollie: *I can talk to you about it later.*

Ross: *Zachary had to take a work call. Please, lay it on me.*

Ollie: *Okay. It was good. Everyone was really nice. I had a lot of fun until . . .*

Ross: *Oh no, did the ex show up?*

Ollie: *She did, and Silas just about froze me out after that. I've never seen anything like it. It was as if he was completely transfixed by her. And oh my God, Ross, if I was actually Silas's girlfriend, I'd be hurting hard right now. She's so beautiful. And the way he looked at her. I actually got kind of embarrassed by his behavior because no one but us knew we were fake dating, so they probably thought he was hung up on her.*

Ross: *Oh fuck, really? Why would he want you to help him out when that's how he's going to act?*

Ollie: *No idea, but it was . . . embarrassing. And then his friend Pacey pulled him to the side, most likely to talk about Sarah. After that, we left and didn't say a word to each other.*

Ross: *He didn't say anything? Brutal.*

Ollie: *Not until we got back to my dorm. He followed me in, and now he's sleeping in my bed.*

Ross: *[side-eye emoji] What? He's sleeping in your bed?*

Ollie: *Yeah, he was exhausted, and I'm pretty sure seeing Sarah drained it out of him.*

Ross: *That makes sense. How are you feeling?*

Ollie: *Confused. Grateful I don't have feelings for him. Glad this is all just an arrangement.*

Ross: *Is the arrangement worth it?*

I think about it. I could go back to my room and call it all off. But then again, it's not like I'm trying to win his affection. This is about business. He's helping me with Roberts, and I'm helping him . . . who knows what I'm helping him do. Didn't feel like much today. Either way, I'm not sure I'm ready to end this just yet, especially since Roberts made this more difficult for me.

Ollie: *It is right now.*

Ross: *As long as you don't get hurt.*

Ollie: *How could I get hurt?*

Ross: *You already said he embarrassed you today.*

Ollie: *But it wasn't personal. It was more of a pretend girlfriend embarrassment.*

Ross: *You're making excuses for him.*

Ollie: *No, I'm not. He acted like a dick the second half of our time together. There's no denying it.*

Ross: *Okay, I just don't want you getting hurt.*

Ollie: *Trust me, not possible.*

Ross: *Okay. Well, Zachary is back, and he was just telling me all about his geology class. This is what happens when you ditch me for a hockey player, I end up taking out our friend who likes to talk about rocks.*

Ollie: *I'll make it up to you. Love you.*

Chapter Ten

SILAS

A door clicks shut in the distance, stirring me partially awake. I open my blurry eyes and catch Ollie walking out of her bathroom.

Her hair is drawn up into a bun on the top of her head, and she's now wearing a baggy pair of sweats and a crop top with no bra. She looks incredibly comfortable and sexy at the same time.

"Oh, you're awake," she says as she stops midway into her room.

"Barely," I mumble. "What time is it?"

"Ten," she says.

"Shit." I rub my forehead. "I'm sorry." I swing my legs over the end of the bed, and I stand, feeling so fucking sore that I groan.

"You okay?" she asks as she entwines her hands together.

"Fucking sore." I hobble over to her bathroom, where I shut the door and take a piss. When I'm washing my hands, I glance up at my bloodshot eyes in the mirror and the frown on my face. The frown that appeared the moment I saw Sarah.

I thought I was prepared to see her. But I was so fucking wrong.

The moment my eyes found her, this dreadful feeling sucked all the air from my lungs, and I froze.

I can barely remember anything that she said other than that whatever she was saying was fake.

It was all fake.

She didn't mean to come work at the Agitators? Bull-fuck-ing-shit.

And the fact that she dyed her hair blonde, how I loved it, and wore the bodysuit I fucking loved on her? It was all premeditated to fuck with my head.

That's exactly what happened too. She fucked with my head to the point that I kept looking back at her to see if she was really that fucking evil. And she was.

Evil . . . but also fucking pretty.

And I hate that I even thought that.

I hate that I felt a little something when she hugged me.

I hate that her smile thawed a part of my heart.

I hated everything about the goddamn interaction.

But most importantly, when Pacey pulled me to the side and told me to get my shit together, I hated that he pointed out that I was ignoring Ollie.

And he was right. I was. Because I didn't know how to act around her. I'm not good at making an ex jealous and flaunting a new girlfriend—even though she's fake. I felt like Sarah was watching my every move.

I push my hand through my hair, knowing I need to talk with Ollie. She deserved to be treated better.

My mouth feels dry, so I wet my finger with toothpaste. I quickly wipe down my teeth, then swish around her mouthwash for thirty seconds before spitting it out. That feels fucking better.

I exit her bathroom and head back into the main space, where I find her sitting cross-legged on her bed.

When she glances up at me, I just blurt out the first thing that comes to mind. "I'm fucking sorry, Ollie."

She looks away and says, "It's fine. No need to apologize."

Yeah, she's upset. From her downcast eyes to the slump of her shoulders, it's plain as day. I fucked up . . . again.

I close the distance between us and hop up on her bed. I hook my finger under her chin and lift so her eyes meet mine. "It's not fine. I was an ass, and I'm sorry."

She tries to look away, but I don't let her. That's when I notice her eyes welling up with tears.

Shit.

"Fuck," she mumbles. "I don't know why I'm getting emotional. This is stupid."

"Your feelings aren't stupid."

"That's the thing, Silas. I shouldn't have feelings about this. It's just . . . ughh," she groans. "I felt embarrassed, okay?" She swipes at her eyes. "And I've been wrestling with this emotion ever since you saw Sarah. I realize that this is all just a job to us, going to these events, but it felt embarrassing when you completely forgot about me. It's more of a vanity thing on my end, but it mattered, and it just felt like . . ." She pauses, gathering her words. "It felt like being with Yonny all over again. Like everyone else in the room is more important than I am, and I'm just an accessory to his agenda. And I know that's how this is supposed to be, but I guess it just hit me different-ly." She swipes at her eyes again. "Fuck, I hate crying."

"I'm sorry," I say again. "I didn't mean to make you feel that way."

"As I said, it's fine." She sets her phone on the charger on her nightstand, then scoots to the far end of the bed, where she slips under her covers. "I'm tired, so I'm just going to go to bed. You can let yourself out."

She turns her back toward me, and I realize I have two

options here. I can either let her be and probably end up fucking this friendship up more than I want, or I can stay and let her know that she isn't just an accessory.

I choose the latter.

I switch her light off, and I pull her covers back and slip under them as well.

Startled, she turns to face me and says through teary eyes, "What are you doing?"

"I'm not going to leave you sad like this. You say it's fine, but it's not."

"I don't want to talk about it, Silas. It's stupid, okay? I'm probably due for my period, so I'm more emotional than I care to admit."

"Doesn't lessen how you're feeling," I say softly. "I treated you like shit, and you don't deserve that, even if you're my fake girlfriend. I can understand where your embarrassment came from, and even though you asked me not to leave you, I still went off with Pacey."

"That was fine. I talked with Winnie, and we had a good conversation. I'm not mad about that."

"Doesn't matter. I still went back on my word." I take a chance and reach out to her, placing my hand on her bare waist. I allow my thumb to caress her skin. "I'm really sorry, Ollie. You deserve better than the way I treated you today."

More tears spring from her eyes as she nods. "Thank you. I'm sorry I'm being so emotional about this."

"Don't apologize. You have no reason to apologize. I really fucked up, Ollie. I'm having a harder time dealing with the idea of Sarah being around than I thought I would."

"I could tell you still have feelings for her," Ollie says quietly.

"That's it, though. I don't," I say. "I was mad. Irritated. Frustrated with her mindfuckery. That's all this is to her, a way to fuck with my head, and it worked. And I'm so fucking mad at myself for letting her have that kind of control that I shut down. I shut down on myself and on you."

"Are you sure you don't still have feelings for her?"

"Positive," I say, gripping her waist. "Did I think she looked good? Of course. That's not something I can turn off, but when it came to how I felt, I was more irritated with her than anything."

She slowly nods. "I can understand that feeling. I was irritated with Yonny the other night. He was kind, nice, and told me I deserved better than when we were together. What was the point of that?"

I rub my thumb along her skin again. "To fuck with you. That's what they do. They try to mentally fuck with you. They try to keep us holding on to what we used to have."

"Did it work for you?" she asks.

"It did. What about you?"

"A little," she admits and then sighs, rolling to her back. I keep my hand on her stomach, and I feel her breath force her stomach to rise and fall. "I hate him. I think that's the first time I truly admitted that. I really hate him. Sure, was I captured for a moment at the fundraiser? Yeah, but afterward, I felt empty and irritated, and I hate that he did that to me." She turns toward me and reaches out to play with my sweater. "Is that how she made you feel?"

"Yes," I answer, feeling like I have a kindred spirit in her. "Really fucking irritated. To the point that I ignored the one person who could force me to smile, even when talking about donkey perversion."

That makes her laugh as she curls into my chest and wraps her arm around my back. I return the embrace, letting my hand float up the back of her short shirt.

"I'm really fucking sorry, Ollie."

"I know. Thank you." She pulls away and sighs. "Now I'm the one who's exhausted."

"I think we both deserve some rest."

"We do." She yawns. "Okay. I'm going to shut my eyes."

"Okay . . ." I swallow and ask, "Do you mind if I stay?"

"Not at all," she says. "As long as you don't snore."

I chuckle. "No need to worry about that." I lift and pull my sweater over my head before I lie back down and snuggle into one of her pillows.

I feel the need to wrap my arm around her and pull her into my chest, but I know that's not the kind of friendship we have, so instead, I tuck my hands under the pillow and get comfortable. I would love nothing more than to take off my jeans, but that would also push my luck.

"Ollie?" I ask, hoping she hasn't fallen asleep yet.

"Yeah?"

"Is your name short for anything?"

She turns toward me again and smiles. "How long have you been wanting to ask that?"

"Day one," I answer.

"Day one, huh?" She smirks, and fuck, it's so cute, especially with her resting on her pillow, free of makeup, a sleepy look in her eyes. "What took you so long?"

"Thought it was appropriate now. I like Ollie, but I was curious if it was a nickname for something else."

"It is, but no one, not even my parents, calls me by my real name."

"What is it?"

"Not sure I should tell you. I don't want you thinking you can use it."

"When would I use it?"

She moves an inch closer till our knees touch and says, "If you were mad at me. Or obsessed maybe. Or in some passionate—yet fake—moment when you call me by my birth name, thinking it will make me weak in the knees. It won't happen."

"Good, because I have zero intention of using it."

"Well, as long as you have no intention of using it . . ."

Her teeth run over the corner of her mouth before she says, "My real name is Oliana. Oliana Owens."

Ollie-ahn-uh.

My lips rub together and test her name on my tongue. "Oliana." I tip her chin up and say, "That's really fucking pretty."

"Don't get any ideas," she says, pointing her finger at me.

"Oliana," I repeat to myself.

"Stop." She playfully pushes at my chest, but I capture her hand.

"It's really . . . really fucking pretty."

Her eyes meet mine, and there's a quiet pause between us when she wets her lips and her fingers slightly claw against my chest.

"What?" I say, breaking the silence.

"Nothing." She smiles.

"Tell me what you're thinking."

"You want the truth?"

"Yes," I answer.

"Well, I'm feeling like I have a touch of whiplash with you. One second, you're incredibly sweet and helping me through this odd arrangement we have, then the next, you ignore me completely, and now you're back to the first guy."

"The real man is the one you're seeing now and the one you saw before the event. The in-between is a part of me that I hate."

"Well, maybe you can lean on me a bit more next time."

"Yeah." I grip her hand that's against my chest. "I think I will."

"Good." She covers her mouth while she yawns. "Now, let me get some sleep."

"Okay. Night . . . Oliana."

"Urghhh," she grumbles. "I knew you would use it."

I CHECK my phone and see that breakfast has been delivered, so I sneak out of bed and pad across the floor. Thankfully, I had them deliver it right to her door. So I crack the door open and pick up the bag of pastries and sandwiches, as well as the four coffees I've purchased because I was unsure of her preference.

I quietly shut the door and bring breakfast back to the main room, where I see her sit up in bed and rub her eye.

"Is that coffee I smell?" she asks.

I pause, right there in the middle of the floor, and stare at her. The light from her window shines in, illuminating her from behind. Pieces of her hair have tumbled out of her bun, framing her face, and her shirt that barely covers her breasts sits extremely tight against her hard nipples. I truly think every crop top she owns is my new favorite shirt because fuck it's hot.

Her eye pops open, and she says, "Uh . . . you okay?" That's when her eyes land on my bare chest, and I watch with satisfaction as they scan me. From the way my jeans ride very low on my hips, up my stacked stomach, and then to my large pecs, at this moment, even though I'm sore, I've never been happier about my workout routine.

"I'm fine, you?" I ask her.

"Good," she replies quickly. "Is that, uh . . . is that breakfast?"

"It is." I walk up to the bed, set the bag on her nightstand, and then check out the coffees. "I have a vanilla latte, caramel latte, black coffee, and a chai. I didn't know what you would want."

"Caramel please," she says as she reaches out her hand. I find the latte and hand it to her while I pick up the black coffee for myself, grateful she didn't choose that one since I really need it. "What's in the bag?"

I pull out the contents and lay them on the nightstand.

"Egg and sausage sandwiches, pastries, and a muffin. Once again, didn't know what you wanted."

"Egg sandwich all day, every day," she says while snagging one. I do the same and then sit next to her. Together we unwrap the sandwiches and take a bite. "I could get used to this," she says.

"Get used to what?"

"Hand-delivered breakfast in bed by a shirtless guy. Sign me up."

"What do you like more? The shirtless guy or the breakfast?"

"Clearly the breakfast." She smirks.

I playfully bump her shoulder with mine.

"You spill the coffee, you clean the sheets. Possibly purchase a new mattress."

"Not a fan of the smell of coffee?" I ask.

"Not in my bed."

I take another bite of my sandwich, then lean my head against her wall. "My dorm was nothing like this when I was in college."

"Oh yeah, Granddad?" she says, causing me to smile. "Tell me, how was it back in the day?"

"You're such a punk, you know that?"

"Makes this friendship more fun, don't you think?"

"Makes me feel like a goddamn geriatric."

She laughs out loud and turns toward me, legs crossed, sandwich in one hand, coffee in the other. "I'm sorry, please, regale me with your tales from ye old college years."

"A punk," I repeat, but she just bites into her sandwich. I take a sip of my coffee then say, "I had to share this space you have with another guy in college. And we didn't have a bathroom. It was a communal bathroom."

"Ooo, how many dicks did you see daily?"

"Really? That's what you're going to ask?"

"Naturally, would you expect anything else from me?" she asks.

I take a bite of my sandwich and then say, "Not really."

"Okay then, so tell me about the penises."

"Yeah, there were a lot of penises, but I was used to it because of playing hockey growing up. We were always showering naked in front of other guys."

"Oh, that's right. Well, what's the biggest penis you've ever seen?"

"That's easy," I say with a wink. "That would be mine."

She rolls her eyes dramatically. "I'm being serious."

"So am I," I say.

"Sure, okay, Silas, you have a huge dong. Now who is the second?"

"Why don't you believe me?"

"Because every guy thinks they have the biggest penis."

"That's not true. I don't think I have the biggest penis. I just think it's the biggest I've seen in person. Online, well that's a different story. Those men are horses."

She snorts and covers her nose with the back of her wrist. "Oh my God, I was not expecting you to say that."

"It's true."

"I know we've talked about this before, but how much porn do you watch?"

"Probably not as much as the average guy. I don't like the fakeness of it. I prefer to just jack off to images in my head."

"Images of who?" She pauses and then asks, "Sarah?"

"No," I answer honestly. "I can't. She fucked me over, and there is no way I'm going back to that, even if she's gorgeous."

Ollie nods. "So then, like who?"

"I don't know, like women I see or celebrities I think are hot. Sometimes I'll just find an image that turns me on."

"Ever think about me?" she asks in a joking tone.

"Keep wearing those goddamn shirts, and I will."

She glances down at her shirt, then back up at me. "This is one of my longer ones."

"Well fuck, I'd hate to see what the shorter one looks like."

"Hate? Really?" she asks.

"Nah, I'd fucking love it. You have hot tits."

"Aw." She presses her hand to her chest. "That's so sweet. I think you have hot tits too."

"Can you not call them that?"

"Well, I'm sorry," she says. "But your pecs are huge." She pokes one with the hand holding her coffee. "I don't think I've ever seen a man as ripped as you. Makes me want to just run my hands all over your body."

"Have at it," I say.

"Oh, nice try, sir. But I'm not going to be subject to one of your jacking-off memories."

I chuckle. "If you run your hands over me, it wouldn't be a memory. It would be a right here, right now kind of moment."

"But that will never happen because we're not a whore-house, remember?"

"Oh, I remember." I finish my sandwich.

"So did you like your roommate back in college?"

"Full-circling this conversation?" I ask her.

"Well, you never got to really talk about your glory days."

"Those weren't my glory days," I say. "Farthest thing from it, actually. I hated my coach. He was the biggest ass in the world and made college a living hell."

"Why did you go there?" she asks. "I'm assuming you had multiple choices."

"It was a great program with great facilities. The coach who recruited me was fired right before I arrived. So it was out of my hands. I suffered through college. And my room-mate wasn't any better because he wasn't a student athlete, so he didn't understand my rigorous schedule."

"Really?" Ollie asks. "That's weird that they'd stick you

with a regular student. My university even has student athlete assigned dorms."

"The other guys on my team roomed with student athletes. Not me."

"So I'm going to assume you two didn't get along?"

"Not so much," I answer. "There were a few times when he was pretty chill, but for the most part, he was a dick. At one point, he was smoking pot in our room, and I had to pin him against the wall and threaten his life. I could have been kicked out of school."

"Ooo, did you ever punch him?"

"I wanted to," I say. "But never did."

She sips her coffee and then says in wonderment, "I truly want to know if we would be friends if we were the same age. Like if you actually went to my university, would we run into each other and be friends?"

"No." I shake my head.

"Why not?" she asks, offended.

"I'd never be friends with you. I'd try to fuck you. But friends, not so much."

"Oh." She smirks. "If we're off the record here, had you tried to fuck me when you were in college, I would have let it happen."

"You would have been disappointed." I chuckle. "Took me a second to figure everything out."

"Probably wouldn't be worse than anything I've experienced so far." She sighs. "Why can't men just understand the concept of the female orgasm?"

"When they're young, they're blind from their own spiraling need for release. The smart ones realize if they want more sex, they have to get good at it."

"And that's what you did?" she asks.

"I did." I wink.

"Huh, well, I guess we'll never know."

"I guess not." I scratch my chest and nod at her. "What

are you up to today?"

"Need to get a workout in. Think I can stop by?"

"You can just come home with me."

"And how do you expect me to get back to my dorm?"

"I have to run some errands, so when you're done, I can drop you off."

Her one brow hooks in the air. "When did you become my chauffeur?"

"If you want to drive yourself, that's fine. I'm just offering." I smooth my hand over my chest and stand from her bed. "But I'm leaving in a few, so you need to decide."

"Well, that was a quick breakfast. You're just going to swallow your sandwich whole and leave?"

"Did you want me to stay?" I ask.

"I don't care what you do with your life."

"Clearly, you do if you're making a comment."

"Only because I'm still trying to finish my breakfast, and you're stating you're leaving in like five seconds."

"So you do want a ride . . ."

"Of course I do," she says. "Honestly, do you think I enjoy driving?"

"Then why make a big deal about it?" I ask.

"Because, Silas, that's what I do."

———

THERE IS no way in hell I planned on lifting today, not after the way my muscles have been screaming at me, but I also need to loosen my legs, so I opted for walking on my treadmill.

What I didn't think about was getting a front-row seat to watching Ollie perform three kinds of squats in leggings that were fit for her ass and her ass alone. They leave nothing to the imagination. They even ride up her crack so I get the perfect defined ass squatting up and down right in front of me. Not to mention, she paired the pants with a sports bra, which only lifts her tits rather than flattens them.

With her hair pulled back in a long ponytail, she's walking around my gym like a goddamn wet dream. I'm over here trying to avoid looking at her so I don't get hard while walking on a treadmill.

But hell . . . look at that ass.

Round.

High.

Tight.

It's obvious the girl spends time on her squats.

And she's doing some heavy weights too. I'm fucking impressed.

I glance down at the treadmill screen and see that I've hit thirty minutes, so I turn it off and thank God that I can step away from the first-class view of Ollie's backside.

I fling my towel over my shoulder, grab my water, and head to my mat, where I pick up a foam roller. Time to experience pain.

I lie down on my side on the roller and roll out my IT band, cringing and trying not to groan the entire time. But motherfucker, does it hurt. It's not like I don't work out during the off-season because I do. It's important to stay in good shape, but it's never as intense as when we're in preseason, and I never skate either. So waking those muscles up again is painful.

"You okay over there?" Ollie asks as she sets her weight on the rack.

"Did I groan out loud?"

"Uh, yeah. It's terrifying."

"Sorry. Just really fucking sore." I roll my leg out more and then switch sides.

"Is it always this bad?" she asks as she puts the weights away and wipes down the bar.

"Yeah. During preseason, there's always a point when our coach decides to ride us hard—and not in a sexual way."

"I would hope not. That's a lot of men for your coach to handle."

I chuckle and continue to roll while wincing. "And it's always around this time when I get incredibly sore."

"The other guys seemed fine."

"They're braver than me."

"At least you can admit that." She picks up her water and walks toward me. "Need some help?"

"Uh, I think I'm okay," I say. "Just going to finish up, then hit up my sauna."

"Sauna?" she says. "You never told me you have a sauna."

"Yes, I did."

"Afraid not. I would have remembered that. Where is it?"

I point. "Door on the left."

Her eyes widen with joy. "Can I use it?"

"You can use anything in here. Towels are in the bathroom. Let me know when you're done, and I'll take over."

"Don't be ridiculous. You can come in with me." She taps my leg. "Don't worry, I'll cover up even though I love sitting in a sauna naked."

"Yeah, so do I."

"If this agreement was a whorehouse, I would tell you to drop the towel. Not to even bother."

I swallow hard. "Yeah, well, good thing it's not a whorehouse."

"Yeah, good thing," she replies with a smirk and takes off. "See you in the sauna."

I finish rolling, giving her a few minutes to get comfy, and when I'm fully stretched and feeling slightly more relaxed, I go to my bathroom, where I strip out of my clothes and wrap a towel around my waist. I've never gone into my sauna with a towel, but there's a first time for everything.

Hand clutching the terrycloth, I walk up to the frosted

glass door of my sauna and open it only to find Ollie stretched out along one of the benches, a towel under her and a towel barely covering her lengthwise. Instead of it wrapped around her body, she just has it draped over the top of her breasts, leaving her side boob on full display, and then positioned thinly between her legs so I get a great view of her entire side.

My groin tightens from the sight, and I inwardly curse for saying something about the sauna. This will be anything but relaxing.

"This is amazing," she says as her chest lifts and her back arches while her leg bends so her foot is flat against the bench.

Fuck.

Me.

"Uh, are you sure you don't mind me being here?"

"Shouldn't I be asking you that?" She rolls her head to the side and glances at me. The corner of her lips turns up. "You know, Sarah is really dumb. I don't know what happened between you two, but for her to not want that"—she motions her finger up and down my body—"she's an idiot." Given I found Sarah with a woman between her thighs, it's not my physique that Sarah walked away from. And I gave Ollie a pretty fair indication of how well I unintentionally disregard people's feelings.

I sit down on the bench. "She didn't want a lot of things when it came to me."

Ollie presses her hand to the towel to keep it close to her body as she rolls partially onto her stomach to look at me. From her turn and use of one towel, her ass comes into full view. And fuck is it so goddamn nice.

My mouth waters.

My body itches to get closer.

And even though I tell my eyes to focus on her face, they betray me and take in her perfect backside.

"I don't understand that. How could she not want you?

I've never been hornier in my life than this past week, thanks to being around you."

I lift a brow in question, and she just shrugs.

"I'm not going to lie about it," she continues. "I'm also not looking for you to relieve that by admitting this. I can handle that on my own. But seriously, I'm sure women all over Vancouver are lining up to jump into bed with you. What was her problem?"

"I guess she just wanted more," I answer, remembering what I walked in on. "Something different."

"Well, I'm sorry she treated you like shit." She flips so she's fully on her stomach now, and she kicks her legs up to the sky while her arms barely conceal her tits. If she were mine, I'd lift her pelvis and fuck her from behind. I'd spank her ass, loving how it would light up with my handprint. And I'd tug on her hair, showing her exactly who was in control.

Me.

Not that sassy mouth of hers.

Not her strong will.

But me.

"So why aren't you dating, then?" Ollie asks. "Why do you think this fake dating partnership is better?"

"I've never dated someone during the season, someone new at least. When I was with Sarah, she knew exactly what to expect with the demands of my job. But I think it would be too hard with someone new, especially with the season starting in a few weeks. Maybe if I met someone right after the end of a season, I could prepare her, but right before?" I shake my head. "It's too much for a new relationship."

"Is it really that taxing?"

I nod. "Long hours, late nights, sometimes gone for over a week, depending on the schedule. It's constant. And it can seem exciting maybe at first, but I know it takes a tough partner to be able to handle it all."

"Did Sarah handle it okay?"

"She did," I answer. "There were things I wish she would have done differently when I was on the road. She didn't like to talk that much on the phone. I tried phone sex a few times, and she wasn't into it. Wasn't into anything when it came to the phone, and some nights, fuck was it lonely."

"You never cheated on her?"

"Never," I say, making eye contact with Ollie. "When I'm with a woman, I'm hers and only hers."

"That's hot," Ollie says. "You always hear these stories about athletes cheating on their partners. I've never really been drawn to athletes for that specific reason. I never want to be cheated on. I can't imagine that kind of pain."

"It's not fun," I say before I can stop myself.

Fuck.

I glance at her, and her eyes widen. She sits a little taller, almost to the point that I can see her nipples. "Silas . . . did Sarah cheat on you?"

I glance away and rub my hand down my face. "I don't want to fucking talk about it."

"Okay," she says quietly. And I know she wants to ask a million questions. I can feel them orbiting her, needing to get them out. And then she says, "For what it's worth, she's an absolute fool."

My eyes land on her again, and she lifts up an inch, but it's just enough for her breasts to almost be exposed. Her teeth roll over her bottom lip as her hand travels down her neck, like a bead of sweat rolling over her skin.

"You're sexy, Silas." Hand clutching her towel, she lifts up to sit on the bench. The towel twists but covers her in all the right places. "You have the kind of body I could worship." She wets her lips as she stands now, the towel a mere loin cloth for her breasts and pussy. "If you were mine, I wouldn't let you out of the bedroom." She comes closer. "I'd make it my mission to have my mouth on every last inch of your skin."

I don't know what she's doing or her end goal, but it's

turning me on to the point that I rest my hands on my lap to hide my excitement.

I want to be touched like that.

I want to be worshipped.

I want to feel fucking wanted.

"You're easily the most attractive, nicest man I've ever met, despite your penchant to be grouchy a lot of the time." She stands in front of me and hinges at the hip so we're eye to eye. She lifts her hand to my cheek and slowly brings her thumb over my lips, dragging it down. I consider sucking her finger into my mouth or pulling her onto my lap . . . possibly laying her across me so I can spank her ass, just like I wanted to when she was working out. "You deserve better," she whispers. "You deserve a woman who not only wants your cock . . . but craves it." And with that, she lifts and turns so all I see is her perfect backside walking away. She glances over her shoulder where she catches my wandering eyes, fixated on exactly what she wants me to fixate on. "I'm going to shower. I'll be in your living room, waiting whenever you want to take me home."

How about never?

How about you come sit on my goddamn lap right now?

How about you let me fuck you so I can get this burning feeling out of my system that seems to develop whenever you're around?

"Okay," I answer in a strangled voice, my cock begging for her touch. "Shower for me, too."

She winks. "Don't think about me while you're in there." And then she retreats to the guest shower.

Don't fucking think of her?

Next to impossible.

I make a beeline for my bedroom, and once I'm inside, I rip my towel off, go straight to the shower, and flip on the water. I step in, gather some soap in my hand, and then perch my arm against the tile as I grip my hard dick and stroke.

"Fuck," I moan quietly.

Don't think about me?

How could I fucking not?

For the past hour and a half, I've been suffering through blue balls as I watched her squat, experienced her stretched out in my sauna, beads of sweat dripping down her soft skin, then getting a show of her ass as she walked away, all tight and high, begging for my hands . . . for my cock.

"Fuck me," I mutter and pump harder.

Ollie in her crop tops, no bra . . . nipples hard.

Ollie in that dress from her fundraiser and her phenomenal tits.

Ollie in her workout outfit . . .

I pump harder, my balls already beginning to tighten.

I bite down on my lip, my impending orgasm seconds away.

Don't be fucking loud.

Don't be . . .

"Oh . . . God." I hear through the bathroom vent, causing my eyes to nearly pop open. Was that Ollie?

It had to be.

Is she, fuck, is she getting off too?

Just the thought of her touching herself in my apartment has me gripping my cock tighter and shooting right over the edge.

I bite down on my forearm as I come all over the shower tile.

My entire body shakes as I steady myself and push off the wall. I slip under the hot water and let it drip down my body as I think about how that was the first time I jacked off to Ollie. And how it won't be the last.

Chapter Eleven

OLLIE

Ollie: *What are you up to?*
   Silas: *Stretching my quads.*
Ollie: *So, riveting stuff, huh?*
   Silas: *Very.*
Ollie: *Well, I have nothing going on, and I figured since you don't have anything going on either, we could make some of our story a reality.*
   Silas: *Why am I now scared?*
Ollie: *Don't be. But if you're up for it, come pick me up at my dorm in thirty.*
   Silas: *So . . . I'm going to have to pick you up? How is that fair? Aren't you the one asking me to do something?*
Ollie: *It's not fair. See you in thirty, don't be late.*
   Silas: *Can I at least ask what the hell we're doing?*
Ollie: *I'll tell you when you pick me up. Now, move along.*

"HEY," I say as I hop in Silas's car and shut the door. He's wearing a pair of black jeans, a white shirt, and a denim long-sleeved jacket with the sleeves rolled up to his elbows, as well as a very Silas-like scowl. "What's with the face?" I ask, pressing my fingers to the furrow in his brow.

"What's with those shorts?"

I glance down at my shorts and back up at him. "Uh . . . nothing."

"They look like underwear."

"Could you imagine?" I laugh and buckle up. "God, that would be uncomfortable." I tug on the sleeves of my cardigan and smile at him.

"Ollie," he says in a dark, unamused tone.

"What?" I ask, and he gives me a look I don't appreciate. "I can see that you're trying to be a controlling asshole at the moment, so I'm going to give you a good ten seconds to change that attitude before I rip you a new one."

"I'm not trying to be a controlling asshole. I just think those shorts are really short, and if we go somewhere in public, we will have pictures taken of us. Do you want those shorts plastered everywhere?"

"Sure, why not?" I say so nonchalantly that I know it's killing him. "If people want to stare at my ass, that's their prerogative. But this bodysuit is comfortable, these shorts are comfortable, and this cardigan gives me all the warmth from the breeze blowing through Vancouver today. Now, unless you have something nice to say, I think we should just forget we had this conversation and move forward."

He grips the steering wheel tightly, the veins in the back of his hand bulging. "Fine, we can forget it."

Wow, he's so convincing. Who knew he would care so much about freaking shorts.

"Are you going to be okay?" I ask. "It looks like you're about to crack a molar."

"It's fine. Just tell me where we're going," he responds on a defeated sigh.

I turn in my seat, plaster a large smile on my face, and say, "The zoo."

His head tilts back and presses against the headrest as he silently says, "Jesus Christ."

I shake his arm. "Come on. It'll be fun. And when we say we've been to the zoo together, this won't be a lie anymore. And you know you're curious about the donkeys."

"I'm really not." He looks at the watch on his wrist and says, "And actually, I just remembered I have somewhere I need to be."

"Liar." I push at his shoulder. "It will be my treat. I'll even get you chicken tenders."

He puts the car in drive. "Wow, I'm really winning today."

⌁

"ARE you really going to be grumpy this whole time?" I ask Silas as I pull him to the side, allowing people to pass us.

"I'm not grumpy," he says, looking down at his zoo map.

"Uh, yes, you are. You barely spoke to me in the car. You grumbled under your breath when I tried to pay, then slapped my hand away, flinging my credit card to the ground—"

"That was an accident."

"And now you're practically trying to insert yourself in that map."

"I'm looking for the tiger section. I like them."

I lift his chin with my finger so he's forced to look at me. "What's the deal?"

His tongue slips over his teeth before he says, "Are we just going to ignore the fact that you showed me your ass the other day and now you're in those shorts . . . are you trying to break me?"

"That's what you're mad about?"

He grips the back of his neck, causing his bicep to pull at his shirt fabric. "I'm just trying to figure you out. This is platonic, right?"

"Uh . . . yeah. Why?" I tilt my head to the side. "Oh my God, Silas Tater Tot—"

"Don't call me that."

"Are you falling in love with me?"

"Jesus." He folds the map and puts it in his back pocket while pushing off the fence.

"You are, aren't you?" I loop my arm through his. "It's okay, you can tell me. I promise I'll be gentle with your heart."

"You're fucking annoying, you know that?"

"I can tell you're trying to deflect, and it's cute." I hold him close as we walk down the pathway, shrouds of jungle-like plants lining either side of the walkway. "But I need to remind you, dear Tatery Totty—"

"Seriously, enough with that shit."

Ignoring him, I continue, "We're just friends."

"Uh-huh. And do friends usually taunt their other friends with their asses in saunas?"

"You thought that was taunting?" I pat his arm. "That was just an artful way to show off the human form. Also, we all have butts, nothing new to see."

"Trust me, that was something new."

"Are you saying I have a nice ass, Silas?"

"You have a really nice ass."

A smile tugs at the corner of my lips. "Well, thank you. That means a lot coming from the king of asses."

He pauses and looks down at me. "King of asses?"

"Oh, have I not mentioned that before? Your glutes are so tight, they could easily crack a walnut."

He chuckles, and I feel him loosen up. "Not sure about that, but thanks."

"See." I shake his arm. "You just needed to loosen up a

bit. Anytime you need a compliment to get that fun-motor revving, you let me know. I have a bunch stocked up."

"Like what?"

"Oh, you know, just things like you have the most amazing pecs I've ever seen in my life. Your shoulders are carved like stone, and not to mention the forearm porn you're offering up today."

He glances down at his forearms. "They're pretty nice, aren't they."

We both chuckle, and I push him lightly to the side. "Okay, no need to inflate the ego. We have a whole zoo to visit, after all."

"Maybe you shouldn't have invited me then," he says, his mouth close to my ear. "Because now I'm going to be insufferable."

———

"I COULD DEFINITELY HAUL MORE than that camel," Silas says as we stare at the very large and beefy camel in front of us.

He has said the same thing about the rhino, claiming he could charge faster.

And the elephant—he could lift more.

And the freaking cheetah—he can run faster.

It's been terribly annoying.

Maybe this is how he feels when I pester him.

"Yes, my dear Tater Tot, you sure can." I pat him on the cheek.

"What did I tell you about calling me that?"

"Do it more?" I ask with a charming smile.

"No. Do it less."

We move away from the camels and head down the path toward the moose. "You can't tell me no one called you Tater Tot growing up."

"People did, and I shut them down too."

"Like who?"

He sticks his hands in his pockets and says, "My grandpa."

"Stop, you did not shut your grandpa down."

He smirks. "In my head, I did."

"Uh-huh, and how did that work out for you?"

"Not great."

"Can't imagine why." We move in front of the moose exhibit and take in the sturdy beast. "Why would you hate that your grandpa called you that? I think it's adorable."

"Because I'm a hockey player and back then, I was scrawny when all I wanted was to be big. The nickname Tater Tot wasn't exactly what I was looking for when all I wanted to be was a big, burly hockey player."

"Aw, you were scrawny?"

"Very," he answers.

"For how long?"

He thinks about it for a second, then answers, "When I was a senior in high school, I started to gain some weight, and college helped me pack on the muscle. I was super fast. That was how I got around the ice without getting hurt as much."

"Are you still the fastest?"

"Sadly, no," he answers. "Holmes is the fastest on the team. I'm second. That dude floats on the ice. Not sure how he does it."

"Probably his good looks carrying him around the ice."

Silas gives me a side-eye that makes me laugh. "What about you? Any nicknames?"

"Just Ollie, which quickly became my regular name. I guess Oliana would be my nickname now, one that you shouldn't use." I lift my brow at him.

"You like that I use it, don't even lie." He drapes his arm over my shoulder, pulling me in tight and, for a moment, I relish it.

Silas is all kinds of tight-lipped and earnest. He takes

things very seriously, holds his cards close to his chest, and never shows weakness, but it's times like this, when he's loose and doesn't mind showing platonic affection, that I truly enjoy. Because I can see his true self, the man he is past the high walls he's erected over the years to protect his heart.

"I might like it a little."

He chuckles. "I fucking knew it."

———

"HERE WE ARE," I say as I walk up to the most prestigious domestic donkey I've ever seen. "Thought you could use this." I hand him a small cardboard tray of chicken tenders. "I even made the special sauce you like."

He doesn't take the tray. Instead, he just stares at it, and with one brow lifted, he looks up at me. "Is that what you were doing when I was going to the restroom?"

"You should never leave me unattended. You never know what I'll get up to." I gesture to the donkey and add, "Isn't it perfect, though? You, me, donkeys, and chicken tenders. Now if only your fly was . . ."

My voice fades as I glance down at his crotch.

My eyes widen right before I let out an ugly, uproarious laughter that shakes the very ground we stand on.

"What?" he says as he looks down, only to find his fly undone. "Motherfucker," he swears under his breath as I laugh so hard, I lean against the fence for support.

"Oh my God." I wave my hand in front of my face as tears tickle my eyes. "You really are the donkey pervert."

"Can you not? People are fucking looking."

"Not my fault." I shake my head, tears now streaming down my cheeks. "Oh shit, I think I'm going to pee myself." I clench my legs together.

"I did not do that on purpose," he says through clenched teeth, trying to block me from the onlooking crowd.

"Which makes it even better. Your subconscious knew. Donkey time meant dong out."

"My . . . my dong was not out," he whispers.

"But it felt a breeze, didn't it?" I cough out a peal of laughter, my cheeks hurting.

"You're real mature. You know that?" He snags the chicken tenders from me and takes a bite of one.

"I'm really not." I laugh some more, now starting to hee-haw like my friend behind me. "I just . . . cannot believe you had your fly down." I dab at my eyes. "It's just such poetic beauty."

"Glad you're entertained."

He moves away from me, and I push off the fence and catch up to him, looping my arm through his again. "Don't be salty."

"Easy for you to say, you aren't the donkey pervert."

My lip trembles.

I attempt to choke down my laughter, but it's no use, and I burst out once again. After a few seconds, I say, "I'm sorry."

"No, you're not," he replies, but this time, there's a smile in his voice, and I know I have free range to laugh as much as I want now.

———

"I BET your fans think you're this cool guy, a real hockey hero with enough swagger to bag every woman in Vancouver, when, in reality, you're kind of a dork."

Silas licks his ice cream cone and says, "As long as they believe I have swagger, that's all that matters."

"Not going to fight against the dork comment?"

He shakes his head. "You've seen me at my worst now. No point."

I lick my ice cream as well and lean my head against his

shoulder. "If this is you at your worst, then what does it say about me that I like you the best like this?"

He pauses, then puts his arm around me, pulling me close. "That maybe you're a dork yourself."

"That's actually very accurate. I didn't think anything about me was cool when growing up. I was not popular, did not have or follow the latest trends, and I was never asked out by anyone."

"Hard to believe," he says.

"It's true. I don't think I hit my stride until college. And that's when Yonny came along, and we know how successful that relationship was."

"The makings of long-lasting love," he jokes as his hand drapes around my arm, and his thumb slowly caresses my skin. The light touch sends a wave of chills up my arms. Even during the years I was with Yonny, he never touched me like this, yet it comes so naturally to Silas, and we're not even together.

"Yes. Man, could you imagine if I was still with him, if I married him? That would be weird. What would my life be like?"

"What would my life be like if I married Sarah?" he asks.

"Treacherous," I answer. "Especially since she didn't appreciate what she had."

"I could say the same about Yonny."

"Yeah, he definitely didn't appreciate me. I mean . . . I love sucking dick, and he never let me play."

Silas lightly chuckles. "If you were mine, I'd let you play any goddamn time you wanted."

"Such a shame I'm only pretend yours, huh?"

"Yeah . . . a shame." He sighs. "But I appreciate what we have. It's made life a bit easier."

"I agree," I say, even though in the back of my head, I have this little voice saying *ask for more*. Because I'm curious. I'm curious what it would be like to have his lips as my own.

I'm curious what it feels like to hold his hand—not for pretend but for real. And I'm curious what it would be like to sit in this moment with him, eating ice cream, and then to simply kiss his jaw just because I can. "Do you ever wonder what it would be like if we were more?" I ask, just as a wave of nerves hits me from what he might say.

"No," he answers, and my heart falls. "But only because if I did, I'm not sure I'd be able to hold back."

"I knew you were falling in love with me."

"Jesus," he huffs before taking a bite of his ice cream cone.

I chuckle because that's better than swooning. *"But only because if I did, I'm not sure I'd be able to hold back."* I need a comeback. "Just admit it, Taters."

"Yup, I'm falling madly, deeply, so far in love with you, Oliana, that I can barely breathe when you're near."

"See . . . I knew it."

I can practically hear his eyes roll.

"THANK you for coming with me today," I say as we're in the car. "I needed the company."

"You did?" he asks when he glances over at me while at a red light.

"Yeah . . . it's actually the anniversary of my grandma's death today, and I always try to do something fun."

"Ollie," he says, his brow furrowed as he reaches over and takes my hand in his. "Why didn't you tell me?"

"Didn't want you to join me because you felt bad for me. I guess I just wanted a normal day, you know?"

"Yeah, I get that." He brings the back of my hand to his lips and presses a soft kiss to my knuckles. It's new, and I know he's doing it as a friend to reassure me that he's there for me, but it doesn't stop the butterflies that take off in my stomach.

We sit in silence, my hand in his as we drive through the

streets of Vancouver back to my dorm. I think about the day and how I teased him awfully but couldn't stop. How he joked around too, but not as mercilessly as me. How we shared ice cream, his arm wrapped around me protectively. How he tried to shield me from fans vying for his attention. *God, he's popular.* The incident with the donkey . . .

It was a mishmash of crazy, by no means a perfect day, but in my heart, it felt perfect.

And that scares me because I feel all warm inside.

He pulls into my dorm parking lot, his hand still holding mine, and instead of dropping me off, he parks his car instead.

"What are you doing?" I ask.

"I'm not going to let you be alone. I'll come up to your room."

He goes to exit his car, but I stop him. "No. That's okay. You don't need to do that."

"Ollie," he says, giving me a look as he turns toward me.

"I appreciate the gesture, but if you didn't know about my grandma, would you have just dropped me off?" He goes to answer, but I add, "Don't lie to me."

He huffs out a heavy breath and looks away.

"That's what I thought. Don't treat me differently. I'm really okay. I had fun, and I appreciate you going to the zoo with me and making me laugh . . . even if it was at your expense."

He turns toward me again and says, "No thank you is necessary. We're here for each other."

"Not like this," I say.

"Yes, like this," he answers as he cups my cheek, his warm, rough palm acting as a comfort blanket.

I lean in to his touch. "This wasn't part of the deal," I say.

"Neither was you showing your ass in the sauna, but that happened."

"Still thinking about that?" I ask.

"Ollie, I'll be thinking about that for a really fucking long time."

His thumb rubs over my cheek, and for some reason, I lean toward him, wetting my lips.

My body is reacting to his touch.

To his soft voice.

To his gentleness.

To our proximity.

"Were you mad I left? Would you have preferred I stayed in the sauna with you?"

He swallows hard, his Adam's apple bobbing. "I'm not sure I should answer that."

"Because you're afraid the truth will scare me?" I ask as I glance at his lips.

"No," he answers as his jaw ticks with tension. "Because we shouldn't be talking about that."

"You brought it up," I say, leaning in closer.

His eyes glance at my lips and then back up, the tension in the car so palpable that I actually can taste it.

I can taste him.

"It's ingrained in my brain." His thumb drags over my cheek, down to my mouth, where he tugs on my bottom lip. His body inches closer, and I prepare myself for his kiss.

It's not like we haven't kissed before, but this feels different.

This feels real.

This feels like we're about to cross a line.

I hold my breath, my eyes connected to his.

What I wouldn't give to taste him again.

To feel his lips against mine.

To have him tug on my hair with his strong hand as he angles my mouth for better pressure.

He takes a deep breath, his eyes flitting back and forth between my eyes and my lips.

God, just do it.

Just kiss me.

End this pounding, aching, searing feeling pulsing through

my veins.

And when he leans in another inch, I feel my heart stop . . . just as he pulls away, putting so much space between us that a wave of cold trickles down my spine, as well as embarrassment.

He pushes his hand through his hair and then swears under his breath before gripping the steering wheel.

"Uh, do you want me to walk you up to your room?"

I blink a few times, trying to regain my composure as I shake my head. "Uh, no, that's okay."

"Okay," he says awkwardly.

"Well . . ." I open the door. "Thanks."

"Yeah, thanks." He looks straight ahead. "Have a good night."

Needing to end the awkwardness, I leave the car and head straight to my building, where I push through the heavy doors and take the stairs up to my floor, not wanting to wait for the elevator.

When I reach my room, I let out a large sigh and lean against my door.

God . . . he almost kissed me.

So close.

And I wanted him to.

Badly.

Fuck . . .

Needing to get the smell of the zoo off me, I strip down to nothing and turn on my shower. I take a long, steam-filled shower, making sure to scrub every part of my body. I scrub for longer than I usually do, and I'm not sure if I'm scrubbing to get the zoo off me or if I'm trying to scrub the thought of Silas almost kissing me out of my head. Either way, I smell heavily of lavender, and I still can't stop thinking about Silas.

When I step out of the shower, I wrap the towel around my torso and lotion up before heading into the main part of my room. I drop the towel and flop back on my bed, naked.

Staring up at the ceiling, I feel my body itching, needing that release, so I reach over to my nightstand just as my phone lights up with a text.

Silas.

I grab my phone and my vibrator and lay back down on the bed. I check the text first.

Silas: *I'm sorry.*

That's it.

That's all he said. Not sure I would expect more. I'm usually the one leading the conversation.

Ollie: *Sorry for what? Almost kissing me?*

Silas: *Yes.*

With one hand, I take the vibrator and move it down to my slit as I part my thighs.

With the other hand, I text him back.

Ollie: *I wanted it just as much as you.*

Silas: *Ollie . . . don't.*

I switch on my vibrator.

Ollie: *Don't what?*

Silas: *You're tempting me again.*

Ollie: *Tempting you would be telling you that as I text right now, my other hand is holding a vibrator against my clit.*

I sink into the feel of the vibration, knowing damn well it's not going to take long.

Silas: *Fuck . . . don't say that shit.*

Ollie: *Why? Does it turn you on?*

Silas: *You know damn well it does.*

Ollie: *Well . . . let it turn you on. You might not be able to kiss me, but you sure as hell can dream about it. Happy masturbating, Silas.*

Silas: *Fuck . . . me.*

I drop my phone to the side and smile to myself as my orgasm starts to climb.

Not sure what's happening between us, but what I do know is that I'm getting under his skin. At this point, I'm not sure if that's a good thing or a bad thing.

Chapter Twelve

OLLIE

"I think something is wrong with me," I say to Ross as I sit next to him in the lecture hall. For such a small class size, we sure do have a large classroom.

"What's it this time?" Ross asks as he brings his coffee to his lips.

Classes started this week. I thought it would be helpful and keep me distracted from this unsettling feeling I have pumping through me, but it's done nothing other than frustrate me.

I haven't really spent time with Silas since the zoo and the almost car kiss. We've seen each other in passing as I've used his gym, but he's been busy with practice and sponsorship meetings with his agent and apparently shooting some commercials as well. I've been keeping up with my internship and getting ready for the new school year.

I turn to Ross. "I'm really horny."

He nearly spits out his coffee. "Jesus, Ollie. Warn a guy."

"I'm sorry," I whisper, seeing that we're drawing attention from around us. "But it's true."

"Don't you have a fake boyfriend to take care of those needs?"

"No," I say. "And please use your whispering voice. You never know who might be listening."

"What do you mean, no? I thought you and Silas were getting along nicely."

"We are. He texts occasionally to see how things are going and asks if I need his help. I tell him everything is fine, but that's it. There's nothing sexual about our interactions." Nothing sexual that goes all the way, at least. It's almost as if we've been edging each other, and that's more frustrating than anything.

"Do you want it to be sexual?"

"If you were in my situation, would you want it to be sexual?"

Ross takes a sip of his coffee and stares at the classroom in front of us. "I would let that man do anything he wants to me."

"Exactly. He's so hot, Ross, it's breaking my will."

"If you like him, then just fuck him."

"I can't," I say. "That's the problem. Our situation is great right now. Plus, I know he says he doesn't, but I think he still has a thing for his ex, and I don't want to be caught in the middle of that. He won't even talk about what happened between them. The last thing I should be doing is fucking his brains out."

"And you would, wouldn't you?" Ross asks with a smirk.

I lean in a little closer and whisper, "I want to suck his cock so hard. I had a dream about it the other night. And I've been itchy ever since."

"Have you seen him lately?"

"No, but I got an email from Roberts yesterday asking how my hockey assignment is coming along. And I'm going to tell you right now. I have nothing. Absolutely nothing. I thought I had an angle for a second, but nope. I can't think of one single thing to write, and what Roberts wants me to write about is out of the question."

"What does he want you to write about?"

"He wants me to try to expose the Agitators owner. I know nothing about him. I haven't even met him, and it's going to look awfully suspicious if I ask Silas a bunch of questions about some old man who pays his salary."

"Yeah, that won't come off right."

"So basically, I have nothing to write, I'm going to fail out of school, and I'll have to live with my parents and eat my words."

"Yeah, that does seem plausible."

"Ross," I say while pushing him.

He chuckles. "I think you should meet up with Silas and talk to him about it. Maybe he'll have some ideas. And also, you can stare at him while he talks and think about all the ways you would love to suck his—"

"Good morning," our professor says while setting his bag on the teacher's desk.

"Good morning," we say collectively.

Ross elbows me. "Text him. See if he's busy."

He's right. Silas might be able to help me with some ideas. And yeah, maybe I miss seeing him a little bit. I always have fun with him, so it might not kill us to get together and have a moment to catch up.

I open my computer and shoot him a text.

Ollie: *What are you up to tonight? Free?*

As I take notes, listening to our professor, Silas texts me back.

Silas: *Yup. Need something?*
Ollie: *Can I come over? I want to talk hockey.*
Silas: *Talk hockey? Am I going to need some alcohol for this?*
Ollie: *Probably.*

Silas: *I'll stop by the store. What time tonight?*

Ollie: *See you around seven?*

Silas: *That works. Want me to pick you up?*

Ollie: *That's okay. Thanks, though.*

Silas: *Let me know if you change your mind. See you tonight.*

Whispering to Ross, I say, "I'm going to his place tonight. Going to talk all the hockey."

"Hopefully, that's not the only thing you do."

Hopefully, it is because I don't think I could handle anything else.

WHY AM I NERVOUS?

Jesus, Ollie, get it together.

You've hung out with this man many times.

Yet this feels different.

Why does it feel different?

Maybe because the last time I was with him, something changed inside me. The way he spoke to me the night of the family skate night. How he apologized without blinking an eye. How he took full responsibility. And how he didn't want to leave me that night.

And then he followed it up with breakfast in bed . . .

I don't know. I've never been treated like that before and found myself loosening up around him. Like in the sauna, where I didn't mind that he saw my ass. That I was thrilled to show it to him, and even more thrilled to think about the possibility of him getting hard over it. And then his genuine kindness toward me on the anniversary of Grandma's passing. *The almost kiss.*

It's all flipped a switch inside me. I want him. The man so far out of my league . . . my *business* partner. Of sorts.

What is wrong with me?

Now I'm just teasing him and myself.

Because I know I'm not going to let anything happen between us. Like I told Ross, Silas has some demons to deal with, and I don't want to be caught in the middle of them. So instead, I'm apparently just going to flaunt myself, driving us both crazy because I'm so fucking horny it hurts.

Hence the nerves.

I'm nervous that I'll say or do something stupid, like I don't know, accidentally trip and fall head first into his lap. Or say something like . . . can I suck your cock as an appetizer?

Urgh, I bet he has the most delicious penis ever. Thick, but not too thick, veiny . . . pierced. If he's not pierced, I would be so freaking shocked.

The elevator dings, and I step off and head to his door. I'm glad his apartment isn't one of those places where the elevator opens up into the actual apartment. I like knowing there's a barrier.

I walk up to his door, and even though I have a key, I knock. As I wait, I glance down at my outfit. I chose a pair of black leggings, thick poofy socks to wear over them, and his sweatshirt because it's chilly out today, and it's really comfortable.

The door unlocks and opens, and when his eyes meet mine, I feel a sense of belonging. It's odd. Like this man completely understands me despite him not knowing everything.

His dreamy eyes scan my outfit before locking gazes with me.

"Nice sweatshirt."

"Thanks." I smirk. "Someone left it in my dorm, and as I like to say, finders keepers."

"It's quite big on you."

"The way I like it." Gripping the straps of my little back-pack, I say, "Are you going to let me in?"

"Sure," he says as he takes a step away from the door, and that's when I notice he's wearing black joggers with no socks and a heather slate-gray shirt that clings to every contour of his body. It's a simple outfit, yet for some reason, he still looks incredibly hot, especially with his hair still wet from a recent shower, showing off his eyes.

"What is that heavenly smell?" I ask as I take my shoes off.

"Got some lasagna and garlic bread from one of my favorite places." He shuts the door, and as he walks by, he leans in and says, "And I got some for you, too."

"Why are you so nice to me?" I ask in a joking manner, but he just shrugs and leads me to the kitchen.

"Help yourself," he says as he pulls the food out of the oven where he's kept it warm.

We each serve ourselves a plate and then we sit at the dining room table—which is nice because I'm usually eating on my bed or at my desk. I like my place, but sometimes a table is a nice change.

I dig my fork into the lasagna, but before I take a big bite, I say, "Thank you for this. I'm starving. All I had was a protein bar today and an iced latte."

He glances up from his plate with a stern look on his face. "Why? That's not enough, Ollie."

"I was really busy. Classes and then I put in a few hours at my internship, then came here."

"No excuse. You need to eat more than that."

"You worried about me, Taters?"

"I am. Can't have you fainting at events."

"Do you have any events coming up?"

"I have a sponsorship party on Friday, but I don't think it's something you have to go to. I'm sure you'd rather go out."

"But do you need me there?" I ask.

"I don't need you there since Pacey and Holmes will be there. I can just hang with Holmes since he won't be bringing anyone."

I pause, slightly confused. "Is something wrong? Did I do something wrong?" Insecurity laces up my spine as I think about our last interaction and how I taunted him with my vibrator. Did I . . . did I scare him off? We haven't hung out since then. And he's checked in a few times, but if I truly think about it, he's pulled away a touch.

"What?" he asks and shakes his head. "No, you're good."

"Okay, well . . . I'd like to go to the event if you want to take me. I feel like you do a lot for me, and I need to be able to be there for you in return. If you're worried I'll embarrass you, I can—"

"I'm not worried about that." He picks up a piece of garlic bread and takes a bite.

I pause for a moment to study him. "I feel like you're acting weird. Like I did something, and you're not telling me."

"You didn't do anything wrong, Oliana." The way he says my real name in such a serious tone penetrates right to my heart.

"Okay." I pierce a saucy noodle. "Well, I'm free."

"It's really okay," he says. "You'll be bored."

And there it is again, him brushing me off. I don't understand. Then again, he never likes to be vulnerable, and I fear if I keep pushing him, he won't want to open up at all, so instead, I decide to change tactics. I'll take care of the Friday event myself.

"Do you know what was boring? My class today on data journalism. I nearly passed out in my own lap."

He scoops up a pile of lasagna. "What is data journalism?"

"Just what it sounds like, learning how to properly use data to write accurate articles."

"You need a class for that?"

"You would be surprised," I say. "What did you major in?"

"Kinesiology."

"Did you plan on doing anything with that?"

"Not really," he answers while picking up his glass of water. "The goal was to play hockey professionally. I didn't have a backup plan, didn't want one. I studied kinesiology to educate myself on my body and understand how to take care of it so I could reach my goals."

"That's actually really smart," I say while taking a bite of my garlic bread. "Do you think it's helped?"

He nods. "Very much. I understand what parts of the body I need to focus on to stay healthy. I understand the recovery process, and I honestly believe it's one of the main reasons I haven't suffered any major injuries."

"That's impressive, actually. How much longer do you think you'll play?"

"Not sure," he says. "I still feel really strong. I can keep up with the younger guys, and my legs don't die out toward the end because I continue to train through the season. It's something I take great pride in."

"I can tell. Do you ever give your body a break?"

"During the summer. That's why I was so sore the night of the family skate event. I go at it hard during the preseason, and my muscles have to get used to the demand again. And with every new year, it seems to get a touch harder."

"How are you feeling now?" I ask.

"Better. I've been able to do some great recovery and focus on what I need to focus on. Lots of ice baths and walks on the treadmill to flush all that lactic acid buildup."

"Are the other guys as smart as you?"

"Not the young ones. They'll learn quickly, though." He points his fork at me. "What about you? Are you feeling sore with your new workout space?"

"I was a little sore in my inner thighs the other day, but for the most part, I feel pretty good. I used your sauna again. I hope that's okay."

"What's mine is yours."

"Which seems incredibly unfair."

"It's not," he says. "We're friends, right, Ollie?"

I tilt my head, studying him. He might not like to show his

vulnerable side, but here, at this moment, I can see it. His question, sort of wondering where we stand. Maybe that's why he's been so distant lately. Maybe he doesn't know, especially after we shared the almost kiss. So to reassure him, I say, "Yes. We're friends."

"Good," he answers. "That means we don't owe each other anything. You ask, it's yours."

"Okay, then the same would go for me. I don't have much to offer, but if you ask, it's yours."

"You have more to offer than you think," he says when he glances up at me, causing the back of my neck to break out in a cool sweat.

"Oh yeah, like what?" I ask playfully.

"You're cool," he says, surprising me. "I love hanging out with my guys, but sometimes it's nice to see a different face, and you're fun to hang out with."

I press my hand to my chest. "Silas Taters, I can't believe you're offering me such a compliment. Coming from the man who nearly had a coronary when I talked about him perverting over donkeys."

"For fuck's sake, I thought we dropped that."

I press my finger to the table. "Donkey pervert is the foundation of this friendship. It will never go away."

"I thought the foundation is you randomly kissing me in a bar."

I roll my eyes at that. "That truth is for you, me, and Ross only because he witnessed the whole thing and questioned me quickly afterward. But everyone else knows us as the people who bonded over a donkey while your fly was down. That's something we need to hang on to."

"Lucky me."

"You're right . . . lucky you."

SILAS DRAPES his arm over the back of the couch as he casually faces me. The rest of the dinner was easygoing. We joked around. He smirked. I laughed. And it felt like things were getting back to normal, which I appreciated greatly.

Now that we retreated to the couch, I feel more relaxed and not so stiff. He seems the same as well.

"What do you do for fun, Silas?"

"Not much," he answers. "Don't have much fun during the season. I'm either working out, playing hockey, eating, or sleeping."

"Riveting," I respond. "What about when it's the off-season? You said you go up to your cabin, right?"

"Yeah, just hang out with the boys. Play games, drink beer, nothing out of the ordinary."

"So you don't have any hobbies?"

"Too busy to have hobbies," he answers.

"That seems boring. You've got to like doing something besides things that coincide with hockey."

"Haven't had a chance to explore. I came right out of high school with a girlfriend and a dream. I was going to play professionally, so when I wasn't training or playing, I focused on Sarah. All my time was taken up with no room to spare."

"I guess that makes sense. Well, is there something you wish you could do? A hobby you wish you could spend more time doing?"

He gives it some thought. "I'd like to cook more. Right now, I have a personal chef who makes my meals and leaves them in my fridge. He comes with me when we go to Banff, and I enjoy watching him work. If I had the energy, I'd ask him to teach me."

"Maybe you should next summer. You won't have hockey, so maybe have him teach you a bit."

Silas nods. "Yeah, maybe I will."

"See." I nudge him with my foot. "I'm already changing your life."

He rolls his eyes and then asks, "What about you? What are your hobbies?"

"Well, I love dancing. I do that when I want to blow off steam or just have fun. I also enjoy scrapbooking, but I haven't done it for a bit. I have some catching up to do."

"Scrapbooking with all those tools and shit?" he asks.

I shake my head. "No, I wish I had the room and the money for that, but right now, it's just simple things I find that I like in magazines or pictures that I print out and write a story next to about the picture. My internship ate up a lot of my time this summer, so I've dropped the ball in adding clippings and pictures to my book, but I'll catch up. I've stashed away everything so when I do have a moment, I can sit down and glue it all in."

"That's kind of cool. Do you have one for each year?"

"Yeah, pretty much. I started back in middle school. It was more of a diary at the time. My mom would purchase my magazines, and I would clip things from them that I loved or print them on the computer. Then I started using pictures with friends, and it formed more into a scrapbook than anything. They're fun to look through because it's like a time capsule in book form."

"Maybe next time I'm at your place, you'll show me."

"Ha!" I shake my head. "No way. You'll make fun of me for the things in those books."

"Like what?"

"Like . . . the Timothée Chalamet phase I went through, or how whenever I see a donut in a magazine, I have this need to cut them out and paste them because I think they're cute. And those are just two things. There's a whole dark side to my scrapbooking of my innermost thoughts and feelings."

"Now I really need to see these."

I nudge him with my foot. "Never."

"We'll see about that."

"Did you ever write in a diary?"

"Does it look like I'm a diary kind of guy?" he asks, looking so hot with the way he raises his brow like that.

"No, but we should never discredit someone for their appearance. For all I know, you could have a secret Bratz dolls collection."

"What the hell are Bratz dolls?"

"Never mind." I sigh.

"Did you have these dolls?"

I wave my hand at him. "That's neither here nor there. I think what we really need to focus on is your diary."

"I told you, I don't have one."

"But if you did . . . what would you write in it?"

"As if I would tell you."

"Come on, Silas. Share a little."

"No."

"Please." I press my hands together, begging him. "I'll be super supportive."

He glances away. "You really want to know?"

Growing excited, I say, "Yes, of course, and I promise, I won't laugh."

"Fine." He exhales sharply. "Dear Diary, Ollie is really fucking annoying. Yours truly, Silas."

When he looks my way, he smirks. I shove my foot at him, causing him to laugh. "You're an ass. I really thought you were going to tell me what you would write in your diary."

"Right now, that's exactly what I would write."

———

"NAKED," I say. "Always naked."

"No fucking way." He shakes his head at me.

"Yes fucking way. I love rolling in the snow, then jumping in the hot tub. The best part is when the snow gets all up in there and then melts away by the hot water. An absolute dream."

"I don't fucking believe you," Silas says.

"That's on you and your trust issues."

"So you're telling me, if I invited you over here for the first fallen snow, you'd go up to my rooftop, roll in the snow naked, and then hop in the hot tub?"

"Hold on." I hold up my hand. "You have a hot tub?"

"Yes, on the roof."

"Well, why the hell did you not tell me about this?" I ask.

"Because that's my sanctuary. I don't need some girl up there, naked in my hot tub."

"Are you telling me that would be a travesty? Because you would be so lucky to see me naked in your hot tub."

"I wouldn't."

I clutch at my chest. "You wound me, Silas . . . or should I say, Potato."

"What did I say about that? Winnie is the only one who can call me that ridiculous name."

"That's not fair, though. I feel like I should have a nickname for you."

"Why?" he asks.

"Well, you call me babe in front of people, so I should be able to call you something."

"Okay, what do you want to call me that's not Potato?"

I give it a second to think of something good, something rich and hilarious, but only one thing comes to mind for some stupid-ass reason.

"I'm going to call you fart face."

"Over my dead body," he roars.

"It's a term of endearment," I defend even though I'm chuckling.

"How is calling someone a flatulent gas cloud a term of endearment?"

"Because I wouldn't dare call other people that. And I think it suits you. When you're grumpy, you always look like you have a fart stuck in you. Therefore, you're fart face."

"Can you grow up like a few years?"

"Would you rather be called something like . . . penis breath?"

"Something is seriously wrong with you." He shakes his head. "You can call me Silas or babe. Those are your options."

"Ew, I wouldn't call you babe. That feels weird to me. I like it when guys call me that, but I can't do it in return."

"Then Silas it is."

"But that's so boring," I grumble. "How about . . ."

"Silas."

"Ugh, fine."

"And I swear to God, Ollie, if you slip up when we're out together, and you just happen to call me fart face, I'm going to murder you."

"You don't give me enough credit. If I slipped up and called you anything, it would be donkey pervert. God, Silas, get it right."

<hr />

"SO DON'T you have questions for me?" Silas asks.

"More like . . . a conversation to have," I say.

"What kind of conversation?"

"About hockey of course. You know, since I know nothing about it. I had some guy at work come up to me and ask if I could get your autograph. I told him to fuck off. I clearly wasn't going to bother you with such menial things. When he left, I couldn't stop laughing at the fact that people want your autograph."

"Why is that funny?"

"I don't know," I say. "Maybe because I don't see you as this big hockey star. I just know you as the guy I kissed in a bar who then became my fake boyfriend."

"Well, maybe you need to see me on the ice to change that mindset."

"Are you inviting me to a game?"

"As my pretend girlfriend, it will be a requirement to show up." He drapes his arm over the back of the couch.

"Ew, will I have to wear one of those jumbo jerseys that looks ill-fitted on everyone?"

"Love the enthusiasm, and no."

"Thank God for small miracles."

He rolls his eyes. "What do you need to know? Let's get this conversation about your favorite sport over with."

"Well, first, I need to talk to you about something, and I don't want you to get mad at me."

"Why would I get mad?"

"You'll see, but promise, okay?"

He studies me for a moment and says, "Okay."

"So . . . when Roberts found out I was dating you, he became quite invested in our relationship. So much so that he pulled me into his office to talk."

"Does he want free tickets or something? The man is rich. Can't he afford them himself?"

"No, that wasn't it. I actually found out that he has a vendetta against your owner. Apparently, Roberts was trying to buy the Agitators, and something fell through. Anyway, he hates your owner and now wants me to use my final assignment as an intern for his company as some sort of exposé to bring down the Agitators brand."

I hold my breath as his brows draw down. "So he wants you to use me, then?"

"Yes," I say, then quickly add, "but I'm not going to."

He looks away and pulls on the back of his neck. I can see the visible change in his demeanor. Once relaxed in his own home, he's now stiff and defensive. "Did you tell him no?"

I wince. "Um, not at the moment that he asked."

"So after."

I fidget. "Not really, but that doesn't mean I'm going to do it."

"That means you plan to exploit me," Silas yells, startling me back.

"Silas, I would never do that to you. That's why I'm here, talking to you about it."

"So I can feel bad that you need a story and just give you permission to pass your assignment? Get the fuck out of here, Ollie."

"That's not why I'm here," I say, standing up for myself. "I'm here because I wanted to talk to you about it and be honest."

"Honest about your intentions of fucking me over?"

"What? No. Why the hell would I do that?"

"I don't know, Ollie. Why wouldn't you tell Roberts no?"

"Because . . ." I stumble, trying to find the right words. "I just thought at that moment that I could think of a better solution. He's my boss, Silas. This internship, it matters to me."

"I understand that, but you're never going to get anywhere without integrity."

"I told you I wasn't going to write the article. Jesus." I stand from the couch. "I came here hoping you could help me think of a different angle. But I guess I was wrong." I move toward his front door and slip my shoes on. He remains seated. "You know, Silas, you can sit there and judge me all you want, but you're not fucking perfect either."

"I never said I was."

"You act like it. You can't tell me that in my position, you would have told your boss no."

"I would have told him to fuck off."

"Bullshit." I laugh sardonically. "You couldn't even tell Sarah to fuck off when you saw her at the event. No, you practically ate her with your eyes. You tell me you don't care about her anymore, but I don't believe it for one second. So don't go throwing stones in glass houses. You tell me to stand up for myself, for what's right. Well, where the fuck are you when it comes to Sarah?"

"That's different," he says.

"No, it's not."

"The fuck it is." He stands from the couch now. "I was going to fucking propose to her. Of course there will be feelings. I can't just shut it off."

"Yeah, well, Roberts holds my future in his hands, and I can't just turn off my goals and desires to make something of myself. Out of everyone, you should understand that." I slip my backpack on and head toward the door. I glance over my shoulder one last time to see if he's going to say something or stop me, but he doesn't, so . . . I leave and go right to the elevator, where I press the down button.

My lips tremble, and my throat tightens as I hold back my tears. I will not cry.

Not over something as stupid as this.

Silas was being an ass, and that's on him. I was coming here to find a solution, and he wouldn't even listen.

That's no reason to cry or get emotional.

It just means . . . I don't need him.

Chapter Thirteen

SILAS

I haven't slept well for the past three days.

All thanks to fucking Ollie.

I'm still pissed.

I'm pissed that she didn't tell her boss to fuck off, and I'm even more pissed that she brought up Sarah. She has no fucking idea about the bullshit I went through with Sarah, so she shouldn't be speaking a word about her.

Water bottle in hand, I walk into the weight room, knowing I'm not going to be alone, and head right to the wind bikes, where I set my drink down and hop on to warm up.

This is fucking ridiculous. I'm not even dating the fucking girl, and she's driving me nuts. I should just tell her the deal is off. I thought this was going to be a good idea, but I was wrong. This is more than I think my mind can handle. I've stayed up until the early morning hours going over our conversation in my head. She claims she wasn't going to write an exposé, but it almost seemed like she was seeing if I could be okay with it.

Never.

I would never be okay with it.

"Dude, you okay?" Posey asks. "You're riding that bike pretty damn hard for a warm-up."

I didn't even realize. I slow down and say, "Looking for a good burn before I get started."

"Brave," Posey says. "I never look for a burn."

He's such a liar. Being one of our defenders, Posey is always in the weight room, trying to keep a leg up on the competition.

"Is Ollie excited about going to the sponsorship party tonight?" Posey asks.

"I don't think she's going to attend."

"Oh . . ." He slows down his pace. "Is there something going on? Is that why you've been in a shit mood the last few days?"

Yes.

"No," I answer. "I think she has other plans."

"I see." He pauses. "Dude, are you not bringing her because Sarah will be there? I hate to admit it, but Pacey said he saw how you looked at Sarah at the ice-skating event. He thought it was concerning, like . . . like you were still in love."

I stop my bike. *Sarah will be there tonight?* Fuck. Why did I think she wouldn't be a part of the event tonight? Of course she is. And then I register what Posey said after that.

I hop off the bike. "I'm not in love with her."

Posey follows me over to the weight rack, trailing closely. "Are you sure? Ollie seems pretty cool, and I don't want you hurting her."

"I'm not going to hurt her," I say as I stack weights for warm-up squats.

"Okay . . . because she seems really young."

"She is," I reply. Younger than I care to admit.

"And you can do damage to a girl that young if your head isn't on straight."

"What are you? Her fucking father? Jesus, Posey."

"No, but I also know when your head is elsewhere, and that's what's been going on lately. I'm worried you're thinking about Sarah."

"I'm not fucking thinking about her," I shout. "Now get off my back."

Posey holds up his hands and takes a step back. "I'm just looking out for you."

"No, you're driving me nuts. I want nothing to do with Sarah."

"You sure?" Posey asks and then glances around the nearly empty weight room. "Because . . ." He pauses and takes a step forward. "Because I overheard her at the ice-skating event after you left. She was excited to have the job so she could be close to you again."

I lift my head. "She said that?"

"Yes, and the last thing I want to see is you getting back together with her. Hell, man, she hurt you so bad you still haven't told us the truth about your breakup and everything that went down. I'm not sure you told anyone."

I haven't told a soul.

"It's none of anyone's business."

"And then this summer, when you started talking to her again—"

"That was brief and won't be happening again. Seriously, we're done. There's nothing to worry about."

"Okay, well, just watch your back because I don't want you to get into a bunch of trouble because of Sarah." He pats me on the back and returns to the bike, where he continues to warm up. See . . . he likes the burn.

As I rest the bar on my shoulders and take a step back from the rack to start my squats, all I can think about is how Sarah will be at that event tonight and that I don't want to be alone with her. I know how Sarah can be. Hell, I experienced it this summer. She can be incredibly convincing, and for some stupid-as-shit reason, I'm easily convinced. But one thing I do know for sure? I am *not* in love with her anymore. I will never love her again.

⊏⊐

I KNOW THIS IS STUPID.

I don't need anyone judging me for what I'm about to do, but I thought about it all fucking day, and I don't have any other options. So as I head off the elevator, I go straight to Ollie's dorm room, ready to force her to go with me tonight.

And knowing her, she'll put up a goddamn fight.

Have we spoken since our fight at my place?

Nope.

Not even a text message.

So she's not going to be expecting me or my request.

Or my lack of apology . . .

Standing in front of her door, I give it two loud knocks, then stick my hands in my suit pockets. I went with a forest-green suit tonight with a white button-up shirt and brown shoes with a matching belt. I paired the outfit with my favorite brown leather-wrapped watch and my signature Tom Ford cologne.

It takes a few seconds, but when she answers the door, I'm subjected to another one of those goddamn crop tops . . . and an angry scowl.

"What the hell are you doing here?"

"We have an event to go to, sweet cheeks," I say, but my voice sounds more menacing than anything.

"You can fuck right off," she says, attempting to shut the door, but I stop her and push my way into her dorm room.

She stumbles backward, shocked by my brazenness.

Hands on her hips, she says, "Oh no, you did not just charge your way in here."

I shut the door behind me and adjust the cuffs of my sleeves as I say, "A deal is a deal, Oliana, which means you need to get yourself dressed and come with me."

"You said you didn't want me to come with you tonight."

"My plans changed. Now get dressed."

"Do you really think you can come in here and boss me around?" Her nipples are hard now, and it's next to impossible not to at least glance at them.

"I'm not bossing you around. I'm telling you that you signed a contract, and now I'm expecting you to live up to that."

"It was a napkin. I could have wiped my nose with it if I wanted to." She folds her arms together and poses in the most defiant stance I think I've ever witnessed.

"A deal is a deal. Now get fucking dressed before I do it for you."

"And what if I don't?" she asks.

I prepared for this question, knowing damn well she would put up a fight. And I hate to do this to her, but she needs to come with me tonight. I need the defense.

"If you don't, then I'm going to go to the owner of the Agitators and tell him about the article."

Her face falls, and her arms drop to her sides. "You wouldn't."

"You don't want to test me."

She stares me down for a few seconds before she huffs and turns toward her closet. "You realize I'm going to hate you until the end of time, right?"

"Whatever gets you dressed up, babe," I say as I make my way into her dorm and sit on her bed. I watch as she digs around in her closet. She tosses a pair of black strappy heels toward the center of the room and then retrieves a long black outfit.

When I think she's going to head into the bathroom to get changed, she doesn't. With her back turned toward me, she pulls her crop top over her head before pushing her sweatpants down, revealing her thin black thong.

My mouth waters at the sight of that rear end again and her bare, muscular back with the rarest of glimpses of side boob as she fits her outfit on. She pulls it up, revealing a black one-piece of sorts with pant legs and a tight-fitted top.

"I need you to zip me up," she says, her back still toward me.

Pushing off the bed, I walk up behind her. I drape her long hair over one shoulder, then rest my hand on her waist. Her back stiffens, and as I grip the small black zipper, I move my hand up her rib cage until I pause right below her breast. Holding tightly, I slowly pull the zipper up, the entire time feeling her breath inflate and deflate her lungs until she's all the way zipped up, and I pull away.

Without a word, she storms off into the bathroom and closes the door.

She wants to play with fire by stripping in front of me? She's going to get it in return.

I sit on her bed again and pull out my phone. I scroll through emails for the next ten minutes, and when she's finally ready and opens the bathroom door, she emerges with her hair pulled back into a high ponytail, a heavy smoky eye, and what looks like fake eyelashes. She topped the look off with bright red lipstick.

Yup . . . she's fucking hot.

Not to mention, the neckline of her outfit cuts down to the spot just below her breasts, once again offering an abundance of cleavage for all to see. It must be her signature move, to show off her breasts whenever she gets a chance. And I'm going to tell you right now, it fucking works.

As she slips her shoes on, I realize one thing. I hate that even though I'm mad at her, I still think she's hot. I don't want to be attracted to her, but it's inevitable. I can't stop it. And I can't stop the way my eyes scan her, resting for a moment too long on her breasts, on her lips, on those eyes.

She stands tall, flips her ponytail over her shoulder, and snatches a clutch from her closet before stuffing her phone, wallet, lipstick, and key in it. She tucks the clutch under her arm and says, "Let's go, master."

Better than fart face. Guess I'll take it.

We're silent the entire trip out of the dorm. I honestly expected nothing less than her glacial attitude.

When we reach my car, I open the door for her and watch her get in, then, taking her seat belt, I loop it over her and click it in. When I pull back, I hear her sharp inhale, only for her eyes to connect with mine in confusion.

"Just want to make sure you don't bolt."

Her face falls. "Aren't you a funny guy?" *No. Just a bit desperate it seems.*

She doesn't bother talking to me, and I don't bother talking to her until we're five minutes from the event.

"You're going to have to act like you like me in there."

"This is not my first rodeo, Potato."

Ah, so we've sunk to that level of pettiness. Guess it's fair, given what I had to say to get her in this car.

"There will be major sponsors here, people who pay me a lot of fucking money, so no donkey pervert story. Just say we ran into each other at the zoo."

"And shield them from the true story of who you are? That's doing them a disservice."

"The real story would be you assaulting me in a bar, but I have enough class to hold back on telling that tale."

She whips her head toward me. "Are you saying I don't have class?"

"Take it as you want," I say as I pull up to valet.

"Well, if that's the way you want to play the game," she says.

"Don't, Oliana," I say in a stern voice. "I swear to fuck, if you embarrass me in there, you won't like the repercussions."

"Oh Potato, I have zero plans of embarrassing you."

Why do I find that incredibly hard to believe? But I don't have time to hash it out with her because the valet is opening our doors.

I hand them the key and then make my way around the car where I meet up with Ollie. She takes my hand and snuggles in close to my side just in time for a few cameras to flash in our direction.

Fuck, I completely forgot about the press.

I turn to Ollie and say, "Don't talk to anyone. Just smile, and I'll guide you inside."

Surprisingly, she does as she's told, and we make it past the press box and into the venue, where we're immediately greeted by Hector Fuentes, the CEO of Skin Leisure, the clothing brand that I recently signed a seven-figure deal with.

"Silas Taters, glad you could make it," Hector says while patting me on the back. "And who did you bring with you tonight?"

"Hector, it's great to see you," I say, turning on the charm. "This is my girlfriend, Ollie Owens."

"Ollie, it's a pleasure to meet you."

"The pleasure is all mine," Ollie says.

"Well, help yourself to drinks and food. There are gift bags for everyone as well. Enjoy the night. We're looking forward to cheering you on this season, Silas."

"Thank you. We're looking good. I feel like we have another shot at the cup this year." I give him a handshake, and then I press my hand to Ollie's back and guide her into the main ballroom. "Need a drink?" I ask her.

"As if you care," she says, smiling up at me, and then grips my hand in hers. "But yes, I'm thirsty."

I don't give in to her need to press my buttons, so hand in

hand, we walk over to the bar, where I find a very familiar face.

"Silas Taters, holy shit." JP Cane walks up to me and holds his hand out.

We shake, and I say, "I didn't know you were going to be here."

"I'm not alone. Brought Ryot Bisley with me. You know us. If there's a place where sponsors are gathering with athletes, we want to be there."

"That's why you own the leading sports app in the world." I bring Ollie forward and say, "JP, this is my girlfriend, Ollie Owens. Ollie, this is JP Cane. He and his brothers, Huxley and Breaker, invested in The Jock Report, something started by Ryot Bisley, his brother Banner, and Penn Cutler. Penn and Ryot both played for the Chicago Bobbies."

"Oh, yes," Ollie says. "I heard about The Jock Report." That's surprising, given she hasn't heard about me. "Wasn't it started because of poor reporting in the media?" Aah, that's why she's heard of it.

JP nods. "It was. Now the athletes have their own voice and can interact with fans without having to worry about an algorithm or having their words turned around on them. Trying to get your boyfriend to join."

"Just haven't had time yet. I promise I will. I'm sure I'll need something to scroll through on our away trips."

JP chuckles, then turns his attention back to Ollie. "What do you do, Ollie?"

"Majoring in journalism, actually," she says with a smile and then leans forward. "Don't worry, I have no intention of reporting on sports or twisting anyone's words. I prefer how-to lifestyle stuff."

And for some reason, I feel like that's a dig at me.

"Lifestyle?" JP asks. "Do you ever cover charitable organizations? Because I have one that could really use some more people backing it."

"Not really, but I know some people who do."

JP reaches into his suit pocket and pulls out a business card. "Email me. I'd love to get in touch. The more of a reach, the better."

"Of course." Ollie sticks the card in her clutch, and we say our goodbyes before ordering our drinks at the bar.

I rest my hand on the nape of her neck as we wait. Talking closely to her, I say, "Were you making a dig at me back there?"

She turns toward me and rests her hand on my chest while she tilts her head back to look me in the eyes. We probably look like the picture-perfect couple. But at the moment, nothing but annoyance, frustration, and a pinch of hate flows between us.

"Did you know that the world doesn't revolve around you, Silas? Crazy thought, I know. But something you might have to come to terms with."

She slides her hand up my chest, to my neck, and then stands on her toes and kisses the bottom of my chin. When she pulls away, she whispers, "If we weren't in a room of people right now, I would knee you so hard in the dick for making me strip out of my sweatpants and put on this uncomfortable outfit."

My jaw clenches, and I'm about to respond when our drinks are placed in front of us. Wanting to get out of earshot, I take her free hand and guide her to a sitting area. I expect her to sit in the chair next to me, but she sits on my lap and loops her arm over my shoulders. Her hand goes straight to my hair, where she lightly plays with it.

"What are you doing?" I ask her, my back stiff.

"Playing the doting girlfriend of course. I mean, you're Silas Taters, after all, and I'm just a lonely college girl who is so lucky to have you in her life, so I'm going to show you that with my body."

"Ollie," I say through clenched teeth as she brings her

mouth to my ear and runs her nose very softly along my cheek, causing my skin to break out in goosebumps.

"Mmm, I wonder where Sarah is. I hope she can see the way you stare at my chest. Don't act like I don't see you."

I keep my breath steady as I lift my Sprite with lime to my lips. I should have ordered alcohol.

"I don't see what the hold up is with her anyway. Sure, she's gorgeous," Ollie says as her lips press against my cheek. "And okay, you guys were high school sweethearts." She kisses me again, this time closer to my mouth. "But did she ever enjoy sucking your cock?"

"Oliana," I say through clenched teeth.

"You know, hearing you say my real name, it's starting to make me feel . . . hot." She squirms on my lap. "Say it again."

I turn to look her in the eyes, and while keeping a neutral face, I ask through thinned lips, "What the hell are you doing?"

"Being the girlfriend. Isn't this what you want? To make Sarah jealous? Well, she's here somewhere, and I'm just trying to show her who you belong to." She leans in even closer and whispers in my ear. "Even if you don't get to fuck my tight, wet pussy."

My breathing picks up, and I can feel my dick harden from the thought of what her pussy would be like, squeezing my cock until I couldn't breathe anymore.

"You don't want to play this game, Ollie."

"Who says I'm playing?" she asks as she stands from my lap and sets her drink down. She leans forward, giving me the perfect view of her chest, and she grips my chin and says, "I'm going to freshen up." Then she presses her lips right to mine.

Soft.

Supple.

Addicting.

I'm so fucking tempted to slip my hand behind her head

and keep her close to me, but I keep my hand still, resting on my thigh as she pulls away.

She rubs her lips together and whispers, "Delicious." And then she walks away, keeping my attention the whole fucking time.

Goddammit. She knows exactly what she's doing, and it's working. She's not going to get back at me with wild, false stories about ridiculous ways we met, but she'll spend the evening trying to turn me on. Well, it's fucking working.

I bring my glass up to my lips just as I see a flash of blonde from the corner of my eye. I turn just in time for Sarah to lock eyes with me. Decked out in a navy blue, off-the-shoulder dress with her hair curled around her shoulders, she looks classically stunning as she approaches me with a large smile.

"Silas," she says as she leans down and presses a kiss to my cheek. I don't return the gesture. "It's so good to see you." She takes a seat next to me and rests her hand on my knee. "This suit looks amazing on you."

"Thanks," I say before taking a sip of my drink.

"Isn't this space gorgeous? I worked with the sponsors on securing the location. I love the vaulted ceilings."

How can she talk to me like everything is okay between us, and we're just old friends catching up? *Like she didn't annihilate me by her unfaithfulness.*

"Oh, and the food selection is supreme. I might have gone to the tasting and had far too many bruschettas than I care to admit."

I can't believe I used to kiss those lips.

Worship those lips.

Wish those lips would slip over my dick and suck until I came. But they never did.

She glances around the room, then leans in even more, her hand now inching up my thigh. "I can't wait for the season to start. It feels like Christmas is coming. I always loved watching you play."

That's the truth. She did.

Even though we had our ups and downs, when she was in the stands, I could always count on her to cheer me on. For the longest time, she was my number one fan, the one encouraging me, telling me to do one more rep.

"And I get to be closer to the ice because I'll be assisting with the on-ice sponsored events. I can practically smell the arena now."

She wets her lips, leaning in even closer, her hand inching up my thigh. Too far.

"What are you doing?" I ask her.

"Talking to you," she says innocently.

"No, what are you doing touching me? I have a girlfriend."

"Oh, I was just being friendly," she says, pulling her hand away just as Ollie walks up to us. And from the look in her eyes, I can tell she's not happy . . . again.

"Sarah, how nice to see you," Ollie says as she bends down to give Sarah a hug. Awkwardly, Sarah returns it.

"Uh . . . Olivia, great to see you."

"It's Ollie," I correct with a venomous tone.

"It's okay," Ollie says while slipping onto my lap. She grips my chin and says, "Sorry for keeping you waiting, baby." She brings her lips a whisper away from mine, and I feel my breath catch right before she closes the distance, melting her mouth to mine. My arm slides around her waist, and I allow myself to get lost in her touch for a second before she pulls away.

She turns her attention back to Sarah. "Your dress is beautiful. Where did you get it?"

"Nordstrom," Sarah says, looking pissed.

"I love shopping there. They always carry classic lines."

"They do." Sarah glances around. "Well, I should get back to the event, make sure everyone has everything they need." She stands and places her hand on my shoulder. "Can't wait to see you out there, Silas. Have a good night." And then she takes off. I bring my glass of Sprite to my lips to wash the delicious taste of Ollie from them. If I don't, I'm going to want more.

"Once again, flirting with the ex," she whispers into my ear.

"I was not fucking flirting," I say through clenched teeth as she runs her fingers over the back of my neck, fucking with my head because it feels so damn good.

"Her hand was on your thigh."

"And I told her to take it off because I had a girlfriend." I squeeze her waist tighter.

"You might not think it, but I can see it in your eyes that you still think about her."

Getting really irritated with this line of questioning, I ask, "Why do I matter to you? Are you jealous?"

"Jealous? Over you?" She laughs. "You and I both know I could do better."

Now that just fucking pisses me off.

I dig my fingers into her side and say, "I'm more man than you could fucking handle."

Her breath becomes erratic as her eyes connect with mine. She's about to open her mouth when I hear Posey say, "There you are. Hey, Ollie, good to see you."

Ollie plasters a smile on her face and waves politely at Posey. "Hey. I'm so sorry, but you're going to have to remind me of your name. For the life of me, I can't keep you all straight."

My most easygoing friend laughs it off. "I'm Levi Posey. The most attractive out of the group. That'll help you remember."

"Oh, I could not agree more. Easily the most attractive."

Posey laughs. "You're dating a smart one, Tates."

Yeah, I am, and she's putting up one hell of a match.

FOR THE TENTH time in five minutes, I grind my teeth together and hold my breath as Ollie's leg rubs against my crotch. I know she's doing it on purpose. There's no other explanation, and at this point, I simply deal with it because if I try to get up, I'll give everyone a goddamn show.

I've also just sat here while Posey and Ollie have hit it off completely, making me even more irritated. Apparently, they both had some magical time in a place called Canoodle in Southern California. They vacationed there separately when they were younger, but when they found out they both had been, they haven't stopped talking about it.

"Did you see the renovated pictures of the Canoodle Cove Cabins?" Ollie asks as her hand sifts through the hair at the base of my neck, making me that much harder. Her nails are just long enough to drive me fucking crazy.

"I haven't. They redid them?"

"Yes, I read a whole article about it. I was writing a piece about must-see small towns, and Canoodle was on there, with the cabins being the number one place to stay. They're beautiful."

"I need to check it out," Posey says just as her leg rubs against my erection once again.

Unable to take it, I lean into her ear and whisper, "Knock it the fuck off."

She just smiles.

"What was your top place to visit?" Posey asks.

"Port Snow, Maine. Followed up by Bright Harbor. They're neighboring towns. Especially during the holidays, it feels like you're walking through a Lovemark movie. I love it there. You need to put it on your bucket list and stop by The Lobster Landing for some fudge."

"Fuck, I love fudge," Posey says. He then slaps me on the leg. "Dude, we should go there this summer before we head up to Banff."

"You realize they're on completely opposite ends of North America."

"Can't afford the plane ticket? Jesus, man."

Ollie chuckles and then presses her lips to my cheek and down my jaw. "He can be such a grouch, can't he?"

"Should have seen him last summer. He was insufferable."

"Fuck off," I say just as Ryot Bisley, a co-founder of The Jock Report, comes up to us.

"Hey, boys, it's been a while." He shakes our hands and turns to Ollie. "I'm Ryot."

"Hello, Ryot. I'm Ollie, Silas's girlfriend."

Ryot smirks. "Maybe I can convince you to convince your boyfriend to join The Jock Report."

"JP was just reminding me," I say. "I promise, I'll join."

"Good, because we have fans asking about you. And you don't have to do much. Interact as much or as little as you want."

"It's pretty simple," Posey says. "I actually like reading the different posts from athletes, and those are the only posts you see, which is fucking awesome. You don't see random commentary from others. It's just straight from the athlete's mouth."

Ollie pauses her seduction and says, "That's such a cool concept. Do you feel like the athletes can connect with their fans on a different level than, let's say . . . Instagram?"

Ryot nods. "The great thing about The Jock Report is that we're not using it as an advertising platform. The Jock Report is for the voices of our athletes."

"If you don't mind me asking, how do you turn a profit?"

"Every athlete and team who have a profile have a shop on the platform. We earn a percentage of those shops as well as from sponsors who sponsor our top ten plays of the week and things like that. And since the feed isn't drowned out by every interest out there, we can charge a higher price because their product will be shown."

"Fascinating," Ollie says. "You could really take that business model and apply it to the top markets."

"You could. It's something the Cane brothers are actually looking into."

"What don't they do?" Posey asks.

"I don't know how they're not exhausted, but hey, I didn't mean to interrupt. I just need to talk to Posey real quick about his shop on The Jock Report. Mind if I steal him away?"

"Not at all," I say, my body cooling down from the brief pause from Ollie's interest in The Jock Report. It's the perfect time to stand up.

"I need another drink," Posey says. "Come with me."

They take off, and I lift Ollie off my leg and stand.

"Aw, are we leaving so soon? I didn't get to get you off."

"Not fucking funny," I say, extremely irritated.

"I'm surprised you can stand from how hard you were. And I wasn't even stroking you. Has it really been that long for you?"

I grip her by the waist and pull her into my chest. Talking into her ear, I say, "Just you fucking wait."

"Is that a threat?"

"Yes," I say as I slip my hand into hers and pull her toward the exit.

We make our way through the crowd, trying to get away with an Irish goodbye, but unfortunately, several people stop me. And every time we stop, Ollie ends up pressing her breasts into my arm, or rubbing me in a way that she knows will turn me on, or even standing on her toes to kiss me. It's become so obnoxious that by the time we get into my car and I start pulling away, I can feel my pulse in my ears.

"Fun night," she says in a smarmy voice that makes me want to give her a taste of her own medicine.

She won't want to mess with me again.

Chapter Fourteen

OLLIE

I don't know if I've ever been more satisfied than I am at this very moment, driving back to my dorm, a fuming Silas Taters next to me.

He thought he could just charge into my dorm, demand I join him, threaten me if I don't, then expect everything to be okay?

Ohhhhhh no.

Not this girl.

I knew going into this event with him that I would have to be reserved in what I said. Frankly, these are networking opportunities for me as well, and making a fool out of myself is not the best idea. But I knew if I turned up the heat, I could teach our friend Silas a lesson.

And I did.

I can tell he's ready to snap from his grip on the steering wheel and the tightness in his jaw.

Guess what, Silas? You deserve it.

Don't fuck with me.

When we pull up to my dorm, I get ready to hop on out, but when he doesn't swing to the front of the building and parks instead, a light trickle of sweat forms on my upper lip.

"What are you doing?" I ask.

He doesn't respond.

He exits the car, walks over to my side, and opens my door. He then undoes my seat belt and takes me by the hand, helping me out of the car.

Uh-oh.

Once he shuts the door, he holds on to my hand tightly as if he's afraid I might take off and maintains his hold all the way up to my dorm. When we reach my door, I turn to him and say, "Well, thanks for walking me up here, but you can go now."

Without a sound, he takes my clutch, opens it up, and pulls out my key. He unlocks the door, parts it open, and says, "Get in. Now."

Okay, so you remember when I was feeling fully satisfied like five minutes ago? That feeling has completely vanished as I walk into my dorm, Silas following closely.

The door closes, and I feel my body still, ready to see what he's going to do next.

He sets my clutch down on the desk before coming up behind me, his chest firm against my back. He dips his head so his lips are right next to my ear. Chills race up my arms from his heady proximity.

"Did you have fun tonight?" he asks in a menacing tone as his hand travels up my back until it reaches the nape of my neck. "Fucking around with my cock, trying to make me hard?"

"I didn't have to try," I say.

Not sure why I decide to poke the bear, but I do.

Unhappy with my response, he moves me up against the wall. His large, muscular chest eclipses my back, and the only reason my face isn't pressed into the white paint in front of me is because my hands are bracing my body.

"It wasn't fucking funny," he says, his tone clear. He's ready to snap.

I swallow hard. "Sorry to say, but you said nothing about not turning you on."

"It's in the fucking contract," he virtually spits. "We don't do that."

"We don't fuck. Nothing says we can't tease," I say, unable to stop myself from mouthing off.

"Is that in the fine print?" he asks.

"Yes," I answer just as his hand finds the zipper to my jumpsuit.

"Good to know," he says in such a sly, knowing voice that I fear what he's about to do.

With one hand on my waist, keeping me in place, he slides the zipper of my outfit down until my back is exposed. His body is so close that I can feel his body heat against mine.

"What are you doing?" I ask.

"Helping you," he says as he lowers the sleeves on my jumpsuit down my arms, and for some reason, I assist him and let them fall all the way off, only to brace myself against the wall again, this time, my breasts exposed since I wasn't wearing a bra. He slides his hands along my bare sides and then pushes my jumpsuit down the rest of the way, leaving me in only my thong.

I squeeze my eyes shut, telling myself I know what he's doing. He's trying to get back at me for what I did at the party. It's clear as day. The easy thing to do would be to tell him to leave. To turn around and put space between us. But I don't seem to open my mouth, and I don't seem to find it within me to step away from him. Instead, I allow him to come up behind me and move his hand along my bare stomach.

"You liked fucking with me tonight, didn't you?" he asks, his thumb trailing up my stomach.

I bite the side of my mouth.

"I was impressed you held it together."

"Do you think *you'll* be able to hold it together?" he asks as his hand moves south to the waistband of my thong. I suck in a sharp breath as his finger runs along the elastic. The soft touch sends zing after zing of arousal down my legs and up my stomach. "Or do you think you'll crack?"

With his other hand, he slips it under the strap of my thong at my waist and holds me tight against his chest with his large, calloused hand. He drags his other hand up my stomach, just below my aching breasts. I want him to touch me.

I want him to touch me all over.

I suck in a sharp breath just as his thumb knocks against the underside of my breast, sending me into a tailspin of need.

"Fuck," I whisper, hoping he doesn't hear me.

But as his grip on my waist grows tighter, I know he did.

His scruffy jaw rubs against my smooth cheek as he swipes his thumb against my breast again.

I grind down on my teeth, telling myself I won't moan. Not for him, not when he's trying to prove a point.

But when he does it again, this time closer to my nipple, I exhale sharply and lower my forehead to the wall.

I can practically feel his smile of satisfaction as he moves his hand back down my stomach, causing it to hollow out as he brings his fingers to the edge of my thong and slowly slides them under.

Fuck me.

I want it.

I want him.

I want his fingers inside me.

His cock.

His mouth.

I back my hips up into his pelvis, and I'm fully satisfied to feel him hard. He might be torturing me, but at least he's torturing himself as well.

"You know you want me," I say. "I've been feeling it all night."

He doesn't answer. He removes his hand from my thong and proceeds up my stomach again. This time, he runs his hand over my breast, barely caressing my nipple, and goes all the way up until he's gripping my throat.

A wave of arousal hits me so hard that I know if he just touched me once, I'd come. That's how turned on I am. That's how much he owns me at this moment.

That's why I'm falling into the way he plays with me.

Holding my neck tight, he whispers, "Swallow."

Unsure of what's going on, I do as he says, and I swallow.

He lightly moans into my ear and says, "That's what it would feel like if my dick was in your mouth. But you would take me deep, wouldn't you?"

"Y-Yes," I say.

His hand on my waist now twists around to the front and slides to the spot just above my slit. Right now, with him gripping my neck, toying with me in a way that has me so hot and bothered that I feel like I could explode, I know he owns me. I might have played with him earlier, but that was nothing compared to what he's doing to me now.

"Ask for it," he says, his lips running along my cheek.

"Ask for what?" I say, barely able to breathe from my pounding heart.

"What you want." He slides his fingers even closer, and I squeeze my eyes shut.

Fuck I want it.

So badly, I'm willing to put aside all of the frustration, the contract, and the entire night, just to come on his hand.

"Touch me," I whisper.

"Where?" he asks.

I swallow again, and he hums in approval. "Everywhere," I answer just as he growls and slides his finger down my slit.

"Soaking," he says as his finger connects with my clit.

"Yes," I moan and rest my head against his shoulder. "Fuck me with your fingers."

"You would like that, wouldn't you?" he says, his voice turning menacing again, and before I can reply, he removes his hand and releases me.

I fall into the wall, empty, cold . . . unsatisfied.

I stand there, stunned, panting . . . in need of release so bad that I place my arm over my breasts to conceal them and turn around to face him.

"You prick," I say. "I never pushed you that far."

He drags his hand over his mouth as his eyes trail down my body. "I told you not to fuck with me."

He moves past me and heads toward the door. "Is this all some kind of game to you?" I ask, walking down the hallway as well, keeping my breasts covered because he doesn't deserve to see them.

"You made it a game tonight," he says, turning on me.

"I made it a game?" I ask. "You're the one who threatened me tonight and forced me to join you."

"I wouldn't have had to force you if you had abided by the contract."

"You didn't even need my help anyway. I saw the way you were sitting so intimately with Sarah."

His eyes turn murderous as he says, "I told her to get the fuck away from me. What part of that don't you understand?"

"The part where you allowed her to touch your inner thigh. And why did you even need me there? I was useless."

"You were anything but useless," he yells.

"Prove it. What could I have possibly offered—"

"A shield," he yells. "You were my goddamn shield. I don't want to be around Sarah, I don't even want to be near her, especially since Posey said she's trying to win me back." He takes a deep breath and pulls on the back of his neck. "I don't . . . I don't want her knowing she has a chance. That's what you're for. That's what this was all about. It's not my goddamn fault that you're using me a different way, a way to get ahead."

My eyes narrow. "I told you I wasn't going to do that article. Jesus, Silas. Are you even listening to yourself?"

"Are you listening to yourself? Fuck, Ollie. I told you I don't want Sarah. If I want anyone at this fucking point, it's you." Frustrated, he growls out an angry "Fuck" before he heads toward the door again.

"Wait," I say, running up to him and standing in front of the door.

In a defeated voice, he says, "Move."

"No, I'm not going to let you leave like this."

"Oliana," he says, unable to look at me. "Just let me go."

"No," I answer again and step up to him. With my hand that's not covering my breasts, I press against his chest. "Why don't you talk to me?"

"Because I don't talk to anyone," he says. "No one."

"Silas, please, you can talk——"

"No, I can't," he says, moving me against the wall again. When his eyes meet mine, I can feel his pain so vividly that my heart actually aches. "I can't talk to you. I can't tell you how I'm feeling. I can't tell you how fucking frustrated I am with you. How irritated I am. How I wish I never met you because then I wouldn't be in this situation of wanting to fuck you so bad that I actually can't think when I'm around you. And I shouldn't want that. I shouldn't want to be buried between your legs because you're not right for me. We are not right for each other." He takes a step back and uses both hands to pull on the back of his neck. "Just move, Ollie. Please. Let me go."

I press my trembling lips together and shake my head. "I want you to stay here."

"I'm not fucking you," he says.

"Then don't. Just stay with me, sleep in my bed, don't be alone."

He shakes his head but doesn't say anything. He just stares at the ceiling, and I can see his resolve wavering. I can see him considering the possibility of staying, so I press him more.

"Please, Silas. Stay with me."

He blows out a frustrated breath and looks me in the eyes. Pain sears through his pupils as he says, "I'm not talking."

"Then don't. You can just lie down with me."

He scans me and asks, "Why?"

"Because it's clear you're hurting."

"I don't need you to fix me," he says, trying to move past me, but I stop him.

"I'm not trying to fix you, Silas. I'm trying to offer you comfort."

"I don't need it."

I press my hand to his chest again. "Yes, you do. And I'm going to tell you right now, if you leave this room, I'm chasing after you, just like this. Nearly naked. Is that what you want?"

He wets his lips, looking me up and down again. "No."

"Then stay. Please, Silas, just stay."

He studies me, just standing there, his Adam's apple bobbing, his damaged eyes taking me all in, wavering with what he should do. And when I think he's going to physically move me himself, he takes a step back and turns back into my room, where he takes his suit jacket off, followed by the white button-up, and drapes them over my desk chair. He undoes his belt and pants but doesn't take them off as he gets rid of his shoes and socks.

When he glances up at me through his hair, I feel a wave of euphoria hit me all at once. He stayed. He might not say it, but he finds comfort in me, in my small dorm, and this is where he wants to be. Not alone in his large apartment . . . but with me.

He heads down the hallway and quietly says, "I'm going to use the bathroom. Can I use your toothpaste?"

I nod, and as he passes me, his hand trails across my stomach before he shuts the door to the bathroom. When he's out of sight, I let out a deep sigh and drop my arm.

God, I have no idea what I'm doing. I'm in way over my head, and I know I shouldn't want him in any way, but that damaged look in his eyes, it's destroyed me. I've never seen such demons, such strength when it comes to keeping everything to himself. I want to help him, be there for him, let him know he's not alone.

I push off the wall and walk over to his white button-up. I let the rich fabric rub between my fingers. Sarah must have really fucked him up for him to need me as a shield. And for him to make that happen, even if it means threatening me. He's that desperate, which if I truly think about it, I don't believe he would have said something. Even though he'd probably never admit it, I know he cares about me. I know he wants to protect me.

And that trust he has, it's very thin, and he's willing to take it away without blinking an eye. Which just means Sarah must have done the same thing.

I pick up his white shirt and fit it over my shoulders, the size difference easily noticeable as I button up the middle buttons. It feels warm, comfortable, like his arms are wrapped around me. And just as I start rolling the sleeves, he steps out of the bathroom and finds me.

The crease in his brow unfurrows.

"Is this okay?" I ask.

Slowly, he makes his way toward me, his every step sexier than the last with the attention he commands from his powerful body. When he reaches me, he pinches one of the buttons that rests just above my breasts as he says, "Yeah."

One word, but it feels like a ton of bricks, knocking me down to my knees.

He wets his lips, and when his eyes connect with mine, I can feel my body tremble with a combination of need and anticipation. But even though his presence electrifies me, I can see something different in his eyes. Not anger, not pain, but vulnerability. It's right there, in his worn, tired irises. He might not say it, talk about it, or acknowledge it, but I can see it, and that makes me feel like I'm something special to this consuming man.

When he steps away from me and heads toward my bed, I walk on shaky legs to the bathroom where I finish getting ready for bed.

I take my time, attempting to calm my racing heart, and tell myself that I'm just sexually charged right now. That's why my mind is clouded with thoughts of Silas, not for any other reason.

After I finish washing my makeup off, I turn off the light and notice that the only light on in the main living area is my nightstand light. Silas sits on the edge of the bed in nothing but his boxer briefs, and I can't help but take in his muscular shoulders, rock-hard pecs, and the contours that wrap around his body from many hours in the gym. He's carved and sculpted his body to perfection.

When he notices my presence, he stands, towering over me in his height, and pulls the blankets back. Without a word, I slip into bed and move against the wall but face him. He slips in as well, turns off the light, and faces me. We both rest our heads on the pillows, and I reach out and press my fingers to his chest.

"You good?" I ask him.

"Okay," he says and then molds his hand over mine. "I'm sorry, Ollie."

"Silas, you don't—"

"Please let me apologize," he says softly.

"Okay."

He places his hand on my cheek, and he says, "I feel like

I'm constantly apologizing to you because I keep fucking up, but that's what I am . . . I'm a fuck-up."

"You're not. You're just hurting."

"That's not an excuse." His thumb strokes my cheek. "Just because I'm hurting doesn't mean I need to hurt you."

I lift my hand from his chest and cup the hand that's on my cheek as I scoot closer to him. "I don't know what happened between you and Sarah, and that's your story to tell someday or keep in. It's up to you, but what I do know is that she hurt you, that she took your trust, and she ran with it. And that makes me sad because I see you walk around, not allowing people to get close to you. I can even see it with your guys."

"It's how I prefer it. Can't get hurt if you're not close to anyone."

"But you're close to me right now," I say, scooting in another inch.

"This is different."

"Is it, though?" I ask.

"It is because even though you're close, I don't think I can fully let you in."

I want to scream why? But I know the answer. I know he's struggling with trusting people, and given his profession and celebrity, I don't blame him. He probably has people asking him for something every day.

So I can pressure him, or I can let him realize that I am someone he can trust and maybe over time, he will let me in.

"That's okay," I say. "I'm just happy I'm close enough." I smile at him, and he strokes my cheek. "But I need you to know something, Silas. I have no intention of hurting you . . . ever. That's why I went to your place to talk about the hockey article because I wanted to figure out a way that wasn't going to hurt you."

"I see that now," he says softly. "I'm sorry I thought otherwise."

"I know why you did. And yes, was I mad about it? Of course. But do I understand? I do. Just know . . . I won't hurt you. It might take you a while to find trust in me, but when you're ready, it's there."

"Thank you," he says quietly. "And you know I'm sorry, right? That I wouldn't do anything to hurt you, even though I made it seem like I would."

"You're a protector, Silas. Not a hurter. If anything, I feel safe when I'm around you. I trust you and your intentions, even if skewed at times by the hurt that rests tightly on your chest."

With a heavy sigh, he rolls away to lie on his back and stare at the ceiling. Why is he pulling away?

I move in closer and rest my hand on his bare chest as I prop myself up on my elbow so I can look down at him. "Did I say something wrong?"

"No," he says quietly.

"Then why did you pull away?"

His eyes meet mine, and he says, "Because you're too . . . fuck, Ollie, you're too mature, too fucking smart, and it's making me think I can do things to you that I shouldn't be doing."

My body tingles with anticipation.

"Like what?" I ask.

"Kiss you, hold you, touch you . . ."

I wet my lips and let my fingers roam his chest as I say, "You can do those things."

He shakes his head. "You deserve better, Oliana. You deserve more."

"Who are you to decide that?"

"I know what I can offer, what you need, and they don't match up. That's why this works, this arrangement. We both get what we need without complicating anything."

"What if what I need has changed?"

He lightly shakes his head. "Don't say that, Ollie. Don't

get yourself wrapped up in this, in me. I'll only end up hurting you."

"I don't believe it," I say. "But I also won't push you." I trail my fingers up to his chin and force him to look at me. "But promise me this, don't pull what you did tonight on me ever again. If you're going to threaten me, threaten me with your cock, not your words. And if you're going to touch me, then you better make me come."

"Then I should probably leave this bed," he says. "Because I have no intention of making you come tonight."

"Do you plan on touching me?"

"I considered holding you," he says softly.

"I think I can make an exception for that," I say as I turn away from him and snuggle into my pillow. He doesn't shift against me right away, he doesn't move at all. So from over my shoulder, I say, "The offer expires."

That gets him moving.

With his large, beefy arm, he drags me into his chest where he buries his head into my hair. I marvel at the way he feels wrapped around me. Warm, safe . . . I don't think I've ever felt like this, like nothing could happen to me when he's near me. And that's terrifying because I know this is just the beginning. I can easily see myself falling for this man, fast and hard.

Chapter Fifteen

SILAS

The sun glitters in through Ollie's white curtains, stirring me awake.

I've paid thousands of dollars to have a comfortable bed I can sleep in at night and for some stupid-ass reason, when I sleep in Ollie's bed, it feels like the best sleep I've ever had. In the back of my mind, I know why, but the front of my mind doesn't want to acknowledge it.

It's too fucking scary.

My brain, my heart, they're not ready for the truth.

"Good morning," I hear Ollie say from over by her desk.

I peep open my eyes to find her sitting cross-legged in her desk chair with a to-go cup of coffee in hand . . . still wearing my button-up shirt. When I saw her in it last night, I had this overwhelming sense to walk up to her and say, "Mine." To let everyone around us know that she belongs to no one but me. And even though it's the only shirt I have here, I'll walk out of this dorm without a shirt on before I remove it from her body. That shirt was meant for her.

"Morning," I say as I sit up in bed and rub my eye with my palm. "What time is it?"

"Eight fifteen. Want some coffee? Ross dropped it off."

"Sure," I say.

She walks over to me and takes a seat on the edge of the bed and hands me her coffee.

"Isn't this yours?" I ask.

"I don't mind sharing, and it's not like your lips haven't touched mine before."

"True." I lean against her headboard, take a sip, and instantly regret it. Fuck, I forgot she likes the sweet stuff. "Jesus," I say, pulling the cup away and handing it back to her.

She chuckles. "Don't be a black coffee snob."

"Ollie, that's not coffee. That's milk and sugar."

"It is not. There's coffee in here. If there wasn't, I wouldn't feel so awake right now."

"It's all in your head."

She pushes at my chest. "Look who woke up on the wrong side of the bed this morning."

"I actually slept great," I say, glancing up at her fresh morning face. She is so fucking beautiful, it hurts. And seeing her like this—in my shirt, no makeup, fresh from bed—makes me want to pull her down on the mattress and claim her.

"So did I." She smirks. "You kept me warm."

"Do you get cold often?"

"There's a draft from the windows. Especially now that the weather is getting colder, I tend to wear more clothes when I sleep, which I hate. I prefer to wear practically nothing."

"How did you sleep in my shirt?"

"Perfect," she answers. "If you weren't here, I would have removed my thong, but I thought I should keep it on out of respect."

"I wouldn't have minded," I say, wishing she slept without it so she was fully naked under my shirt.

"I'll keep that in mind for next time."

She hops off the bed and says, "What are you up to today?"

"Meeting up with Holmes to go over plays and get ready for the season. Our first game is in a week and a half. I want to make sure we're game ready. We also study our opponents and their weak spots. Although they could have worked on them over the off-season, it's always good to be prepared."

"I guess I had no idea you study film."

"All fucking season," I say as I move the covers off the bed. I reach for my pants and shuffle them over my legs.

"Is that why you don't have a lot of time to do anything?" she asks.

"Yeah, pretty much."

She glances down at my shirt, then back up at me. "Oh, do you need this?"

"Keep it," I say. "It looks good on you."

Her cheeks blush, and she smirks over her coffee cup. "You know, Silas, some people might consider that flirting."

"Consider it a compliment," I say as I reach behind her and grab my jacket. I shake it out, then slip it over my shoulders, only to button it up in the middle. My chest is easily visible, but it's not a far walk to my car.

A playful smile on her lips, Ollie scans me up and down and says, "Very Timothée Chalamet of you, Silas. Although, nothing screams walk of shame more than what you're wearing right now."

"Too bad I didn't get any action to make it a true walk of shame."

"That was by your doing."

"Trust me, it was the best decision for both of us." I slip my phone into my pocket, and with keys in hand, I head down her hallway. She follows, and when I reach the door, I turn toward her.

She leans against the wall, one foot propped up against it, and tilts her head to the side, waiting for my next move.

I want it to be me pressing her into that wall and taking advantage of her mouth. I want her hands all over me.

But not just that. I want to continue to feel her comfort. Last night, I felt so vulnerable, and she ignored her pain and helped me with mine. She didn't hold anything against me, something Sarah would have done when we were together. She forgave me and my stupidity, then asked me to stay—not for her, but for me—because she didn't want me to be alone.

It's made me look at her differently.

It's made me want her in a different way.

It's made me consider what it could be like if we took a step forward.

And that's terrifying because I don't think I'm ready. I don't think I'm prepared to be there for her the way she needs it. I don't think I can be the man she needs. It's why I need to control myself around her and tread carefully.

It's why, at this moment, with her looking so goddamn beautiful, I can't take what I want.

So I move in close to her, snag my index finger under her chin, and say, "Thank you for last night."

"No need to thank me, Silas. That's why I'm here."

"Still . . . thank you." And then I lower my head. I hear her slight intake of breath right before I kiss her cheek and then push away, keeping my hands at my side so I don't happen to reach out and do something I'd regret later. "Have a good day, Oliana."

Her head rests against the wall as she says, "See you, Potato."

OLLIE: *How was the film time?*

Silas: *The film time? Is that the technical term?*

Ollie: *In my head it is.*

Silas: *It was good. Have a headache from watching so many yester-day. But I feel prepared.*

Ollie: *Did you take any pain relievers?*

Silas: *Yes, Mom.*

Ollie: *And here I thought I called you Daddy.*

Silas: *You just made me spit water all over my shirt.*

Ollie: *Then my work here is done.*

Silas: *What are you up to?*

Ollie: *Working on a stupid paper, going to take a break soon.*

Silas: *Cool.*

Ollie: *You know, this is the point in the conversation where you would realize that I'm going to be free soon and you're free, so then maybe we can hang out.*

Silas: *Don't think that's a good idea.*

Ollie: *Afraid you might fall madly in love with me?*

Silas: *Afraid I might want to fuck you.*

Ollie: *Once again, not a bad feeling to have.*

Silas: *We have a no whorehouse policy.*

Ollie: *Good answer. I was testing you.*

Silas: *Oh, were you now?*

Ollie: *Yup. You passed.*

Silas: *Now I can say I truly accomplished something this weekend.*

Ollie: *You're welcome.*

———

OLLIE: *Excuse me, Potato, what is the meaning of this package you sent me?*

Silas: *What are you talking about?*

Ollie: *Don't play dumb. I know you dropped this package off at my dorm. There's a weighted blanket inside, along with a fancy coffee maker and the fixings to make a latte . . . with an Agitators mug.*

Silas: *Oh yeah, that might have been from me.*

Ollie: *Why did you send this all to me?*

Silas: *Because you said it was getting drafty in your dorm. Thought you might need something to keep you warm . . . while I'm gone.*

Ollie: *Okay . . . okay . . . hold up . . . Silas Taters, you realize that's flirting, right? You're straight up flirting with me.*

Silas: *I call it being a good friend.*

Ollie: *I call it you want me bad, and even though you won't admit it, you're showing me with this thoughtful gift.*

Silas: *Perceive it how you want.*

Ollie: *I will. You want me.*

Silas: *Sure, if that's what you want to believe.*

Ollie: *It's not whether or not I believe it, Silas. I fucking know it. Also . . . thank you so much. This was really sweet. I can already feel how warm the blanket is. If only it smelled like you.*

Silas: *See, that would be flirting.*

Ollie: *Uh-huh . . . okay.*

———

OLLIE: *Weird, I came home to another package. But this was just a bottle of cologne.*

Silas: *Huh, wonder who sent that to you.*

Ollie: *I wonder. It actually smells just like you.*

Silas: *Super weird.*

Ollie: *You realize this changes everything.*

Silas: *You realize everything has already changed.*

Ollie: *Why are you holding out on me?*

Silas: *It's for the best.*

Ollie: *Then why send me gifts?*

Silas: *Just because we aren't together doesn't mean I don't want you not thinking about me.*

Ollie: *This is all kinds of messed up.*

Silas: *It got messy the day you kissed me in that bar.*

———

SILAS: *Do you think you can make it to my first game? I have to set tickets aside.*

Ollie: *When is your first game?*

Silas: *Tuesday.*

Ollie: *This Tuesday?*

Silas: *Yeah.*

Ollie: *Uh . . . I think I can. I just need to rearrange some things.*

Silas: *It's okay if you can't be there.*

Ollie: *No, I can, but . . . do you think you could get a ticket for Ross too? I don't want to go alone.*

Silas: *Of course.*

Ollie: *Perfect. I can't wait to see what this hockey thing is all about.*

Silas: *Jesus.*

Ollie: *Do I need to dress warm?*

Silas: *Yes, but don't worry. I got you.*

Ollie: *What does that mean?*

Silas: *You'll see.*

Chapter Sixteen

OLLIE

"Happy Birth . . . why are you wearing that?" Ross asks as I open the door to my dorm room.

"Do you not like it?"

"No, I do. You look hot, but why are you wearing Agitators paraphernalia when we're supposed to be going to a bar tonight?"

Yeah, this Agitators sweatshirt doesn't really scream dance club, but it sure does look like I'm going to a hockey game. Silas sent over a sweatshirt, a winter hat, a shirt with his name on the back, and even socks. There was a note also that said, *dress warm*. But knowing I was going to the club after this to celebrate my birthday, I put on a pair of faux leather leggings, black booties, and a shoulder-less tube top. I slipped the sweatshirt on over it, skipped the hat, and prayed that I could keep warm with hot cocoa.

"Silas invited me to his first game tonight, and I thought I should probably go, but he gave me two tickets. One for you and one for me."

"Hockey?" Ross asks with a crinkle of his nose. "On your birthday?"

"It's fine. We'll go to the club after. Trust me, I still want to get my dance on."

"Are you sure this is what you want?" he asks as I grab my mini backpack and head out of my dorm.

I loop my arm through Ross's and say, "Yes. Plus, we can get nachos, and I know how much you love nachos."

"I do like nachos," he says as we head to the front of the dorm where an Uber waits for us.

"Does the driver already know we're going to the arena?" Ross asks.

"He does."

Ross shakes his head at me. "I feel bamboozled."

"The night is young, Ross. We have all the time in the world to celebrate. Now get in the car. I don't want to be late for . . . uh . . . the shoot off?"

"I believe the term you're looking for is puck drop," the driver says as we buckle up.

I lean forward and ask, "Do you know about hockey?"

"Been watching all my life." He pulls out onto the main campus road.

"Mister, we are going to need you to give us a crash course."

⸻

"THIS IS where my nipples fall off," Ross says as he shivers next to me.

"Stop it. It's not that cold." My clattering teeth beg to differ.

"And how did he get these front-row seats for you?" Ross asks, looking around at the people who are banging against the glass, begging for the attention of the Agitators who are warming up.

"I don't know. Magic?" I stand on my toes and glance around, looking for Silas. I have no idea what number he is or what he would look like in a jersey, so I scan for his last name. "Do you see him?"

"What? Sorry, I'm distracted by the man beside us who has mustard in his beard." Ross speaks louder. "Excuse me, sir, you have mustard in your beard."

"Oh hell, really?" the boisterous man says. "That's what I get for scarfing down three hot dogs before the game."

Horrified, Ross turns toward me and mouths, "Three," eyes wide and shivering.

I try not to laugh as I scan the ice, not seeing him. That's until the crowd erupts and a blur of black and purple flies across the ice, then stops suddenly in front of another player, shooting ice all over him. The crowd cheers, pictures are taken, and I glance around as children, women, and grown-ass men start calling for Silas to look at them.

"I think he's arrived," Ross says. "And who did he get ice on?"

I catch a glimpse of the name on the back and see that it's Posey.

"Oh, it must be something they do every game because that's his friend Posey." I ask mustard beard, "Does Silas do that every game to Posey?"

"Yeah, the crowd loves it."

"See." I elbow Ross in the side. "Look at me knowing stuff."

"Congrats, who figured you knew about ice shards?"

"Better than nothing." I snuggle into Ross and give him a little shake. "Lighten up, it is my birthday after all. And guess what I read on the way over here when Sal wouldn't stop talking about the rules of hockey?"

"Something you should have been listening to . . ."

I roll my eyes. "I clocked out after ten minutes. But I did see that there is an openly gay player on the team."

"Who?" Ross says, nearly using my head as a stool to get a better look. "Where is he? I'll be the judge of him."

I chuckle and hold my phone up to Ross. "His name is Ian Rivers. And he's hot."

Ross brings the phone closer and studies the picture. Slowly, a smile starts to form on his face. "Well now . . . let's go Agitators."

I chuckle and steal my phone just as a player comes zooming up to the Plexiglas, causing the crowd to scream. When I look up, I find a familiar frame in front of me. Stick in one hand, Silas lifts his helmet, showing off his beautiful blue eyes. My heart skips a beat at the sight of him in his gear, his smile stretching from ear to ear as he offers me a simple wink before lowering his helmet again.

Butterflies take off in my stomach, and it feels like at this moment, with thousands of people surrounding us, no one else exists besides him and me. My God, he is gorgeous. *Awe-inspiring.* Especially in his gear. I'm seeing the appeal that this crowd's already aware of. He taps the glass with his fists, then takes off.

My eyes track him as he skates swiftly away.

I watch him juggle a puck on his stick.

And I don't tear my eyes away when he loops around the ice offering knuckles to his teammates.

I might not know anything about hockey.

And I might be in a fake relationship with a hockey player.

But I know one thing for sure. Silas Taters just stole a little piece of my heart.

———

"OH MY GOD," I yell as Silas is slammed against the Plexiglas. I turn into Ross and cover my eyes. "What on earth is this brutality?"

Ross loops his arm around me and says, "I've never been more captivated in my entire life." And then to my horror, he yells, "Get the fucking puck!"

"Ross, don't yell at them. They're trying their hardest."

"No, they're not when they can't score a freaking goal. What is this shit?"

Mr. Mustard leans in and says, "This is normal for hockey. There aren't many high-scoring games."

"Wait." Ross turns toward him and asks, "You're telling me, we sit here for five periods—"

"Three," I correct, because I did learn something from the Uber driver.

"Ah, that's right, we sit here through three periods with an expectation of one goal?"

"On average, one to three," Mr. Mustard says.

"Well, that's just . . . thrilling," Ross says with excitement as he screams again. "Slam him, Posey. Slam him against the wall."

I'm not sure what I've created, and I'm not sure I like it.

SILAS IS SO FAST on the ice.

I don't think I've ever seen anything like it.

He's smooth and quick on his feet. He's able to turn at a moment's notice, and then how he handles his stick. Hockey must be one of the hardest sports to master.

The puck is on the other side of the . . . uh . . . rink? Is that what we're calling it? And a bunch of guys are fighting over it. It reminds me of little kids playing soccer when a small group huddles around the ball, trying to get it.

But this is much more . . . brutal. Elbows fly, bodies are

shoved, and there was even a fight between Posey and another player where Posey upper-cutted the guy. I've talked to that man. He's so nice in person, but to see him just go at it with another guy was shocking.

All of a sudden, the crowd erupts, and I glance down the rink to see what's going on. Out of nowhere, Silas skates down the ice, twisting his stick, handling the puck. He passes it over to Holmes. Silas slides behind the goalie, and then with two flicks of the wrist, one from Holmes and one from Silas, they score.

A siren goes off, a red light flashes, and I swear on my two tits, the crowd cheers so loud that I fear the arena might collapse.

"Yessssssss," Ross screams while shaking me. Then he turns to Mr. Mustard, and they belly bump.

I laugh while I watch Silas hold his stick up and celebrate with his boys.

I have to admit, this is probably one of the hottest things I've ever watched.

⸻

"ARE YOU SURE THIS IS ALLOWED?" I ask as we walk down a cinderblock-lined hallway.

Right before the game ended—the Agitators taking the game two to zero—an attendant told us to meet her after the game at the top of the stairs. I assumed she was sent by Silas, so I listened.

But now that we're walking through the inner depths of the arena, I'm slightly nervous.

"Yes," Carrie says. "This is very much allowed."

"Do you think we'll see Ian Rivers?" Ross asks, now wearing an Agitators shirt and holding a giant foam finger that Mr. Mustard bought him. Before we left, they exchanged phone numbers and plan on meeting up to watch another game together. When I tell you I don't recognize my best friend, I mean it. In the last few hours, he's completely transformed. I even considered leaving the game after the second period, but Ross was glued to the Plexiglas. He wasn't going anywhere.

"I'm not sure. Ian keeps to himself a lot. He usually slips right out of the locker room and is usually the last to leave."

As we turn the corner, we see a few people standing by a door, and I recognize one in particular.

"Ollie," Winnie says with a bright smile on her face. "Ah, it's so great to see you." She wraps me in a large hug and then looks up at Ross. "And who do we have here?"

"This is Ross, my best friend," I say. "He recently became a huge fan of hockey, and when I say recently, I mean tonight."

Winnie smiles. "Isn't it thrilling?"

"I'm pretty sure I'm living on some sort of sports high, and that's never happened to me in my entire life. Now I get it. I understand why grown-ass men cry over sports."

Winnie and I both laugh. "Pacey, the goalie, is my fiancé."

"Really?" Ross asks. "He was amazing tonight. Mr. Mustard was telling me he's one of the best goalies in the entire league."

Winnie's cheeks blush as she says, "I don't know who Mr. Mustard is, but I could not agree more."

"And holding the other team to no goals, such a thrill to watch. Got a win for this girl's birthday." Ross hugs me close.

"It's your birthday?" Winnie asks. "Oh my gosh, happy birthday."

"Thank you," I say just as the locker room door opens, and Hornsby pops out.

He offers us a quick wave. "Going home to my girl. We'll catch up later."

"Who was that?" Ross asks breathlessly.

"Eli Hornsby," Winnie answers. "Also known as Prince Charming. The prettiest face you will ever see."

"And he, uh, he has a girl?"

Winnie chuckles. "A girl and a baby on the way."

"How unfortunate," Ross says just as the door opens again. This time, it's Silas.

His eyes lift from where he adjusts his sleeves, and an adorable smile spreads across his face when he spots me.

He's so dreamy . . .

My stomach twists in nervous knots from the pure sight of him in a suit, hair freshly wet from a shower, his face still covered in a thick scruff that I know would feel good against my skin. And with his bright eyes set on me and me alone, I wait in anticipation to see what he'll do.

How he'll greet me.

People are watching, so will he be intimate?

Will he just give me a hug?

Take my hand in his?

"Hey, baby," he says, causing my entire body to turn into a puddle of swoon. And to my utter delight, he slips his hand behind my head and brings his lips to mine, where he presses a deep, sultry kiss that nearly makes my shoes fly off right here in the middle of the Agitators hallway.

It's the kind of kiss you dream about when you see someone for the first time in a long time.

There's passion behind it. Strength in his grip all the way to his fingertips.

It brands me, cuts deep to my very soul.

And when he slowly pulls away, just enough for our eyes to meet up, I can see everything he wants in his mysterious eyes. He wants me.

He wants this.

If only I can convince him to take the leap.

Unlocking our gaze, he slips his hand behind my back and holds me close to his chest. I know this is all for show, that what's going on isn't real, but that doesn't negate the fact that with every touch, every look, he takes my breath away. I can't pinpoint the moment when this thought process happened, but what I do know is that over the past few weeks, my shield has been lowered, and I'm starting to see Silas in a completely different light.

I'm starting to see him as the man I want as mine.

"Oh my God, I still can't believe I get to see this joyful smile on Potato's face," Winnie says. "It makes me so happy, especially since when I first met you, you were a giant curmudgeon."

"Were you a curmudgeon?" I ask Silas, looking up at him.

"Maybe a little."

"Maybe a lot," Winnie says.

Silas pats Ross on the back. "Did you enjoy the game?"

"More than you would have expected," Ross says, keeping his eyes plastered on the locker room door.

"Well, now that the game is out of the way, what else do you have planned for Ollie's birthday? Just going to go home . . . and have fun?" Winnie asks.

I feel Silas glance at me while his grip grows tighter on my back. I don't have to look up at him to know he's not only pissed I didn't tell him it's my birthday, but he's also embarrassed.

"Actually, we were just going to go dancing, maybe grab some drinks," I say, filling in so Silas doesn't have to answer.

"Ooo, fun. Well, I won't keep you." She asks Silas, "Where was Pacey in the process of coming out here?"

"He got held back by some reporters. He should be out soon."

"Okay, thanks." Then she gives me another hug. "Maybe we can get together some time, celebrate your birthday without the guys."

"Yeah, that sounds great." I wave, and with Silas's hand

adhered to my back, we make our way down the hall. Ross reluctantly walks next to me.

"Great game," I say awkwardly. "I've never been to a hockey game before, so that was something else. Ross here really got into it."

"Might be my favorite sport, ever," he says. "By the way, is that, uh . . . Ian Rivers guy available?"

"I think he has a boyfriend. At least I know he's been dating."

"Dammit," Ross says, disappointment heavy in his voice. "The good ones are always taken."

"Where are we headed?" I ask as we reach a door at the end of the hallway.

"My car," he says.

The fall wind whips up around us as we step out into the starry night. Silas brings us over to his Tesla, and he opens the door for Ross but keeps me put.

"I just need to talk to Ollie real quick."

"Not a problem," Ross says. "I'm going to see if I can find any information on this alleged boyfriend. I have some gay friends around the city who are rich in gossip. They must know something."

Oh Ross.

Silas shuts the door and brings me to the back of the vehicle, where he pins me and very carefully, in a low and controlled voice, asks, "It's your fucking birthday today?"

Yup, I knew he would be angry.

"It is." I swallow.

"You know, this happened with Eli," Silas says. "Penny didn't tell him it was her birthday, and he nearly lost it. I didn't think much of it until I was standing in front of Winnie, and she's asking you what you're going to do the rest of your special day."

"Silas, it's not a big deal—"

"And when I asked you to come tonight, and you said you

needed to move some things around, were those birthday things?" He's speaking so low, I know Ross can't hear him.

"Yes, but like I said, it's not a big deal. We had a good time. And Ross and I were going to go out after the game, so no biggie."

"It's a big fucking deal to me, Ollie."

"Why? It's not like you're my actual boyfriend," I say, even though it doesn't quite feel right saying that, especially after the kiss we shared only moments ago. "I don't expect you to do anything for my birthday."

"You should know me better than that." His hand brushes over my cheek. "I would have done something for you. I would have made it special."

"You did make it special. I loved watching you play." I tug on the lapel of his suit jacket. "You were really hot out there."

His jaw grows tight as he says, "Don't say things like that."

"Why not? It's true. You were sexy on the ice. I couldn't take my eyes off you."

"Oliana," he says, his voice growing dark before he rests his forehead on mine. "I'm struggling here. Please don't distract me."

"What are you struggling with?" I ask as I find the waistband of his pants and pull him in a touch closer. "I thought you were sexy on the ice."

"You're changing the parameters of this agreement."

"As if you don't want to," I say, growing slightly frustrated with him. "You're telling me that kiss we had back in the hallway was all fake for you?"

His eyes flash open to mine. "You know it wasn't."

"So then . . . what's the problem?"

"I told you what the problem is." He puts some distance between us. "And that's beside the point. We're talking about your birthday."

"There's nothing to talk about. You clearly don't want to extend this relationship into something more. You're not my boyfriend. Therefore, you don't need to worry about my birthday. Enough said," I reply, now just irritated with him. "Now, if you'll excuse me, Ross and I have some dancing to do." I attempt to leave, but Silas pins me to the car.

"You're not going without me."

I roll my eyes. "Come on, Silas. You don't like dance clubs."

"You don't know that."

I pop my hip out and cross my arms. "So you're telling me you'll go to a dance club with me and Ross and dance?"

"I didn't say I was going to dance, just that I'll go with you."

Well, this ought to be fun.

If there is one way to get this man to change his mind about our situation, to give in to the way he feels about me, it's having him watch me dance with other people. I want more with him, but it seems like the only way I can break him is to flaunt myself and make him so rabid with jealousy that he has no choice but to claim me.

Maybe this will turn out to be in my favor after all.

"Okay." I smile. "Let's go."

He eyes me, probably trying to gauge where my head is at, but I just smile at him and move myself to the passenger side of the car. This time, he allows me.

He wants to be stubborn? Fine, let's see if I can crack him.

━━

SILAS PRESSES his lips together when he scans me one last time as we head into the club. I can still remember the look on his face in the car when I disrobed from my sweatshirt and showed off my shirt underneath. The only way I can think to describe it is what Sandy from *Grease* wore in the last scene, with the off-the-shoulder sleeves but with no bottom half. So my entire torso is on display. And boy, oh boy, did Silas give me a look. I loved every second of it.

When we enter the club, the music filters through my veins, and all I want to do is go straight to the dance floor, but because Silas is who he is, we're directed to a roped-off VIP section guarded by bouncers. I've never been in one of the suites that overlooks the entire club, but they're nice. Cushioned seats, a server, privacy if you need it.

"Mr. Taters, if you need anything, please let us know."

"Thank you," Silas says. "I think just those drink orders. And I believe Levi Posey and some friends will be joining us shortly."

"Of course," the host says before taking off.

Ross turns toward Silas and says, "Is Ian Rivers coming?"

"I think he might be."

"Dear Jesus. Is he bringing his partner?"

Casually, Silas says, "According to Posey, Ian isn't involved anymore. I checked for you."

Ross shrieks and turns toward me. "I need to go to the bathroom to freshen up." He kisses me on the cheek and takes off, leaving me alone with Silas who takes a seat on the bench and stretches his arm across the back.

When we make eye contact, he motions with his finger for me to join him, so I do, but instead of taking a seat next to him, I straddle him and sit directly on his lap. His hands fall to my hips, and he wets his lips as he stares at me.

"You know . . ." I trail my fingers up his stark black shirt. "You never actually told me happy birthday."

In probably the most seductive voice I've ever heard, he says, "Happy birthday, Oliana."

"That's better," I say while I move my finger to the open part of his shirt. "So you invited some of your guys to join us?"

"I did."

"And did you do that so you can touch me without having to hold back?"

His jaw grows tight.

"Because you know, you're free to touch me whenever you want. You don't need people around to do it."

His jaw ticks before he says, "I invited them to fill up the space in here, and I know they'd want to celebrate after the win. Plus, it seemed like Ross was really interested in Ian."

"He is. You should have seen him." I run my finger over Silas's pec. "He was a true fanboy out there. Pretty sure I witnessed a hockey fan being born tonight. And he made friends with the guy next to us, even exchanged numbers so they can talk hockey. I can't wait to see how he acts when Ian gets here. That was sweet of you."

"I'm sure Ian will be happy about it too." His hand comes up to my rib cage. "Were you going to go out in this without me?"

"Yes," I answer unapologetically. "Do you have a problem with that?"

"I shouldn't," he says, his thumb rubbing along my skin.

"But you do."

"Yeah, I do."

His eyes connect with mine, and I just smile at him. "Well, good thing this is a fake arrangement, right? Because at the end of the day, it doesn't matter."

Ross enters the VIP section along with the server, who drops off our drinks. Silas didn't order alcohol, just a seltzer water with lime, while Ross and I both ordered cocktails.

I hop off Silas's lap and say, "Let's go dance, Ross."

He glances at Silas almost as if he's looking for permission, but I hand him his drink before he can give it. I loop my arm through his and pull him through the curtained area and out onto the dance floor.

"That man is going to eat you up tonight," Ross says before taking a very large sip of his drink.

"Doubtful," I say, taking an equally large sip so my drink doesn't spill when I start dancing. "He won't act on it."

"I don't know about that," Ross says, glancing over my shoulder. "He's staring you down right now."

"Good. Let him stare."

"So is this something you want? Because the kiss I witnessed in the hallway was more than some fake kiss."

"Tell me about it. Everything feels so real with him, but he won't admit to it. He won't let himself cross that line, and I'm so frustrated with him that I'm ready to piss him off."

"Oh, like you pissed him off at his sponsor event?"

"Exactly," I say. "He wants me. I know he does, but he doesn't think he's good enough for me, and that's infuriating. So, let's see how he feels when I dance with other people."

"Ollie, please, for the love of God, don't get the man thrown in jail. It won't look good for him."

"I won't. I'm just going to help him realize exactly what he's missing out on."

"I'll pray for his safety tonight."

I start moving to the beat as I say, "It's my birthday, and guess what, Ross? I deserve a freaking treat. And that treat is sitting over there in that VIP section, watching my every move."

"He truly is . . . like a lion stalking his prey."

"Good, let's hope he strikes."

Chapter Seventeen

SILAS

I dig my fingers into the couch for the tenth time in five minutes as I watch Ollie grind against Ross. All I can think about is how I wish it was me. How I wish I had my hand pressing into her stomach, keeping her close to me, letting her do all of the work.

But my head is screaming at me no.

I'm not in a position to start anything with her.

Not when I'm still struggling with how Sarah broke me.

Not with the new season.

And especially not with the way I want to physically claim her until she can't fucking walk.

"Are you really in here alone?" Posey asks as he steps into the VIP section with Holmes and Rivers.

"Yeah," I answer, though I keep my eyes ahead, watching Ollie.

"Why? Your girl is out on the dance floor. Don't you want to dance with her?" Posey asks, taking a seat.

"She's having fun. I'm not going to wreck that." I glance at Holmes and say, "Surprised to see you here."

"He's attempting to get a certain someone out of his head," Posey says.

"Dude, come on," Holmes bemoans. "You said you weren't going to say anything about her."

"I just mentioned it, nothing more." Posey lifts a bottle of beer to his lips that he must have grabbed on his way in here.

"I told him to go for it," Rivers says. "Holmes is a catch. You're telling me she wouldn't choose you over some other guy?"

"She won't," Holmes says as he sinks into his chair and lifts his beer as well. The server appears at that moment and brings the boys more bottles.

When she stands tall, she says, "There are some girls who want to come join you boys. Would you like me to let them in?"

"In a second," Posey says.

When the server leaves, I raise my brow at him. "Getting into trouble tonight?"

"Celebrating our first victory," he replies. "And attempting to find a girl for Holmes. Rivers, you're on your own, bud."

"Actually, Ollie's good friend Ross is interested," I say just as I look out toward the dance floor and catch a guy grinding into Ollie.

Red-hot anger flashes through my body in seconds, and I find myself standing just as Ross filters in. "Hey," he says. "Uh, who all is here?"

I don't even bother with introductions. I blow right by him and head toward the dance floor. He's outgoing enough to fend for himself.

I have one thing on my mind, and it's to get that fucker off Ollie immediately.

Not that it *really* matters, but Sarah's betrayal was private, unseen—thank fuck. But if Ollie is photographed with another guy so soon into our "relationship", it will be very, very public.

Let's be real, Silas. This has nothing to do with paparazzi.

Okay, Ollie might not be mine, but she isn't going to be someone else's, that's for damn sure.

Mine.

My fists clutch at my sides, my jaw is so tight I think I might crack a molar, and with every step I take forward, I feel myself growing angrier and angrier until I reach them and tug on the guy's arm, pulling him away.

"Silas," Ollie says in shock.

"Dude, what the—hey, you're Silas Taters."

"I am, and you're dancing with my girl. So unless you want to know what it's like to have your face beaten in by a professional hockey player, then I suggest you leave her the fuck alone."

The guy holds up his hands and takes a step back. "Dude, I had no idea."

"Beat it," I growl.

The man gets the hint, and without another word, he takes off.

"Was that necessary?" Ollie asks, arms folded, looking just as angry as me.

"Don't fucking test me tonight, Ollie. I'm not in the mood."

"Excuse me, but I'm pretty sure it's my birthday. Therefore, I can dance with whoever the hell I want."

"It might be your birthday, but my boys are also here, which means you shouldn't be dancing with anyone but me."

"Is that really the reason you just scared the piss out of that poor guy? Or is it because you can't stand the thought of another man touching me?"

My jaw works to the side as I look away. She's got me pegged. I could give two shits about my boys being here. What I care about is her being close to another man.

Touching another man. Even looking at another goddamn man.

"Answer the question, Silas."

"Both," I say. And when a satisfied smile crosses her face, I know I'm fucked.

How could I not be fucked?

Ollie is easily the sexiest woman in this club. Hell, the sexiest I've ever seen. She has me by the balls, even if I want to believe that's not the truth.

"Then dance with me," she says as she slides her hand up my chest and around my neck, pulling me onto the dance floor. "I want to feel you against my body."

"Ollie," I groan as she spins and presses her backside to my front. She starts moving to the music, and I just stand there, letting her rub against me, enjoying every goddamn second of it.

She moves my hand around her waist and presses it against her bare stomach, just like I envisioned. As she moves against me, her ass grinding into my pelvis, I find myself growing more and more frustrated with holding back rather than just taking what I want.

Maybe for a moment, just a moment, I can give in.

I can take.

So I allow myself to loosen up, and I pull her in even closer as I move my hips with her. Her hand grips the back of my neck, anchoring herself in place, and I explore her body with my hands as we dance together, in unison, like this is what we were meant to do our entire lives.

Everything else around us fades, and it feels like just me and her out here on the dance floor. There isn't a fake contract, there aren't complications, and there's nothing to worry about. It's just the two of us.

She grinds into me. I bite my bottom lip, holding her right where I want her, and together, we move, her ass making me harder with every beat of the music. I grow so hard that my body starts to float from the euphoria of it all. All intelligent thoughts dissolve, and I'm left with pure animalistic behavior.

I want more.

I need more.

With one thing on my mind, I move her over to a wall where I spin her around and prop one of her hands against the wall as my other hand moves up her body just below her breast.

"Fuck, you're hot," I say as I lean close and move my mouth against her ear.

"I want you inside me," she says, her leg snaking around mine, sending a beat of electricity up my spine.

My will bends, and I press even closer into her pelvis, showing her how much she turns me on. When she lets out a light moan, my body tenses, prepping for more. I grip her by the ass, lift her up so she circles her legs around my waist, and pin her against the wall, her center lined up with my hard-on.

"Why didn't you tell me it was your birthday?" I ask as I thrust my cock into her pelvis.

"Didn't think you would care." Her hands thread through my hair.

I thrust again, and this time, she lets out the sexiest fucking moan I've ever heard. "When it comes to you, I care about everything."

"If you cared, then you wouldn't torture me," she says as she moves her forehead against mine. "I want you, Silas. I want you so much that I think about you at night when I'm pleasuring myself. I think about you in the morning, wondering if you missed me from the night before. I think about you so much that it makes it hard for me to concentrate during the day. Please tell me you feel the same about me."

I thrust against her again, and again . . . and again, my breath becoming labored as a trickle of sweat rolls down my back. Her grip on me becomes deathly as she whispers, "Tell me, Silas, tell me you want me."

"Of course I fucking want you. Jesus Christ, Ollie."

Keeping her right where I want her, I thrust again. Her head falls against the wall, her panting growing heavier. I lower my mouth to her neck where I nip, lick . . . trail kisses along the column, all the way up her jawline. I lift her chin so our mouths line up, and as I stare down at her, my need for her driving my every move, I wet my lips.

"Do it," she says breathlessly. "Kiss me, Silas."

My breath is heavy in my chest as I stare down at her luscious lips. Fuck do I want to kiss her so bad. I want to relive the moment from the hallway, sink back into her embrace, and get lost for hours. But even though my pulse is beating so fast I can hear it in my ears, I also know . . . I can't.

"I want to deserve you."

"You do," she says, her hands gripping me tightly.

"I don't," I say as I pause my hips, realizing what I'm doing. Dry-humping Ollie in a public place is not the smartest idea where anyone could see us. So I lower her to the ground despite her protest.

"Don't," she says. "Please, Silas, don't pull away."

If only it were that easy.

I take her hand in mine, and I move her through the dance floor and back to the VIP booth. Ross is already chatting up Ian while Posey is talking to a girl, and Holmes is talking to two. I hope he knows what he's doing.

"Hey, man," Posey says, easily reading my expression. "You out?"

"Yes," I say. I glance at Ross and catch his attention. "You good if we leave?"

"Perfect," he says.

"Good." I grip Ollie's hand even tighter and say, "Let's go."

I'm halfway out of the VIP suite when she says, "I don't want to go."

But I don't listen as I pull her through the club and out the front door where I hand my valet ticket to the valet.

"Silas, I said I wasn't done."

"I know what you said."

"Then release me so I can go back in."

"No," I answer.

"You can't control—"

I yank her into my side and speak closely to her ear. "Don't argue with me. Not right now." And then lightly, I press my lips to hers, enough to keep her quiet but not too much to get me any more worked up.

The drive back to her dorm room is quiet. I have nothing to say because I'm wavering between what I should do and what I shouldn't do.

My conscience is causing my head to spin and my body to be at war with my mind.

The frustration climbing up my spine becomes so monumental that I feel like I can't breathe. I blackout the entire way there. When I park, I don't even remember how we got here. All I know is that I'm about to combust.

I like Ollie. When I first met her, sure, I thought she was hot, but I also knew she'd be someone who could help me. I never considered building feelings for her. But her patience, her tenderness, and her understanding have slowly peeled away at my resolve. And then seeing her with another guy tonight nearly wrecked me.

I'm buzzing with so much adrenaline from the win, from the club, that when we get up to her dorm room, and she opens the door, I push her in and slam the door. Her eyes widen as I approach her and with one arm, I scoop her up and deposit her on her bed.

"Silas," she says, breathless.

I remove her shoes and socks, then grab her leggings and peel them off her body until she's only in her top and red lace thong.

Her hands fall to her face and she says, "Please don't be teasing me."

I move over her and force her to look at me. "Do you remember when we made our contract?"

"If you stop this because of the whorehouse——"

"Do you remember the contract?" I ask, my patience wearing thin.

"Yes," she says.

"Do you remember the extra condition you gave me? You owe me a favor."

"Yes, I remember," she says, her breathing becoming heavy.

"I know what I want my favor to be," I say as I pull her up and then rest my hands on her shirt. I slip my fingers underneath and pull it up and over her head, revealing her matching lace strapless bra.

"Wh-What is it?" she asks.

I reach around her back and find the clasp of her bra. With one flick of my fingers, I undo it and watch as the fabric falls to her lap.

And fuck me . . .

Her tits are so fucking sexy. Round, tight, with dark nipples pebbled from the air, they're aching for my touch, for my mouth.

I push her back down on the mattress, and as I thread my fingers into her thong and start to tug it down, I say, "I want you to allow me to fuck you with my tongue tonight."

"Is that even a question you need to ask?" Her chest heaves as I lower her thong down her legs and all the way off.

I stare down at her, completely naked for me, and I realize there is no way I'll have any self-control. She's easily the sexiest woman I've ever been with. With round, high tits, a narrow waist, and a bare pussy, she's making me sweat just looking at her.

"Fuck," I mutter as I slide my hands up her thighs and run my thumbs over her pussy. "You're so hot, Ollie."

Her legs spread, and she opens for me while her hands fall to her breasts. "Please don't play with me, Silas." Her head twists to the side. "I've wanted you to make me come for so long. I need it tonight. Please."

Seeing her desperation match the desperation I feel inside makes me feel even more connected to her. I like knowing I haven't been the only one suffering.

I remove my jacket and toss it to the side and then untuck my shirt and unbutton it. The entire time, I watch her play with her nipples and move her pelvis, seeking attention. Just watching her has my cock straining in my pants. I leave my shirt open and bend down. Placing both my hands on her inner thighs, I spread her even wider, causing her to gasp.

I make eye contact with her as I lower my mouth, and right before I stick my tongue out, I take a deep breath.

Her eyes widen right before I press my mouth to her slick pussy.

"Oh fuck," she groans as her pelvis pushes up, seeking more.

Hands still on her thighs, I take long, languid strokes with my tongue. She squirms beneath me as I lap away at her, never fully pushing all the way in against her clit, just staying around the outside, prepping her for what's to come. If this is her response already, I can't wait to see what else she does.

I lift only slightly and say, "Hold your thighs for me."

She lets go of her breasts and grabs her thighs, keeping them spread for me. Instead of going back to her pussy, I trail kisses up her tight stomach to just below her breasts.

"Suck them, Silas. Please . . . please suck them."

"That wasn't part of the agreement," I say as I drag my tongue between her breasts.

"Please," she begs, the sound so desperate that I give in and press tiny kisses along her breasts, but once I reach her nipple and see how hard it is, I lose another level of self-control. I cup her breast in my hand, squeezing it hard as I suck her nipple between my lips.

Together, we moan.

I don't know how long I've wanted to play with her tits, but Jesus Christ, they're better than I imagined. Soft, velvety, and bigger than I expected. Fuck, I could spend hours playing with them.

I nibble across her tit, making sure to leave my mark before I work my way to the other one. Her pelvis lifts toward me, feeling out my hard cock, and I allow it because what little pressure she's able to obtain keeps me satiated as I play with her breasts.

Sucking.

Nipping.

Licking.

Squeezing.

"I love your tits, Oliana," I say, my voice ragged from how turned on I am. "But I think I might love your pussy more." I kiss my way back down her stomach, past her pubic bone, and right above her pussy. With two fingers, I spread her wide, exposing her clit, and then lower my tongue to just above it.

And I hover, letting her feel my heavy breath and the scruff of my jaw against her inner thigh.

"Silas," she moans. "Please."

I love how vocal she is. I love that she doesn't shy away from what she wants but simply asks. It's so sexy.

With my hand that's not spreading her, I move it back up her body, and just as I pinch her left nipple between my fingers, I press my tongue against her clit.

"Oh my . . . fuck," she says, her eyes squeezing tight.

From her delicious response, I do it again.

And again.

And again.

"More," she begs. "I need more."

I press my tongue against her slit and lightly flick at it, creating a vibration against the nub that causes her to release her legs and grip my head, her fingers digging into my scalp.

"Fuck, Silas. Oh my God . . . keep . . . going."

I keep my eyes on her, watch her reaction as I continue the relentless pace, and as I see her body grow tighter and tighter and her breathing pick up, I know she's getting close, so I lift, releasing her.

"No," she cries and sits up on her elbows. "Silas, don't do this to me."

I reach out and cup her face. "Baby, where's your vibrator?"

"In . . . in my nightstand," she says, her eyes wild with anticipation.

I reach into her nightstand and find a purple vibrator. I switch it on to make sure it works, and then I say, "Hold your legs again."

She does as she's told, and I run the dildo along her slit, letting her arousal lube it up before I slip it inside her. She groans and tightens when I turn it on. I let the subtle buzz work her back up. Her eyes stay fixed on me, traveling down my chest to my abs, and right to my pants where my hard-on is pressing urgently against my suit pants. She wets her lips, and I know what she wants after this, but she won't be getting it.

No, just this.

Only this.

"How close are you?" I ask.

"Very," she squeaks out.

"Good," I say right before I lower my mouth to her pussy again and press my tongue against her clit, flicking short, tight strokes once more. Her moans grow louder. Her body tenses. Her breath seizes, and her mouth falls open as a guttural moan spills past her lips.

"Fuck . . . fuck," she says as her body convulses, and she comes.

It's the sexiest thing, seeing how I can control her, how I can make her feel the most euphoric feeling anyone can ever experience. Her response was unlike anything Sarah ever gave me, and it's made me feel . . . powerful. *It also confirms that Sarah and I were so incredibly incompatible.* But not this woman in front of me. We couldn't be more sexually compatible.

I slowly pull away and turn off the vibrator, letting her catch her breath on the bed. I remove my shirt and then tug on her arm to lift her up. Her worn-out body allows me to put the shirt on, and then I kneel in front of her and button a few of the middle buttons before laying her back down on the bed. I hover over her and lean down to kiss her forehead.

"Happy Birthday, Ollie."

With that, I grab my suit jacket, and without turning around, I head out of the door, praying no one sees me exit her dorm with a massive fucking erection. I'll be dreaming about her all fucking night when I pleasure myself and deep into my dreams.

OLLIE: *I can't believe I'm waking up alone.*

Silas: *If I had stayed, I would have had my dick halfway down your throat.*

Ollie: *A birthday present I would have gladly accepted.*

Silas: *A present I wasn't willing to give.*

Ollie: *So was last night all you were willing to give?*

Silas: *Come outside and find out.*

I set my phone down and lean my head against the headrest of my car as I stare out the window, watching a couple of college kids stumble out of an Uber and make the walk of shame toward the building.

I'm still trying to comprehend how I let myself snap last

night. Do I regret it? Fuck no. Everything about Ollie turns me on—from her mind to her body to her moans to her fucking mouth. I'm addicted. It's why I'm here, this morning, needing to see her before I head off to the weight room.

It takes her a few moments, but when I see movement from the building door and I look over, I nearly swallow my tongue as she comes walking out in the shirt I put her in last night, the front tucked into a pair of joggers. She's pulled her hair up into a messy bun on the top of her head, and from the way her breasts sway against my shirt, she's not wearing a bra.

I open the door for her from inside my car, and when she hops in, she moves in close to me, places her hand behind my neck, and pulls my lips to hers. I was not expecting her to kiss me, but fuck me, I can't stop it.

I let her explore my mouth. Her lips are so soft as they float against mine. Her tongue is curious as it dives against mine. Her forceful grip on my neck keeps me in place. I sink into the kiss longer, matching every stroke of her tongue with mine. She leans in closer, one of her hands falling to my chest, then down to my stomach . . . then . . .

I pull away, breaking the kiss, and gasp for air as her devilish eyes smile at me.

"That's how I should have been greeted this morning," she says. "Maybe with another orgasm." She grips my hand and holds it as she faces me. "Why did you leave?"

"I shouldn't have been there in the first place. I couldn't . . . fuck, you cracked me at the club, and I needed to . . ." I bite the side of my cheek. "Shit, I needed to make my mark."

"You did. My inner thighs are red."

"Really?" I ask. "Are you okay?"

"I'm more than okay. I really wish you'd stayed, Silas."

"You know why I didn't."

She rolls her eyes. "Back to this again? God, you're driving me crazy."

"I'm not trying to," I say.

"So what . . . you just decided to eat me out last night, and that's it? Back to just seeing each other at important events?"

"Ollie, you know I can't offer more right now."

"No, I don't know," she says, her annoyance evident in her voice. "It's so frustrating. And you know what, Silas? I can't wait around forever. If you don't want to be with me, then—"

"I have something for you," I say, quickly cutting her off so she doesn't have a chance to finish that sentence, a sentence I don't want to hear.

"What?" she asks.

"I've got a present for you."

Confused, she says, "I thought last night was my present."

"I got you something else." I reach into the center console and pull out a flat jewelry box. "Here." I hand it to her.

"Silas," she says softly as she takes it. "You really did get me something." When her eyes flash to mine, she asks, "Why?"

"Because you mean something to me. Even if I frustrate you and you don't understand me sometimes, you matter to me. And you've made a difference in my life. I want you to know that."

She lets out a sigh and leans her head against the window. "Dammit, Silas."

"What?" I ask.

She softly shakes her head. "I'm ready to freaking scream at you, and then you do something like this. You do something kind. Just like yesterday, I'm ready to scream at you for pulling me out of the club, and then you go and give me the best orgasm of my life." Her eyes connect with mine. "Best orgasm . . . of my life."

I wet my lips, my body humming from the compliment.

"Can't you make up your mind on what you want? I feel like I'm being strung along," she continues, her voice now more sad than angry. And that makes me feel like shit.

"We made an arrangement, Ollie," I say softly. "I'm

fucking terrified of what will happen if we don't follow that agreement."

Because I like you.

Because I can get lost in you.

And because I don't know what I would do if you hurt me.

"We aren't following the agreement, Silas. We haven't been. And meanwhile, you're hurting me in the process because you know how I feel about you. You know I want you, and you give me hope with experiences like last night. And the worst part is, I know how you feel about me. You want me. I can see it in your eyes. But if I'm off base here, I need you to tell me that's not the case." Her eyes lift to mine. "Tell me right now." I can't. I can't tell her I don't want her because that would be a huge lie, one that she would see right through. So when I don't say anything, she continues, "See, you can't even say it. So if we both want each other, why are we not together?"

"It's complicated, Ollie." I rub my hand against my forehead. "I told you that."

"Yeah, you did," she says with a sigh as she hangs her head low.

Fuck.

I hate making her feel like this.

I hate that dejected look on her face.

I wish I could be more for her.

Shoulders slumped, she carefully opens the jewelry box, revealing two gold necklaces, each with a thin gold bar as the pendant.

Trying to move past her disappointment in me, I say, "This is called a high-low necklace. It represents the highs in your life, your accomplishments, your joy, and the lows in your life, the moments you've struggled or felt like the weight of the world rests on your shoulders. I figured with moving forward in your career, you might need a reminder of the journey you're on to accomplish the goals truly important to you."

Her finger runs over the thin chain before she glances up at me. The anger is gone, and a hint of sadness is left over, but there's also gratefulness. "Silas, this is incredibly thoughtful." She hands it to me, and I panic for a second before she says, "Will you put it on me?"

"Of course," I answer. While I take the necklaces out, she leans closer to me. When our eyes meet, I feel this instinctual urge to kiss her again, to claim her. To let her take me up to her room and strip down where I would spend the day in bed with her.

Getting lost in her would probably result in one of the best days I've had in a very long time.

Instead, I slip the necklaces on and watch as she gently touches them. "I love it. Thank you."

Then she tilts her head to the side, studying me briefly before she pinches my chin with her forefinger and thumb, brings me in close, and then delivers a gentle yet enticing kiss on my lips.

"You're welcome," I say when she pulls away, my lips wanting so much more.

"I'm assuming you're leaving," she says.

"Yeah. I have to hit up the weight room today and review some film. Game tomorrow."

"Will you be home later?" she asks. "I want to get a workout in."

"Yeah, probably. I'll leave you alone, though."

"Please don't." She hops out of the car and turns to face me. Standing there, in my shirt and my necklace, I feel my heart beat wildly as I see just how I've claimed her. And I know, if I took off those pants of hers, I'd see where else I claimed her. "Hopefully, see you later." She shuts the door and walks away, my eyes glued on her ass.

I grip the steering wheel tightly, remaining frozen in place. You will not chase after her.

You will not fucking chase after her.

—

"YOU DID A LOT OF GRUNTING," Posey says as we sit in our lockers, fresh from a shower after spending an hour lifting weights.

"So," I say, knowing he's right. I did a lot of grunting because I was fucking frustrated. I'm sexually frustrated, and the entire time I was lifting weights, all I could think about was how great Ollie's pussy tasted and how I wanted so much more.

"Last time you grunted that much, something was bothering you. So . . . is something bothering you?"

"No," I answer as I lean against my locker, not having the energy to get dressed.

"Something tells me you're lying. Did something happen with you and Ollie last night?"

"Yeah," I answer, just absolutely exhausted to do the runaround on this conversation. "I licked her pussy."

"Uh . . . is that a bad thing?" Posey asks, sounding confused.

Mentally worn out, I realize that I need someone to talk to about the real reason Ollie and I are together—someone to work through this—so I turn toward him and say, "Yes, because we've been pretending to date each other, and last night, I lost control and ate her out."

"Uh . . ." He blinks a few times. "What?"

"We aren't really a couple. We've been faking it. But you can't tell anyone."

"Dude, come on. You know I hate fucking secrets, and what do you mean you've been faking it? Why?"

"Because I didn't want to hear it from you guys, constantly babying me with Sarah around, and I wanted to keep Sarah at arm's length. Ollie needed some help too, so we formed an agreement."

"Well . . . shit," he says. "I really thought you two were together."

"We're not." Fuck, it feels good to get that off my chest.

"But from the sound of it, you want to be."

I shake my head. "No, I mean, yes, I want her. Fucking bad. But I don't think I'm ready. I'm still carrying baggage from Sarah, and we just started the season. I don't think it's good timing."

"Well, as much as I would like to be helpful, I really don't think I'm the one to talk to. I'm not good with secrets, and if you tell me any more than you already have, I know I'll end up blabbing. So best we keep this at what it is, an unfortunate slip of the tongue."

Just then, my phone beeps, and I glance at the screen to see it's from Ollie.

I swipe at my screen to read it.

Ollie: *I just fingered myself to images of you last night.*

"Fucking hell," I say as I drag my hand over my face.

"What?" Posey asks. I flash the screen at him, and I watch as his mouth falls. "Jesus fuck."

"See what I'm dealing with? You have to help me."

Posey shakes his head. "No, I won't get wrapped up in everyone's issues. I'm one man. I can't handle it all."

"What else are you handling?"

"Well, I just got done nursing Pacey and Hornsby back to a solid, healthy relationship with their girls. I'm working on Holmes and making sure he doesn't jump off a cliff from his unrequited love. I can't fucking take you and the mess you're in as well."

"Too bad," I say. "I need advice. What the fuck do I do?"

"How the hell am I supposed to know? Do you see me with a girl? This is really a question for Hornsby or Pacey."

"Neither of them are here. You're here, so help me. This is how she always is, trying to get me fucking turned on so I crack."

"So then just tell her no."

"I have," I say. "She's adamant. And for some reason, I keep falling further and further into her trap. I'm going to fully break. I can feel it."

"Then break." Posey throws his hands up in the air.

"I told you . . . I can't."

"Then I don't know. Tell her that you hope she had a pleasurable time."

"That's shit advice."

"Told you I wasn't cut out for this."

Grumbling under my breath, I text her back while Posey slowly leans toward me, trying to see what I'm typing.

"What, uh . . . what are you saying back?" he asks.

"What you told me to say. Hope she had a pleasurable time."

"Noooo," Posey practically yells as my finger hits send. "Don't say that."

"I already did. It's sent. What the fuck, man?"

"What are you what the fucking me for?" he asks. "You said that's shit advice. Why did you use it?"

"Because I'm losing my goddamn mind!"

OLLIE

"YOU KNOW, I really don't want to be a part of this," Ross says as he spins in my desk chair with a huge smile on his face.

Things went really well for Ross last night.

Really well . . .

"I sat here and listened to you give me a detailed description of how you sucked Ian Rivers off at his place. And you know that was shitty because of how much I've wanted Silas to let me do that."

"I know, but did you have to say you fingered yourself?"

"Yes, I have to get his attention. Telling him I fingered myself is getting his attention."

My phone beeps with a response, and with a sarcastic smile, I say, "See, got his attention."

"What did he say?"

"Oh, now you're interested."

"Obviously, you have me invested. Just tell me."

"Bet you he says something like . . . I wish I could taste your fingers."

"Oh, that's hot."

"That's because Silas is hot," I say as I swipe to see the text message. Clearing my throat, I read it out loud. "Hope it was a pleasurable . . . time. What?"

"That's what he said?" Ross winces. "Ooof, that's brutal. It's like your crazy uncle accidentally received the text, and instead of making you feel bad, he tried to help a girl out."

I study the text, confused. "I really expected him to say more."

"Maybe you scared him away with the fingering."

I give Ross a death stare. "I did not scare him away. Maybe he just needs a touch more pushing." I crack my fingers and say, "Watch a master at work."

⸺

SILAS

"IT'S NOT MY FAULT," Posey says while slipping his briefs on under his towel. "I told you I didn't want to be a part of this.

I've expended all my helpfulness to Hornsby. That took it out of me."

"That was months ago. Don't you recharge?"

"I'm not a fucking battery."

My phone beeps, and before I can even consider looking at the text, Posey swipes it out of my hand.

"What the fuck are you doing?"

"Stealing this nightmare from you so you don't embarrass yourself even more." He opens the text and then grips the side of his locker while coughing.

"What? What did she say?"

"Holy shit." He looks up at me and points the screen at me to read.

Ollie: *It would have been more pleasurable if you were here to lick my arousal off my fingers. I just had to do it for you.*

Fuck . . .

"Dude . . ." Posey is speechless, and that's saying something. "What the hell did you get yourself into?"

"I fucking told you. She's torturing me."

"You need a good response."

"I fucking know." I try to take the phone back, but Posey keeps it.

"I'll type it out, you nimrod. We don't need any mistakes this time."

"What are you going to say?"

"Uh, what we're both thinking." Going to the emoji, he double-taps on the eggplant emoji, and before I can stop him, he sends it.

"Dude!" I snag the phone away. "Two eggplant emoji? She's trying to dirty talk, and you give her two eggplant emoji?"

"That is dirty talking. She got two penises to rise at the same time."

I give him a stern look. "Don't fucking bone out over my girl."

"Ha." He points at me. "You said my girl."

"Urggh, I fucking hate you right now."

———

OLLIE

DING.

"I don't want to know what he says. I'm still shook that you said you would taste your own fingers." Ross leans forward. "Who the hell says that?"

"Me, that's who," I say as I swipe open his response. When two eggplant emoji pop up, I groan out loud.

"Was that a sexual groan or an irritated groan? I honestly can't tell at this point."

"Irritated." I show him Silas's response.

"Eggplant emoji? What is he, freaking sixteen? That boy has no class."

"He has class," I say as I clutch the necklace he gave me today. "I just think . . . maybe he's trying to hold back or something."

"Frankly, I'm embarrassed for him. What's he going to do next? Text water droplets."

Ding.

We both look at each other. "If that's water droplets, I'm going to kick a wall," I say.

Together, we look down at the screen to find two eggplants . . . and two water droplets.

"Dear God," Ross whispers.

———

SILAS

"YOU FUCKING MORON!" I say while whacking Posey with his own towel.

"What? Water droplets are in."

"They're not in," I say defeatedly as I toss his towel to the floor. "Jesus fuck, what have you done?"

"Spared you the humiliation of saying something stupid."

"Spared me?" I guffaw. "You made this worse."

"How so? In a subtle way, I told her you were turned on. Can't get any better than that. Trust me, it works."

"Yeah, where's your proof? I don't see you walking around with a girlfriend."

"Hey, you're the one who asked me for help. If you didn't think I was qualified, you never should have confided in me."

"Obviously," I reply as my phone dings. Posey reaches for it, but I swat his hand away. "Get the fuck away."

I turn my back toward him and open the text.

It's a picture of Ollie, showing off her cleavage, the necklaces I gave her on full display. I wet my lips as I stare at it for a few seconds, taking in every last bit of her from her full lips to her gorgeous eyes to her ample tits that I got to suck on last night . . .

My phone is ripped from my hands, and Posey is staring at the photo. "Holy shit," he says.

"Give me that."

"No way, you're going to fuck this up." He takes off toward the middle of the locker room in his briefs. I grip my towel and chase after him.

"I'm going to fuck it up? You're the one who's been fucking it up this whole time."

"Uh . . . pretty sure I'm the one who got you this picture with my expert texting. By the way, you're welcome."

"She feels bad for me," I say as I chase him around.

"Nah, she's turned on by your eggplants and droplets. Told you I know what I'm doing."

"You know shit." I leap over a chair, but he dodges me and runs to the other side of the locker room.

"Watch daddy work his magic." Posey starts typing away as he's moving about the room.

"Do not fucking text her."

"Oh, I'm texting her. Next pic she sends will be a nude."

"Give me my goddamn phone," I say as I pick up a water bottle and chuck it at him, hitting him directly in the hand and knocking the phone to the floor and across the room.

We glance at each other, and in slow motion, we move through the locker room and both dive for the phone at the same time, clashing against each other. My towel loosens, his legs tangle with mine, and we grapple on the floor, army crawling toward the phone until we both reach it at the same time.

That's when I see what he texted her back.

Silas: *Oye, my dick.*

What in the actual fuck?

"Oye, my dick?" I scream. "That's what you fucking wrote? Oye, my dick? What the hell is wrong with you, Levi?"

He pauses, a pinch to his brow. After a second, he says, "I'll admit, that wasn't my best work. You can blame yourself. The pressure of running around the locker room hindered my ability to be clever and sexy."

Just then, the locker room door opens, and Hornsby walks in, only to stop dead in his tracks when he sees me and Posey tangled up together.

After a few seconds of awkward silence, Hornsby finally asks, "Why is your dick on Posey's knee?"

"Is that what that is?" Posey asks, glancing down. "Dude, congrats on the soft penis. Like a velvet cloud."

I kick at him. "Get the fuck away from me."

Chapter Eighteen

SILAS

In case you were wondering, there was no recovering from "Oye, my dick."

The text messages ran cold after that, and any chance we had at a nude pic vanished. Not that I wanted one. In a weird way, Posey did me a favor by writing "Oye, my dick" because I wanted to drive her away, and that about did it.

Now that I'm walking into my apartment, knowing she's here working out, I'm dreading every second of seeing her. She'll definitely give me shit for killing the buzz. But at least I'm not walking in here to a sexually charged Ollie, ready to pounce. Nope, she's probably as dry as the fucking Sahara Desert after oye, my dick. I think everyone is dry after that.

Not to mention, I can't get the feeling of my penis on Posey's knee out of my head.

I'm all sorts of fucked up, and I know the one thing that I need is some peace. And the place I find most peace is in the sauna.

After setting my bag and keys down in the entryway, I head to my bedroom, where I strip out of my clothes and wrap a towel around my waist. My mind immediately flashes to my penis and Posey's knee, and I mentally curse my disturbed brain.

I go to charge my phone just as a text lights up the screen. Wondering if it's Ollie, I click on it but see that it's Hornsby.

Hornsby: *I gave it an hour, but I can't fucking take it any longer . . . Taters and Posey were wrestling naked together, and I walked in on it. Taters's penis was on Posey's knee, and they both liked it.*

Jesus fucking Christ.

I pinch the bridge of my nose and take a few deep breaths. My phone dings, and I mentally prepare for what's to come.

Pacey: *Uh . . . what?*

Holmes: *Like . . . they were both naked?*

Posey: *NO! Taters was naked. I was respectful enough to put on underwears.*

Taters: *I was about to put on my briefs. Also, only a child calls it underwears, you nitwit.*

Posey: *Do you really want to call me names after what we went through together . . .*

Pacey: *It seems like there's meaning behind those ellipses.*

Hornsby: *There was meaning throbbing between the two of them on the ground.*

Taters: *Fuck off, there was no throbbing.*

Posey: *The eggplants beg to differ.*

Pacey: *What eggplants? Your eggplants?*

Holmes: *I'm really fucking confused.*

Hornsby: *I believe they were in the midst of a sexual tryst.*

Taters: *For the love of God.*

Posey: *HA! Taters wishes. He couldn't handle me.*

Hornsby: *Seems like he handled you just fine . . . owning you with his penis on your knee.*

Posey: *I will admit to the group, I thought his penis felt nice. Honestly, it's made me look at bologna in a different light.*

Holmes: *I can usually handle these text chains, but sorry, I'm out.*

Pacey: *Levi, I think you need help.*

Hornsby: *I keep hearing skin slapping together.*

Taters: *There was no fucking slapping!*

Posey: *Why do I hear it too?*

Taters: *That's it. I'm out too.*

I set my phone down and leave it on my nightstand as I exit my bedroom.

Sauna, that's what I need. I need the fucking sauna to clear my mind.

I glance through the window on the gym door, and when I see that Ollie isn't there, I heave a sigh of relief. Looks like oye, my dick really did scare her off. Pleased and also humiliated, I walk into the gym and head straight for the sauna, where I turn it on. I consider removing my towel but then think better of it, just in case Ollie shows up.

I take a seat and stretch my arms across the upper bench as the heat starts to seep into my skin.

This is exactly what I needed.

I shut my eyes, let out a deep breath, and then sink into my seat just as the door opens.

Fuck . . .

"Funny finding you here," Ollie says.

I slowly open my eyes and see her standing in front of me, a fresh soap smell coming off her, wrapped in a towel.

"Uh . . . hey," I say. "Get your, uh, workout in?"

"I did. And I took a shower but then thought, you know, I would love some sauna time."

"Well, if you want to be alone, I can leave."

She shakes her head. "No, you're exactly who I want in here." And then, she lets her towel loose, and it falls to her feet.

Hell . . .

Looks like oye, my dick didn't scare her at all.

My mouth goes dry from the sight of her—naked,

gorgeous, and so fucking perfect in every goddamn way. I'm useless. Completely and utterly useless as she walks up to me, leans forward, and presses a light kiss to my lips.

"Mmm, I missed these lips," she says as her hand touches my thigh. "And I missed the way you smell." She draws her hand inward. "And I missed the way it feels when you possess me with your voice." Her hand strokes along my bulge.

"Ollie," I groan.

"Tell me you don't like that," she says as she palms me.

Involuntarily, my legs slightly part.

"Making more room for me?" she asks as her thumb glides over my stiffening cock.

"Ollie . . . I . . ." Fuck, I can't think when she's stroking me over the towel like that.

"You what?" she asks as she rests one knee on the bench and brings her breasts up to my mouth. My lips part, and she gently places one of her nipples right on my lower lip.

I suck her in.

"Silas," she moans. "I love your mouth." She lifts up and brings her other leg to the bench, where she straddles my lap.

Immediately, my hands fall to her hips, where I keep her firmly in place.

"Tell me you love my tits."

I nibble on her nipple for one second only to remind myself not to give in. But . . . fuck, they're so perfect. "I love them," I admit.

"Good," she says as her hands fall to my shoulders, and she starts to lightly rock her hips over my lap.

Too good. Feels too fucking good.

My head falls back as I ask, "What are you doing?" It's a stupid question because I know exactly what she's doing.

"I'm not messing around anymore," she says as her hands climb up my pecs, her nails digging into my skin. "I'm voiding the contract. I don't want you as pretend anymore." She brings her hand to the back of my head and rubs her nipple along my lips. I part them and suck in the hard nub again. "I want you for real, as mine. I'm claiming you."

Claiming me.

It triggers this overwhelming need within me to be claimed. Something I desperately want. Something I realize suddenly . . . *Sarah never did.*

My hands float up her sides until I reach both of her breasts. I palm them and squeeze, causing her to hiss. "I'm not mentally ready for you," I say, speaking the fucking truth. I might want her, I might want to be claimed by her, but I don't think I can give her everything she needs.

"Let me help you be ready, Silas."

"I'm fucked up, Ollie." I bring her other breast into my mouth as her hips pick up their pace. Faster, harder. I exhale sharply as her pelvis teases me.

Taunts me.

Pushes me to want more even though my brain tells me to stop.

"Aren't we all a little fucked up?" she asks.

"I don't trust people," I groan out as I move my thumbs over her nipples.

"I'll earn your trust." She tips my head back and runs her tongue along my neck. "Let me be the one who takes care of you." Her tongue runs along my lips right before she kisses me again. I go to kiss her back, but she pulls away, leaving me wanting more. Her lips pepper kisses down my neck.

To my chest.

She slides off my lap between my legs.

She continues to press kisses to my stomach, then lower . .

.

Fuck me, I know what she wants. She's made it really fucking clear, and I'm not sure I'm ready because the moment her lips touch my cock, I know I'll be lost. There will be no stopping her.

What am I talking about? There's no stopping her now as

her hands slide up my thighs to the knot of my towel. Her hungry eyes glance up at me as her fingers toy with the knot. My breath is heavy in my chest as I curl my hands into fists in anticipation. When I don't stop her on the first tug, she smiles and parts my towel completely, letting my stiff cock stretch up my stomach.

Her eyes widen right before she wets her lips.

"Oh . . . my . . . God," she whispers as her fingers trail along my Jacob's ladder piercing. "I knew it." Her eyes are in awe as she moves her head closer. "I knew you would have the most perfect penis I've ever seen." And then, in one fell swoop, she licks from the base of my balls all the way up to the tip.

My stomach bottoms out from the onslaught of her delicious mouth, and a low moan falls past my lips. "Fuuuuck."

Satisfied with herself, she spreads my legs wider and tugs me closer to the edge as she opens her mouth and draws me in, all the way back to her throat.

"Jesus." Feels so fucking good.

Warm.

Wet.

Tight.

So good I can't stop her.

She could do whatever she wanted at this point.

One of her hands wiggles between my legs, just below my balls, where she cups them and gently rubs her thumb between them while her other hand squeezes the base of my cock.

"God, Silas. I could suck you all fucking day." She takes me deep again, pulls up, then dips down over and over.

She doesn't gag.

She doesn't even make a noise.

She just continues to make me lose my mind, one pulse after the other, and when I feel myself start to climb, she lifts to only the tip where she sucks but pumps the base with her hand.

"Fucking hell, Ollie. Your mouth is making me crazy."

Her teeth line the edge of my tip, and I hiss right before she laps at me with her tongue, then takes me to the back of her throat.

My hand floats to her hair, gripping it tightly because I have nothing else to grab. As she pumps up and down, making my balls tighten, I know that after this, nothing will be the same.

Her mouth is sinful.

Her hands are immoral.

I've never in my life had someone suck me like she does, and it's evident in the way that my chest hitches, attempting to find air. And by how I'm desperate to hold on to anything as I feel my body tremble, tingle, and prepare for what's to come.

She brings me to the back of her throat, then presses her lips around the head and sucks so goddamn hard that my pelvis flies off the wood seat of the sauna.

"Baby," I groan as my body tightens and my cock swells in her mouth. "I'm going to come."

Her mouth pulls off my cock, and I gasp in frustration. Her smile nearly makes me scream in a demand to have her finish what she started. She swirls her tongue around each one of my piercings until she reaches the tip again, sucks hard, pulling me to the edge. She deep-throats me again, and I explode.

My hand tightens in her hair. "Fuck. Your mouth . . . so . . . hot." And with that, I come down the back of her throat. She continues to suck me until I'm completely sated and resting against the back of the sauna, unable to move.

"Delicious," she says as she moves up my body, trailing kisses.

Bringing her body to a stand, she sets her foot on my seat and then props one of her legs on the bench behind me, bringing her soaking pussy right up to my mouth.

So fucking hot. She knows just what she wants, and she doesn't mind asking.

I glance up at her, and from where I'm sitting, I can see that she's in need of relief as well, so I slide my hand to the back of her ass, pulling her in closer, and press my tongue to her clit where I swipe long strokes, flattening my tongue so I reach every inch of her.

"I'm already so close," she says. "I love your cock, Silas. I want to suck it again."

That makes my tongue flick faster, more persistent. I want to make her come hard and fast.

Her hand falls to my head, and her fingers dig into my scalp, just like last night. Her tits bounce above me, her legs shake next to me, and her lungs search for air, just like mine.

"Silas," she gasps. "I'm close."

I bring two fingers to her entrance and curve them up inside her, causing her back to arch and for her to nearly lose her balance, but I catch her by the ass and stabilize her as I scoop my fingers and flick her clit.

"Oh . . . God . . . oh fuck. Silas!" she yells right before her body shivers, and a feral moan falls past her lips as she rides my fingers and tongue, pulling out every ounce of pleasure from her orgasm until she's completely done.

Watching her orgasm will never get old. Ever.

I remove my fingers, and with her eyes set on mine, I suck on them. Her heady eyes fall shut briefly as she lowers her leg and then carefully lowers herself to the ground.

Hand to her chest, eyes on me, she drifts backward to the wall of the sauna, putting just enough distance between us that I'd have to get up to pull her back onto my lap.

Skin red.

Sweat dripping down her chest.

Her eyes are wild as they scan me, taking me all in.

And as she heaves, staring me down, I know she's feeling

the same thing as I am. That was unlike anything we'd ever experienced.

I don't know if it freaks her out, but it creates a tsunami of concern in my head, and I can feel my brow crease as I think about how easily I could get attached to her and how easily she could break me.

She takes a few deep breaths, studying me, and then without a word, she bends down, picks up her towel, and wraps it around her body. With one final look, she opens the door and disappears.

What did I just do?

———

"SO . . ." Posey says as he comes up to me in the training room where I'm warming up my legs and rolling them out on a foam roller.

"So what?" I ask, grumpy as shit.

Why am I grumpy? Because yesterday, I had my cock sucked so hard I'm pretty sure I don't even remember my whole name. I realized that even though I want to control myself around Ollie, I can't seem to keep my distance. I'm scared. I'm unsure. And the one person I want to talk to is the person I'm terrified of.

Not to mention, I haven't heard from her since she left the sauna.

Not one goddamn word.

"How did yesterday end?"

"I'm not talking about this," I say.

Posey startles me as he sits next to me and leans in so close that I can smell his freshly applied deodorant. "It ended well, didn't it?"

"No." I push at him, but he remains unmoved.

"Liar." He smiles. "I've known you long enough to know

when you've had sex." He pokes my cheek, and I swat his hand away. "You had sex."

"Can you just leave me the fuck alone?"

"It was my texting, wasn't it?" He puffs his chest and cracks his fingers. "I've still got it."

"I didn't have sex," I say quietly and then whisper, "She just . . . sucked me in the sauna."

"Sucked you in the sauna." Posey shakes his head in mirth. "That is a title of a porn waiting to happen. Was it good?"

"Of course it was fucking good," I say. "I'm obsessed with the girl and everything about her."

"So why so grumpy?"

"Because I haven't talked to her since. I have no idea what's going on. I'm fucking terrified, and—"

"There you boys are," Sarah says as she walks through the doors of the training room. "I have a few things for you to sign that we're giving to important sponsors. You're the two I'm missing."

Of course she takes this moment to walk in here. This is the luck of my goddamn life. Teeth clenched, I avoid the low cut of her shirt and how she's purposely bending in front of me.

But the thing is . . . her appearance, her need to show off her tits, it does nothing for me. Absolutely nothing. The only emotion I feel when she's in the same room as me is anger.

Because of her, I don't trust people.

Because of her, I can't be the person I need to be for Ollie.

Which, in return, makes me despise her.

She hands me the pictures and a Sharpie, and while offering her the cold shoulder, I sign them.

"You were great the other night," she says, clearly not getting the hint. "I loved seeing you out on the ice again."

I cap the marker and toss it to Posey, who signs the pictures as well.

"Are you not going to say anything about my shirt?" she

asks, and when I look up, I see that she's wearing a shirt with my name and number.

"Why are you wearing that?" I ask.

A confused expression crosses her face. "Because I'm your number one fan."

It's comical how clueless she is.

"If you were my number one fan, you wouldn't have fucked other people when I was away. For months."

It's the first time I've said it out loud.

It's the first time I've truly acknowledged what she did to me.

And I know it's the first time Posey is hearing it.

"Silas," she says quietly.

I take the pictures from Posey and shove them at her. "They're signed. Now leave."

To her credit, she backs away slowly and then turns around to leave. Instead of my eyes falling to her retreating ass like they used to when we were dating, I go back to my foam roller, feeling Posey's eyes on me.

"Don't, man," I say, swallowing hard.

"I won't," he replies, understanding completely.

"And please . . . please don't say anything to anyone."

He grips my shoulder. "Your secret is safe with me, man. Promise."

━━━

SECOND GAME DONE. We brought home the win, and luckily, despite my personal life, I was able to forget it all when I was out on the ice. Scored a goal and had an assist. I've been known to bring my personal grievances into a game, but I just felt numb this go-around.

So fucking numb.

Like nothing from the outside world could penetrate me. Nothing.

Not Sarah.

Not Ollie.

Nothing.

But now that I'm driving home, all I can think about is how I want to see Ollie. How I want to talk to her about . . . everything. I want to know where her head is at. And I know I won't be able to get any sleep if I don't talk to her.

I drive over to her dorm, and instead of going up to her place, I park my car and grab my phone to shoot her a text.

Silas: *Hey, I'm outside your place.*

I let out a long sigh as I squeeze my eyes shut, wondering how the fuck I got here.

The plan I laid out for myself two years ago didn't have me sitting in a college dorm parking lot, pining after a girl I know I shouldn't while dodging my ex. My plan was to marry Sarah. To have kids. To buy a house and win some more goddamn championships. But for the past two years, it's felt as though nothing fits. As though I've been drifting. Yes, I know Sarah's infidelity has played a large part of that, but I should be fucking over it by now. And I am. Over Sarah. Even though I still feel angry. *Does that ever go away?* But now with Ollie in my life, it feels as though I'm almost grasping something really good, yet things are also falling apart, and there's nothing I can do about it. It wasn't supposed to be like this. I just don't understand it.

My phone dings with a response.

Ollie: *I'm not there. Ross and I took off for the weekend.*

What?

Fuck.

Silas: *When do you get home?*

Ollie: *Late Sunday.*

I rub my hand over my forehead and swear under my breath.

Silas: *We leave for some away games on Sunday.*

Ollie: *Oh. Okay . . . well, do you need me?*

Yes.

I need you here, so I can speak to you in person, so I can work out these tumultuous feelings buzzing inside me.

Silas: *No, I guess not.*

Ollie: *Cool. Well good luck on the away trip.*

I study her text, and I wonder what the fuck is going on. She's acting like nothing happened between us over the past few weeks—like I'm a mere acquaintance—yet she was determined she wanted more. What, now she doesn't? I don't know how to handle that.

I consider asking Posey, but I think we all know how that went last time. I need to get this off my chest. I need to talk it through, and even though I don't want to tell anyone else my issue, I know I probably don't have a choice. Not if I want my head on straight for the game.

I pull out of the parking lot and head for Pacey's place.

———

"ARE you fucking kidding me right now?" Pacey asks as he stands in his doorway, wearing nothing but a pair of boxer briefs.

I know exactly what he was planning on doing. It's what we all like to do after a game, when the adrenaline is still coursing through us. And I interrupted him.

"I'm sorry, man. But I really need to talk."

He must notice the slump in my shoulders and the defeat in my voice because his harsh expression softens, and he lets me in.

I kick off my shoes, and just as I look up, Winnie appears in a robe, her hair slightly messy.

Hell, I really did interrupt them.

"Sorry, Winnie," I say. "I didn't mean to interrupt anything."

"It's okay," she says softly. "What's going on?"

I pull on the back of my neck. "I need some advice."

"Okay, sure. Do you want me to get you a drink?"

"Nah, I'm good."

"Well then, come sit down."

We all take a seat in their living room. Winnie sits on Pacey's lap, and he loops his arm around her like the happy little couple that they are.

"What's going on?" Pacey asks. "Everything okay with Ollie?"

"Not really," I say and let out a deep breath. "Uh . . . Ollie and I aren't really together."

"What are you talking about?" Winnie asks.

"It was all fake. We met at a bar. She needed me, and I needed her, so we formed an agreement. Since Sarah started working at the Agitators, I thought it would be easier to pretend I was with someone than have you fuckers constantly ask how I'm doing, or have Sarah assume she could get back together with me."

"Jesus," Pacey mutters.

"Anyway, as you probably can see what's coming, I developed feelings for Ollie, and she developed feelings for me."

"Well, that's a good thing," Winnie says with a bright smile.

"It is when you have your head on straight. Unfortunately, that's not me, and I've been pushing her away. I'm just so fucked up from Sarah that I haven't been able to get over the feeling of distrust. All Ollie wants is for me to give her a piece of me, and I haven't been able to. And now . . . well, I think she's pulling away. She took off for the weekend, and I won't see her until we get back from our away trip. I feel like that's too goddamn long, and I don't know what to fucking do."

Pacey nods. "You like her, yeah?"

"Yeah," I answer. "And I fucking shouldn't. I mean, Jesus Christ, she's still in college. We're clearly in completely different phases of our life, but I can't stop thinking about her.

I want so much more when I'm around her, but my brain won't let me. It's like there's a mental block up there."

"Maybe because you never talked about what happened with Sarah," Pacey says quietly. "And I'm not asking you to tell us, but dude, how can you move on if you've never dealt with what put you in this headspace to begin with?"

"He's right," Winnie says softly. "It's not easy moving on from any kind of heartbreak, especially if you keep it inside you and never let it free."

"I know this, yet I'm so fucked up that I can't seem to get myself to talk about it."

"Are you afraid you're going to be judged?" Pacey asks.

"Maybe. I also don't want to revisit it. I mean, fuck, Pacey, I was going to propose to her."

"I know, man," he says. "But it might be good to get it off your chest."

"Have you told Ollie everything that happened?" Winnie asks.

I shake my head. "I haven't told anyone."

"Maybe you should tell her," Winnie suggests.

"That would mean that I'm committing myself to her."

"Isn't that what you want?" Pacey asks.

"I mean, I want her, but I . . ." I swallow hard. "I just don't think I'm good enough. I don't think I'll be what she needs. And then what? I end up in the same position I'm in now? And she's going places. She has a future in front of her. I'm not going to thwart that with the restrictions of hockey life."

"Who says it needs to be thwarted?" Winnie asks. "I do my own thing, and I'm still able to be with Pacey and work on our relationship. We might have ups and downs, but we still make time for each other. Our schedule might revolve around hockey, but our life doesn't."

"I don't know . . ."

"Let me ask you this," Pacey says. "How would you feel if

you called her up tonight and ended things with her? Just called it all off."

I consider the idea. No more visits to her dorm. No more teasing. No more of her sweet, mind-melting kisses. No more witty text messages.

"Like shit," I answer.

"Then there's your answer. You might be scared, doubtful, and not ready, but you're also not ready to let her go. What's going to be more fulfilling? Navigating through a new relationship together? Or suffering apart?"

He makes sense. I'd rather be with her.

"But what happens when I tell her about Sarah, and she doesn't want to be with me? I don't think I could take it."

"That's not going to happen," Winnie says.

"How do you know?" I ask.

"Because I've seen the way she looks at you. I saw how she reacted when you kissed her outside the locker room. I'm honestly shocked that you said you've been faking it because nothing about her reactions around you is fake. That girl likes you . . . a lot, Silas, and I think she's ready to be there for you in any capacity. She's not going to scare easily."

"You really think so?" I ask, feeling so insecure that I actually hate myself for it.

"Yes, I really think so," she answers, then leans forward and places her hand on my knee. "You're a good man, Silas. A caring, thoughtful, protective, loyal man and you shouldn't be living in Sarah's shadow any longer. Don't let her take away a good thing in your life. Because if you don't go after Ollie . . . Sarah wins."

Chapter Nineteen

OLLIE

"What do you think? Please don't lie to me," I say to Ross as we hang out in the hotel we're staying in for the weekend. One of the companies Ross worked with closely over the summer gave him a free staycation trip. So we're staying in a very fancy hotel in Vancouver for the weekend.

"I think Roberts is going to hate them all."

"Ugh," I groan. "But I need to turn in something to him this weekend. I'm already behind."

"Maybe because you've been consumed with sticking your tongue down a certain hockey player's throat instead of asking him questions."

"Can you even blame me?"

"No." Ross shakes his head. "I really can't."

"What the hell am I going to do, Ross?"

"Well, I can tell you one thing, he won't want to hear about snacks at a hockey game."

"The nachos were phenomenal, though. That seems like a Vancouver secret."

"I'm not denying the quality of nachos we had at the game, but I am questioning your sanity. Roberts won't give you credit for your internship if you turn in an article about nachos when he wants an in-depth article on the Agitators organization."

"Yeah, well, I have zero information regarding the Agitators other than they treat their families and players with respect."

"So maybe go with that," Ross suggests. "It might not be what Roberts wants, but it's a twist on the story. You could start it off with how intimidating the organization is, but you were surprised to find they were nothing but welcoming, especially to a newcomer."

"Yeah, that could work," I say, my mind starting to turn with ideas.

"See, that's what I'm here for," Ross says as he tugs on the lapels of the hotel-provided robe he's wearing and then sips champagne from his champagne flute like a freaking king.

"You're really living up this moment, aren't you?" I ask as I set my computer to the side and lie on my stomach across my bed.

"I don't ever get sent gifts, so yes, I'm going to soak it all up."

"I feel like you're still on a high from being with Ian Rivers."

Ross smirks. "That too."

"Have you heard from him?"

"I have. He texted me this morning and asked how I was."

"How cute," I say. "Are you planning on meeting up again?"

"He wants to take me out on a date when they return from their away trip. I told him I'd love to." Ross stares up at the ceiling. "He has easily the nicest body I've ever seen."

I think Silas could give him some competition, but that's just me.

"Well, I'm glad you went for it." My phone lights up next to me, and I see it's from Silas.

I swipe open the text.

Silas: *Can we talk?*

I twist my lips to the side, concerned.

"What's that look for?" Ross says.

"Silas wants to talk."

"So talk."

"I don't think I'm ready."

"What do you mean?" Ross asks as he wets the rim of his champagne flute with his tongue.

I sit up and cross my legs on the bed. "Okay, so I went to his place yesterday to work out. I knew he was going to come home, so I took a shower and found him in the sauna. Well, let's just say, things happened in there."

"What kind of things?"

I run my finger over the comforter and say, "I gave him head, and then he returned the favor."

"You saw his penis?" Ross turns toward me now, fully invested. "I won't ask for details, just tell me . . . was it pierced?" I nod, and Ross groans. "God, that's so hot."

"So hot, but when we were done, I saw this almost dead look in his eyes."

"Really?" Ross asks. "What do you mean?"

"Like . . . he was upset that I seduced him, and I don't know, it made me feel awful. Like, I assumed that once he finally had a taste of me, he'd give in to his feelings, but instead, he looked upset, pensive. I don't know, I think I messed things up, and him wanting to talk is him wanting to call everything off."

"Ah, I see," Ross says. "Well, there's only one way to find out."

"Yeah, but I don't want to find out. I just want to lie here, drink champagne, and believe I'm not about to get my heart ripped out of my chest."

"You like him that much?" Ross asks.

I flop on my back and nod. "Yes, I like him that much."

—

SILAS: *I know you're busy with Ross, but I'd really like to talk with you.*

I stare down at the text, my chest twisting in pain, my gut churning with uncertainty. Ross is currently taking a bath, enjoying every aspect of our suite as I sit here with a computer on my lap, attempting to write a story that I know Roberts will reject.

Knowing I need to text Silas back, I pick up my phone.

Ollie: *Maybe we just save the conversation for when you get back.*

I set my phone down but immediately see that he's texting back, so I pick it back up.

Silas: *I can't wait to have this conversation.*

My lip trembles as I stare up at the ceiling. Dammit. Yup, he wants to break things off.

I'm so stupid.

The sauna idea was so stupid.

Pushing him too hard was so stupid.

Because look where it's gotten me. Instead of slowly trying to win him over and make him feel comfortable, I've created chaos in his life, and now he wants to get rid of that chaos.

Ollie: *Well, I'm busy at the moment. Maybe we can talk later, okay?*

I flip my phone face down and ignore the buzz from his text as I focus on my article. Come on, be intelligent, Ollie. Write something intelligent.

Don't focus on the fact that Silas is about to destroy your heart.

299

———

"I COULD GET USED TO THIS," Ross says as he picks up another Danish from the Danish basket. "Room service was created by someone who loves people, truly, from the depth of their souls loves people. Who doesn't like to laze about their room, with an impeccable view, I might add, and eat pastries from a basket?"

Taking a sip of my coffee, I offer him a smile.

I got no sleep last night—absolutely none. I received a few more text messages from Silas, but I left them unanswered because I honestly can't handle the emotions swirling through me. I've done everything, and I mean everything, to get this man to give in to his feelings and give me a chance, but I've failed every step of the way, and that's . . . that's embarrassing.

I honestly thought I had a chance at being with him, that I could change his mind, but at the end of the day, when it all comes down to him letting go of his past and moving forward with me, he won't do it.

And I know he doesn't like Sarah anymore—he's told me that several times—but she still controls him. She still has the upper hand, and I can't compete with that. I'll never be able to.

I just don't want to hear him tell me that we're done. I'll be crushed, and I'm not sure I'm ready for that.

"You know, I can see that you're trying to act like everything is okay, but I can tell it's not," Ross says.

"I don't want to talk about it. I feel like that's what we've been doing the entire time we've been here."

"Because you've had a sour face the entire time. Look at the cart in front of us, Ollie. There's a freaking pastry basket right there. It's our dream, and you're sad."

I hug my pillow to my chest. "It's because I'm sad."

"Maybe you should talk to him."

"And what, have him tell me it's over?"

"Wouldn't it be better than living in this limbo? At least if he does break it off, I can invest in a pastry basket to go so we can eat our feelings."

I lightly smile. "Very true."

My phone dings with a text, and I know it's Silas. On a heavy sigh, I open it up, but instead of a text from him, it's from Winnie. Why is she texting me?

Winnie: *Hey, I know you're away right now, and I really don't want to get into people's business, but Silas is really trying to talk to you, and I think you need to hear him out. They're leaving in an hour.*

I sit taller and stare down at the message.

"What is it?" Ross asks.

"It's Winnie, Pacey's fiancée. She said Silas really needs to talk to me." I press my hand against the necklace he gave me. "What if he has something important to tell me? What if something happened to him? I don't think she'd text me if he was going to break up with me. Do you?"

"That would be pretty shitty if she did."

I type back a text.

Ollie: *He does? Is he okay?*

Winnie: *He just really needs to have a conversation with you. If you want, I can give you the address of their private airport.*

Ollie: *Please, I'd love that.*

I hop off the bed and run to the bathroom, where I flip on the shower.

"I'm assuming you're going to go talk to him?" Ross asks from the bedroom.

"Yes, but first, I need to get this stink off me."

———

ALL I'M GOING to say is thank God for Winnie because there is no way I'd be able to get through the gates of this airport without her calling ahead and making arrangements. Even at that, as I sit here in the front reception, I have a security guard watching my every move. It's incredibly uncomfortable knowing at any moment, he'd have no problem tackling me to the ground and dragging me out of here by the foot.

I felt bad leaving Ross, but he told me he had no issue. He was going to take one more bath before he checked out, and having some alone time was just what he needed since, apparently, I brought down the climate.

I told him I owed him big time, packed my stuff, and quickly skirted out of the hotel.

I wish I had more time to fix my hair and makeup, but I didn't want to miss Silas. So I went with a fresh face, hair in a high ponytail, and I'm wearing his hoodie and a pair of leggings. I easily could pass off as a fangirl . . . hence the security.

As my foot bounces up and down, waiting for Silas, a few players trickle in. No one that I know, though. I feel like I maybe saw Holmes, but I can't be sure.

I check the time on my phone and glance around, hoping Silas comes soon. He hasn't texted this morning, which makes me believe he gave up, and I don't blame him. You can only text a person so many times before you realize they don't want to talk.

The door opens, and Pacey walks in, followed by Hornsby . . . and Silas. I stand from the chair I've been waiting in, and my mouth goes dry as he glances up and spots me.

He stutters to a stop as he tries to understand what I'm doing here. Pacey sees me too, so he offers to take Silas's bags. Silas hands them off, and then, looking so good in a three-piece suit, he walks over to me.

"Hey," I say as a greeting.

"Ollie." He sounds breathless. "What are you doing here?"

"Uh, well, you said you needed to talk, so here I am."

"I wanted to talk last night," he says.

"I know, but I was, uh, just not up to it."

He glances over his shoulder. "Yeah, well, I'm not going to have this conversation here."

Oh God! He *did* want to break up with me. And here I am, like a freaking fool, thinking that it's something else. Of course he doesn't want to break up with me in the middle of the airport reception area. No one wants a crying person in public.

"Right." I try to smile, but my lips tremble, deceiving me. "I get it." My eyes water. Dammit, Ollie, hold it together. "We can just, uh . . ." A tear floats down my cheek, and I quickly swipe it away. "We can talk when you get back."

I turn to walk away, but he steps in front of me, his hand on my stomach. "Ollie, wait." He lifts my chin. "Why are you crying?"

I will my tears to stop as I hold back my emotions, my throat feeling so thick with emotion that it makes it hard to speak. So softly, I say, "I know . . ." I clear my throat. "I know you want to end our agreement, okay? I'm just . . . I'm not handling it well."

I swipe at my eyes again.

"What makes you think that?" he asks.

I look around and notice no one is near us, so I say, "I saw it in your eyes the other day, Silas. You don't want this, and that's okay. I get it. Does it hurt because I really like you? Yes, but it's something I can get over." I try to walk away again, but he stops me.

"I don't want you to get over it," he says softly. "I don't want you to get over me."

"What?" I ask, surprised.

"Ollie." He cups my face and runs his thumb over my tear-soaked cheeks. "I wanted to talk because . . . because I don't want this to be an agreement anymore. I want us to be real."

Hope springs in my chest as more tears fill my eyes. This time, they're tears of joy. "Really?"

"Yes, but I need to work through some things." He wipes away another tear. "Did you think this whole time I was going to call things off?"

I nod, feeling foolish.

"Ollie, come here." He pulls me into his strong chest and wraps his arms around me. He lowers his head and speaks closely to my ear. "I'm losing my mind over you. There's no way I could just end it."

I cry into his chest as he holds me.

"I'm sorry it's taken me so long to get here," he whispers again. "But I don't see a situation where I don't try to make this work for us. I just . . . I just need to talk to you."

I glance up at him and run my finger over the scruff on his jaw. "I'm sorry I didn't answer your texts. I was so sick to my stomach."

"I'm not going anywhere, baby. Okay?"

I nod and then lift on my toes, pressing a kiss to the bottom of his mouth. He cups the back of my head and angles my jaw for better access to my mouth. Before I know what's going on, his lips are on mine, and his tongue swipes against mine. I grip his suit coat as I let him take me for a ride, his mouth doing all the work.

It's delicious.

It's meaningful.

Nothing about this kiss is dead.

It's full of passion and everything I'd ever want when it comes to this man.

When he slowly pulls away, he cups my head and hugs me one more time. "Fuck, I wish I didn't have to leave."

"Me too." I smooth my hands over his chest. "Will you call me when you land?"

"Yeah, babe . . . will you answer?" He lifts a brow at me, and I chuckle while nodding.

"Promise."

"Good." He kisses me one more time and sighs. "I have to go."

"Okay, safe trip. Text, call, FaceTime, send me nudes . . . all of the above."

"You do the same," he says and offers me one more kiss before taking off. He steps away, glances over his shoulder, and smirks at me.

Be still my heart . . . he's so freaking sexy. When he's out of sight, the security guard comes up to me with an expectant look on his face.

I turn toward the exit and say, "See, I told you I wasn't lying."

"All right, move it along."

SILAS: *Hey.*

Ollie: Is that really going to be your opening line?

Silas: It was going to be "send me a picture."

Ollie: Aren't you on the plane?

Silas: Yes, but we can still text.

Ollie: Oh, I see, so what you're trying to tell me in a not-so-subtle way is that you miss me and can't wait until you land to communicate.

Silas: Basically.

Ollie: Well, I will have you know, I sobbed in my car when I left the airport.

Silas: Why?

Ollie: Because I'm happy and mad at myself for not talking to you yesterday. I could have spent the night with you. Instead, I spent the night in fear, my stomach twisting in knots.

Silas: If it helps, I felt the same way.

Ollie: Can I ask you something?

Silas: *Ask me anything.*

Ollie: *In the sauna, were you mad at me?*

Silas: *Was I mad at you? Are you fucking kidding? Ollie, that was . . . fuck, I still think about your mouth on my cock.*

Ollie: *But afterward, you seemed angry. I was afraid I pushed you too hard.*

Silas: *I wasn't angry, and if I was, I was probably angry with myself for giving in when I've been so determined to hold back.*

Ollie: *Are you sure?*

Silas: *Positive. I wanted you to stay.*

Ollie: *Why didn't you stop me?*

Silas: *Something we can talk about later. Can I FaceTime you tonight? I really need to get some shit off my chest.*

Ollie: *Yes, call anytime.*

Silas: *Thanks.*

Ollie: *Can I tell you something?*

Silas: *Yes.*

Ollie: *You have the nicest cock I've ever seen, and I've watched a lot of porn.*

Silas: *LOL.*

Ollie: *Seriously, I dream about it. I want my mouth on it again.*

Silas: *Babe, you're going to make me hard on the plane.*

Ollie: *I'm just telling you the truth. I loved every second of sucking your dick, and I want to do it again.*

Silas: *Christ.*

Ollie: *Miss you already.*

Silas: *Miss you.*

SILAS: *Finally in our hotel.*

Ollie: *Call me whenever, just in my room.*

I've thought about this conversation all night and what he might say, what we might talk about. I've even tried to figure out what I should wear, which seems so stupid because it's a phone conversation, but I feel nervous.

I decided to opt for his sweatshirt and keep things the way he left me, but I'm cuddled into the weighted blanket he gave me, surrounded by the scent of his cologne.

My phone rings, and I quickly answer it, holding it in front of me.

His handsome face appears, and I feel everything in my body relax.

"Hey," I say softly.

"Hey, babe," he says as he lies on his hotel pillow.

"How was the flight?"

"Fine."

"Where are you right now?"

"Las Vegas," he answers.

"Ooo, are the boys headed out on the town?"

"Probably some of the guys. Most of us are tucked into our rooms."

"Run across any women trying to claw their way into your bed?"

"There were some in the lobby, but security doesn't let them up. You need a key card to get up to the rooms. And you realize you don't have to worry about that with me."

"I know," I answer. "I just find the whole thing fascinating. Life of a professional athlete, it's a different world." I pause and say, "Hey, that might be a good article to write. Would you mind that? If I wrote about your general grind and commitment to play your sport?"

"No, that's fine. We've had articles written about us along the same lines."

"That's not getting too close to comfort for you?" I ask.

"Not at all. Roberts might like it."

"Better than my nacho idea." I sigh. "I've been struggling with this article, and Roberts has been harping on me for a first draft. I've pushed him as far as I think I can go when it comes to extra time. I started writing something about how welcoming the Agitators are, but there wasn't much meat to it. I think I could work with this."

"Feel free to ask me anything."

"Thank you. I appreciate that." I get comfortable on my bed. "So . . . what do you want to talk about?"

"Us," he answers.

"What about us?"

He rolls his teeth over his bottom lip and says, "This would have been easier in person, but I really need to just . . . to just say it."

"Okay," I say, listening intently. "I promise, whatever you have to say, it's safe with me."

"Thank you, baby," he says softly, then looks away. It takes him a few seconds, but he finally says, "I was going to propose to Sarah." Oh, this is the conversation he wanted to have. Well, now I feel like an even bigger ass because it *would* have been better in person. "I thought she'd be the girl I spent the rest of my life with." I know this, so I just nod. "And I had a ring picked out and everything. After a game one night, I came home, looking for her." His eyes dart to the side, and I can tell this is really hard on him.

"It's okay, Silas," I say. "Take your time."

"I came home and found her in our bedroom with another woman and a man watching them."

My breath freezes in my lungs as I try to comprehend what he's saying. Sarah cheated on him . . . with another woman and a man?

"Oh my God, Silas. I'm so sorry." No wonder he has trust issues. How can I not feel for this man?

He drags his hand down his face and whispers, "Fuck, I've never said that out loud before."

"I can understand why. That must have been so hard on you."

"It was," he says. "I was . . . I was devastated. We rarely

had sex, especially toward the end of our relationship, and now I knew why. I just keep wondering, how long was she cheating on me? She suggested it definitely wasn't the first time she'd cheated. So how long was I the idiot who didn't know what she was doing when I was gone? She said four months, but fuck, I don't believe her."

"Have you asked her?"

He shakes his head. "No, probably best that I don't fucking know. It will only make me angrier. And I'm trying to release this anger. I want to be able to be healthy for you, Ollie, that's why I'm telling you this, why it's been so hard for me to open up to you, to let you in."

Yeah, she stole his trust and made it impossible for him to put himself out there again. I don't know how someone recovers from a situation like that.

"I get it. And I'm so sorry Sarah put you through that. She didn't deserve you, and she proved that. I don't have much to say that will be helpful other than I'll be patient with you. I'll give you time. I promise I won't push, and I'm sorry I pushed before."

"I'm glad you did," he says. "Or else I never would have let you in. You pushing has helped me move past this fear I've been holding on to."

"What fear is that?" I ask.

"That maybe I don't deserve anyone. That something is wrong with me. That I'm not loveable, and that's why Sarah cheated on me."

"Silas." I sit up. "Please don't believe that, not even for a second. Because the man I've grown to know is worthy of everyone around him. He's loyal and protective and so fucking loveable. The people who hurt us are the people who are hurting inside. They hurt others because they don't know how to deal with their hurt. Sarah is the one in the wrong. She's the one who isn't worthy or loveable, not you."

He doesn't say anything, just stares off to the side.

"Did you hear me?"

"Yes," he answers. "Fuck." He rubs his eye with his palm. "I'm sorry."

"What are you sorry for?"

"For not being strong enough."

"You can't be perfect all the time, Silas. No human is. The best thing about us as humans is just how imperfect we are. It shows how we've survived, how we've journeyed through life. It gives us wisdom and practice for how to protect our future. There is no need to always be strong, especially with me."

His eyes connect with mine through the phone, and I can see how much tension has eased from them. "How are you so fucking smart?" Because for the first eighteen years of my life, my grandma made sure to tell me that. That every setback brings about growth. Endurance. Even though my dad tried to tell me otherwise.

"All my years of being told I won't amount to anything," I say. "You quickly learn how to drown out the hate and build on it instead."

"I'm good at drowning out the hate and using it as fuel on the ice."

"That's different. Sports are different. That's physical. What Sarah did to you, that's emotional, and being emotionally vulnerable is harder than shooting a puck past a goalie." I wet my lips. "But I'm so glad you shared with me, Silas. It means more to me than anything, and I promise, this stays between us."

"Thank you." He pauses and then asks, "Does all of this make you look at me differently?"

"Yes," I answer. "But probably not in the way that you're thinking. It makes me fall for you even more. Because now you've let me see a piece of your heart. I see your warmth. Your fear. It makes you more human, and I love that. If anything, you're even more sexy than before."

That causes him to smirk. "If that was even possible."

"Oh my God." I roll my eyes, causing him to laugh.

"In all seriousness, babe, thank you. It will take me a second to process all of this, and I can't promise it'll be easy. I'm still struggling with trust. I still have that deep-rooted fear of opening up to others, so I'll need you to be patient with me."

"I'll be patient, Silas, because you're worth it."

Chapter Twenty

SILAS

Silas: *What are you up to?*

Ollie: *I'm in class right now, pretending to take notes on my computer. In reality, I'm texting you and looking through an article about the type of training you do.*

Silas: *Why read an article when you can ask me?*

Ollie: *I can't just have one source. It's good to have multiple. Also, I'm bored out of my mind and didn't know what you were doing, so this was an easy thing to do to keep my mind sharp.*

Silas: *Keeping your mind sharp should include paying attention in class.*

Ollie: *Uh-huh, and how often did you pay attention?*

Silas: *Often enough.*

Ollie: *For some reason, I don't buy it. I feel like you fucked around a lot.*

Silas: *Nah, I liked learning about muscles and shit. It was the gen-ed classes that nearly destroyed me.*

Ollie: *A waste of time if you ask me. No geography class would convince me to change my major. That's for damn sure.*

Silas: *It was English lit for me.*

Ollie: *Was it because they weren't reading Harry Potter?*

Silas: *Pretty much.*

Ollie: *What are you doing?*

Silas: *Just got done warming up my legs. Now watching Posey eat a bologna sandwich, and I'm utterly disgusted.*

Ollie: *I think he needs a woman.*

Silas: *I think there might be one, but I can't be sure. Ever since the bar, he's been a bit off.*

Ollie: *You mean "oye, my dick" off?*

Silas: *I'm so fucking glad I told you that was Posey.*

Ollie: *I'm still on the fence about that.*

"HOW ARE THINGS WITH OLLIE?" Pacey asks quietly as we sit on the bus, heading back to our hotel. We're staying an extra night in Vegas, then traveling to Arizona tomorrow morning.

"Good. I, uh, I told her everything that happened with Sarah."

"How did she handle it?"

"Really well. It felt like a weight was being lifted off my shoulders."

"So you feel better? You're going for it?"

My phone buzzes in my hand with a text message from her.

"Yeah. She makes me feel good. She oddly makes me feel whole."

"That's good, man," Pacey says. "I can feel your relief. I feel like you've been carrying around this heavy weight for the past few years, and now it seems like you're not alone in carrying it."

"I'm not," I say as I glance down at her text.

Ollie: *Congrats on the win. Call me when you get to the hotel.*

—

"DO YOU ALWAYS WIN THIS MUCH?" Ollie asks as she lies in front of her phone. She told me she got a tripod to hold her phone so she doesn't have to hold it while she talks to me. And from the view I have down her sports bra, I agree it was an amazing purchase.

"We're champions, babe. That's what we do."

"Ooo, look at you all cocky."

"You have to be, or else you're eaten alive out there on the ice."

"This might be a stupid question, but have you gotten in any fights?"

"More than I can probably remember. It always happens. Tension runs high during games, and hockey is already a physical sport."

"Well, I don't like that. I don't want to see you get hurt."

"To get hurt, you have to lose the fight. I don't lose."

"You're oddly turning me on."

"Yeah?" I ask with a lift of my brow.

"Yeah, but it could also be from sitting here, staring at you without a shirt on. Seriously, Silas, your body is incredible."

"Thanks, babe."

"And I haven't been able to properly explore it the way that I want to." She playfully pouts.

"Whose fault is that?"

"Yours," she says in an accusing tone. "If you had opened up a little sooner, you'd already know what it feels like to be inside me."

"Babe, don't torture me."

"You realize I love sex, right? I love the feeling of an orgasm, and I haven't had many delivered by men. Yonny is the only other guy who's been inside me. And he wasn't super into anything, not even my mouth."

"I would give up my entire savings to have your mouth on my cock right now."

"Me too," she says while she wets her lips. "God, I'm so on edge right now. I need you, Silas." She sits up and lifts her sports bra over her head, revealing her tits.

"Fuck . . . me," I say, my dick growing hard in seconds.

"Nothing feels right when you're not here." She grips her breasts and pinches her nipples. "Nothing feels the same. Now that I know what it feels like when you give me an orgasm, I can't even do it properly for myself."

"Do you need some help?"

"Yes," she says.

"Then strip. Strip down to nothing and spread your legs in front of the camera. I want to see that wet cunt."

"God," she moans as she strips out of her sweatpants and then rests on a pillow and angles her body so I can see her face, her sexy tits, and her pussy. Her legs are completely spread.

"Babe, that's so fucking hot."

"Tell me what to do, please. Make me come, Silas."

Seeing how much she needs it, how much we both need it, I say, "I want you to glide your fingers up and down your body and around your breasts without touching your nipples." When she starts moving her hands, I say, "Just like that, baby. Slower, I want you to feel how soft your skin is."

"I want it to be you touching me."

"Soon, Ollie, but just pretend it's me. Know how much I want those tits in my mouth, how I want to suck, squeeze, and pinch them. I want to lick them, bring them into my mouth, and spend hours worshipping them." Her breath grows rapid. "Glide your fingers closer to your pussy, tease yourself the way I'd tease you. Get close to your slit but don't touch yourself."

Her hand lowers and, when she gets close enough, her

pelvis lifts. "Don't fucking touch that cunt. It's mine." She groans and drags her hand back up her body. "That's it, baby, I'll let you know when you can touch yourself."

"Don't make me wait."

"Don't tell me how to make you come," I snap.

Her teeth roll over her bottom lip, and a slight smirk passes over that beautiful mouth of hers.

"Spread your legs more." When she does, I say, "Run your fingers along your inner thighs. But don't touch your pussy."

She brings her hands down to her thighs, her fingers dragging over her velvet skin.

"Make circles so close to your pussy that you can feel yourself get wetter and wetter with each pass."

Her nipples pucker, and her body starts to tighten as she looks for that touch.

"Fuck, you make me so hard," I say as I slide my briefs down and grip my cock.

"Let me see," she says, looking up at the phone.

I point the phone at my erection, and she moans as her fingers slide close to her pussy.

"Don't fucking touch yourself, Ollie."

"I'm not," she says, her voice distressed.

"Then lay your hands by your side."

"Silas, please."

"Do it."

She releases herself and just lies there, stark naked, legs spread.

"Fuck, just look at you. I wish I was there, eating that wet pussy. Sucking on your clit, driving my dick so hard inside you that you can practically taste my cum in the back of your throat."

Her chest rises and falls, her hands itch at her side, and she wets her lips.

"Silas, I need more."

I pump at my cock. "Pinch your nipples, baby. Make yourself moan."

Her hands go straight to her breasts, and she plays with them, moaning, saying my name, calling out with every pinch. My cock grows thicker in my hand.

"My dick is so hard, Ollie. Shit . . ." I pump harder. "Finger yourself. I need to see you pleasure yourself."

"Finally," she says as she slides two fingers against her clit, and she starts making small circles. "Oh fuck," she yells. "Silas, I'm so wet. Oh my God."

"That's it, baby, keep up the pace. I need you to match my strokes. Pinch your nipple too. I want you to mark yourself." My hand is frantic on my dick now, precum sliding down the side. "Jesus, I'm right there."

"Me too. Oh fuck, Silas . . . oh my God." Her body tenses, her legs fall open even more, and her hand moves so fast that it sends a hot wave of heat over me as I watch Ollie pleasure herself. It's such a goddamn turn-on that in seconds, my cock swells, and my chest fills with a sense of euphoria.

"Fuck, I'm coming," I say right before I fall over the edge, my cum traveling up my stomach.

"Me . . . too," she says. I watch her entire body spasm as her body shudders with pleasure. "Silas," she says. My name coming from her mouth sounds so sweet.

When she finally catches her breath and looks up at me, she has a semi-satisfied look on her face. "I want you, Silas, when you get home. I need you."

"I need the same thing," I say.

She sits up and takes the phone in her hand, bringing it so only her beautiful face is in view. "Will you take me out on a date?"

"I will."

"Will you let me sleep over at your place?"

"It will be a requirement."

She smiles. "Is this what it's going to be like? When you're gone, this is what we do?"

"I sure as fuck hope so," I answer.

"Good, because I can manage this."

BAG AT MY SIDE, I roll it off the elevator and toward my apartment. We had a two-game stint out on the road, which is nice, starting off easy. We remain undefeated, which is an even better start to the season than prior seasons. It seems as though we're all clicking on the ice, and Coach is very happy about it.

On the flight home, I saw Posey sitting in anguish, and I tried to ask him what was going on, but he wouldn't say anything. I wonder if that's why he got in a fight during our game. Something must be bothering him, but none of us can tell what it is.

I'm sure he'll speak soon. He always does.

When I reach my apartment door, I unlock it and then swing it open, only to find Ollie sitting on the couch, watching TV. When her head whips around to look at me, the most beautiful smile I've ever seen greets me.

This.

This is what I've missed.

Coming home to someone. Someone eager to see me.

I set my bag to the side and shut the door just as she comes running up to me. She leaps into my arms, wraps her legs around my waist, and plasters her lips to mine.

Probably the best welcome home I've ever received. "Oh my God, you smell good," she says as her lips move across mine. "I missed you."

I spin us around and pin her against the door. "I missed you too," I say, running my hand through her hair as my lips move over hers. "Fuck, I missed you."

She releases me and pulls my shirt that she's wearing over her head, leaving her completely bare up top.

"Hell," I mutter as I grip her breast tightly in my palm. "I can't wait. I need to be inside you."

"I need you, too."

So with my girl in my arms, I walk us back to my bedroom, and I lay her on top of my bed, then reach for her sweats and pull them down, revealing a tiny black thong. I tear it right off her and then strip out of my hoodie and shirt and let them fall to the floor. Her eyes fall over my chest as her hand goes between her legs, where she starts massaging herself.

"Are you on birth control?" I ask her.

"Yes," she answers.

"Can I fuck you bare?"

Her voice catches in her throat, and she nods. "Y-Yes."

My spine tingles with anticipation, and I shed my jeans and socks, only to sit on the edge of the bed and lie all the way back, my cock stretching up my stomach.

"Ride me," I say. "But don't let me penetrate you. I want to see just how slick that pussy is." I scoot back toward the headboard as she straddles my legs. I take her tits in my hands as she lowers her pussy over my cock. "Ride those piercings, baby."

Her eyes turn hungry. She connects her body to mine, and her head falls back in ecstasy as she slowly moves her slick center over my cock.

"Oh my God, Silas, this feels . . . this feels incredible."

"You feel incredible," I say as she falls forward. Bringing her breast into my mouth, I focus on her areola and nipple, swirling around them with my tongue, flicking and then nibbling just enough that she sucks in a sharp breath of air. With my hand, I do the same thing to her other breast as she continues to rock on me.

"I can come just like this," she says, her hands falling to

my chest, her pelvis lifting just slightly to get a better angle. "Fuck, I'm already close."

"Then come. Use me, fuck me like this. Make your voice hoarse."

Her lips roll together, her eyes squeeze shut, and her pace picks up, her thrusts becoming harder, deeper. So aroused, so wet, she doesn't stop. Her body flushes, her stomach hollows out, and I watch as she tightens only to let loose.

"Fuck!" she yells as her body undulates over mine, over and over again, riding her orgasm out until there is nothing left to take, and then she collapses on top of me. I roll her over to her back and lower my head between her legs where I press my tongue to her nub, causing her to jerk in response. I press again, seeing how sensitive she is, and when she widens her legs, I flick my tongue against her clit. She moans, her back arching, her arm falling over her eyes as her body twists and writhes. "I can't, I can't come again."

"Relax, baby," I say, and she loosens up. I take that moment to drag my tongue slowly over her slit. Once, twice, three times.

Her breath catches.

Her mouth falls open.

And in seconds, she's falling apart against my tongue as well, her moans creating such need that when she's fully sated, I flip her over to her stomach, take a pillow, and shove it under her pelvis to keep her propped up.

I smooth my hand over her tight ass and give it a hard slap, loving the way she moans and the echo of her skin filling the air.

"Your ass is perfect," I say, sliding my fingers down her crack. "Have you ever been fucked here?"

She shakes her head. "N-No."

"You will be," I say, slapping her ass again. "Now that you're mine . . . your entire body is mine to fuck with. Got it?"

"Yes," she says as her hands curl into the comforter.

"But I need this pussy."

I move my thumb over her arousal, swirling it around her entrance, and position my cock where I want it. I'm so goddamn ready for this that I can't take a breath before I start sliding inside.

"Fuck, this pretty pink hole is so goddamn tight." I pause, catching my breath. "Babe . . ."

She feels like a virgin. I can barely get myself inside.

"I need you to relax."

"I am relaxed," she says. "Just push, Silas. I'm fine, I promise."

Gritting my teeth, I push in harder and slide in a few inches. "Mother . . . fucker," I grind out, my cock ready to explode from how tight and warm she is.

"More," she says, bucking her hips against me.

I can't deny her what she wants, so I push deeper into her until I bottom out, fully inside.

"Jesus, are you okay?" I ask, feeling lightheaded, fucking dizzy from the grip she has on me.

"I'm so perfect," she answers and starts moving her hips.

"Babe, don't move. Please . . . fuck." She moves her pelvis, and I match the thrust because I'm so desperate for the warmth, for the friction. "I won't last."

Nope.

I'm going to come in less than thirty seconds.

"I'm sorry," I say as I grip her hips and start pumping. "Fuck, I'm sorry." I can't control myself. I can't stop. I pump harder and harder, thrusting so fast that I start to black out. The grip her pussy has on my cock is so intense that I can't fucking see straight.

I lose all sense of everything around me. All I seek is my pleasure. This release I need.

I thrust.

Over.

And over.

And over again.

I'm pounding so hard, and our skin slaps together so loud, I swear to God my neighbors can hear us.

"I'm there, oh shit, I'm right there," I groan. Blackness crowds my vision, a rocket of pleasure shoots right up my spine and explodes straight out of my cock. "Uhhhhhh, fuuu-uuuck." I still, holding her hips. I come inside her, just as her pussy spasms around me, and she comes for the third time, making my orgasm last longer. *I can't fucking breathe.*

I fall off to the side and feel my chest heave as I try to catch my breath. Slowly, my vision comes back just in time to see Ollie lying on top of me. My hands go around her, and I pull her in tight.

"Never in my life have I ever come that hard," I say.

"Me . . . neither. Or that much." She kisses my chin and then my cheek, my nose, and then my mouth. I part my lips and allow her to make out with me for a few seconds before she releases me and rests her head on my chest. "Silas?"

"Hmm?" I ask, stroking her back.

"I think you just ruined me for all men."

"Good." And then I add, "See what happens when you fuck a real man?"

She chuckles. "I can admit when I've been proven wrong. Dating an older man is so much better."

"Damn right, babe."

"ARE you really cooking me breakfast, or am I imagining this?" Ollie asks, coming up behind me and kissing my bare back while her hands rest on my hips.

"I hope you like omelets."

"Love them," she says as I turn off the stovetop and turn to face her.

She's wearing one of my shirts, and it looks so good on her. I truly wonder how I got this lucky to call her mine.

I lift her chin up and say, "Morning."

"Good morning." Her hands go around me and dip under the waistband of my briefs, where she grips my ass.

"You're going to make me hard."

"Good."

"Breakfast first, then I'll fuck you."

"Fine, but eat fast."

I chuckle and then remove her hands from my ass. "Grab us coffee from the pot."

She looks over at the coffee maker and says, "For a man who has all this money, I'm surprised you don't have a fancier machine."

"No need when I like it black," I answer. "Don't worry, there's creamer and shit in the fridge for you."

"Aw, did you get that just for me?"

"I did," I answer.

She pulls two mugs off the tree mug stand next to the coffee maker and then fills them up. She then goes to the fridge, where she pauses for a moment. "Silas, there are five different creamers in here."

"I didn't know what you would like."

"When did you get them?"

"This morning," I answer as I put the very large omelet on the plate and then split it in half. I serve her the other half and then grab the whole wheat toast from the toaster and spread butter over both slices. Together, we take the plates, silverware, and cups to the table. I sit and then tug on her hand to sit on my lap.

"You know, there is a perfectly good chair right over there," she says as I kiss her neck.

"I know, but I've been jealous of watching my friends sit with their girls like this. It's my fucking turn."

She loops her arm around my shoulders and kisses my cheek. "That's actually really cute."

I smooth my hand over her thigh and pick up my fork. "You know, I don't think I ever thanked you."

"For what? Making you blackout when I sucked you off last night?"

I lightly laugh. "No, not that, but this mouth"—I lightly kiss her—"it's fucking sinful."

"Thank you."

"But that's not what I was talking about." I rub her thigh gently. "Thank you for being patient with me. I still have a lot to work out in my head, but I appreciate you not getting frustrated with me."

"Like I said"—she drags her thumb over my lip—"you're worth it, Silas."

I nip at her lips, and she smiles, returning the kiss before turning back to her breakfast. "So I have a lot of things I want to do with you."

"Like what?" I ask.

"Well, first of all, I want to try my vibrator on you. I also have this cock ring I've been eyeing that I want to strap you in. Also, how do you feel about some light bondage?"

I chuckle. "Jesus, Ollie, I thought you were talking about like regular activities."

"Are cock rings not regular activities?"

"No." I laugh some more and then kiss her shoulder. "But I'm game for whatever you want."

"Really?"

"Really. Just don't hurt me. I still have to play hockey. If my balls are beaten up and bruised, I'm going to have a hell of a time skating."

"I love your balls. I would never hurt them."

"Well, that's not something I've ever heard."

"Because my predecessor didn't know how to appreciate her man." She kisses my chest and draws her hand down on my balls where she lightly cups them. I breathe out a deep sigh, so fucking content as she handles me. "Do you get waxed?"

"Yeah," I answer.

"I thought so, I've never seen them hairless like that, and I feel like I couldn't get enough of them in my mouth last night."

"Yeah, I could tell."

She scoops up some egg and then says, "Can I ask you something, and I'm not asking to get praise or anything like that, just genuinely curious?"

"Sure."

"Well, Yonny never truly liked getting his dick sucked, and I don't know why. He didn't like sex that much in general, and I always thought that was weird. Do you think that has anything to do with my . . . rather aggressive technique?"

"Fuck . . . no," I answer. "That was all on him. Baby, when I say you're easily the best I've ever had, I mean that."

She turns toward me. "Really?"

"Really."

She twists so now she's straddling me, and that's when I realize she's not wearing any underwear. I slip my hands under her shirt and then pull it all the way off her body and deposit it on the floor. I then take my already hard dick out of my briefs and whisper, "Fuck me."

"I've been waiting," she says right before she lifts up, poises my cock at her entrance, and slams down.

Christ . . .

She is absolute heaven.

Chapter Twenty-One

OLLIE

Ollie: *I had a hell of a time covering up all your bite marks this morning.*

Silas: *Am I supposed to feel bad about that?*

Ollie: *A little sympathy would be nice.*

Silas: *Not sorry. Let everyone know who you belong to when they ask about them.*

Ollie: *I'm going to start nibbling your dick, so your teammates know who *you* belong to.*

Silas: *I welcome it. Nibble away.*

Ollie: *Don't threaten me with a good time.*

Silas: *Pretty sure that would be a good time for me.*

Ollie: *Have I told you how much I love your dick?*

Silas: *Not nearly enough.*

Ollie: *I think about it constantly.*

Silas: *Once again, don't make me hard in front of my guys.*

Ollie: *Can't you control yourself?*

Silas: *Can't *you* control *yourself*?*

Ollie: *No. Get used to it.*

Silas: *At least you're honest.*

Ollie: *Will you come to my place after the game tonight? I have plans.*

Silas: *I'll be wherever you want me to be.*

Ollie: *Good answer. Good luck tonight.*

Silas: *Thanks, baby.*

━━

"YOUR SMILE IS CONTAGIOUS," Ross says as he comes up to my booth in the student union, where I'm munching on a salad. "And you did a shit job covering your hickeys."

"I was just telling Silas how I had a hell of a time covering them up." I save the article I'm working on and turn my attention to Ross, who sits across from me. "How are you?"

"Good." He smiles. "Saw Ian last night."

"Did you?"

Ross nods. "He took me out to this really nice steak restaurant. We spent the whole night chatting about nothing and everything, and when it came time to say goodbye, he asked if I wanted to go back to his place."

"Please tell me you said yes."

"Of course I did." He leans forward and whispers, "Hockey bodies are unlike anything I've ever touched."

"Tell me about it," I say, thinking about Silas and his naked self.

"Broad chests, tiny waists, muscles everywhere." Ross sighs. "I honestly feel inferior when I'm around him. I feel like I have to try harder."

"Stop it," I say. "You have an amazing body, and if Ian didn't think so, he wouldn't be inviting you back to his place."

"True." The corners of his mouth pull up. "He is such a dom, Ollie. He owns every part of the bedroom."

"That's so hot."

"Is Silas the same way?"

"He is," I say, thinking about our night together. "He likes to control every aspect of what we do. He tells me what to do but also asks what I need. He's considerate and thoughtful. He prefers to pleasure me, and I prefer to pleasure him, so sometimes it feels like we're fighting over who gets to make the other come."

"I could see that in him. I can also see that in the bite marks all over your neck."

I press my hand to my neck. "Things got a little out of hand last night."

"Everyone on campus can see that."

"Do you have any bite marks?" I ask.

"No, but Ian loved smacking my ass last night, so that's a touch sore."

I reach across the table and take Ross's hand in mine. "Oh my God, Silas did that to me. I've never been spanked before, and I swear to you, I almost came when he did it the first time."

"Really? I had to get used to it, but once I did, I really enjoyed how he slapped it and then soothed his hand over where he smacked me."

I shake my head in disbelief. "How did we get so lucky? Doesn't it feel weird that everything is falling into place for us?"

"It does. I feel like something is brewing that can't be good."

"Or you can think about it like we've earned this in life," I say, trying to find the positive in all of this. "Just because things are going right, doesn't mean they're going to go wrong."

"I know, but my dating life has been tragic at best," Ross says. "And yours has too. Yonny was anything but a good boyfriend. He was terrible, and then you randomly kiss some guy in a bar, and he happens to be the sex god you've always dreamed of? Doesn't that feel like too good to be true?"

"A bit," I say, thinking about it. "But I think Silas and I were supposed to meet each other. Was it a risk just randomly kissing him so I could prove Candace wrong and shove it in her face? Of course. But it feels like we were meant to meet that night. He helped me feel confident and beautiful again, while I helped him find value in himself after being cheat—uh . . ." I glance away. Fuck. "I mean, after he and his ex broke up."

Ross pauses and studies me. "What were you going to say?" I roll my lips together, mentally cursing myself. "Were you going to say Silas was cheated on?"

Panic eclipses me. "No, he, uh . . . they just broke up. That's it. I wasn't going to say cheated." As if my panic is believable. God, how could I have said that out loud? So casually? I swore to him I would never say anything, and here I am, almost dropping the bomb. What the hell is wrong with me?

Absolute betrayal. Tears fill my eyes as my throat grows tight.

Ross notices my panic and reaches across the table to take my hand. "I won't say anything, I swear on my life, Ollie."

I nod, believing him, but still hating myself. "Okay . . ."

He squeezes my hand. "I promise."

"Thank you," I reply solemnly.

"Hey." He squeezes my hand again. "It's going to be okay. You two were meant to find each other. I know it." I nod as a tear slips down my cheek. "Don't be upset."

I swipe my cheek. "I swore I wouldn't say anything." I take a deep breath and pick up a napkin to blot my eyes. "God, I'm an idiot."

"It's okay, Ollie. Hey, how about we talk about something else? How's the article?"

Yeah, let's talk about anything other than the betrayal that caused Silas to close off his heart.

"Good," I answer, shaking the panic from my voice. "I'm almost done. I have a few finishing touches, but I really hope Roberts likes it. I dove into the daily life of a hockey player, what they deal with, their commitments, and I even touched upon the Agitators organization. How they protect their players at all costs, and how the players are held to higher standards. But it's why they're champions. I really hope it's what Roberts is looking for."

"I'm not sure it's what he'll be looking for exactly, but I also believe it will be captivating and he'll let it slide."

"I hope so," I say. "I really worked hard on it."

"Did you let Silas read it?"

"Yes, he read it this morning and approved. Then he went down on me."

Ross chuckles. "That man loves pussy, doesn't he?"

I laugh and nod, feeling a touch better. I know I can count on Ross. I'm glad it was him I slipped up to and not someone else. "He does. And I love that he loves it so much."

"I bet you do." Ross wiggles his brows.

I STEP into the quaint coffee shop and look around. Exposed beams run along the ceiling while a variety of plants open up the space, making it feel like a jungle. Hence the name Jungle Café. I've never been here, but from the pine wood floors to the delicious aroma and the adorable booths that extend at least seven feet high and connect bulbed lights from one end to the other, there's no doubt I'll be bringing Ross here to get some work done.

From the corner of my eye, I catch someone waving, so I turn and find Winnie with two large cups in front of her.

I weave through the tables and sit in the seat across from her. "Oh my God, it's adorable in here."

"I know. It's my favorite place to do my work." She hands me one cup. "Caramel latte, just for you."

"You're so sweet. Thank you."

"I'm just glad we got to find some time alone to sit and talk." Winnie is probably the cutest person ever. Such a bright smile with golden-blonde hair and a welcoming personality. It's obvious why Pacey fell for her and quickly at that. They make such a cute couple.

"I'm grateful. This whole dating a hockey player thing is completely new to me."

"Well, I'll be your guide and help you through the unexpected bumps. Also, it will be nice to know someone who is going through it as well."

"Aren't you close with Penny, Hornsby's girl?"

"Yes," Winnie answers. "But she's also been super pregnant, so she's on a different level."

"Ooof, I don't want that to happen to me for a bit."

Winnie chuckles. "You have a lot of time to worry about that. Unless . . . you're not careful with Silas."

I lift my coffee to my lips. "I'm careful. Very careful."

"Good." She smirks. "I'm really happy Silas found you. I know I said that before, but I am. He's such a good guy. It's so nice to see him happy."

"Well, he makes me happy too."

"I hope this isn't too presumptuous, but he told Pacey and me about your fake arrangement."

"I figured he did."

"How on earth did you have the confidence to just go up to him and kiss him? I doubt I could ever do that."

"Desperation makes us do funny things." I set my coffee down. "There's this girl I work with who I can't stand. She's the type of person who acts cordially to your face while sneaking in insults, and then when you're not around, plots how to take you down."

"Oh, don't you just love people like that?"

"Yeah, they're the best," I say with an eye roll. "Well, she's been out to get me ever since I took one of her Post-it Notes, and she hasn't let up. She was even put in charge of the end-of-summer assignments and gave me hockey, something I knew nothing about. The night we found out was the night I met Silas. She goaded me at the bar we were hanging out at, and that's when I discovered she was dating my ex."

Winnie winces. "Oof, that could not have gone over well."

"It did not. I wanted to save face and said that my boyfriend was at the bar too. When they didn't believe me, I saw Silas by himself, walked up to him, and told him I was going to kiss him. When he didn't tell me no, I did it."

Winnie chuckles. "That's so amazing."

"After that, we made an agreement to help each other out, which you know about already. Honestly, I didn't think it would turn into this, but if I look back at it, I wonder how it could not. Silas is unlike anyone I've ever met. The way he makes sure that I'm okay, that I have everything I need . . ." I press my hand to the necklaces he gave me. "He's truly everything I want."

"That makes me so happy. You two are seriously the cutest."

"Thank you. I kind of wish we didn't start this relationship during the season, because it makes it more difficult, but we're working it out."

"It's hard for sure," Winnie says. "But it has its bonuses."

"Oh?" I ask.

Winnie glances to the side. "Have you experienced the post-game adrenaline sex yet?"

I perk up. "I mean, we've had sex after his game, and it was the most incredible sex of my entire life."

Winnie slowly nods when bringing her cup to her mouth.

"Expect that after every home game. Every . . . home . . . game."

My palms start to sweat at the thought of those kind of orgasms rolling in every other day. "Seriously?"

"Yup. I even asked Penny, same thing with her. They have so much energy and adrenaline that they become rabid beasts after games. I don't even bother with clothes anymore when Pacey comes home. He knows exactly where to find me, naked and in bed."

"Is Pacey the best sex you've ever had?"

"Hands down. What about you and Silas?"

"He is," I say, my chest feeling full for this man. "He's the best all around."

"It's so freeing to be able to talk about this stuff with someone. I can't talk to my best friend Katherine about it because she's a touch uptight and prudish. And then Max, my other best friend, well, he keeps asking me when I'm going to introduce him to Ian Rivers."

I wince. "Uh . . . I might have had Silas introduce my friend Ross to him."

"Noooo," Winnie says, biting down on her finger. "Shit, did they hit it off?"

I slowly nod. "They did."

"Crap." Winnie leans against the back of her seat. "Max is absolutely going to kill me."

I chuckle. "I'm sorry."

Winnie waves me off. "Don't be sorry. It's my fault. I should have whored him out sooner. Ugh . . . what the hell am I going to say?" Winnie taps her chin. "I don't suppose your friend Ross and Ian would be interested in a threesome?"

"I could always ask," I say as we both laugh.

MY DORM DOOR opens and clicks shut.

Anticipation sears through me as I wait on my bed.

I've been thinking about Silas all day. I even watched his game with Ross. They won again, and Silas scored as well as Holmes. He looked so smooth out there on the ice. I'm truly impressed by his talent.

After the game, I came back to my place and slipped out of my sweats into a pair of lace underwear that barely covers my butt. I paired it with a black crop top, something I know he loves. I considered the whole naked thing, like Winnie said, but I also really liked the idea of Silas peeling my clothes off.

He steps into the main part of my living space, and when I see him come into view, dressed in a suit, hair wet from his shower, I feel my entire body heat as if I'm standing over a fire, flames ablaze.

His eager eyes roam me from head to toe, and when he reaches my face, he says, "You look fucking good, babe."

I smile. "So do you."

He unbuttons his suit jacket and removes it, setting it on my desk. He also kicks off his shoes and closes the space between us. Gently, he slips his hand behind my head and lightly kisses me, increasing my need for him immediately.

I grip his shirt tightly as he slips a hand under my under-wear and digs his fingers into my skin. I moan against his mouth, and he brings me to the edge of my bed, where I sit, releasing his mouth from mine.

Standing in front of me, with an obvious bulge in his pants, he undoes the buttons of his white shirt. Then he untucks it, letting it hang open so I get a glimpse of his well-carved body. He then undoes his belt and pants and lets those hang open as well.

"You had a good game today," I say as I stand and push his shirt off his rock-hard shoulders.

"You watched?" he asks as my hands go to his pants, and I push those down as well, leaving him in only his briefs.

"Yes, Ross and I watched. He's really getting into hockey. He was texting Mr. Mustard throughout the game."

Silas steps out of his pants right before I tug him onto the bed and have him rest against the headboard. I straddle his lap and sit right on top of him.

His hands immediately fall to my rib cage, his thumbs teasing my breasts. "Do you know how many times you wore one of these crop tops and all I wanted to do was lift it up to suck and play with your tits?"

"Every time?" I ask, drawing circles on his chest.

"Yes. Every goddamn time." He lets out a steady breath.

"Did you ever think about me while you touched yourself?"

"Many times," he answers. "Too many times than I care to admit."

I flick my finger over his nipple and feel his pelvis shift under me. "I find it so hot thinking about you jerking off to the thought of me." His hands reach up under my crop top and cup my breasts. "Did you ever feel satisfied after?"

"Never," he answers, his voice growing deeper as my hips move over his. "I always felt like I needed more, that I needed the real thing."

"You have the real thing now," I answer.

"Yeah," he breathes as I grind down on him. "And I'm trying not to lose my goddamn mind as you move over me. I can't just sit here and talk as if all my brain cells aren't disintegrating by the second."

I smirk. "Then tell me what you want to do to me."

"Fuck you. Hard. Fast. And then do it all over again." He rolls my nipple with his fingers.

I chuckle and shake my head.

"What?" he asks.

"Winnie was right."

"She was right about what?"

I pepper kisses along his jaw as he pinches my nipples now,

causing a wave of arousal to shoot between my legs. "That there's a post-game sex adrenaline you guys have." I kiss his cheek, then his lips, then his jaw.

"There is, and if I don't fuck you soon, I'm going to lose my goddamn mind."

I chuckle and lift my arms for him to remove my shirt. "Well, fuck me then."

He quickly removes my shirt, then rolls me to my back and pulls on my underwear. He tears them off and tosses them to the ground before spreading my legs and lowering himself.

"Hold on," I say, pausing him. "I want you to put something on first."

The confused look on his face is so cute. "You want me to wear a condom?"

"No. In my nightstand is a cock ring. Put it on."

His eyes turn dark before he reaches and pulls open the drawer of my nightstand and finds the black cock ring. He holds it up between us and says, "Put it on me."

He doesn't have to ask me twice. I have him sit back so I can pull his briefs off. When his erect penis comes into view, I can't help myself. I dip down and suck in the tip.

"Babe," he says, shifting my hair to the side so he can watch my mouth. I give him a few pulls before I release him and slip the cock ring around the base of him, and then with a smirk, I turn it on. His body jolts, and his hands grip the mattress. "Fucking hell."

"Does it feel good?" I ask as I roll my tongue around the head again.

"Yes," he says, his head falling back to the headboard. "Fuck yes, it feels good."

Satisfaction races through me as I slip his cock inside my mouth. I feel the vibration against my tongue, and as I take him deeper, I enjoy the constraint I have on him, the tension in his thighs, and the stiffness in his body. Nothing is sexier to me than being able to make a man come from my mouth. I love having that kind of control. That kind of power.

I pull up to the tip and then swirl my tongue down his piercings, taking time on each one. When I reach the base where the cock ring is vibrating, I move back up, nipping the entire way.

"Shit." He clenches his jaw. "More. Suck me in deep again."

Loving that he loves my mouth, I part my lips and bring him to the back of my throat again. His girth doesn't bother me, nor does his length. I revel in it. And since I don't seem to have a gag reflex, I'm able to bring him deep.

I repeat my pulsing over his strained erection a few times until he releases a loud growl, causing me to pause. I glance up just in time to feel him lift me up off his dick and toss me backward on the bed. His crazed eyes meet mine. "I'm coming in that perfect cunt, not in your mouth."

Mmm, yes, please.

His strong hand slides up my stomach, over my breasts, and up to my neck, where he grips me.

"I need to fuck you badly," he says. "I'll eat you out after, but I need release. Now."

"Then fuck me, Silas."

He positions his cock at my entrance, I spread even wider for him, pulling on my knees so he has better access, and he slides into me, one agonizing inch at a time. The vibration from the cock ring immediately hits me in just the right spot, and I know at that moment, with his hand on my throat and his massive cock stretching me out, I don't stand a chance.

"Be rough," I say. "Make me feel every inch of your massive cock."

His eyes go wild, and he starts pumping hard, so hard that I slide across the bed until I'm right against the wall.

"Fuck me harder," I say, his hand still gripping my neck, making me feel completely owned by him.

Because he's pumping so aggressively into me, I release my legs and push one hand against the wall to steady us while my other hand grips his shoulder, where I dig my fingers into his back. "Harder, Silas. Fill me with your cum."

"Goddammit," he says as his hips pulse in and out of me, his abs firing as his body moves. The veins in his neck protrude, his muscular pecs bounce, and his grip grows tighter around my neck.

"You're so big inside me. I can feel every inch of you."

He pumps again.

And again.

And again, hitting me directly in the G-spot, sending me into a swirl of euphoria, my orgasm right there, ready to fall over.

"I'm going to masturbate to this when you're gone," I say. "To this very moment."

He moans as he stretches tall, giving me an amazing view of his delicious abs. If he wasn't so desperate, I would push him so I could lick every inch of his stomach.

"I never want to stop fucking you," he says as he pulses and pauses, then pulses and pauses. The new friction matched with the vibration of his cock ring has my toes curling.

"Punish me. Choke me. I'm right there. Harder, Silas."

"Fuck," he says right before releasing himself and turning me onto my stomach. He props my hips up and slaps me so hard in the ass that tears spring to my eyes right before a wave of lust pulses down my legs. And then he does it again, the slap so loud that it echoes against the walls.

And just as he spanks me again, he inserts himself inside, making me feel so full that my stomach bottoms out.

"Fuck me deep, Silas."

On another growl, he wraps my hair around his knuckles and tugs my head back right before spanking me so hard in the ass that I cry out in pleasure.

"Blister me," I cry. "Again, Silas."

He pulses inside me and spanks me again.

"Make me red."

He grunts and slaps me again.

And again.

And again, until my pussy starts to convulse.

It's too much. All of it. His cock. His control. His hand.

My orgasm pulses up my body, and with one more thrust, I spasm around his cock and scream his name.

"Ahhhhh . . . fuck." He pumps a few more times, grumbles something unintelligible, then stills, his hands shaking my pelvis as his cock swells inside me, and he comes.

We moan together. Our orgasms matched right before we slowly tumble down from euphoria until we both collapse on top of the bed, the cock ring still vibrating.

"Jesus, Ollie," he says as he reaches between us to turn off the cock ring and remove it. I feel him toss it to the side, and then he rolls and pulls me with him. I curl my leg around him and rest my head on his shoulder. He rubs his thumb over my side while I trail my finger up and down his chest. "Fuck," he breathes out heavily. "That was . . . fuck . . ."

Probably the best way to describe it.

"You turn me on so much," I say.

"Same, babe." He kisses my head and takes a deep breath. "Give me a second, and I'll be between your legs again, giving you what you deserve."

I press a kiss to his chest. *It's not just the sex.* I mean, the man can fuck like there's no tomorrow. But not only that, he makes me feel cherished. As if there is nothing better to him than the enjoyment *I* experience. That makes me feel . . . treasured. I love it. "You're what I deserve."

Chapter Twenty-Two

SILAS

I was with Sarah for over a decade, and never once did I feel what I feel about Ollie.

I think I loved Sarah. I'm not going to take that away from our history, but I don't think I loved her the way I thought I did. Our love grew apart over time.

With Ollie, there's this obsession. An obsession to make her happy, to make her feel fulfilled. An obsession to be near her, to hold her, to possess her.

An obsession to never let go of her, and knowing I have another away trip coming up, I actually feel sick that I have to leave her.

She curls closer into my side, warm, naked, needy.

She hasn't let go of me all night, and I haven't let go of her. She makes me feel desired, and Sarah never made me feel that way. I always felt like I was chasing her. Chasing her to give me attention or any piece of her. But now that I think about it, she was always looking for something else, someone else. *We never would have lasted. And now I'm so fucking glad I found that out when I did.*

Ollie shifts, and her hand draws down my stomach.

Hell . . .

She finds my morning erection and lightly runs her fingers over it.

"Morning," I say, my pelvis shifting upward unintentionally.

"Mmm . . . morning," she says right before she travels her mouth down my body, right to my cock.

"Baby," I groan as I make room for her body.

She swirls her tongue around the tip, and I place my hands behind my head and watch her delicious mouth drive me fucking nuts.

We spend the next half hour using our mouths, hands, and bodies to bring each other pleasure to the point that we're both sweating, tangled between each other, and completely spent.

"Ollie," I say, out of breath. "Baby, you have to stop telling me to fill you up with my cum."

"Why?" she asks with a laugh. "That's what I want."

"I know, but it makes me wild."

"That's how I like you. Wild. Out of control."

"You're going to break me."

She twists into me and asks, "Are you telling me I have to take it easy on my geriatric boyfriend?"

My brow rises as I turn toward her, causing her to laugh. "I'm not fucking geriatric."

"Could have fooled me with all the cracking your bones do."

"That's just part of being an athlete."

"A geriatric athlete."

"Oliana!"

She laughs and straddles me. "Are your feelings getting hurt?" She traces her hands over my pecs.

"Yes."

"Aw, my poor baby." She kisses my lips and then hops off, leaving me cold and wanting more.

"Come back here."

She slips my shirt over her body and buttons the middle button. "I need some breakfast. You've fucked me hungry."

"And you're calling me the geriatric one." I slip my hands behind my head and say, "I could go all day, baby."

"Says the man who was breathing heavily last night and had to take a break between rounds."

I sit up on my elbows. "I'm the one doing the fucking pumping. Excuse me if I don't want to cramp up."

She laughs some more and then goes to her mini fridge, where she pulls out two yogurts.

She tosses one at me and then pulls out spoons. I scoot back to the headboard and sit up while she sits right on top of me, just the way I like it.

I pull off the lid of my yogurt and do the same for her. She hands me a spoon, and together, we eat breakfast.

"Did you turn in your article?" I ask.

"I did yesterday. I haven't heard anything yet."

"It was a good article, babe," I say. "I don't see how he won't like it."

"Thank you. I really appreciate your help on it. Before I turned it in, I made a few changes, but I feel like it'll give me the credit I need, and then after that, I just have to breeze through the rest of the internship until the end of the year."

"Your grade doesn't depend on the rest of the year?" I ask.

"No, the extension of the internship is just experience. That's why the extension was so good because it's paid and great for the résumé."

"What do you plan on doing after you graduate?" I ask.

"Hopefully find a job that suits what I'm working toward . . . not sports."

I chuckle. "But now your boyfriend is a professional

hockey player, giving you the inside look. You could be very valuable to someone looking for a sportswriter."

"Oh yeah, very valuable. I couldn't even tell you a single rule about hockey, let alone write about it."

"So what happens if you get a job that's not in Vancouver?" I ask, wanting to gauge where she's at.

"Are you worried I might not be at your beck and call for your post-game adrenaline?"

"No." I bring my hand to her thigh. "I just want to know what your plans are."

Playfully, she asks, "Are you growing attached to me, Silas?"

"I am," I say, completely serious, which changes her expression. I set down my yogurt and grip her waist. "I really like you, Ollie."

"I really like you too, Silas."

"I want you to have the world in front of you, all of the opportunities, but I also want to know that I have a chance of being in that future."

She sets her yogurt down as well and rests her hands on my chest. "You're in my future, Silas. I don't know what that future will be, but you're in it. I honestly can say this is the happiest I've ever been."

"Me too, Ollie." I slide a strand of hair behind her ear. "How do you feel about everything so far, with the season and the time apart?"

"Good," she answers. "I had coffee with Winnie, and it felt nice to talk to someone experiencing the same thing as me."

"You don't fear I won't be there for you?"

"I don't have that fear at all."

"Because if you do, you can tell me."

"Silas," she says, placing her hand over my heart. "I promise I can handle this. So far, I've seen you almost every night besides the nights you were on the road. And those nights, you called me. I have no worries about you not being there for me. And I have no need to go looking for comfort elsewhere if that's what you're afraid of."

"I don't want to be afraid of it," I say as I droop my head. "But I feel this heavy weight in my chest when I think about you and how I feel." I look her in the eyes. "It's really fucking strong, Ollie. You brought me back to life. I don't want to lose that. I don't want to lose you."

"I'm not going anywhere," she says, then leans in to kiss me. "I'm yours, Silas. Only yours."

━━━

"YOU LOOK HAPPY," Holmes says, walking up next to me as we head down the hallway. Another game day, another chance to add a win to the tally.

"I am happy," I say. "Had a great morning with Ollie."

"You feeling her?" Holmes asks.

"Yeah, man. A lot. She makes me really fucking happy." Leaning in close, I say, "I think she's the fucking one."

"Really?" Holmes asks, surprised.

"I know it's pretty early, but I swear to God, I've never felt this way. Even with Sarah. This is a new level of connection— of . . . possession—I have inside me. I haven't told her, but hell, dude, I love her. The feeling is so strong in my veins that I need to be around her all the goddamn time."

"And you trust her?" he asks, making me think he might have had a talk with Pacey.

"I do," I answer. "I trust her with everything in me." When I told her about Sarah, she floored me with her compassion and empathy. She showed maturity beyond her years. But her anger on my behalf proved that she values trustworthiness and honesty as much as I do. "She's far more mature than I expected and has adapted to being the girlfriend of a hockey player much easier than I anticipated. So far. I'm happy."

344

"I can tell. You're on top of your game, too."

"I feel like I've shed this weight I've been carrying around. The weight of what Sarah put me through. Now that Ollie has come along, it just feels different. Right. Like everything is in place."

"Morning, boys," Blakely says, cutting us off in the hallway. Blakely works for the Agitators and has been helping with Penny's job regarding social media. Blakely is also the girl Holmes has a huge crush on.

"Uh, hey, Blakely," Holmes says, his body growing rigid next to mine.

I thrive for these moments. And I know I shouldn't because my friend is clearly uncomfortable. But I love watching him squirm. It makes me realize he's not the robot he likes to portray himself as, and that light that keeps him motivated is stronger.

"Ooo, Halsey, that suit looks amazing on you. Is it new?"

I catch his cheeks blush as he shakes his head. "No, had it for a bit."

"I love it. You should wear it more often."

Why do I feel like he's going to wear it every day for the rest of his life now?

"Thanks."

Just to stir the pot a bit, I nudge his shoulder. "You going to compliment her dress?"

Holmes flashes a death look at me right before he says, "Uh, you look beautiful, Blakely."

Okay, I was just looking for a dress compliment, not a full-on I'm in love with you compliment.

"Oh . . . thank you, Halsey." She glances down at her plum dress. "Since I have to be on the ice today before the game, I thought I would dress in Agitators colors."

"Purple looks really good on you."

I swear to God, I see heart eyes sprouting from Holmes.

He's going to get so much shit when we get to the locker room, and he knows it.

"Thank you." She clears her throat. "Um, well, I have to go gather some things——"

"Ugh, there you are," I hear Sarah say as she walks up to us in a pair of skintight black pants and a purple top that dips low in the front. "Oh hey, Silas." She smiles, and it's crazy that I used to like that smile—now it just seems maniacal. Like she's plotting revenge.

"Hey," I say, hand in my pocket.

She turns to Blakely. "I talked with the guys, and they'll be able to use the new purple rug we got for the ice. They're unpacking it now."

"Oh, awesome."

"Let me know if you need anything else. I'm going upstairs to work on a few graphics."

"Okay, sounds good."

"Okay, catch you later." She walks by me and runs her hand down my arm as she passes. "Good luck today." And then she's gone.

When she's out of earshot, Blakely whispers, "She was telling me the other day that she's trying to get you back. I don't know what your history is, but I would be careful because aren't you dating someone?"

"I am. Sarah can try all she wants, but it's not going to happen. I'm happy with Ollie."

"Okay, good. Just checking. All right, I'll let you boys get to the locker room." She moves by us. "Good luck tonight, Halsey."

"Thanks," he says quietly as we move away.

When we're out of earshot, I say, "That was fun."

"Not a fucking word," he grumbles.

And I leave it at that because why torture him anymore?

SILAS: *Where are you?*

Ollie: *Back of the bar.*

I move through the crowd, trying not to draw attention, but that's nearly impossible after another big win. Undefeated has never felt so good.

Posey follows me as well as Holmes and Rivers, and we head to the back of the bar where Ollie is waiting with a round of beers.

God, this girl. She's perfect.

"Hey, baby," I say as I plant a kiss on her lips.

"Hey, handsome," she says, kissing me back. "Congrats on another win."

"Thank you." I give her another kiss and slip my arm around her waist, keeping her close as she hands out the beers.

Ross appears, and I give him a nod just before he walks up to Rivers and kisses him as well. Rivers then slides his hand into Ross's and pulls him off to the side to a private booth.

"Guess we won't be hanging out with them," Posey says before taking a sip of his beer.

"I didn't think we would," Ollie says. "They really like their privacy." She then looks up at me. "No goals tonight. What was that about?"

"Two assists, babe, that's just as good."

"Is that what you're convincing her?" Posey asks with a laugh. "Dude, you're pathetic."

"I might not be well-versed in hockey," Ollie says, "but I know that bullshit he just spewed is inaccurate."

Posey lets out a boisterous laugh while I give my girl a look.

"What?" She shrugs. "It's true."

"You're supposed to back me up."

"Not when you're making a fool of yourself."

"Hell, I think Ollie is the best thing that's ever happened

to you. Please tell me you're bringing her to Banff when this season is over. We could use her to cut through your bullshit."

"Yeah, she's coming with me," I say as I kiss her forehead, only to feel her go stiff in my arms. Confused, I glance down at her to see if everything is okay, and that's when I hear a familiar voice.

"Great game, boys," Sarah says, coming up to us.

Jesus, is she following us around today? Is there an air tag on me that I don't know about?

"Uh, thanks," Posey says.

Sarah grips my arm. "Amazing assists."

"Hey," Ollie says, swatting at Sarah's arm. "Don't touch him."

The abrupt demand startles me, only to make me inwardly smile. Ollie is claiming me.

"Excuse me?" Sarah says.

"I said don't fucking touch him, especially in front of me. That's disrespectful as shit. I know you might be from a different generation, but I'd appreciate if you didn't set back feminism and act like a man-stealing bitch. Accept the fact that you're not together anymore and move on."

Oh hell, I think I just got hard.

Sarah's brows narrow as she says, "You might be his girl-friend at the moment, a flavor of the week, but Silas and I have over a decade of history. If I want to touch him, then I'll fucking touch him."

"Don't," I say to Sarah. When her eyes connect with mine, I repeat, "Don't. I honestly don't want you near me. I'm just tolerating it because it's part of your job, but outside of the arena, don't come near me."

"Silas," she says, looking insulted. "I know we've had our disagreements—"

"Disagreements?" I say, my voice a harsh whisper. "I think you remember it incorrectly because what you did to me wasn't a disagreement. What you did went against everything we promised each other. I'll never forget it. I'll never forgive it." Ollie's arm tightens around me, offering me support. "You have absolutely zero chance of ever winning me back, so for the love of God, leave me the fuck alone."

"Zero chance? Really? I see the way you look at me, Silas."

I grip Ollie even tighter.

"You're mistaking distaste for lust. There isn't anything in this world that would make me change my mind. We're over. So save your dignity and move the fuck along."

"Wow," she says, shaking her head. "You're really going to take this girl you barely know over me? We have history, Silas. I know you. She doesn't. And when she breaks your heart because she's too immature, too inexperienced to date someone of your caliber, I'll be sitting back, waiting."

"Don't hold your breath," Ollie says. And fuck, I love her. I love her so goddamn much.

Without another word, Sarah walks away, flipping her hair over her shoulder.

"Oh shit," Posey says before laughing. "You pissed her off."

"Good, maybe she'll stay away once and for all."

I spin Ollie toward me and lift her chin so her lips are near. "I'm going to fuck you so hard when we get to my place."

A smile stretches across her beautiful face.

"I'm counting on it."

I lightly kiss her, only for Posey to clear his throat. "Can you two not? Some of us are struggling romantically and would prefer not to watch you two go at it."

I lift my lips from Ollie's and then turn toward Posey. "Some of us? Does that include you?"

"What? Me?" He points at his chest. "No, I'm not struggling. I'm fine." He pats Holmes on the back. "Just looking out for our dear friend Halsey here."

"Don't," Holmes says, peeling Posey's hand off his shoulder. "I'm good."

"Not from what I saw this morning," I say.

"Ooo, what happened this morning?" Ollie asks.

Holmes gives me the death glare, and I say, "Sorry, dude, she's a part of me now. What I know, she knows."

He takes a long pull of his beer before saying, "Just ran into someone . . ."

"Blakely," I say, filling in for him.

"And I don't know, just told her how beautiful she looked. That's it, we're not talking about it anymore, or I'm going to fucking leave."

"Dude." Posey shakes Holmes. "You said that to her? That's huge. What did she say? Did she blush?"

"I said we're not getting into this," Holmes says, always in a bad fucking mood.

"She blushed," I answer for him. "And she said he looked really good in his suit."

Posey's mouth drops open. "Holmes, that's your in."

"It's not," he says, setting his beer down. "Have you forgotten she has a boyfriend?"

"No," Posey answers. "But things change. Look at Taters. He was with Sarah for over a decade, and that changed." He glances at me. "Sorry, had to use you as an example."

"It's fine," I say as I kiss Ollie's forehead.

"She's happy, and I'm not going to fuck around with that. Now, we can either change the subject, or I can leave." From the expression on his face and the dead-set tone in his voice, I know he's serious. And I have to respect the man. Blakely is not available, and she does appear happy, so I respect the fact he's not going to chase after her. I shouldn't tease him, really.

"Ollie turned in her final paper for her internship."

"What was it about?" Posey asks.

"You guys," she says, sounding so sincere and full of love. "Talked about your day-to-day journey and what you do to prepare for a season. Talked about the Agitators and how welcoming they are as a team to newcomers."

"When does it come out?" Posey asks.

"Not sure. I still haven't heard from my boss about it."

"He hasn't said anything to you?" I ask.

Ollie shakes her head. "No, but I guess no news is better than bad news." She turns to the boys. "He wanted me to do some sort of exposé about the team and the owner, really dig for some dirt. But I wouldn't."

"What a dick," Posey says. "That's a total conflict of interest."

"That's what I said, but he apparently didn't care." Ollie sighs. "Oh well, hopefully, he enjoys what I put together."

"He will." I kiss the top of her head.

━━

"I CAN'T BELIEVE you leave again tomorrow," Ollie says as she comes up behind me in the kitchen, where I'm grabbing a glass of water. Her hands go around my waist, and she hugs me from behind.

"I know. This is how it'll be for the next few months." I turn around to face her. "Are you going to be okay?"

"Yes, I'm just going to miss you."

"Well, if you want, you can stay here when I'm gone."

She glances around my apartment and then back up at me. "It's way too big."

I chuckle. "Then take some of my clothes home with you, so you can wear them while I'm gone."

"That I can do." She stands up on her toes and presses a kiss to my chin. "Do you ever think how crazy it is that we got here? Ross was talking about it the other day, how happy we are. We're kind of waiting for something bad to happen."

"Why would you wait for that?" I ask. "Live in the moment, babe. This is real."

"That's what I keep telling myself, but then, it's nights like tonight when it feels too good to be true."

I move her back to the counter and lift her up and sit her on it. "What do you mean?"

Her fingers move over my dress shirt, and she plays with the buttons, slowly undoing them one at a time. "Despite Sarah's interruption, it was nice. Yonny never let me hang out with him and his guys like that. I was never welcome, and tonight, I felt like I belonged."

"You did belong. That's how it is, Ollie. It's you and me. I don't care who I'm with. I want you there with me."

She parts my shirt open and tugs on the belt loops of my pants. "When you say things like that . . . that's what makes me believe this is all too good to be true." Her fingers toy with my zipper.

"It's not. This is how you're treated with me, Ollie."

She slips her hand into my pants and cups me. I place my hands on her shoulders and take a deep breath. Fuck. "You realize this is how you're treated with me, right?" she asks as she slowly massages my balls. "You're desired. You're wanted. You're needed. You're cherished." Her hand slides up my shaft and pulls me out of my briefs. "I'm yours, no one else's."

Sliding off the counter, she kneels in front of me and pulls me into her mouth. My hands fall to the countertop in front of me, and as she sucks me into her warm mouth, I have the same thought as Ollie.

This feels too good to be true.

It feels like everything is going my way.

And as my girl kneels before me, I can acknowledge I have the same fears. Sarah believes I'll get tired of Ollie and go back to her. She is so fucking deluded. But I fear that Ollie will get sick of this lifestyle, see that the grass is really greener elsewhere, and I'll be left with another broken heart. I just hope to God I'm wrong.

I hope this isn't too good to be true.

Chapter Twenty-Three

OLLIE

"Silas?" I groan as I stretch my arms above my head. Light falls into his bedroom from the bathroom, and I glance over to see the door closed.

From the nightstand, I glance at the clock and let out another groan. Six thirty.

Ugh.

I have class this morning starting at eight thirty. Silas is probably getting ready for his away trip since they leave today. Grumbling, I flip the warm covers off me, letting the chilly air hit my naked body. I push my hand through my hair and make my way to the bathroom and hear the shower turn on.

I open the door and catch Silas slip into the walk-in shower surrounded in black marble tile. I stare at his muscular ass, the divots in the side and the dimples on his lower back. When he turns and lets the water drip down his body, all the way past his dick, my mouth waters. I need him. Even though

I had him several times last night, I won't see him tonight, which means I need to get in as much Silas as I can.

I walk into the bathroom and head straight for the shower. He spots me from the corner of his eye as he's wetting down his body, and a sexy smile spreads across his face.

"Morning, baby."

"Good morning," I say as I slip into the shower. "Can I join you?"

"You don't even need to ask," he says as he takes my hand and brings me under the water. "How did you sleep?"

"Okay," I answer. I push the water over my head and then look up at him. "I felt like I was trying to claw you as much as I could."

"I could tell." He kisses my forehead. "I loved it."

He squeezes some shampoo into his hand and rubs his hands together before he gently massages it into my scalp. "When do you leave today?"

"Wheels up at three."

I close my eyes as his strong fingers dig into my scalp. "Then why are you up so early?"

"I woke up around five for some reason and couldn't get back to sleep. I didn't mean to wake you."

He helps me under the water, and I rinse my hair. "It's fine," I say. "I'm glad you did. I have two classes this morning, and I probably would have missed my first one if you didn't wake up."

When I'm done rinsing my hair, I switch positions with him so he can warm up while I put conditioner in my hair. Being the good man he is, Silas made sure that I had all the products I use daily in his apartment. He washes his hair as I comb through my conditioner. His eyes remain on me the entire time.

"What?" I ask as I set my brush down.

"Just keep thinking about how hot you are."

"Oh yeah?" I ask as I grab his soap bar and suds up my hand.

His eyes fall to my hands and then back to my face. "What do you plan on doing?"

"Soaping you up," I say as I reach for his semi-hard cock and pull it into my hand.

He smirks and then grabs the soap from me and does the same, but to my body. His hands pass over my breasts before he turns me around so my back is to his chest, and his hands travel up my body.

"Why do I feel like you have something else in mind?" I ask as he kisses up my neck.

"Because I do," he answers.

"Then fuck me until I'm too sore to move."

"Hell," he mutters right before he nips at my neck, pulling the skin between his teeth and making his mark.

I let him because I wear his markings with pride.

It might look trashy from an outsider looking in, but to me, they're reminders of who I'm with and why I'm with him.

As his mouth works around my neck, he plays with my breasts, one of his favorite things to do. He plucks at my nipples, pulls and squeezes them, and creates such a wave of arousal that I start to move my ass along his erection.

"That's it, baby. Let me feel that ass against my cock."

I push harder into him and rotate as he drags his mouth up my neck. He slides his hand up my throat and then turns my head so my lips meet his. It's a short but passionate kiss, enough to make me want more. He reaches behind him and switches on the handheld showerhead. He rinses off our soap and then brings it to the front of me, right in front of my pussy, and says, "Spread."

I do as I'm told, and the water blasts right against my aching clit.

"Silas," I moan.

"Hold this here."

I grip the showerhead and place it exactly where I want it against my clit as he bends me forward. With the hand not holding the showerhead, I brace against the tile and hold my breath as I feel him position his cock against my entrance.

"Don't take your time, Silas. I need your dick now."

Hands gripping my ass, he pushes inside me in one large thrust that nearly has me crumbling against the wall.

"Goddamn," he shouts. "This tight pussy will be the death of me."

He works his erection in and out of me at a demanding pace, and all I can do is brace myself as he builds both of our orgasms to the precipice.

The vibration of the water bouncing off my clit combined with his wet strokes has me clawing to hold on longer.

"Jesus, I'm already there," he says, pumping faster.

Thank God.

"Me too," I squeak out as the first tingle of an orgasm zings down my legs. "Fuck, Silas . . . I'm . . . I'm . . ." I can't get out the words because together, we both groan, our orgasms making us incoherent.

I push against him, he tugs, and together, we slowly ride down the high.

On a deep breath, I stand and lean against his chest, where he holds me tightly.

"Shit, Ollie. I'm sorry."

"Why are you sorry?" I ask.

"Because I wanted that to last longer, but the minute I was inside you, there was no chance."

I turn toward him and use the showerhead to rinse his chest. "I was right there with you."

He pinches my chin. "How can I still come that fast with you? It's fucking embarrassing."

I chuckle. "I think it's all the spanking, pinching, tools, and dirty talk," I answer. "We don't give each other a chance."

"You're right about that." He takes the showerhead from me. "How did this feel?"

"Phenomenal, but your dick felt better."

"Good answer." He presses a kiss to my lips, and then we get lost in each other's mouth once again. This time, we turn off the water.

"DID SILAS GET YOU THAT SWEATSHIRT?" Ross asks as he examines the black hoodie I'm wearing that says Property of the Vancouver Agitators.

"He did," I answer as we wait at our favorite coffee kiosk on campus for our drinks to be made. Thanks to post-shower sex on the bathroom floor, I was almost late for my first class. Silas was insatiable this morning, and no matter what I did, he wanted more.

Not that I didn't want it, either.

But I barely made it out the door with clothes on. He gave me this sweatshirt this morning, one that fits better, and then sprayed me with a touch of his cologne before kissing me goodbye.

The entire drive to campus, I wore a huge smile on my face.

Throughout my first class, I kept thinking about him and everything we've done in the past twenty-four hours.

Even now, when getting coffee, all I can think about is how Silas would hate my order and cringe at it.

"I like it," Ross says. "I'd ask Ian to get me one, but he's pretty much opened his entire closet to me. So I can take what I want."

"And what did you take?"

Ross smirks. "A few things."

"Ollie," the barista says, setting two drinks down on the

counter. I grab them and hand Ross his order, and together, we head toward our class.

"So, hear anything from Roberts?" Ross asks.

"No, and I'm sort of getting nervous about it. Don't you think he would have said something by now?"

"I don't know," Ross answers as the fall wind whips around us. It's getting to that point in the year when a hoodie just isn't going to do it anymore. "Roberts is a weird guy. He doesn't praise very often. I turned in my paper and heard nothing. It published and all was good. So I think it's better not to hear something."

"That's what I was thinking, but—"

"Hey, hot stuff."

I pause and turn to the side just in time to see a large mass of a man wrap his arms around me and scoop me into a hug. I'm about to start kicking when I smell a very familiar cologne.

"Silas?" I ask, completely off guard.

When he pulls away and I see his handsome face, partially hidden behind sunglasses, I nearly squeal.

"Oh my God, what are you doing here?"

"Thought I'd spend the morning with you since I don't have to be at the airport until later." He glances up and nods. "What's up, Ross?"

"Hey, Silas. Risky coming to a campus where you're worshipped."

Silas just shrugs and then brings his lips to mine. "Surprised?"

"Yes," I say, still trying to grasp that he's here, with me, at my school. "I have to go to class, though."

"I know. Figured I'd just go with you, then take you out to lunch. You good with that?"

The corners of my mouth tilt up. "I'm perfect with that."

"Good." Silas loops his arm over my shoulder, and

together, we all walk. "How are things with Rivers?" Silas asks Ross. "He doesn't talk much in the locker room."

"Things are great," Ross says, that ever-present smile on his lips whenever Ian is mentioned.

"Ian is a real daddy . . . if you know what I mean," I say, causing Ross to push at my shoulder. "What?" I ask. "It's true."

"You don't need to tell Silas that."

"Sorry to say, whatever I know, he probably knows," I reply.

"So you two actually talk? That's shocking since Silas's dick is always down your throat."

Silas nearly chokes on his own saliva as I laugh. "I'm a good listener." I wink.

Ross leans forward so Silas can see him, and he says, "And just so you know, since we're spilling secrets here, congrats on the piercings, Silas. She is positively infatuated with them."

Silas lets out a deep chuckle. "So I've heard."

We make our way through the crowd of students, and I don't know if it's because no one's paying attention or Silas did a good job covering himself with a hat, glasses, and hoodie, but we go undetected. When we reach the classroom, thankfully, it's a larger one, so we can sit in the back.

When we sit down, I notice just how big Silas is for the seat, his shoulder expanding into my space, but I welcome the comfort of having him near.

As I take out my laptop to take notes, I say, "Now, no distracting me. Got it?"

"How would I distract you?"

"Uh, touching, talking . . . breathing."

"You don't want me to breathe?" he asks, a raise to his brow.

"It will remind me how you breathe in my ear when you're ready to come. There will be none of that."

"You have to let him breathe," Ross says. "Having a giant

hockey man pass out in the middle of class will bring more attention than you want."

"Fine," I huff. "You can breathe, but that's it."

"Understood," he says. "And just to clarify one more time, there's a strict no-touching policy?"

"Very strict."

"No handholding?"

"Would that be touching?" I ask him.

"Yeah."

"Then no . . . no handholding. Just sit there and try not to turn me on."

He stretches his arms in front of him and says, "I can't make any promises since I'm so alluring to you, but I'll try."

"The cockiness is actually making me dryer by the second."

"Can we not?" Ross asks as he sips his coffee. "I don't want to think about your wet nether regions."

"I sure as hell do," Silas says.

I point at him. "That's exactly what not to do. No comments like that. Just sit there and be quiet."

The professor walks in before I can shoot off any more warnings to Silas. Class starts, I prep my notes with a header, and just as the professor starts talking, a text message pops up on my computer.

Silas: *You look really pretty.*

I glance over at him, and he points to the front of the class and whispers, "Pay attention."

I roll my eyes and focus up front even though I can smell his addicting cologne waft toward me every time he shifts.

I start typing something the professor said when another text pops up on my screen.

Silas: *That sweatshirt looks hot on you too.*

My nostrils flare, and when I glance in his direction, he points at the front again.

He's in so much trouble.

So instead of turning toward him, I type him back.

Ollie: *What happened to no distractions?*

Silas: *Can't a guy tell his girlfriend he thinks she's pretty?*

Ollie: *Not when she's trying to pay attention in class. This might be how you acted when you were in school back in the day, but not me.*

Silas: *Using the term "back in the day" will get you spanked, and you text me all the time from class, so don't try to be Miss Studious just because I'm here.*

Ollie: *Threatening me with a spanking? Oh no, I'm shivering in my boots.*

Silas: *I can taste your sarcasm it's so heavy.*

Ollie: *Do you really think a spanking is a punishment? You know I only get wetter when you slap my ass.*

Silas: *Fine . . . then your punishment will be no fellatio.*

Ollie: *Ew, don't use the term fellatio. God, Grandpa.*

Silas: *I'm surprised you even knew what that was. Fine, no sucking my cock.*

Ollie: *That's fine. I can handle that.*

Silas: *Liar. You're itching to blow me right now.*

Ollie: *You're vulgar.*

Silas: *LOL. Says the girl who tells me to fill her with my cum every goddamn time we're together.*

Ollie: *That's not vulgar. That's just an honest request.*

Silas: *I love how you're able to run circles around the truth. Truly inspiring.*

Ollie: *I'm studying to be a journalist after all. We have to run around the truth a bit.*

Silas: *Studying to be a journalist? Seems more like you're occupied with texting your extremely hot boyfriend.*

Ollie: *Yes, my extremely hot boyfriend who is thirty-one and sitting in a college class because he's so attached to me that he can't spare a moment without smelling my pheromones.*

Silas: *Is that what the oniony smell is?*

I gasp and poke him in the side, causing him to laugh,

drawing some attention from the students around us. Silas adjusts his glasses and sinks lower into his chair.

I see him type away on his phone, and I try to pay attention to what the professor is saying, but it's no use as another text from him pops up.

Silas: *You're going to get yourself thrown out of class. Is that the goal?*

Ollie: *The goal is to pay attention, but you're distracting me.*

Silas: *It's because I like you, and I think you're cute.*

Ollie: *We would never have been able to be in class together if we were the same age.*

Silas: *We wouldn't even be talking to each other if we were the same age.*

Ollie: *Why do you say that?*

Silas: *I was a dweeb in college. Didn't have dick piercings, which I know is a huge plus for you. Barely had any tattoos, and my head was shaved.*

Ollie: *Oh my God, I need to see pictures.*

Silas: *Maybe one day if you're lucky. But you must earn the opportunity.*

Ollie: *Sucking your dick every night hasn't earned me that opportunity?*

Silas: *It's brought you closer. These are sacred pictures. But back to us knowing each other in college. I would never have gone for it because I was with Sarah. I never would have even talked to you.*

Ollie: *What if you came to college single? Then what? Would you have talked to me?*

Silas: *Still no. You would have been placed in the too pretty catalog.*

Ollie: *Now you're just being ridiculous.*

Silas: *I'm not. It's the truth. You're gorgeous, Ollie. I would have been intimidated.*

Ollie: *Nope, not falling for it. I'm not reaching over and holding your hand because you're being all cute and telling the truth. Nice try, fella.*

Silas: *Wasn't looking for a handhold . . . but it would have been nice. I like holding your hand, makes me feel at home.*

"Oh my God," I mutter right before I rest my hand on his thigh. From the corner of my eye, I see his grin stretch from ear to ear. His hand encapsulates mine, and he gives it a good squeeze.

For the rest of class, he sits there, holding my hand while I take one-handed notes on my computer.

And honestly, I'm not even mad about it.

"DID YOU SEARCH THIS PLACE OUT?" I ask Silas as we sit at a small, hole-in-the-wall deli where we ordered pastrami sandwiches.

"I might have looked up delis near your campus. Being the sandwich lover you are, I assumed you already knew about this place."

"I don't, and I feel embarrassed about it."

"You should," he says as he unfolds his sandwich. It smells amazing.

I lift the pickle that comes with the sandwich and take a bite. As I chew, I lightly moan. "Oh my God, so good." Silas stares at me, a pinch in his brow. "What?" I ask him.

"Can you please not moan? I don't want to have a boner while eating a pastrami sandwich."

I chuckle. "You need to control yourself."

"Won't happen when you're around. Sorry. Control your moaning."

"Can't when a pickle hits me in all the right spots."

"You hear yourself, right? You hear how that can be taken out of context?"

I smirk. "Maybe I wanted it to."

He shakes his head at me. "You're so fucking dirty."

"Pot calling the kettle black. Not sure I've ever met a dirtier man than you."

"You haven't lived long enough," he says as he lifts his sandwich to his mouth. "Talk to me when you're thirty."

"First of all, I don't plan on having experience with anyone else, and also . . . when I'm thirty, that means you're forty. Will you even be able to walk around with me, or will Granddad need a cane?"

"Make fun of me all you want," he says, taking a bite of his sandwich. He chews and swallows. "But when I'm forty, I'll still make you come harder than any other man."

My cheeks blush as I realize that is so true.

"So what are the plans for when I'm gone?" he asks as he wipes his mouth with a napkin.

"Wallow in self-pity because my fine-ass boyfriend won't be around."

He wiggles his eyebrows. "Just the answer I was looking for."

I nudge his shoulder with mine playfully and say, "I don't know. Probably try to catch up on schoolwork. Watch the games with Ross now that he's an addict. Work out of course. Not too much."

"Are you behind on schoolwork?"

"Just a little. I'm not one who likes to procrastinate. It's why it really bothered me to take so long on that article for Roberts. I just like to get my stuff done and not have it hang over me. But ever since I started seeing this guy, he seems to consume a lot of my time."

"Hmm, he sounds like bad news." Silas takes a bite of his sandwich.

"Yeah, he's not too bad. But I figured the best time to catch up is when you're on your away trips. Kind of works out nicely. Spend time with you, catch up on schoolwork."

"Are you going to be going out?"

He's fishing for information, and I don't know why, but I find it endearing in a weird sort of way.

"Are you asking if I plan on going out to clubs and dancing the night away while my boyfriend is gone?"

"You said it," he says, and I know he's joking, but there's also a layer of insecurity inside him. He might trust me, but he still battles that niggling doubt. So I make it easy on him.

I press my hand to his and say, "I don't plan on going out, not without you." He glances up at me, those ice-blue eyes piercing my very soul, and I have this overwhelming sense of affection for him. Consuming and almost paralyzing because, at this moment, I know . . . I know I love him.

My heart is screaming at me to say it, to tell him how I truly feel. But my brain is slamming on the brakes. It might not be the best idea, not when he still seems a touch flighty and not sure of himself. I don't want to scare him away. That's the last thing I want.

"If you wanted to go out . . ." He pauses and swallows. "That's your choice, and I'd be fine with it."

I set my sandwich down and face him. "I appreciate that, but just so you know, I don't need that in my life. I have you now, and that's all I need. So don't worry about me when you're gone, okay?"

He nods and then lets out a deep sigh. "I'm sorry. I'm still trying to regain that sense of trust." He presses the heel of his palm to his forehead. "Sarah really fucked me up."

"I get it, and I have no problem being patient while you figure it all out. But I need you to know something about me, Silas. I hate cheaters, so I'd never become one. I'm with you, so in my mind, that's that."

He presses his finger under my chin and brings me in close. He stares at me for a heartbeat, and for a moment, I almost think he's going to say exactly what I'm feeling—it seems like it's on the tip of his tongue—but then he closes the rest of the space between us and kisses me lightly on the lips.

"Thank you for understanding me."

"No need to thank me," I say as I grab my sandwich. "We understand each other, hence this giant sandwich in my hands. You know what I like."

"I do." He smirks. "Sandwiches, pickles, and my cock."

"In precisely that order."

His brow raises, causing me to laugh. "That exact order?"

"Yup, that exact order."

———

TO: *Ollie Owens*

From: Alan Roberts

Subject: Article

Miss Owens,

Your article has been reviewed and although it was not what we asked for, we've deemed it adequate. It'll be published in the next few days.

Please note, you have gained credit for your internship, although barely. I suggest in the future, when you're given an assignment, you execute it correctly.

As for your internship for the rest of the year, it is up to you if you would like to stay. I have other candidates more than happy to come back to the office for experience, candidates more willing to listen and execute assignments properly.

If you'd like to move forward, I suggest we have a conversation about advancing your career and what that takes.

Sincerely,

Alan Roberts

I read the email a few more times, my heart pounding in my chest.

I passed, but . . . Roberts is also not happy, and if Roberts is not happy, then that means I could be fucked. Future employers will see his name on my résumé, they'll call for a reference, and if he tells them that I'm not a team player or that I don't listen to instruction, that could be very bad.

I press my hand to my forehead in distress. Sure, it was a long shot that he'd like the article, given he wanted something else from me, but I wasn't expecting such a negative, scathing response.

Needing to talk this through in private, I quickly make my way to a conference room, lock the door, and dial Ross's number.

On the second ring, he answers, "Hey girl, I was just about to text you. Those cider donuts you like are back in stock at the store. Want me to grab you some?"

"Uh, sure," I say, my voice shaky.

"What's wrong?" Ross asks, clearly able to read me so well.

"Roberts emailed me."

"Oh shit, did he not like the article?"

"He claimed it was adequate. I passed and got a credit for the internship."

"Well, that's a good thing."

"Sort of. He wasn't happy in the email and made a dig that if I don't want to listen to the assignments, other candidates would gladly take my position for the extended internship."

"He said that? Damn. That's not good."

"I know," I say on a groan. "I've worked so hard to get to where I am, Ross. What am I supposed to do now? What if he gives me another assignment on the Agitators? I can't write that piece. But if I go against him, he could seriously make sure I don't ever get a job after college, and then what? I go back home?"

"Okay, I can hear you're spiraling a touch. First of all, you got credit for the internship, so that's good. That's all you needed, so pat yourself on the back. And you did it without compromising Silas. Now, as for the rest of the internship, I'd take it one day at a time. Meet with him, feel out Roberts and see where his head is at. It would be best if you probably reminded him of where you excel, maybe even come in with a few assignment ideas, how you can be beneficial to the company, and see what he says from there."

"That's a good idea," I say, feeling the tension slightly ease from my chest. "If I go into the meeting prepared, then I can at least provide him with options rather than him dictate. I mean, he will dictate, but if I can sell myself on the lifestyle brands while emphasizing my piss-poor hockey reporting, maybe he'll ease up."

"I think it's a great idea. And before you meet with him, please talk to me about your ideas first. We don't need you going in there with anything lame. You need to wow him."

"Oh, I will," I say. "Trust me, I won't do anything stupid, not with so much on the line."

"Good," he answers. "Okay, so yes to the donuts?"

I chuckle. "Are the donuts for me, or are they for you?"

"You know I always use you as a scapegoat when it comes to pastries."

"Yes to the donuts."

"Okay, I'll grab two boxes just because I know you love them so much."

"Uh-huh." I laugh. "We can eat them tonight while we brainstorm some ideas."

"Sounds perfect. Have fun at work."

"Thanks, text you later." I hang up and then open up my text thread with Silas.

Ollie: *Got an email from Roberts today (finally). Said that I got credit for the internship. Only took him long enough.*

Lucky for me, Silas texts right back.

Silas: *Babe, that's awesome!*

Ollie: *I feel relieved. Now I just have to talk with him about my journey and where I'm headed in the company.*

Silas: *Got to love those conversations. When is the article being published?*

Ollie: *A few days he said.*

Silas: *I'll look out for it so I can print it and frame it.*

Ollie: *You know that's not the first article I've written, right?*

Silas: *Who said framing it was for you? I like to frame everything that has my name on it.*

Ollie: *Oh my God.*

Silas: *LOL. Seriously though, you can add it to a scrapbook for us. You know, create one of those so we can look back at how we started.*

Ollie: *I've actually collected a few things for a scrapbook with you in it.*

Silas: *Really?*

Ollie: *Yeah, just some things like a napkin from the bar where we first kissed, and pictures we've taken, and some pamphlets from the zoo . . .*

Silas: *Well fuck, babe, that's really cute. Is there anything I can look at yet?*

Ollie: *No, it's just a collection right now, but hopefully, once I catch up on everything, I can put together a little book for us.*

Silas: *I can help.*

Ollie: *You'd want to help with my scrapbook?*

Silas: *Hell yeah. Do you need supplies? I can get you one of those letter-cutting machines.*

Ollie: *A Cricut? That's okay. LOL. I like to keep it simple.*

Silas: *Well, you let me know if that changes. I'd be more than happy to grab some things for you.*

Ollie: *Thank you. But if you really want to help, then that could be something fun we do together, when of course we're not fucking.*

Silas: *Fucking first, then scrapbooking.*

Ollie: *I feel like we're becoming so domesticated.*

Silas: *How do you feel about that?*

Ollie: *Perfect.*

Chapter Twenty-Four

SILAS

"I'll have the steak as well," Pacey orders. "Medium. Thank you." He hands his menu to the server.

"Great. If you need anything else, just let me know. Enjoy."

Holmes, Posey, Pacey, and I all reach for a piece of bread at the same time. I go with the pumpernickel, Posey dives for the rye, and Holmes and Pacey are stuck with plain.

While we butter our bread, Pacey says, "See that picture Hornsby sent of Holden? His kid is cute as shit."

Hornsby and Penny just had their baby. We met him the other day, and to our surprise, they named him Holden after Halsey's brother who passed away. Holmes felt so honored. He even teared up when he held little Holden. It was a nice moment for all of us.

"Of course the kid would be cute," Posey says. "They're both really good-looking people."

"That means shit," I say. "It's really up for grabs when it comes to the kind of baby people can make."

"Thought about it, have you?" Pacey asks. "Considering children with Ollie?"

"Oh fuck, no," I say, shaking my head. "Neither of us is ready for that. She still has to graduate, and I know her job is really important to her, so she'll put any sort of child thing on hold for a while. Plus, I don't think I'm ready for that. I'm barely ready—*mentally*—for my relationship with Ollie. I mean, I'm getting there, and I think we're solid, and I trust her, but a baby? I'm not mentally ready for that."

"What does Ollie want to do when she graduates?" Holmes asks.

"Online contributor," I answer. "She really enjoys discussing lifestyle-type things. When she graduates, she hopes to receive offers from a few places. Apparently, the guy she's interning with has a lot of connections. It's why she's sticking around with him."

"Is that going to take her away from Vancouver?" Holmes asks as he sets his butter knife down and then takes a bite of his bread.

"I sure as hell hope not. We talked about how we want to stay together, no matter what happens, and who knows, maybe by the time she graduates, things will be more intense between us."

"Like wedding bells?" Pacey asks.

"I mean, I could see it happening," I say, pulling on the back of my neck.

"Really?" Posey asks. "I feel like you've barely been together."

"Is there a certain timeline that has to be followed to have that kind of thinking?" I ask him.

Posey shakes his head. "No, but I'm just surprised is all. You wouldn't tell us what happened with Sarah, and now that you're with Ollie, I just want to make sure you're healed, you know? That you're not jumping into something too quickly."

"Where the hell is this coming from?" I ask him. "You're the one who was helping me text her the other day."

"Ah, so you admit that I was helping you." Posey points his finger at me.

I pinch the bridge of my nose. "I really hate you. You realize that?"

"Dude, we're about to have the best steak we've ever put in our mouths. Let's not throw hate out there," Pacey says. "And to hop on what Posey is saying, I think we just want to make sure you're okay. We like Ollie, we've seen a change in your life since she's been around, but you can't fully give yourself to her until you've healed. We just want to make sure you're there."

"You all feel that way?" I ask.

I glance at Holmes, and he just nods.

"Hornsby, too," Posey says. "We just care about you."

"Well, I appreciate it," I answer, not getting mad at them because how could I? If I were in their position, I'd probably be doing the same thing. "I wouldn't say I'm one hundred percent, but I'm getting there." I glance around the table and realize that maybe if I talk about it more, it will help me heal. Clearing my throat, I say, "I haven't really said anything, but, uh . . . Sarah cheated on me. That's why we broke up. I caught her with a woman and a man." That last part stings, and I wait for my guys to react, but when I look up, all I see is compassion in their eyes.

"Shit, dude," Pacey says. "I'm sorry."

Holmes grips my shoulder and gives it a squeeze, not needing to say anything, just keeping it at that.

When I look up at Posey, he's shifting his fork around on the table.

"What's going on in your head?" I ask him.

When his eyes meet mine, he says, "This might not be

what you want to hear, but . . . what a bitch. Does she realize she'll never find another man with a Jacob's ladder piercing? All I can think is big mistake . . . huge."

What a fucking idiot, but it makes me laugh.

I grip my water and say, "I think you're right, Posey."

"I know I'm right. Not many men are man enough to get that done. She'll regret it."

"What thoughtful insight," Pacey says with a hint of sarcasm. He then turns toward me and says, "How are you dealing with getting that off your chest?"

"Seems to get a touch easier every time I say it." I lean in a little closer so I don't have to project my voice. "I think I kept it in for so long because it was embarrassing. Like . . . I wasn't man enough to keep Sarah happy, and she had to go somewhere else to find that happiness."

"That's not on you," Holmes says. "That's on her."

"Was it, though?" I ask. "I know I tried a lot with her, but the season's strain wore on us year after year. If I supported her, maybe she wouldn't have strayed."

"Dude, you were a good boyfriend to her," Pacey says. "You put in the effort, she didn't, and I'm not just saying that. I'd tell you the truth if I thought you were at fault. But you weren't. What Holmes says is right. That was on her, not you."

"And now she'll regret it," Posey says, tapping his nose and winking at me.

Sometimes I wonder why we're friends with him.

"I think accepting that truth will take me a moment, as well as learning to trust again."

"Trust is hard," Holmes says. "Trusting anything, even life." Quietly he adds, "Not wanting to lose what's close to you again. It's tough."

I know he's referencing losing his brother, and it's one of the first times I've heard him say anything like that. He normally keeps quiet, especially regarding his brother, which makes me wonder why he's offering a slight glimpse into that part of his life.

"It is," I say. "But Ollie is helping me with that trust. She's patient and understanding. She knows all about Sarah, and she's reassured me that she would never treat me the way Sarah did. I don't know, with Ollie, I just feel lighter, more put together, like the worst is over, and now I'm starting to head out of the other end of the dark tunnel."

"She seems legit," Posey says. "When she defended you in the bar in front of Sarah, I almost kissed her on the lips I was so pleased."

"Dude, no," I say. "Don't even think about kissing her."

"I'd never do it." Posey rolls his eyes. "I was just full of glee that I thought of kissing her."

"Full of glee?" Pacey asks.

"Yeah, you should know that emotion. You were a gleeful fuck when you first met Winnie. Remember how he slunk around the cabin, chasing after her?" Posey says.

"I did not chase after her."

We all scoff at that because Pacey was immediately infatuated. None of us were even allowed to consider looking at Winnie.

"I might have followed her, but I didn't chase," Pacey clarifies.

"That sounds better," I say.

"I'm glad she's everything you're looking for," Holmes says to me. "Ollie seems pretty cool."

"She is," I say, a smile coming to my face as I think about her.

The last few weeks have felt like a whirlwind, and in some way, we've been able to build a foundation together. A foundation of appreciation and friendship. And from there, it's grown. It's grown into something I never thought I'd feel again—love for a woman. But even at that, I think the love I have for Ollie is greater and more meaningful than anything I ever had with Sarah. Experiencing both relationships, I can easily say that.

I think Sarah always had one foot out the door, whereas Ollie truly cherishes me. She appreciates me. And she wants me for me, not for the wealth and assets. Sarah, especially later in our relationship, rarely . . . *loved* on me. It's completely different with Ollie. And I can't see her changing because she's truthful to her core. Sarah isn't, and I know that now. I can see more clearly how selfish she actually was. Everything is different with Ollie.

The feeling I have when she looks at me.

The emotions I experience when we're intimate.

And the way I respond to her—when I talk to her, text her —it's so different from the sense of obligation I had with Sarah. Perhaps that's from the newness of our relationship, but I feel like an active, willing participant rather than someone waiting for the shoe to drop.

Ollie has awoken me, and I'll never take that for granted.

I glance up at my friends and say, "Thanks for being there for me. I really appreciate it."

"No need to thank us," Posey says, mouth full of bread. "That's what we're here for."

———

SILAS: *You awake?*

Ollie: *Mmmm, yes. You going to call?*

I sit up in bed, the morning light shining in my hotel room, and I go to FaceTime. Last night when I got back to my hotel, it was pretty late so I just called Ollie for a bit, but now that I'm awake, I want to talk to her more. We have time before I need to be at the arena, so I might as well spend some time with my girl.

The phone rings a few times, and then her beautiful face comes into view.

"Good morning," she says all sleepy-like as she twists in her sheets.

"Morning," I reply and then notice her bare shoulder. "Babe, are you naked?"

"I am. What about you?"

"I have my briefs on."

"Take them off," she says as she slides the sheets down, and I get a front-row seat view of her perfect breasts.

I prop the phone up on the nightstand next to me and shimmy out of my briefs only to drop them on the floor.

"You're already hard," she says.

"Woke up with a hard-on. Had a sex dream about you last night."

"Mmm, tell me what I did," she says as she moves her hands over her breasts.

My mouth waters from the sight of her. "We were at my place, making dinner together."

"You don't know how to cook." She smirks.

"Didn't stop me from trying in my dream. You were wearing one of my button-up shirts with nothing else."

"Sounds about right." She pinches her nipples, and I grip the base of my erection and squeeze.

"I propped you up on the counter, laid you down, and explored every inch of your body with my tongue."

"Did you undo my shirt and let it fall open?"

I nod. "Yeah, and I sucked on your tits for what seemed like forever."

"I love when you do that," she says as I start to move my hand up and down. "Were you hard in your dream?"

"So fucking hard, like I am right now."

"Let me see," she says, her beautiful eyes fluttering open. I take the phone, and I turn the camera around so she can see my hand on my cock, pumping. "God, that's so sexy."

"Let me see you touch your pussy," I say as my grip grows tighter.

She picks up her phone as well and offers me the same angle. Her bare pussy comes into view right before her hand slides over it, and her finger glides over her slit. "Silas, I wish this was your tongue."

"Me too, baby," I say as a light sheen of sweat breaks out over my skin.

"What else happens? Did you fuck me on the counter?"

Knock. Knock.

I glance over toward the entryway of my door.

Fuck, is that housekeeping? I put up the do not disturb. They should leave me alone.

"Silas."

"Huh? Oh sorry, what did you say?" I ask.

Knock. Knock.

"Dude, open up," Posey says.

"Is someone knocking on your door?" Ollie asks.

"Yeah," I grumble as I flip the camera around. "I think it's—"

The door beeps to unlock, and it opens. Posey, Pacey, and Holmes come charging in. I have about two seconds to cover myself up before they see me.

"What the actual fuck," I yell as I turn the screen of my phone face down so they can't see Ollie. This is why I shouldn't give a spare key to the guys. I thought it was a good idea, given I tend to sleep through an alarm occasionally, but this is not cool.

"We need to talk . . ." Posey's voice dies down as he takes in the scene in front of him. "Uh . . . were you . . ."

I pick up the phone, and luckily, Ollie is covered and waiting for me. "I'll call you back, babe."

"Okay," she says right before I hang up.

"What the hell is going on?" I ask. As my three friends all exchange glances. "What?" I shout.

"Was that Ollie?" Pacey asks.

"Yes," I say, annoyed. "And you're fucking interrupting."

"Sorry, but . . . you need to read this," Posey says as he walks up to me and hands me his phone.

Completely confused, I look down at the screen and read the headline of an article.

"Even Hockey Players Can't Have it All."

Byline: Ollie Owens.

I glance up at them. "Is this Ollie's article?" They nod. "Well, Jesus, why are you barging in here? I've read it already."

"Have you?" Pacey asks.

"Yes," I say. "Before she turned it in."

Posey looks almost gray as he says, "So you were cool with her talking about . . . about what happened with Sarah?"

"Wait, what?" I ask as my heart stills in my chest, all air escaping from my lungs.

"It's, uh . . . it's in there," Holmes says as he pushes his hand through his hair in distress. "How she cheated on you."

"No, the fuck it's not," I say, tossing the phone back. "She wouldn't have written that."

"Dude," Pacey says softly. "It's in there."

"Where?" I say, swimming in the lane of denial.

Posey picks up the phone, and he scrolls through it. Then hands me the phone.

My eyes zero in on the start of the paragraph.

And after a long road trip, where the boys are beaten up and ready for a homecooked meal, there's nothing more they want to go home to than their family and loved ones. Unfortunately for Silas Taters, that wasn't always the case. The Agitators paint their organization as picture perfect, but when you lift the veil, you're offered a glimpse into another side of the story, a side where their players can't seem to make their loved ones happy. It's probably not the first time this has happened, but it's the first confirmed time on record that our Agitators aren't perfect. Silas Taters's former girlfriend cheated on him.

The phone slips out of my hand as my eyes remain fixed on the spot in front of me.

No.

There's no fucking way.

She wouldn't do that to me.

She cares about me. She knows the damage. She understands the trust issues I suffer. She wouldn't use me as a piece in her article . . . right?

I read through it.

I approved it . . .

And then something sticks out in my head. The day she told me she turned it in, she said she made some changes. Were these the changes?

"Silas," Holmes says softly. "What can we do, man?"

"I . . . I don't fucking know," I say as I lean back on the headboard. "I don't fucking believe it." Then immediately, I ask, "Who wrote that? What's the name on the article?"

"It's Ollie," Pacey says. "Byline, Ollie Owens."

"You told her about Sarah and what happened, right?" Posey asks.

"I did, but . . . she swore she wouldn't say anything to anyone." I shake my head, unable to comprehend this. "She wouldn't do that . . . would she?"

My mind flies fast with ideas, with notions of what could have happened, but out of all of the scenarios, one thing keeps sticking out in my mind . . . her need to prove herself. Her need to do right by Roberts.

My lips roll together as my teeth grind down.

"Silas . . ." Posey asks.

"She wouldn't fucking dare," I say, rage taking over the shock.

"Tates, maybe we get you out of bed, showered, talk about this," Pacey suggests, but I shake my head.

"No, I need you to leave. Right fucking now." My fists clench at my side.

"I don't know if that's a good idea," Holmes says.

"I said fucking leave," I yell, startling all three of them.

Pacey nods his head toward the door, and Holmes follows him. Posey hangs back for a second and says, "I'm here for you, Silas. If you need me, you just ask."

I don't say a word, I just stare at my phone, rage beating through me. What if this was Sarah? What if she had something to do with it?

Or what if . . . the girl I thought I fucking loved has decided to fuck me over . . . just like Sarah?

I whip off my covers and go to the shower, my anger so heavy in my chest that I feel like I can't breathe. I can only imagine what the comments section is saying, what other news sites are going to read the article and then toss their own spin on me. Because that's what they do. One article comes out with the news, and the rest just circulate it with additional "facts."

So now everyone will fucking know about my private life.

Everyone will know the kind of man I am.

How I can't make a woman happy.

How I'm a fucking loser who a girl cheats on.

My biggest, darkest, most embarrassing part of my life is now out on display. *I've been played for a fool again.* She came after me, pushed me . . . all to get fucking ahead in her career.

I slip into the shower once the water is warm, and instead of washing my body off, I feel myself lean against the tile as I try to catch air into my lungs.

Fuck, how could I be so stupid?

She's used me from the very beginning.

From the very fucking beginning, and I chose to look past it.

I slide down to the bottom of the shower and push my hands through my hair as the water surrounds me. My eyes well with tears, and as I curl my fingers into fists, I feel my tears fall. Nothing feels worse than this. Ollie swore she'd never cheat on me, and perhaps that was true. But her promises didn't extend to using me for her career, did it? No one had to know about what Sarah did, and their ignorance meant I was saved from the embarrassing scrutiny.

And my heart? It feels as though it's been ripped right out of my chest.

I've given Ollie so much of myself, things Sarah never knew about. I was ready to see a new future. A happier future. But that was only possible through trust. And trust has once again been shattered.

Sarah might have bent me, but Ollie . . . she just fucking broke me.

Chapter Twenty-Five

OLLIE

Ollie: *Hey, is everything okay?*

Ollie: *Silas, I haven't heard from you. Just checking in.*

Ollie: *When you get this, just text or call, or anything. I want to make sure you're okay.*

I stare down at my phone as I sit in class, waiting for it to start, my stomach churning. Something happened. The boys charged into his room, told him something, and now he's not responding. I don't know if it has to do with us, something with the team, or maybe with Hornsby.

I sent a text to Winnie as well, asking her if she's heard anything, but she hasn't responded either.

And now that it's a few hours later with no answer to my phone calls or texts, I'm starting to freak out.

The door to the classroom opens, and I glance up just in time to catch Ross walking in, a look of almost disgust on his face.

"Surprised to see you here," he says as he takes a seat.

Uh, what's with the attitude?

"Why?" I ask. And then I realize maybe Ian told him something. "Wait, do you know something about the team? I was in the middle of . . . things with Silas when the boys busted into his room, and I haven't heard from him since. He won't answer my calls or my texts."

"I'm not surprised," Ross says with pursed lips.

What the actual hell.

He digs through his backpack, and I stop him and turn him to look at me. "What's going on?"

"Ollie, you know I love you, and I'd do anything for you, but that article. Girl, are you really that desperate to impress Roberts?"

"What are you talking about?" I ask. "Was it released?"

"Yeah, and it's already trending." He shakes his head. "I can't believe you wrote that about Silas after you promised him."

"Wrote what?" I ask as I grab my phone and search for the article. When it comes up and I read the headline, I already know something is off. That's not the headline I chose. My eyes scan over the text, rapidly floating through the text until it gets to one part.

One single paragraph that causes all the blood to drain from my face.

"Oh my God," I whisper. "I . . . I didn't write that." My eyes scan through the paragraph over and over. "Ross, I didn't. I would never do that."

"It has your name on the article," Ross says.

Tears fill my eyes as I look up at him, panic causing my throat to grow tight. "But I didn't put that in there. I would never do that to Silas. I . . . I don't understand." My breath escapes me, and I panic for air, my breathing becoming labored.

"Shit," Ross says as he scoops up our things and then takes me by the hand, right out of the classroom and into the hallway. "Deep breaths, Ollie." He guides me to a corner and then sits us both down.

"I didn't do it. I w-would n-never." My teeth start to chatter, my body spasming with every second that goes by where this article is published.

"If you didn't do it, then who did?" Ross asks.

I glance at him and say, "You're . . . you're the only one I accidentally told."

His brow creases. "If you're implying—"

"No, I'm not." I shake my head. "I know you wouldn't do that to me." I press my hand to my forehead and try to think. "I just don't get it. That's not how I turned in the article. Who changed it? Can someone change it? That's not allowed, is it?"

"I have no idea," Ross says. "Obviously, someone did change it. Who did you turn the article in to?"

"Roberts," I say. I sent it directly to him. "I don't get how he would know about the cheating. Silas hasn't told anyone. And I don't know who else would know about the article."

"The only correlation is . . . you," Ross says, stating the obvious.

"Fuck," I say as I pull out my phone and dial Silas's number. I bring it up to my ear, and it rings three times before going to voicemail. When the phone beeps, I say, "Silas, it's me. I really need to talk to you. Please call me."

I hang up and then lean my head against the wall.

"Why didn't you tell him that you didn't write that part in the article?"

"Because he's not going to listen to the voicemail," I answer, knowing Silas too well. "There's no point." I draw my legs up to my chest and grip them tightly. "I think I'm fucked."

SILAS

"MAN, YOU HAVE TO EAT SOMETHING," Posey says as he takes a seat next to me at a table in the arena while my phone buzzes on the table. Another phone call from Ollie, but I let it go to voicemail.

"I did. I had a protein bar," I say.

"That's not enough, and you know it." Posey passes a plate of pasta salad toward me. "Come on, man. Eat something."

"I don't want to fucking eat something," I say as I lean back in my chair. "Fuck, Levi, does it look like I want to eat something?"

He pauses, studying me. "It looks like you want to punch your fist through a wall."

"Accurate," I say as my leg bounces up and down at a rapid pace.

"Have you spoken to her?"

"What the hell would I say? Thanks for throwing me under the bus for your own career gain? Thanks for spreading my dirty laundry for the fucking world to see?" I shake my head. "No. Fuck her."

"Okay, I can see where your head is at, but maybe something to consider, what if, I don't know . . . what if it wasn't her who wrote it?"

"What the fuck are you talking about? That's the article she wrote. I read it before she turned it in. She told me she made a few changes. The part of me being cheated on, those were her changes. And why the hell are you defending her?"

"I'm not defending her. I'm just trying to figure this all out, okay? It doesn't seem like Ollie would do that to you."

"And you think you know her better than I do?"

"From what you know of her, is this something she would do?"

I glance away, my anger overtaking my common sense.

"She knew about Sarah. She was one of the first to know. How did it end up in her article?"

"I . . . I don't know," Posey says as he scratches the back of his neck. "All I know is that I've seen the way she looks at you and cares for you. It's hard to believe she would do this." He pauses and then says, "What if . . . what if it was Sarah?"

"What do you mean?" I ask.

"What if Sarah went and told someone? I mean, she did have that altercation with Ollie at the bar. Maybe Ollie pissed her off, and Sarah went in for revenge?"

I run my tongue over my teeth, giving that idea thought. "How would she even know who Ollie was, that she was writing an article to begin with?"

Just then, the person of question, Sarah herself, walks into the cafeteria. It's rare when marketing people go on trips with the teams, but because she's been helping fill in for Penny, some duties have been split.

Sarah glances around, and when she spots me, she heads right for my table.

But this time, instead of her trying to attack me with her sex appeal, she has a worried expression on her face.

"Silas, can I have a word with you?" she asks as she wrings her hands in front of her.

"Whatever you have to say can be said in front of Posey."

She glances at Posey and then back at me. I wonder what's going on in her head. Is she guilty? She has to know about the article. I swear everyone knows about it at this point. That thing spread like wildfire.

"Okay." She clears her throat. "I wanted to talk to you about that article that was written. I'm already getting emails from other news outlets asking for an interview, for a comment. My name is being tossed around because I was your last girlfriend, and now my boss is questioning me. Why . . . why did you have her write that? I know I hurt you, but this is playing with my livelihood now."

"So . . . you didn't have anything to do with this article?"

"No," she says in disgust and shock. "Why would I want to put that out in the world? I'm ashamed of what I did, Silas. I don't want to be known as a cheater. There are comments in that article of people tearing me apart. Do you really think I would want to add that kind of disaster to my life?"

I've known Sarah for a very long time, and I know when she's being manipulative, when she's lying, when she's sad, angry, and telling the truth. And I know, from the depths of my soul, that she had nothing to do with this.

She swipes at a tear and whispers, "I don't want to lose this job."

"You won't lose your job," I say. "I'll make sure of it."

"Dude . . ." Posey says. When I give him a death glare, he doesn't back down. "She fucked you over. Made you feel like absolute shit. Made you self-doubt, and you're just going to jump in and protect her like that? What the fuck, man?"

Sarah stiffens next to me. "Everyone makes mistakes, Levi."

"That wasn't a mistake," he says, his voice harsh. "That was messing with my boy. You realize the kind of man Silas is? He would do anything for the people close to him, and you cheated on him, God knows how many times. Frankly, it's disgusting you think you can ask for help without even apologizing or owning up to what you did. You're a shit person, Sarah. Simple as that. If your name is being dragged around, then you fucking deserve it."

"Levi," I say, trying to calm him down.

"What? It's true. You deserve better. Don't sink to her level."

"I'm not sinking to her level, but I'm also not going to just sit back when the girl I was with fucked us both over. Sarah shouldn't lose her job because of what she did to me." Even I'm not that petty.

"The whole reason you were even with Ollie is because of

Sarah," Posey practically yells. "Like where's your fucking head at, man?"

I know he's right.

Sarah doesn't deserve my empathy.

She doesn't deserve anything from me.

Yet for some reason, I feel bad for her.

"I don't know." I rub my hand over my forehead before I stand from the table. I look down at Sarah and say, "You had nothing to do with this article?"

"I swear, Silas. I wouldn't do that to you, and I sure as hell wouldn't do that to me. I know you don't trust me, and I get that. I do owe you an apology. What I did to you, how I treated you, it was awful and I'm sorry. I saw how badly I hurt you, and I wouldn't do that again. Maybe I was jealous of Ollie, but I'd never be vindictive, especially if it hurt me in the end too."

Because it always revolves around Sarah. That's something I need to remember.

I just nod and take off toward the locker room.

Where the fuck is my head at? Great question.

I'm angry.

I'm hurt.

And I'm trying to figure out why the girl I thought I loved would do this to me.

Maybe what it comes down to is I got played.

Simple as that.

OLLIE

"DID YOU WATCH THE GAME?" Ross asks as he comes into my dorm room.

I shake my head as I bury myself further into my bed, where I've stayed for the past three days.

Thankfully, I haven't had to go to work because it was a weekend, and I skipped out on classes on Friday, so I've just remained planted here, unmoving, not wanting anyone to communicate with me besides Silas.

And he hasn't said one word to me.

Not a single one.

And I don't blame him.

From his vantage point, another woman he loved betrayed him. If only he would listen to me.

Ross takes a seat on my bed. "Silas got into another fight."

My gut squeezes from the thought of it. The other night when we were watching, Silas got into an altercation with another player. I watched as he tossed his gloves to the ice along with his helmet and upper-cutted another player. That other player did the same.

The sight of them grappling nearly made me throw up.

"Was it bad?" I ask.

"The player caught Silas right in the face. The announcers were saying it looked like Silas just gave up and wasn't invested in the fight at all. And from where I sat, it seemed like he wanted to be punched. It was their second loss in a row, and Mr. Mustard was complaining about Silas and how he needs to get his head in the game."

"I'm sure it's not, thanks to me."

"But you didn't write that piece in the article."

"I know that, and you know that, but he doesn't. For all I know, Silas is reeling right now. He trusted me when his trust was hard to earn, and look what happened. He's hurting, Ross, and all I want to do is fix it."

"So fix it," Ross says. "The guys come home tonight. Ian told me. Go to his place and force him to talk to you. He can't avoid you if you're in his apartment. He deserves the truth."

"But I don't know what the truth is. All I know is that I didn't write it."

"So explain that to him. Let him know that you plan on getting to the bottom of this."

"I don't know, Ross." I sigh. "Maybe I should just give up. He's probably better off without me."

"That's bullshit, and you know it." Ross comes closer and places his hand on my leg. "Ollie, you've been significantly happier since you've been together. He even said it himself that he was learning to trust again."

"That means nothing when I lost that trust."

"Well then, tell me this," he says. "You said you love him, right? Are you just going to give up on that? Do you think you could get over him?"

"No," I say. "But I don't think I have a choice. I think it's inevitable."

"It is if you don't try." He pushes at my leg. "Just go over there, talk to him. Get him to listen to you."

I pull my weighted blanket that smells like him closer to my face. "And what if he doesn't believe me?"

"He will. Trust me. You just need to talk it out. Okay?"

I roll my teeth over my trembling lip. "I don't know."

"You'll regret it if you don't. Talk to him, make sense of it all." Ross is right. I can't imagine ever feeling how I feel for Silas for anyone else. He's such a good man. Private, thoughtful, caring, kind, funny . . . just perfect. I can see my life with him. Through ups and downs, wins and losses, good assignments and bad assignments. I can see how we balance each other out. *And I can't just let that go. Let him go.*

I take a deep breath and say, "Okay."

Chapter Twenty-Six

OLLIE

From the moment I stepped into Silas's apartment, I knew this was a bad idea.

The last thing I'm sure he wants to see when he gets home after a brutal road trip is me, but Ross is right. If I'm going to have any chance at salvaging this relationship with Silas, then I need to talk to him. And the only way I can do that is if I'm at his place.

Doesn't make it any less intimidating.

Because I have this horrible feeling that this is the end of us. That there is no coming back from this. And the more I think about that, the more I can't hold back my emotions. Because I love this man. I love him more than anyone I've ever loved, anyone I've ever been with.

He's made me feel beautiful again.

He's made me feel like I matter.

He's put a smile on my face every day, and the knowledge

that it could all end after tonight has my stomach in absolute knots.

I got a text from Ross about a half hour ago letting me know that the boys landed, so Silas should be home any minute.

I check my phone for the time just as the front door unlocks.

Nerves shoot through my veins, and as the door opens, I brace myself for what's to come.

I stand from the couch, wearing his sweatshirt and a pair of leggings, hoping and praying he'll give me a chance.

He steps into the apartment wearing a stunning dark gray three-piece suit that clings to every part of his body. He rolls his suitcase inside, then shuts the door behind him and locks it. When he turns around and spots me, he freezes.

His lips thin.

His brow turns down.

And I immediately know I'm not welcome.

"What the fuck are you doing here?" he asks.

Hands trembling, legs about to give out, I take a step forward and say, "I really need to talk to you."

"About what?" he asks as he tosses his keys on the entryway table and walks over to the kitchen. That's when I catch the black under his eye as well as the swelling. My heart aches, knowing I'm the reason he has that. I'm the reason he's had such a rough few days. I'm the reason his team now has two losses.

"About the article," I say.

"Nothing to talk about," he replies as he grabs a beer from his fridge and pops it open. "You decided to take advantage of me to gain momentum in your career. Simple as that."

He downs what seems like half of the can.

"I . . . I didn't write that," I say.

He lowers his can of beer and looks me in the eyes. "Do

you really expect me to believe that? You wrote that fucking article. I read it before you turned it in. That was yours."

"Yes, it was," I say, my voice barely above a whisper from how tight my throat is. "But that part about you, it wasn't written by me. I wouldn't do that to you, Silas."

"Wouldn't you, though?" he asks. He takes another gulp of his beer and then sets it down on the counter. "You were desperate to make something of yourself, to impress Roberts, so what would stop you from using me? Seems like it's worked out for you. The story is everywhere."

"I wouldn't do that, Silas. I wouldn't do that to the man I love."

"Love?" He scoffs with an ugly laugh. "You don't fucking love me, and don't even try to claim that you do," he says while reaching into the fridge for another beer. "No one would ever write that about the person they love."

"Silas, I didn't write—"

"You fucked me, took what you wanted, and left me bleeding," he says, his voice growing angrier. "Was it worth it?" He tips his beer back and chugs.

For the third time, I say, "I didn't write that—"

"Don't fucking bullshit me, Ollie," he yells and slams his beer on the counter next to his empty can. "I don't want to hear your excuses. Before you turned in your article, three fucking people knew about Sarah cheating on me." He holds up three fingers. "Me, Sarah . . . and you."

"Well, did you ask Sarah? Maybe she said something."

"She came up to me, horrified because her life has drastically changed. She's getting harassed, about to lose her job, and her name is being dragged through the mud. She wouldn't have done that to herself."

"And you believe her?"

He takes a step forward. "Why the fuck would she damage her image to make you look better to your boss?"

It's a good point.

"You're out of options, Ollie. You sure as hell know it wasn't me who said anything. No one else knew, so tell me again how this is not your fault."

I can't.

I have no answers for him.

No reason as to why or how this happened. I'm just as confused as he is.

"I'm . . . I'm sorry, Silas."

He shakes his head. "Get the fuck out of here. Leave your key on the table."

"Silas, please. Just give me a second to figure this all out. I can talk to Roberts and see what happened."

"What the fuck do you not understand when I say get out of here?" he asks, yelling. He flings his arm toward the door. "Leave. You're dead to me, Ollie."

"Silas . . . you don't—"

"Leave!" he yells. "Now. Get the fuck out of my life."

And with that, he walks toward his bedroom without looking back. And I know, that's the last time I'm going to see him.

That's the last time I'll talk to him.

There's no coming back from this.

A sad, heartbreaking reality I'll have to face.

OLLIE: *Five minutes and counting.*

Ross: *How do you feel?*

Ollie: *Nauseous.*

Ross: *You can do this.*

Ollie: *The only reason I'm doing this is so I have answers.*

Ross: *I know. You've got this, Ollie.*

"Mr. Roberts will see you now."

I tear my eyes off my phone and lightly smile at Roberts's assistant as I stand up. "Thank you," I say before pushing through Roberts's glass doors and straight into his office, where I find him typing away on his computer.

"Miss Owens, is this about the email I sent you?" he asks, eyes still on the computer.

"No," I say as I sit in one of the chairs across from his desk. "I was hoping to speak to you about the article."

He moves his mouse around, clicks a few times, then finally gives me his attention. "What about it?" he asks. "It's picked up a lot of traction. I'd think you would be happy to see your name everywhere."

One would think.

"Well, there was a part in the article that I didn't write, and I was wondering where it came from."

"What part in particular?" he asks as he presses two fingers to his temple.

"The part where it talks about Silas and how his girlfriend cheated on him."

"Ah, well some changes were made in the editing process. It probably was added then."

"Added? That's what everyone is talking about. How can you be so casual about it being *added* in there when I didn't write it, but my name is on the article?"

He picks up a pen from his desk and tilts his head to the side, silently studying me. "Do you have a problem with the article, Miss Owens?"

Nerves flit through me as I slowly gulp. I don't want to make him mad, but I also want to get to the bottom of this.

"I do." It feels like my internal organs are shaking from his stern look. "You see, that information about Silas was private. It should never have been available to the public."

"Private?" he says. "Funny, because my source heard you talking about it with your friend."

"Talking about it? I never—" I pause, my mind flashing to my lunch with Ross, where I accidentally told him.

"I can tell from your expression you know exactly what I'm talking about."

"That was . . . that was accidental," I say. "That wasn't public information."

"You should know anything said out loud is public information, Miss Owens. Or have you not learned that in your years studying to be a journalist?"

"But who . . . how . . ."

"It doesn't matter," Roberts says. "The information was brought to me, and I thought it was an integral element of our article that was missing. Frankly, it was boring up until that point."

"But you can't do that," I say, growing angry. "You can't just change my article like that."

"Yes, I can. It's in the contract you signed when you first joined the company. I can change anything you write. And I did."

"But that messed up my relationship with Silas. You . . . you hurt us."

"Are you looking for an apology?" he asks, a maniacal smile passing over his lips.

"I'm looking for some decency," I say. "Good God, where's your integrity? You're talking about a man's private life here, one that's being dragged through the mud."

"You're talking about the same thing that happens to every professional athlete and celebrity out there. They're in the limelight, and they know the consequences. They get paid a lot of money, so their private lives are fair game."

"No, it's not. They're humans. You shouldn't have the right to destroy someone based on the narrative you believe is correct in your head."

"Are you telling me how to run my business? A college student, really, Miss Owens?" He tosses his pen on the table and then folds his hands together. "I suggest you stop and think about what you're saying to me."

"I know exactly what I'm going to say to you." I stand from my chair and say, "You're a pathetic man who has made millions bashing other people's lives. You're a sorry excuse for a human, and I truly hope that when it's your time, karma comes back to bite you so hard in the ass your mustache falls right off."

His jaw ticks, and he stands as well. "That was a mistake, Miss Owens."

"What are you going to do? Fire me?" I ask. "I already quit. I will not subject myself to a man who deems it suitable to pry in other's lives to fulfill some farsighted Napoleon complex you're embodying."

"You think this conversation will remain within these walls?" He shakes his head and then presses his finger into the desk in front of him. "I'll make sure you never get a job within this industry. You can count on that."

"If that's what's going to make you sleep better at night, then go ahead. I don't give a fuck. You're a tiny man with a fat ego. I feel sorry for you."

"You won't get credit for this internship. Insubordination."

"Fine," I say as I head toward his door. "Do whatever you want. You already took away the most important thing in my life. Feel free to take away the rest." And then I fling his door open so hard that it clashes against the wall, startling his assistant right out of her chair. "Your boss is a lying mother-fucker with a tiny dick. Have fun."

And with that, I go straight down the elevator, through the bustling hallways, and straight to my desk, where I grab my purse and fill it up with my belongings, including the picture of Silas.

"Where are you going in such a hurry?" Candace asks as she pops up out of nowhere. "Can't be the article that has you all in a tizzy."

The tone in her voice feels slimy.

Too slimy.

Like . . . like she knows something.

Slowly, I turn around and say, "That article, you don't happen to know who edited it, do you?"

"Who do you think edited it?" she asks with a smirk. "Every article went through me."

My nostrils flare.

The hairs on the back of my neck stand to attention.

And I clutch my bag as I take a step forward so we're nearly nose to nose. "Did you put the cheating part in the article?" I ask through clenched teeth.

As if in slow motion, Candace's expression morphs from smug to full-on demonic as the corners of her mouth lift like the Grinch. "Roberts practically begged me to liven it up, and since you were so indiscreet, spreading your boyfriend's dirty laundry everywhere, I thought the information was up for grabs."

"You overheard us. You were there in the cafeteria?"

"You should really learn to keep your voice down."

The rage of a thousand men takes over my body, causing my blood to boil. How fucking dare she?

I should have known.

She was out to get me from the day I used her Post-it Note.

"You . . . bitch," I mutter, causing her to smile even broader if possible.

White-hot anger blisters through me.

My fists clench at my side.

And before I can stop myself, I grab her head, and I slam my forehead against hers, headbutting her straight into the wall behind her.

I don't even register the pain.

I don't bother to say anything else to her.

Instead, I bump into her on my way down the hall, and while I pass her desk, I sweep my arm across her neatly organized pens and Post-it Notes and trash it all to the floor before reaching the elevator and pressing the down button.

I don't realize the full extent of what I've done until I'm in my dorm, with ice on my forehead, and an email from my adviser that I'm going to have to repeat my internship, which will delay me from graduating.

Fucking . . . great.

The worst thing? The pain in my head and the pain from failing is no comparison to the pain in my heart from losing Silas.

TO: *Ollie Owens*

From: Professor Wheeler

Subject: Scheduled Meeting

Miss Owens,

Since you failed to show up to our meeting regarding your future here in the journalism department and you didn't obtain credit for your summer internship, it's with deepest regards that I'm recommending to the dean that you're excused from the School of Journalism, effective after the semester is done.

You will maintain credit for the classes you've taken this semester, given you pass them, but unfortunately, we will no longer be able to offer you any more classes in the journalism department moving forward. I believe you are aware of the circumstances that brought you to this point. And since you were on a partial housing scholarship, I have the difficult job to tell you that you no longer will have access to those funds at the semester's end.

If you have any questions, please feel free to contact me. I would advise that you sit down with a school-provided counselor to figure out what your next moves should be.

Sincerely,

Professor Wheeler

ROSS: *Want me to come over?*

Ollie: *No. I just want to be alone.*

Ross: *I don't like you being in your room all by yourself.*

Ollie: *I love you for caring, but I just want to sit here and cry alone.*

Ross: *Can I at least bring you something? Maybe find Candace and accidentally run a razor over her head, right down the middle perhaps? I have impeccable accuracy. I also know where Professor Wheeler's office is. I can stick a dead fish in it somewhere.*

Ollie: *I'm not going to stop you if that's what you choose to do.*

Ross: *I'll keep a razor in my pocket at all times, then. The fish, well, that will have to be specifically planned. But seriously, anything I can bring you?*

Ollie: *No, I'm good. Thanks.*

I set my phone down, then press my palms against my eyes and let out an ugly sob.

This is so unfair.

All of it.

The loss of the internship, the loss of credit even though I performed everything required. I even wrote an article that was within the scope given to me.

Yet I'm losing everything.

My job.

My dreams.

My housing.

My man . . .

I'm not going to negate the fact that I'm the one who slipped up. I'm the one who broke Silas's trust. Even if it was accidental. That's on me, but what Candace did? I'm still trying to wrap my head around it, how someone can be so maniacal.

How one mistake can have such an adverse effect on the outcome of my life and everything that was important to me.

Then again, that's what Silas must think of me. That I took a piece of his life and sold it for gain. And he's dealing with a shitstorm from the media. I know, because I've looked. Sarah too.

All because of Candace. There's no doubt in my mind that she's Roberts's favorite right now, something I strived for throughout my internship, but now, now it feels like a baseless desire.

Why would you want to team up with a man like that? With someone who has absolutely no heart or awareness for the people around them? Someone who would derail a person's future with zero regard for how adversely it will change their life.

I grab a tissue from my nightstand and blow my nose before wiping my eyes again.

At least I felt like I made the right decision by choosing to leave.

And headbutting Candace. I hope she has a concussion. I can still hear the sound it made when our heads collided.

Sure, it cost me my graduation and reputation, but I walked away knowing I did the right thing.

As for what I'm going to do now? I have no freaking clue. Roberts not only got me kicked out of the School of Journalism, but he'll prevent me from obtaining any internship or job here in Vancouver, which means, I have to go back home.

The thought of walking back there with my tail tucked between my legs only to see my dad's "I told you so" face creates a whole new level of nausea. Something I can't think about right now, even though I probably should since my time here is quickly dwindling.

Sighing, I slowly climb out of bed and fill up my water glass. That's when I see the box of things I collected while dating Silas and all the little items I saved to put in a scrapbook.

Maybe because I love self-inflicting pain apparently, or

maybe because I miss him more than anything, I pick up the box and carry it to my bed. I set my water on my nightstand, then flip open the box. I swipe away my tears, making way for fresh ones, and pick up the first thing at the very top. The picture frame I brought into work of him. I never changed the picture out of pure spite. Nope, I made everyone stare at his abs.

I set the picture down and then pick up another one. It's a selfie of the two of us. He's kissing my cheek, and I'm smiling. I choke down a sob as I stare at how incredibly happy I was. How happy he was.

I set that down and grab the map we used at the zoo. It's folded in half from where Silas stuffed it in the back pocket of his jeans. I remember watching him do that and thinking it was an odd thing to think was hot. But I did. I thought it was so hot, and I had to check myself because we were still friends.

Another picture of us, this one is of me sleeping on his bare chest.

The labels to the yogurts we shared together.

Napkins from the bar.

Another picture of us from one of the events we went to together. I found it online and printed it out.

Agitators paraphernalia.

A business card from . . .

I stare down at the business card, remembering when I got this. We were at the sponsor event for Silas, and I was trying to break him by fondling him all night. But there was a break in my pursuit to drive him crazy. That was when we spoke to JP Cane and Ryot Bisley . . . the owner of The Jock Report.

JP handed me his card in case I could help him with his charities.

I rub my lips together and once again swipe at my eyes as an idea forms in my head.

I grab my phone from the nightstand and text Ross.

Ollie: *I think I have an idea.*

He must be on Ollie watch because he texts back right away.

Ross: *Uh, an idea for what?*

Ollie: *It's kind of crazy, but I think it might be the solution I need.*

Ross: *Are we talking about stalking Silas? Creating a PowerPoint on how you didn't fuck up but sort of did in a small way? I really think we need to just let him be for now.*

Ollie: *Not about Silas, he has asked me to leave his life, and I'm going to respect that.*

Ross: *Okay, then a solution for what?*

Ollie: *Leaving school.*

"I'M ACTUALLY SWEATING for you right now, and you know how much I despise perspiring," Ross says into the phone.

"I know, I'm sorry."

"Are you sure this is a good idea?" Ross asks.

"No, but what else am I going to do? Go back to Oregon? That is the last-case scenario."

"I know, but The Jock Report? They just ran an article about your article and how the media manipulates stories for views."

Yeah, that didn't bode well for me. After I told Ross my plan, we pooled together our money and bought the cheapest airplane ticket we could find to Los Angeles and then put the hotel on my credit card. I'm here for twenty-four hours with a mission to talk to JP Cane without an appointment. And with a big black mark on my name.

"It won't be easy," I say. "But I need to at least try. I'm all out of options."

"Okay, but call me as soon as you're done."

"I will."

"Good luck. Love you."

"Love you too," I say before hanging up the phone and

sticking it in my purse. Dressed in a deep purple pantsuit and a white blouse, I clutch the strap of my purse and walk through the doors of Cane Enterprises. I know Ryot Bisley is one of the owners of The Jock Report, and JP is an investor, but since he's the one I made a connection with, he's the one I'll try talking to first.

When I reach the front desk, I casually say, "Hello, I have a meeting with JP Cane."

I don't.

The assistant looks up at me and says, "ID?"

I smile and dig into my purse for my ID. When I hand it to her, I'm almost worried she's going to run some quick background check, but instead, she scans it and then prints out a visitors pass for me that I stick on my shirt.

"Through security, top floor."

I smile and say, "Thank you."

I work my way through security, get searched, and then head to his office. The building is beautiful. Full of live plants and modern lines, I could see why working for Cane Enterprises would be relaxing even though the demand for success is high.

When I reach the floor I'm supposed to be on, there's another receptionist, so I stop at her desk. "Can I help you?" she asks.

"Yes, I, uh, I don't have a meeting, but I would like to see if JP Cane has any availability today."

Without even checking, the woman shakes her head. "I'm sorry, he has no time in his schedule."

Exactly what I thought was going to happen.

"I understand," I say. "I actually met Mr. Cane up in Vancouver at a sponsor event, and he gave me his card." I flash the card at her. "He said to contact him. Well, I'm here in Los Angeles for the day and really need to talk to him."

"And as I said, he doesn't have any time in his schedule."

"What if . . . what if I just wait around, see if something opens up?"

"You are more than welcome to see if that happens, but I can't guarantee you anything."

"I understand, and I appreciate the chance." I glance behind me at two leather armchairs. "Would it be okay if I sat there?"

"That would be fine," the receptionist says.

"Thank you." I smile kindly. "I'm Ollie, by the way. Ollie Owens."

"Ollie, it's nice to meet you. I'm Terri."

"Terri, thank you for letting me crash in your waiting area for the day."

I walk over to one of the chairs, and just as I take a seat, the elevator doors part, and three extremely attractive men step into the lobby.

Huxley.

JP.

And Breaker.

I know what they look like and what they do for the company, thanks to careful research. I've even researched their personal lives and noted that they're all married.

Each with a cup of coffee in hand, they greet Terri, and as they're walking by, JP glances over at me and pauses for a moment. Faded recognition crosses over his face as he points his finger at me. "How do I know you?"

"The sponsor event in Vancouver. Ollie Owens," I say. "I was with Silas Taters."

"That's right," he says. "Ollie Owens?"

"Yes," I say.

"She's hoping to slip in to see you today," Terri says. "I told her your schedule is full, but she's willing to wait to see if there's an opening."

He slowly nods, keeping his eyes on me. He lifts his cup to

his lips and takes a sip. "Well, looks like you're going to have to wait." And with that, he takes off.

Dammit, and for a second, I thought he'd meet with me quickly.

Looks like I'm here for the long haul.

I take out my phone and send a quick text to Ross.

Ollie: *Schedule full. Waiting in the reception area to see if there's an opening. JP saw me, recognized me, and made me repeat my name. I think he knows I'm the one who wrote the article. Do you think this is a lost cause?*

Ross: *I was afraid of that. They're very passionate about The Jock Report, and your article goes against everything they believe in.*

Ollie: *I get it. Do you think I should leave?*

Ross: *What do you think?*

Ollie: *I could admit defeat. Or I could hang in here and hope he gives me a chance.*

Ross: *I'm guessing you're going to wait.*

Ollie: *I don't think leaving is an option.*

OLLIE: *Two hours and counting and nothing. Not even a peep.*

Ross: *What have you been doing?*

Ollie: *Writing in my notepad about how much I miss Silas.*

Ross: *That has got to be the saddest two hours ever.*

Ollie: *I cried at one point and realized I needed to stop.*

Ross: *The receptionist is going to judge you.*

Ollie: *Trust me, I think she already has.*

OLLIE: *Just saw JP leave for lunch with his wife. I almost cried just from the sight of them holding hands. I miss Silas.*

Ross: *Pull it together, woman.*

Ollie: *I know. It was a weak moment.*

OLLIE: *I want to stand and stretch so bad. I've been sitting in this chair for six hours. I need mobility.*

Ross: *Don't stretch. Don't do anything to draw attention to yourself.*

Ollie: *So don't perform jumping jacks?*

Ross: *Jesus, no.*

Ollie: *This is torture.*

Ross: *Hang in there.*

OLLIE: *Everyone is leaving the office. It's past five. What do I do?*

Ross: *Has JP left?*

Ollie: *No. Seems like everyone else has filtered out.*

Ross: *Well, stay put until told otherwise.*

Ollie: *I feel so pathetic. It's clear he knows who I am from the article, and the last thing he wants to do is talk to me.*

"Miss Owens?" Terri says. I look up to see her standing next to her desk, her purse strapped on her shoulder.

"Yes?" I ask.

"Unfortunately, I'm going to have to ask you to leave. It's time for me to go home, and I can't let you be here by yourself."

"Oh . . . yeah, I understand that," I say, feeling heartbroken.

I stand from my trusty chair and pick up my purse.

"I'm sorry, Miss Owens."

"No need to apologize," I say. "I get it."

Terri gestures her arm to the elevator, and I follow suit. Terri has been nice all day. She even offered to grab me something for lunch. Who does that? Offers a complete stranger lunch? I declined, not wanting to put her out, but even though this has been a shitty day of waiting in a chair, at least someone was nice to me, a person who probably doesn't deserve it.

Terri presses the elevator button, and as the elevator dings, I hear, "Ollie, come back here, please."

I look over my shoulder to catch JP standing in the hallway, hands on his hips.

Oh dear God.

A wave of nerves streams through my veins, and I think about turning around and bolting for a moment. But this is it, my one chance. So with my chin held high, I thank Terri, and then head back to his office. He props his office door open, and I follow him in.

A corner office, of course. It's full of rich tones but isn't pretentious like Roberts's office. And instead of sitting behind his desk, which is intentionally intimidating, he sits in one of the armchairs in the sitting area of his office.

"Have a seat," he says, gesturing to the chair across from him.

I sit up straight, trying not to look defeated or exhausted from the day, battling my nerves up until this point.

"I'm interested to know why you waited all day to talk to me," he starts. "Last I remember, you were dating Silas Taters, but from the article you wrote about him, I'm assuming that's no longer a topic of conversation."

Yup, I knew he read the article.

Clearing my throat, I say, "I would love to have a conversation with you where I speak openly and honestly about my situation."

"Please, so would I," he says, crossing his ankle over his knee and leaning back in his chair. "Tell me why you're here."

"For a job," I say, which causes his eyes to slightly widen before he lightly chuckles.

"Okay, you're here for a job. Tell me why you think you would be a good fit for Cane Enterprises."

Here goes nothing.

"This past summer, I was an intern with Alan Roberts, as you know, headed into my last year of college. For my end-of-internship assignment, where I would get credit for all my work, I was assigned hockey as my general topic."

"Ah, so the article was your end-of-the-year topic?"

I nod. "I also met Silas at the end of summer. I had no idea who he was, but we became friends quickly, and from there, the relationship grew. When Alan Roberts found out I was dating Silas, he asked me to look into the Agitators organization and to write a 'gotcha piece' exposing the dark secrets of the organization."

"While you were dating Silas?" JP asks as he props his chin up on his hand.

"Yes, I told Roberts that was a conflict of interest, and I wasn't comfortable doing it. He persisted. I chose not to go in that direction but rather provide a lifestyle piece on what it's like to be a professional hockey player. It was the best I could do, given my background is in lifestyle and that I know nothing about hockey. I gave the article to Silas so he could read it over to make sure he was good with everything in it."

"He was?" JP asks, surprised.

"Yes, so I turned it in. Little did I know, Roberts had asked a girl at the company to run edits on it. She offered up the information about Silas being cheated on, and they stuck it in the article without my consent." I take a deep breath. "From there, everything has fallen apart. Silas, rightfully, has ended all communication with me. When I found out what Roberts did, I quit on the spot, not wanting to work for a company that would do such a thing to someone. I, uh . . . I headbutted the girl who added the cheating part and left." JP smirks. "I lost credit for the internship. Roberts and the head of the journalism department are close, and he told her about it. I was cut from the school for not earning credits for my internship, and I've lost my housing scholarship because I'm no longer in the School of Journalism. Instead of graduating this coming summer, I have to start over." I take another deep breath. "That's why I'm here, because I've not only researched Cane Enterprises and everything it represents, but I've also researched The Jock Report, and after going through the hell I've been through the past week, I know, deep in my soul, I want nothing more than to help lift the voices of those who deserve it. I know you're not in charge of making decisions for The Jock Report, but I am hoping this conversation might be a foot in the door."

I end there and wet my lips, so freaking nervous as he sits there and studies me.

"How do I know you're telling the truth?"

"It's a great question, and frankly, I don't have any way of proving to you that Roberts made the switch other than forwarding you the email I sent Roberts with the original article." I pause and take a deep breath. "This summer, I fell in love with the most incredible man I've ever met. I had no idea men like him—noble, honest, funny, selfless, and respectful—existed. I'm absolutely gutted that this happened to him. I'm trustworthy, I'm a hard worker, and if that means putting me on probation or—"

"What's Roberts's number?"

"Huh?" I ask.

JP pulls out his phone. "Give me Roberts's number. I'm going to call him."

"Oh, uh . . . okay. But, he, uh, he won't say nice things about me."

"I'm not looking for nice things. I'm looking for the truth." I hand him my phone with Roberts's number on display, and as he dials, he asks, "What's the name of the person who edited your article?"

"Candace," I say as my palms start to sweat.

JP nods and then puts the phone on speaker. It rings a few times and then, "This is Roberts."

"Alan Roberts?" JP asks.

"Yes, who is this?"

"Sorry for the cold call, this is JP Cane from Cane Enterprises."

Roberts's voice loosens up as he says, "Oh, JP, to what do I owe the pleasure?"

Just hearing his gruff voice makes me want to stick my hand through the phone and pull his mustache off.

"I was approached by a former employee of yours, looking for a job. An Ollie Owens?"

"Really?" Roberts says. "That's bold of her."

No, it's not, you moron. What am I going to do, just sit in a corner and not work at all?

"Yes, well, she told me this story about how she wrote an article, but you changed it in the editing process. It was a real woe is me sob story." JP keeps his eyes down while he speaks to Roberts, not allowing me to see his facial expressions. "I'm not interested in her, but I am interested in hearing about the girl, Candace, who changed the article. She clearly knows how to grab readers' attention."

"Ah, so she told you about Candace adding that piece?" Bingo! Thank you, Roberts. "Candace is the kind of employee anyone would be lucky to have. She takes action, but unfortunately, she'll be offered a job here at the end of the school year. Can't let you poach her from me."

JP chuckles. "Dammit, I thought you were going to say that. Well, keep me in mind if someone like Candace comes up. I'm looking for someone who could help grow the business."

"Of course."

They exchange a few more pleasantries, and then JP hangs up. He fiddles on his phone, then leans back in his chair.

When his eyes connect with mine, he says, "You were fucked over."

It must be the validation of what happened because I can't stop myself as I start to cry and nod. "I was. And I lost everything, even Silas. And granted, part of it was my fault. I . . . I let it slip to my friend Ross what happened to Silas, and Candace was apparently eavesdropping. That's how she knew." I shake my head. "That little slip-up made me lose the best thing that ever happened to me . . . Silas."

JP studies me for a few more beats. "How are your editing skills?"

"I took multiple classes, and I was actually certified this summer."

He nods and then places his hands on the armrests and lifts from his chair. Confused, I do the same. "Well, I can't promise anything, but I'll put in a word for you with The Jock Report."

"Oh, thank you. That means a lot."

He nods. "I'm sorry you lost Silas. I know what it feels like to love and to lose. The worst pain a person can experience." He grabs a pad of paper from his desk. "Write down your contact info here, and I'll be in touch."

"Thank you," I say as I take the pen from him and write down my name, number, and email address. I'm almost tempted to toss in Ross's number too in case he can't get ahold of me, but I think better of it.

"I'll walk you out," JP says, guiding me toward the elevator.

"Thank you," I say again. And for the first time since I read the article, I feel a sliver of hope that maybe something will go right for me. I've lost Silas for good, I know that. And even though I thought living in Canada was my future, it might be LA where I end up. *That's better than going home and seeing the disappointment in my father's eyes.*

"IT'S BEEN A WEEK," I say as I sit on Ross's bed while he streams the game. "I was sure I'd hear something from him by the end of last week. But nothing."

"He helps run a billion-dollar enter—get the puck!" he yells. "Yes, go, fucking go." My eyes fall to the computer on Ross's lap, and I catch sight of Silas screaming across the ice, his hockey stick out in front of him, sprinting toward the puck. He collides into the boards, but somehow kicks the puck with his skate toward Rivers. Rivers brings it around the goalie's net and passes it to Holmes, and within a blink of an eye, Holmes shoots the puck in the goal, scoring. "Yesssss!" Ross screams while pumping his fist.

I sink down into his bed, unable to watch. Especially a celebration. It's too painful to see Silas's handsome face. It's been a few weeks since we've talked, and all I can wonder about is if he's moved on. If he's been with someone else. If he's . . . if he's gone back to Sarah. The thought makes me so ripe with nausea that I have to take deep breaths.

"Sorry," Ross says. "I was saying that he has a big company to run, it's probably going to take him a second. I'm sure you're not the first thing on his list."

"Probably not," I say as I curl into his pillow. "How does he look?"

"Silas?" Ross asks.

"Yeah."

"You really want to know?"

No.

But I can't help myself.

"Yes, I do."

"He looks good," Ross says. "Thicker scruff, but he looks good, clear eyes."

I swallow down my emotions. "Good," I answer just as my phone rings. I sit up and stare at the Los Angeles number. "Oh my God, Ross. I think it's JP."

"Really?" he asks as he turns down the volume on his computer. "Answer it."

I push my hair behind my shoulders, straighten up, and then lift the phone to my ear while accepting the call. "Hello?" I ask.

"Ollie, this is JP Cane."

"Oh, hi, JP," I say, my nerves just about to fray every last inch of me. "How are you?"

"Good," he answers. "I had a moment to speak with Ryot, Banner, and Penn, and they all agreed with the popularity of the app, they need to take on another editor. I gave them your name and qualifications, and they're ready to make an offer." Tears well up in my eyes.

"Oh my gosh, that's . . . that's amazing," I say.

"I can send you all the details in a moment as well as connect you with the guys so you can introduce yourself."

"Wow, that would be fantastic. Thank you so much."

"Of course. And hey, I hope that broken heart heals soon."

A tear floats down my cheek. "Me too. Thank you, JP."

"Don't let me down."

"I won't. I promise. Thank you."

I hang up and drop my phone to my lap as I press my hands to my eyes and cry.

Ross scoops me up into a hug. "You got it, didn't you?"

I nod against his shoulder. "I did." When I pull away, I say, "Looks like I'm moving to Los Angeles."

Ross's face falls flat, and his grip loosens. "Wait, you're moving?"

"Yes, the company is in LA."

"Yeah, but I thought." He grips his hair. "I thought you'd work remotely."

I shake my head. "I can't stay here, Ross. Firstly, I'm no longer a student and my study permit visa will be terminated." The joy of being an international student. You only have three months to leave after your studies have finished, or by the date on your study permit, whichever comes first.

Although, of course, it's more than that. "But also, Silas is plastered everywhere, and when it's not his face, it's the Agitators logo. Even if I could stay, it's just too painful. I have to think of it as another opportunity for a fresh start."

"Well . . . fuck," he says softly. "I wasn't expecting that. I mean, yeah, of course. You're no longer a student, but fuck."

"I hate that I'm leaving you though, Ross." I hate that I'm leaving without a degree . . . *and* a broken heart. But it's life.

"Going to miss you, girl."

"Going to miss you right back."

Chapter Twenty-Seven

SILAS

"Come out with us, man," Pacey says as he slips his shirt on.

"I'm good," I answer.

"That's not the right answer," Posey says as he buttons up his shirt. "We just took another win, and we deserve a chance to celebrate your fucking hat trick. Now come on. You're coming."

"I don't need to celebrate." I slip my shoe on and then the other. "I'm fine just going home."

"Well, we're not fine with it," Hornsby says. "Penny has already told me I can go celebrate because Holden is sleeping, so we're fucking celebrating." Hornsby shakes my shoulders. "Three fucking goals, man. That's something to celebrate."

Knowing they won't leave me alone, I succumb to their demands. "Fine."

Posey fist-pumps the air. "Great, you can ride with me."

"I can drive myself."

Posey laughs at that. "As if we would let you just drive,

allowing you not to show up. No, dude, you have to be escorted."

Dammit. They know me too well.

"Fine," I say as I slip my suit jacket on. "But I'm leaving when I want to fucking leave."

"You're required at least thirty minutes," Pacey says.

"No, two drinks," Hornsby counters.

"Two big alcoholic drinks," Posey says.

I glance at Holmes, and he just shrugs. "I agree with them."

"Wow, dude." I shake my head. "Fine, two large alcoholic drinks."

"Thatta boy," Posey says, shaking my shoulders. "Let's hit the road."

He pushes me toward the exit, and together, we walk past the media and out of the arena. When we reach Posey's car, he goes to my side and opens the door for me.

"What the hell are you doing?"

"Making sure you don't go anywhere," he says and then nods to the car. "Get in."

"You're being ridiculo—"

My voice falls as Posey buckles me in himself. When he's done, he pats me on the leg and then goes to his side of the car.

When he's settled, I say, "That was taking it too far."

"Felt right to me."

He pulls out of the parking space, the other guys following closely. "So . . . what do you want to talk about?" Posey asks.

"Probably not what you want to talk about."

"And what do you think I want to talk about?" he asks.

"I don't know . . . my love life and how I'm a recluse now who doesn't hang out with you four, so that's why you've pressured me into going out with you tonight."

"You said it, not me. So let's chat about that."

"There's nothing to chat about."

"Sure there is." Posey makes a left and heads toward downtown. "Have you heard from Ollie at all?"

"Wow," I say. "Less than a minute. I thought you'd at least give it five minutes before you brought her up."

"Nah, no beating around the bush over here. Got to get straight to the point. So have you?"

"No. She took my advice and got out of my life."

"Okay, so no correspondence at all?"

"No," I answer.

"And how do you feel about that?"

"Good," I respond even though that's a lie.

I don't feel good at all.

I actually can't fucking sleep at night.

My body's on autopilot as I move through the motions, never feeling anything. When I got in those fights after I found out about the article, I didn't feel a goddamn thing. When I came home and confronted her, I felt nothing. When I scored the hat trick today, there was zero joy within me.

I'm just dead inside.

And when I go home and lie in my bed wishing for my mind to stop whirling about Ollie, I can't stop thinking about how I wish she was in my bed with me, naked and curled into my side. How I miss her sweet moans as I drove inside her. How I miss her witty remarks when we're joking around. How I miss her never-ending hugs, her addicting cuddles, and her mind-blowing kisses.

I miss her so goddamn much that the only time I ever feel anything is at night, when I'm alone and wishing she was there. That's when I feel pain.

It's why going out tonight sounds slightly appealing because it will cut down on the time when I'll be alone, feeling that pain.

"Why don't I believe you when you say you're good?"

"Because you're annoying," I answer.

"Well, at least your maturity is intact," he says, annoying me even more.

———

IT'S TOO FUCKING CROWDED in here.

The music is too loud.

And even though it's an Irish pub that gives you the sense that you're back in Ireland with its creaky floorboards, Gaelic band, and large pints, I want nothing to do with it.

"I don't know about this," I say to Posey as he pushes me through the crowd cheering for us.

"We have a private space in the back, don't worry." He guides me through a curtained-off area and into an open room with high-top tables and chairs scattered throughout.

Well, that's slightly better.

"Guinness?" Posey asks me.

"Sure," I answer as I sit at one of the tables just as the guys filter into the back. Winnie is attached to Pacey, which I half expected. And then Rivers walks in with Ross right by him.

Fuck.

I haven't seen Ross since the article's release, which is one reason I avoided going out. I didn't want to see him, especially since Ross and Ian are getting pretty serious now.

I turn away from him, hoping he doesn't approach me, given the awkward elephant in the room. And what is he going to do when he goes back home? Is he going to report to Ollie about what state I'm in? Does she even care?

Probably not.

If she was willing to throw me under the bus, I'm pretty sure she doesn't care about me at all.

And that's what fucking stings the most. Is that I'm lying awake at all hours of the night, devastated over losing her, over her fucking me over, and she's probably fine. Living her best life under Roberts's command.

Christ, what the hell was I thinking, coming to this?

Really bad idea.

I need to leave.

I move off my stool and turn around just as I come face-to-face with Ross.

Of fucking course.

"Silas," he says.

"Ross," I reply. Rivers is only a few steps away, his eyes on us. I'm sure ready to pounce on me if I disrespect his man.

"Can I speak with you?"

"Yeah, I don't think I want to do that," I answer. "I was actually just on my way out."

I slide to the side, but Ross slides in front of me. The balls on this guy because I have about forty pounds of muscle on him.

Rivers comes up behind him, equal height as me, and says, "Listen to him."

Now, I could take Rivers. We might be almost evenly matched, but my pent-up anger will win out. But nothing screams low team morale than getting into a fight with one of your own, so I reluctantly sit back down while Ross takes a seat next to me.

"Thank you," Ross says just as Posey drops my drink off in front of me. Rivers must tell him to leave us alone because it's just me and Ross, probably one of the last people I want to talk to. "First of all, I don't want you to think I'm trying to get you back together with Ollie. She's moved on, but I think she deserves her truth to be told to you."

She's moved on?

Like . . . with another man?

It's two stupid words—moved on—but because I still have these crazy feelings for her, it cuts me deep.

"Ollie was telling the truth. She had nothing to do with

your private information going in the article. It was Candace. She edited the article, had the information about you, and slipped it in."

"How would Candace know about that?" I ask. "It doesn't make sense."

"Ollie and I were having lunch at the union one day. She was gushing about you, how you've made her feel special again and given her confidence." My gut churns again. "And she was rambling of course and started to say how she's helped you ever since you were cheated on, but she never got the full sentence out before she stopped herself and started to freak out. I guessed what she was saying, and she begged me not to say anything. I, of course, would take that to my grave not only to protect you but to protect my girl who was so distraught. Unfortunately, Candace was sitting right behind us and heard."

My body starts to tingle with dread as I try to comprehend what he's saying. "But . . . but she said it," I say, grappling for anything.

"And regretted it the minute it came off her lips. She wasn't gossiping, she was talking about how happy she was, and it just slipped." Ross's jaw grows tight. "And the fact that you didn't give her a chance to explain that really pisses me off."

I don't say anything because frankly, I don't know what to say.

"Ollie is the most loyal person I've ever met, so loyal that she confronted Roberts and quit on the spot when she found out the truth. She ended up losing credit for her internship, was kicked out of journalism school, and lost her scholarship for housing . . . because of you. Because of protecting you. She fucking loved you so much, and you couldn't even let her explain."

Ross shakes his head and gets up from the table.

"I understand you're hurt, Silas. I've been in your position

421

before on many occasions. But the difference between you and me is that I've learned who to trust and who not to trust. And I can assure you, Ollie Owens is a person you can trust. She's not a person you throw away."

Rivers comes up behind him and possessively grips the back of Ross's neck. "She lost everything, Silas. Every fucking thing she cared about. Could you imagine what would have happened if she hadn't lost you *as well* in all of this? She probably wouldn't have had to leave. Although, maybe moving on is the best thing for her."

He starts to walk away, but I stop him, standing as well. "What do you mean she's moved on?"

"Afraid she found someone else?" Ross taunts. "It would serve you right. If you truly loved her, Silas, you would have listened to her and then made your decision, but you didn't give her that chance. Shame on you. You don't deserve to know what she's doing now."

And with that, he moves away, Ian at his side.

I back up and slowly sit down on the stool behind me, my mind whirling.

Holy fuck.

Was that . . . was that the truth?

Was that what she was trying to tell me all along?

A sickening feeling consumes me as I think about the last time I saw her, when she came to my apartment. When she tried to tell me the truth, and I wouldn't let her. I wouldn't believe her, and then I yelled at her to get the fuck out of my life.

And then she lost everything.

Her dreams.

Her goals.

She was kicked out of school?

Jesus Christ.

"You okay?" Posey asks.

"No." I shake my head. "I'm not." I glance up at Posey. "I fucked up, man. I fucked up big time."

━━

SHE'S MOVED ON.

Those three words have played over and over in my head all night, keeping me awake.

All I could think about is the look on her face when I told her to leave.

It haunted me last night.

Over and over again to the point that I pulled up her name in my phone, tempted to call her, but then I reminded myself what Ross said.

She's moved on.

I shouldn't call her if she's with someone else.

I don't want to come back into her life when clearly, she's been able to let it all go.

Not me, though.

I can't let this fucking go. It's eating me alive.

I push through the weight room, feeling the sleepless night heavy on my shoulders. I have no energy to work out, so I'm just going through the motions now.

My eyes are bloodshot, my muscles are exhausted, and my brain fucking hurts.

"Hey," a voice says as I walk up to the warm-up bikes. I look toward the weight racks where Rivers is about to load up his bar.

"Hey," I say as I set my water bottle down.

"You look like shit."

"Feel like it," I say as I sit on the bike but don't move.

"Any of this have to deal with what Ross said to you last night?"

"All of it," I say as I grip my forehead. "Dude, please . . . please just tell me if she's with someone else."

He faces me and leans against the rack, arms crossed. "Ross didn't want me saying anything to you." He pushes his hand through his hair and says, "But fuck, I can't have you getting in fights out there again. We just got our groove back."

"Just fucking tell me," I say, the pain so evident in my voice.

"I have no idea if she's with someone else," Rivers says. "But when Ross said she'd moved on, he meant she actually moved."

"Moved?" I ask. "To where?"

"Los Angeles."

"What?" I ask, feeling my fucking heart tumble to the ground. "She moved to Los Angeles?"

Rivers nods. "Yeah, she got a job with The Jock Report as an editor."

"Fuck," I mutter. "And she's down there now?"

"She is," Rivers says. "Ross was really upset about it, hence why he had to talk to you last night. He needed to get it off his chest."

"I understand that," I say and hang my head. "I fucked up so hard, Rivers."

"You did," he says. "But there's always a way to make it better."

"She moved. How can I make that better?"

"Distance doesn't matter, especially if you love her, and I'm assuming you love her."

I nod. "Even when I thought she hurt me, I never stopped loving her. Never."

"Then there's your answer. She might not live here now, but that shouldn't stop you. If you want your girl back, then get her back."

I PACE MY APARTMENT, trying to get the courage to make a phone call. But I'm chickening out, so scared as to what would happen . . .

Silas: *I can't do this.*

Posey: *Yes, you can.*

Pacey: *We went over this. You want her, go get her.*

Hornsby: *Coming from experience, if you love her, don't let her go.*

Holmes: *You won't feel right until you do.*

Silas: *I hate that you're all right.*

Posey: *So execute the phone call and text us after. I'm frothing at the mouth for an update.*

On a deep breath, I dial the number and bring the phone to my ear. Sweat builds up in my palm, and I hold my breath when the phone is answered.

"Hello?"

"JP?" I ask. "It's Silas Taters."

"Aah, I've been expecting your call. Let me guess, you're ready to join The Jock Report?"

"Something like that," I say. "I think I need your help. I'm in LA in two days. Think you can help me win my girl back?"

"I thrive for moments like this. I'm in."

Chapter Twenty-Eight

OLLIE

Ross: *You know, the Agitators are in town if you want to go catch a game.*

Ollie: *I think you know the answer to that.*

Ross: *If you want to have dinner with Ian to catch up, I can let him know.*

Ollie: *You know I love him, but I don't think I'm ready to see any hockey player.*

Ross: *He'll be sad, but I'm sure he'll understand. Did I tell you that he asked me to move into his place?*

Ollie: *NO! That's so exciting. Are you going to do it?*

Ross: *I told him I was slightly apprehensive since I have the dorm and I don't want to lose that, you know just in case something happens between us, but he said I could keep it and he wouldn't be insulted. He understands the need for security.*

Ollie: *You found yourself a good one. So, is that a yes, then?*

Ross: *It's a yes. I'm moving in this weekend when they return from their away trip.*

Ollie: *Send me pictures of your his and his closet.*

Ross: *It will be beautiful.*

Ollie: *I have no doubt in my mind.*

"Hey, Ollie," Ryot Bisley says as he comes up to my desk.

Let me tell you the difference between Roberts's office and The Jock Report office. Instead of cubicles, it's all open seating. We all have laptops, and we can come and go as we please, hook up to any station, and get comfortable. There are recliners, private rooms for concentration, and games like ping pong and air hockey all through the space so you can take a mental break. It's truly amazing here.

"Hey, Ryot," I say, setting my phone down.

"I have a new client who just signed on, and I was hoping you could help him with his article. It's his first time, and he's a bit self-conscious about his editing abilities."

"Well, that's what I'm here for. I'd be more than happy to look over it."

"Great," Ryot says, then hands me a printed-out piece of paper. Odd, we usually do everything online, but this will work. "If you could make it a priority, I'd appreciate it."

"Sure, I'll get to it right now," I answer.

"Thanks, Ollie. Let me know if you have questions, and when you're done, just bring it to my office."

"Sure, not a problem." Ryot takes off, and I walk over to the community office supply table, grab a red pen and highlighter, and then sit in one of the recliners.

Once I'm comfortable, I lift the paper and read the title.

"The Truth About Silas Taters . . ."

What the actual fuck.

I look up toward Ryot's office and see that he's disappeared behind his door. This is not an article I want to read. It's not an article I should read because who knows what he's going to say, something that might hurt me. It's been several weeks since Silas threw me out of his life . . . and I don't feel anywhere near healed. *Will I ever stop hurting?*

But I can't tell Ryot I can't edit the piece because when I took this job, I swore to myself not only will I be the most loyal employee to the men who gave me a chance, but that I would do anything they asked.

Anything.

And this is anything.

"Fuck," I mutter as I squeeze my eyes shut.

You have to do this. There's no option. So just read it and get it over with.

On a deep breath, I focus my eyes back on the paper.

"The Truth About Silas Taters."

Written by Silas Taters

You might know me as a starting forward for the Vancouver Agitators, for my quick feet on the ice, and my ability to conceal a puck until the last minute, tricking the opposite team's goalie.

Others unfortunately might know me from a recent article that was released about my personal life.

Either way, you know of me, and I figured I should set the record straight.

This past summer, a girl in a bar kissed me. I wasn't expecting to fall for her, nor was I expecting her to make me feel wanted, needed again.

But she did.

In a few short weeks, I found myself falling hard for this girl.

Who is this girl? Ollie Owens, the girl who wrote the infamous article about me.

I know what you're thinking, how could you fall for someone who'd write an article about me in such a negative way? Here's the thing, the article she turned in wasn't the article that was published.

Her words were manipulated.

Her truth was skewed.

And because of her loyalty to me, to the Agitators, and to the fans, she confronted the offender who changed her article, only to lose everything, including me in the process.

Why am I telling you this? Because this is why The Jock Report exists, so you can hear our story rather than a story construed by someone else looking for clicks.

Was I cheated on? Yes.

Was that private information that shouldn't have been put on a public forum? Yes.

Will there be consequences for the person who changed the article? Yes.

I'm going to end this by saying I'm not good when it comes to this social media stuff, and I'm sure as hell not good at writing articles, but what I'm good at is admitting when I'm wrong.

And I was wrong about Ollie Owens.

Losing her will be my biggest loss to date, and that includes last year's championship run.

Tears stream down my face as I stare at the paper in front of me, wishing and hoping my eyes aren't deceiving me.

"Reading anything good?"

My eyes dart up and find Silas standing in front of me wearing a pair of jeans and a black polo. His hands are stuffed in his pockets, his beard has been trimmed to look like scruff, and those gorgeous blue eyes I've fallen in love with stare right at me.

"Silas," I say, just above a whisper.

He kneels in front of me and reaches out to take my hand. He wets his lips and says, "I'm sorry, Oliana." Hearing my full name nearly rips me apart. "I'm so fucking sorry. I should have given you a chance to talk to me, to tell me your truth, but I was so caught up in the hurt from Sarah, seeing it be repeated that I, fuck . . . I said things to you I never should have said."

He reaches out and swipes the tears from my cheeks.

"I know I fucked up, and I have no reason to ask this, but if you would give me another chance, a chance to prove to you that I do deserve your love, then I promise I'll never fucking hurt you again."

"Si-Silas," I say, my throat so full of emotion.

I thought of this moment, dreamed of it actually, that

maybe, just maybe he'd give me another chance. But every time I woke up, I knew it wasn't a reality. Silas was too hurt, too damaged, and it was on me for not protecting his heart like I should have.

But now that he's here, in front of me, I know this is my chance.

I scoot forward, on the edge of my seat, and grip his hand with both of mine. Speaking directly to him, I say, "I love you, Silas. I love you so much that I haven't been the same without you. What I did, telling Ross about—"

"He told me you didn't do it on purpose, that it was a slip-up. I believe him. I believe you."

That makes my eyes water all over again. Of course Ross approached him.

"I still shouldn't have said anything."

"Baby, it's okay," he says as he leans in closer. "I'm the one who should have been more understanding."

I shake my head. "I should have protected you."

"You did," he says, cupping both of my cheeks now. "You stood up for me, you lost everything for me, and fuck . . . I . . . I love you, Oliana. No one has ever done that for me, and I felt like such a piece of shit, knowing that I treated the most precious thing in my life so carelessly. It won't happen again. I swear on my life, it won't happen again."

"I believe you," I say.

He brings his forehead to mine and whispers, "Can I have you back? Please tell me you're mine again. I can't fucking sleep. I can't concentrate. I feel so goddamn sick without you. Please, Ollie, please come back to me."

The desperation in his voice.

The grip he has on me.

His words.

They're everything I need and so much more.

"I'm yours, Silas. Always have been, always will be."

And then his mouth is on mine in a crash of kisses that

steals my breath away. His hand smooths up the back of my head, holding me tightly as I grip his cheeks, allowing him to swipe my mouth with his tongue, tempting me to open. And I do. Because I can't deny this man anything.

I love him.

He's mine.

And I'm never letting go.

Like that first night, when I walked up to a complete stranger in a bar, I kissed this man as if he were mine. And just like that moment, I claim him. Kissing him like he's mine, but this time . . . he actually is.

Epilogue

SILAS

"Can I have this drawer?" Ollie asks.

Standing in front of my dresser, wearing a pair of sweatpants and one of her famous crop tops, is my girl, looking so fucking good.

It's taken a few weeks to work out the logistics, including applying for a work visa, but Ollie is finally back in Vancouver and living with me.

"Baby, you can have any drawer you want," I say, coming up behind her and bringing her into my chest. I kiss along her neck and add, "Take whatever you want. It's yours."

She chuckles and tilts her head to the side, giving me better access. "You can't possibly be ready to have more sex."

"I'm always ready," I say as I slide my hand under her crop top and grip her breast.

"Silas," she reprimands, turning around. "We need to unpack. I can't just live with these boxes everywhere."

"It will get done," I say, backing her up against the dresser.

"Not when you're leaving tomorrow for away games."

"All the more reason to fuck you," I say, tugging on her shirt.

Laughing, she pushes at my chest. "How about this? You give me an hour of unpacking, and then the rest of the night, I'm yours to do with whatever you want."

"Whatever I want?" I ask with a questioning brow.

"Whatever, but you need to put in the effort of unpacking."

"I can do that," I say as I slip my hands under her shirt again and play with her nipples.

"Silas," she says, her head falling back.

"Yes, baby?" I ask, lowering my mouth to her breast, only to be stopped by the palm of her hand.

"No, sir. Unpacking first, then sex."

"Ugh," I grumble and then pull away, my erection tenting my goddamn sweats. "See what you do to me?"

Her eyes fall to my lap, and I see that hungry look.

"Goddamn you," she says right before she pushes me back on the bed and then pulls my sweatpants down to release my cock. Looking me in the eyes, she says, "Real quick, and then you give me two hours of unpacking."

"Whatever you want, baby, just give me that tight cunt."

She slides her sweats off, showing me that she's wearing nothing underneath, and then she hovers above my lap and positions my cock at her entrance. In one fell swoop, I'm fully inside her.

"Fuck," she says while her hands float up to her breasts. "God, I'll never get over how big you are inside me."

I grip her hips and encourage her to ride me. Which she does.

She rides me hard.

Her hips undulate over mine, and I sit back, fucking loving every second of this.

From the moment we made up, we've tried to spend as

much time with each other as possible. She came back to my hotel, thanks to Ryot letting her leave early, and I made love to her for the first time. It was slow, torturous, and we took our time, reacquainting each other until we climaxed at the same time. After that, I fucked her on every surface of that hotel room. And when we were completely spent, we formed a plan.

She didn't immediately go back to Vancouver because she wanted to spend more time with The Jock Report team and discuss her remote options with Ryot, which wasn't a problem at all. She felt bad for abandoning them, but Ryot not only encouraged her to return to Vancouver—because he'd prefer his employees are happy—but assisted in getting her work visa expedited. So now, whenever I go to LA for a game, we agreed she'd come with me to catch up with the team.

But now that she's here, in my home, moved in with all her belongings, I can finally breathe.

I have all the plans to propose to this girl because I know she's the one, but I also figured we have time. I don't want to scare her off because we just got back together, but this summer, I have a feeling when we're in Banff, it's going to happen.

"Silas, your cock, it's so good."

I squeeze her breasts as she continues to ride me, over and over again until I feel her start to tighten up.

"You close, baby?"

Her lips press together as she nods.

So close she can't even say it.

"Then let me feel you come," I say, right there with her.

She rides me a few more times, and when her mouth falls open and a silent moan escapes her, I feel her convulse all around my cock, which drives me wild.

I pump up into her a couple of times, and when my balls tighten, I prepare for my orgasm as it rips through me.

I grind out swear words as she falls on top of me, her hair like a curtain around us.

After a few seconds, she asks, "Will this ever get old?"

"No," I say. "Never."

I lightly kiss her lips. "I love you, baby."

She smiles against my mouth. "I love you, too."

I wrap my arms around her and take a deep breath.

All is right in the world.

The Agitators have had the best start to a season in history.

I've been able to forgive Sarah and move past the hurt her actions caused.

I can see my life clearly. Sarah's definitely my past and Ollie is unquestionably my future.

My girl is now living with me, working in a role she loves.

And there is no doubt in my mind that we have a bright future ahead of us because she's mine. I'm hers, and it all started with a surprising, soul-changing kiss.